MIDNIGHT HUNGER

CLOSE CONTACT
AROUSED
TABOO
EIGHT INCHES

Published by Kensington Publishing Corp.

Books by Todd Gregory

EVERY FRAT BOY WANTS IT

Books by Sean Wolfe

CLOSE CONTACT
AROUSED
TABOO
EIGHT INCHES

Published by Kensington Publishing Corp.

MIDNIGHT HUNGER

TODD GREGORY
CHASE MASTERS
SEAN WOLFE

KENSINGTON BOOKS

KENSINGTON BOOKS are published by

Kensington Publishing Corp.
119 West 40th Street
New York, NY 10018

Special book excerpts or customized printings can also be created to fit specific needs. For details, write or phone the office of the Kensington Special Sales Manager: Kensington Publishing Corp., 119 West 40th Street, New York, NY 10018. Attn. Special Sales Department. Phone: 1-800-221-2647.

Kensington and the K logo Reg. U.S. Pat. & TM Off.

ISBN-13: 978-0-7582-3536-7

Printed in the United States of America

Contents

Contents

MIDNIGHT HUNGER

Blood on the Moon

Todd Gregory

Chapter One

"Happy Mardi Gras!"

The woman was obviously drunk as she threw her arms around Cord Logan and pulled him close and tight to her soft breasts. She pressed her mouth on his before he had time to react and push her away. His entire body stiffened and he winced. Her mouth had the nauseating taste of sour rum and stale cigarettes. He pushed her arms away from him. Repulsed, he pulled his head backward and took a step back, almost bumping into a weaving guy in an LSU sweatshirt carrying a huge cup of beer. She stood there in the middle of Bourbon Street, grinning at him. She looked to be in her mid-thirties, and heavy strands of beads hung around her neck dipping down into her cleavage. Her lipstick was smeared, making her look kind of like a drunken clown. Her hair was bleached blond with about three inches of dark roots growing out of her scalp, and was disheveled and messy—her hairspray had given up on it hours ago. Her blood-shot eyes were half-shut, and she tilted her head to one side as she looked at him, her sloppy smile fading. She was wearing a low-rise denim miniskirt over stout legs and teetering heels.

Her red half-shirt with THROW ME SOMETHING MISTER written on it in gold glitter revealed a roll of flab around her middle and a fading sunburst tattoo around her pierced navel. She tried to grab his head and kiss him again, but he deflected her arms.

She narrowed her eyes, going from "happy drunk" to "mean bitch" in a quarter second. "What's a matter? Don't you like girls?" she jeered at him, weaving a bit on her heels. She put one hand on her hip, replacing the smile with a sneer.

What? He stared at her, and froze for a moment as horror filled him.

For that instant, everything seemed to stand still. The dull roar of marching bands in the distance, the rock music blaring out into the street from the bars lining Bourbon Street, the shouting and yelling of the revelers, all faded away as he stood staring at her squinting eyes.

Don't be stupid, Cord, no one can tell just by looking at you.

The spell was broken when a strand of purple bands flew between them, hitting the pavement with a clatter. Cord involuntarily took another step back. The woman squealed with excitement and bent over, her T-shirt falling open at the neck to reveal a cavernous blue-veined cleavage. She stood up clutching the beads in her fist, a look of triumph on her face. She turned around, Cord forgotten, and lifted her shirt, showing her bare breasts to the crowd of men holding beads on the balcony. She shook her shoulders, making the large breasts sway from side to side, and she started yelling up at the men on the balcony. They all began whistling and catcalling. The beads began to fly— Cord grabbed a strand of gold ones just before they hit him in the face. He slipped them over his head and moved on down the street before she remembered him and tried to kiss him again.

You're being silly and paranoid, he scolded himself as he dodged beads falling from the sky and the drunks pleading and fighting over them. *No one can tell you're gay, and no one here knows you.*

He started walking faster through the crowds on Bourbon Street. Everyone was apparently drunk. He caught a glimpse of a couple in a doorway, her skirt hiked up and the man's hairy ass clenching as he penetrated her. New Orleans, it seemed, was everything he'd always heard about the city. He heard his father's voice in his head, *New Orleans is a city of sin, a modern-day Sodom.* He'd always wanted to come here, from the first time he'd seen a Mardi Gras parade on television. After rooming with Jared Holcomb for two years at Beta Kappa fraternity up at Ole Miss in Oxford, Mississippi, and listening to his stories about the modern-day Sodom where he'd grown up, it became an obsession for him to come down.

And finally, he was here.

His parents didn't know he was here, and they would definitely not approve. When Jared had suggested that he and some of the other brothers come down for Mardi Gras, he'd added, "Don't tell your parents." Jared was always lecturing him about breaking free of his parents, but it wasn't as easy as Jared made it sound. Cord was an only child, and his parents hadn't liked the idea of him going to Ole Miss. They wanted him to go to the University of Alabama, which was only about forty minutes from where they lived in Fayette County, close enough for them to drop in on him unexpectedly. He'd held firm, though, and they'd finally resigned themselves to it. But his father had called the preacher at the Oxford Church of Christ, and any time he missed a service or a Bible study, they knew. He hated the Church of Christ, hated everything about it and the way it had twisted his parents into bigots. How many times had he sat there, at either White's Chapel in Fayette County or at the church in Oxford, squirming as the preacher droned on and on about how homosexuals were an abomination in the eyes of the Lord, destined for the fires of hell for all eternity? If it wasn't the homosexuals, it was the feminists, or the blacks, or the illegal immigrants, or the godless liberals. The sermons were never about love, but almost always about hate and intolerance—which, no matter how many times he read the gospels, he'd never been able to find a single time Jesus had said anything of the sort. Oxford was his first step away from his parents and family, and he was determined to never return to Fayette County to live. He planned on applying to grad school once he was finished with his degree, and maybe even going on to his doctorate. His parents expected him to get his degree, get an Alabama teacher's certificate, and get a job at Hubbertville High School, where his father was the principal and his mother the home ec teacher. His granduncle Duncan, the current history teacher, was waiting for Cord to replace him so he could retire.

They'd planned his entire life for him—but it never occurred to them that he might be gay, that getting away from that corner of northwest Alabama and never returning was his main goal in life.

He kept walking up Bourbon Street, weaving his way around and through the crowds on the street. He stayed in the middle of the street to avoid beads flying down from the balconies. Every so often he'd see a woman lifting her shirt and even a guy dropping his pants. As he passed a muscular young guy wearing a baseball cap backward and a Kappa Sigma shirt, the guy dropped his pants and wiggled his hairy bubble butt for a group of women on a balcony, and they showered him with beads. He grinned. *This would kill Mom and Dad,* he thought as he caught a strand of red beads shaped like hearts and slipped them over his head.

He was still a little nervous, but it had been even easier losing his fraternity brothers in the mob of drunks on Canal Street watching the Endymion parade than either he or Jared had imagined. Jared was more than his roommate; Jared had, over the two years they'd shared the corner room at the big Beta Kappa house on fraternity row, become his best friend and partner in crime. Jared was the only person in the house he'd confessed his attraction to men to one night when they were doing shots of Jägermeister, and Jared had kept that secret for him—had even gone with him to Memphis shortly after he turned twenty-one to go to his first gay bar. He'd been too nervous to talk to anyone and didn't know how to react when guys stared at him and smiled. Jared had just rolled his eyes at him. "How do you ever expect to get laid when you won't even look at anyone?" he'd said, exasperated, turning back to the bar and waving the muscular stripper over, slipping some ones into his orange bikini and getting him to let a very nervous Cord touch his muscles. On the way back to Oxford, Jared said, "You need to come to New Orleans for Mardi Gras this year—there's a whole area of the French Quarter that's all gay bars." At first, it was going to be just Cord and Jared—but then Jared had invited Gordon Zupke and Brad Avery to come with them. "Safety in numbers," Jared had told him, "but it'll be really easy for you to slip away from us and head to the gay bars—you'll see."

They'd arrived late last night, and were all camping out in the carriage house behind the Holcombs' big house on State Street.

They'd spent Saturday afternoon on St. Charles Avenue watching the Iris and Tucks parades, sucking down beers and catching beads before heading back to the Holcomb house to get ready for the Endymion parade that night. While Gordon and Brad were showering, Jared had worked everything out for Cord's escape that night.

"We'll stake out a place on Canal Street for the parade," Jared had said, passing Cord a joint. "About ten o'clock, just melt away into the crowd—no one will notice for a while that you're gone. I'll pretend to text you and say that you've hooked up with a chick . . . they'll get that and forget about it." He grinned and winked at Cord. "Just make sure you make up some good details to tell us tomorrow. The gay bars are easy enough to find—just walk down Bourbon Street and you'll eventually get to them. You can't miss the rainbow flags hanging from the balconies." He took the joint back. "And have a good time, bro. Make the most of it. This might be the only chance you get on this trip to get down there."

And it had worked just as Jared had said it would. The crowds on Canal Street were at least ten people deep, and around ten o'clock, Cord had just stepped back away from his friends and melted into the crowd.

The night was warm but damp. The air hung heavy with moisture, like it was trying to form into rain but just didn't have the energy. The street lamps were surrounded by halos formed by the light dissipating into a slight mist, and the sky was covered in clouds that looked pale red. Every so often the moon would peek out from behind its cloud cover, and it, too, looked reddish, as though it had been dipped in blood. As he passed by a strip club, he saw his reflection in the glass covering pictures of nude women with their nipples blurred out. His dark brown hair was mussed a bit, and his black T-shirt molded over his upper body, showing off the muscles he'd earned playing sports in high school and kept up in the gym at Ole Miss. He was wearing a pair of baggy jeans that hung off his hips, showing his black Calvin Klein underwear. He frowned at his reflection, wondering if he was good looking enough to find someone.

Stop being so nervous, he scolded himself as he straightened his hair a bit. *This is your chance to find out if this is what you really want. And if it's not, well, then you can just forget about it all and get on with your life.*

He started walking again. He ducked around people and kept his eyes moving to watch for beads flying down from the balconies. He hadn't been paying attention that afternoon at the Iris parade and had been clocked but good in the forehead by some medallion beads that left a bruise just over his left eyebrow. "It makes you look rough," Jared had laughed, winking. "The boys will like that."

He bought what was advertised as a "big ass beer" from a vendor, marveling that he wasn't carded. He'd been twenty-one for several months, but still got carded whenever he'd tried to get into a bar or buy liquor in Oxford. But in New Orleans he hadn't had to flash his ID even once—it was like they really didn't care how old you were as long as you were buying liquor. He took a big gulp out of it and kept walking. A pair of girls in matching yellow T-shirts tried to hand him condoms, but he just smiled and shook his head as he kept walking.

"Are you sure?" one of them called after him. "Hot as you are, you're going to need some!"

"Aw, thanks," he called back. He laughed. *Maybe I'm better looking than I think I am,* he thought, and kept walking. He took another gulp from the massive beer. His watch read twenty after ten. He was just beginning to think he wasn't going to find the bars, that Jared had just been fucking with him, when he saw a rainbow flag fluttering in the slight breeze—and just across the street another one.

He stopped and stood there for a moment, staring at the two bars facing each other across Bourbon Street. There were crowds of men on the sidewalks and the street in front of the two buildings—almost exclusively men. Up on the balconies of both bars were crowds of men holding beads and watching the guys on the street. He swallowed. The gay bar in Memphis had been crowded, but it had been nothing like this. He could hear loud, thumping dance music coming from both places. He took a deep breath and stood there, just watching the guys. He shook his head and smiled.

It was, as Jared had said, a smorgasbord. Old, young, tall, short, white, black, brown, skinny, fat, smooth, hairy, muscular— every possible body type he could imagine. Some of the guys were shirtless, others were wearing leather, all of them drinking and laughing and having a good time.

No one seemed to be in the least concerned about going to hell.

"Okay, here you go," he thought to himself, downing the rest of the beer in a few quick chugs. He tossed the empty cup into an overflowing garbage can and walked into the intersection. *Which bar should I go into?* he wondered to himself as a shirtless man walked in front of him. He gaped at him. He was about Cord's height, his head was shaved, and he had bright blue eyes. *He looks like one of the guys on the porn sites,* Cord thought to himself.

The shirtless man stopped and looked at him, his face breaking into a huge smile.

"Damn, you're a cutie," he said, reaching out and lightly punching Cord in the shoulder.

Cord felt his face turning red. "Thanks," he managed to stammer out. *God, you're a dork,* he thought to himself. *Say something else, idiot!*

The shirtless man kept smiling. "How old are you?"

"Twenty-one."

"I'm Clint." He stuck out his big hand, which seemed to swallow Cord's. Cord swallowed. The man was gorgeous, even if he was in his forties or so. His big muscular chest was dusted with black hairs, and his stomach was solid and sculpted as well. The waistband of a pair of white 2xist underwear peeked out over the top of his tight faded jeans. "I'm from Dallas. Where are you from, little boy?"

"Cord from—" he bit his lip, trying to decide if he should admit where he was from, then decided to throw caution to the winds. What did it matter, after all? "I go to Ole Miss."

"Aw, you are just a baby," Clint said in a teasing voice. "You having fun, Cord?"

Cord nodded. "I've never been here before."

"Never?" Clint went on grinning. "Welcome, then. Bit overwhelming, isn't it? I remember my first Mardi Gras." He rolled his eyes. "Well, I remember arriving, and I remember leaving, but everything in between is a bit of a blur. But I know I had fun." He winked.

Cord laughed and relaxed a bit. "I got in last night, but didn't make it down to the Quarter. Which bar—" he hesitated, "is more fun?"

"Baby, they're all fun!" Clint laughed. "I'm heading over to Oz to meet my friends—come on along with me. There's a killer DJ playing there tonight. You like to dance?"

In his head, Cord heard his father's voice. *Dancing is a sin. It just provokes lust.* He dismissed the voice. "I love dancing."

"Come on, then!" Clint grabbed his hand and started pulling him toward the bar. "What are you waiting for?"

"Cool." Obediently Cord followed him across the street. They got into a line leading into the door to the right. He could see the place was crowded, and he caught a glimpse of a pair of muscled legs dancing on the bar. He gulped, and once he was through the door, he paid the twenty-dollar cover, got a stamp on his left hand and a plastic armband attached to his right wrist once he showed his ID. "Have a good time," the man working the register said and waved him inside.

He took a few steps into the crowd and his jaw dropped. Everywhere he turned to look there were sexy men. Smoothly muscled men in Day-Glo bikinis were dancing on the bar, their cocks bouncing inside the material. All the bartenders were shirtless and moving fluidly to serve the thirsty crowds pressing against the bar. He bumped into another shirtless guy and started to say "excuse me," but the guy just smiled and said, "Happy Mardi Gras!" Another guy charged behind him gave his butt a light squeeze. The dance floor was packed with shirtless men dancing to a remix of Lady Gaga's "Just Dance." Clint motioned to him. "Come on," he shouted over the music, "let's get a drink." Cord gulped down the rest of his beer as Clint shouldered his way up to the bar. "What do you want?" Clint said into his ear.

"Bud Light," Cord shouted back as another hand gripped his butt. He spun around, but the guy was already disappearing into the crowd. Clint pressed the cold bottle into his hand. "Thanks!" Cord took a long pull on the beer and shook his head. The bar in Memphis had been nothing like this. His mind was going into overload; he didn't know which way to look. The dancer on the bar directly in front of him winked, turned around, and shook his hard ass at him.

"Take your shirt off!" Clint winked as he uncapped his bottle of water. "Relax and have fun!"

He started to shake his head in protest. In his mind he heard the preacher last Sunday at the Oxford Church of Christ railing against the declining morals in the country. *All you have to do is turn on your television and see practically naked people cavorting like there's no heaven or hell, hedonistic sinners risking their immortal souls. . . .*

He took a deep breath, set his beer bottle down on the bar, and pulled his shirt off over his head.

"Sweet," Clint winked as Cord tucked his shirt through his belt. Clint reached over and gently tugged on Cord's left nipple.

Cord gasped as a volt of lusty electricity shot through his body. His dick stiffened inside his jeans. He quickly picked up the beer and took another drink. It tasted a little weird, but then the big-ass beer he'd just finished hadn't tasted right, either.

Clint grinned at him. "Nipples are wired, huh?" He stepped in closer and put his arms around Cord, pulling him into his powerful torso. His hands dropped and gripped Cord's ass, pulling their crotches together as he pressed his lips against Cord's. Cord moaned as Clint's tongue pressed through his lips, and he sagged against the bigger man's body. Clint nuzzled on his neck for a moment, and Cord began to tremble. "My friends are out on the dance floor," Clint finally said with a smile, breaking the spell somewhat. "Come on, pretty boy, let's go dance."

Cord just nodded, unable to say anything, and followed Clint through the crowd on the dance floor.

Lady Gaga mixed into "Single Ladies" by Beyoncé, and Cord tried to not bump into any of the guys on the dance floor as Clint pulled him through to a group of about six or seven shirtless muscle guys dancing in a circle. He really couldn't hear any of the names as Clint introduced him around, but they were all good looking, their bodies amazing. *I feel like I've stepped into a porn movie,* he thought. The guy he was standing closest to was named Jean-Paul. Jean-Paul fixed him with a stare that had him shaking in his shoes. Jean-Paul had shoulder-length light brown hair and piercing green eyes that almost seem to glow in the black lighting on the dance floor. He, too, was shirtless, his torso lean, hairless, and muscled. His jeans hung low on his hips, so low that his pubic hair was slightly exposed in the front, as was the top of his butt in the back. Jean-Paul reached out with the index finger of his right hand and traced a line from Cord's neck down his body, stopping just before it reached his crotch. Jean-Paul gave him a sardonic smile, an eyebrow raised, and Cord smiled back, swallowing deep and hard.

What have I gotten myself into? he wondered again as he took another drink from the beer. Clint winked at him as he started dancing. Despite the beer buzz, Cord felt a little self-conscious; he rarely danced at the fraternity parties, and wasn't really sure he knew how. But a quick glance around the dance floor showed that most guys just tried to move to the beat of the bass back-line, so he started doing the same. Clint moved around behind him and began grinding his crotch against Cord's ass—and Cord could feel the erection rubbing against his backside. Clint brought his arms forward around his waist, and then

Jean-Paul stepped in front of him and began playing with his nipples, flicking them lightly with his index fingers. Jean-Paul thrust his crotch forward into Cord's, and put his arms around him, sandwiching him in between the two shirtless studs.

"Single Ladies" became Rihanna's "Take a Bow," and Jean-Paul put his lips at the base of Cord's neck and began flicking his skin lightly with his tongue.

Cord's entire body began to tremble. Jean-Paul smiled at him, and whispered in his ear, "You're very beautiful."

Cord swallowed and just smiled back at him. Jean-Paul slid a hand into the front of his jeans, and Cord's knees buckled a little. Clint's hand was stroking the crack of his ass behind him. He glanced over to the stage, where two hot guys were kissing each other as they danced.

"You've never been with a man," Jean-Paul whispered again. His breath was warm against Cord's ear, and goose pimples came up on his arms. He looked into Jean-Paul's eyes, a deep pool of green, and—

And he was back in high school, the dance floor was gone, and he was lying on his bed with his friend Terry, lying naked on Terry's bed as they watched a porn movie and masturbated. Terry was watching the television, but Cord was watching Terry, with his lean hairy body, stroking himself as on the television some large-breasted blond woman was sucking a big dick while taking one in her ass, Terry's eyes were closed, and Cord wanted more than anything to put his mouth on Terry's dick, to taste him, to see what another man's cock felt like, to do what the woman was doing in the video, to suck and lick and worship Terry's long skinny cock. . . .

Cord shook his head to clear it. He was feeling fuzzy, the way he did when he'd smoked too much pot. Things didn't seem real. Jean-Paul's outline almost seemed to glow in the flashing lights over the dance floor. "No," he said finally, "I've fooled around some—" his mind flashed back to watching Terry masturbate to the porn video—"but I've never . . ." his voice trailed off. He couldn't say the words.

Jean-Paul leaned in and kissed him again, and Cord felt himself going weak in the knees, his head spinning somewhat. Jean-Paul's fingers closed around his cock and gave it a little squeeze. Cord gasped, his breath coming in sudden gasps.

It felt great, intense, and if Jean-Paul had undone Cord's pants right then and there, he would have let him. Out of the corner of his eye he saw one of the sweaty guys on the stage at the end of the dance floor slipping out of his pants, revealing a black jock.

New Orleans is a city of sin.

He never wanted to leave.

Clint's hand was completely inside the back of his jeans now, a finger probing deep inside the cheeks, searching, and Cord started to tremble as Jean-Paul began stroking his cock in front. His entire body felt wired, eroticized. The slightest brush of skin against his sent volts of electric desire through him. His balls began to ache for release, and in a brief moment of clarity he realized he could come right then and there on the dance floor if Jean-Paul didn't stop—

As though he'd read his mind, Jean-Paul stopped what he was doing and smiled. "Let's go back to my place, shall we, my young pretty boy." He bit the lower lobe of Cord's ear, sending him into another uncontrollable shiver of ecstasy. "Would you like that, Cord? Would you like to get naked and make love all the night long?" he whispered.

Cord couldn't speak, he just nodded.

With a smile, Jean-Paul signaled to the other guys, and they walked off the dance floor. They slipped through the crowd out onto the street. Jean-Paul took his hand, tracing his index finger in Cord's palm. Clint walked on the other side of him, his arm around Cord's shoulders. A chilly wind blew over them as they headed up St. Ann Street, and Cord shivered. Clint squeezed him more tightly. "It's not far," he grinned. The others walked behind them, and Cord's mind raced. *Is this going to be an orgy?* He swallowed nervously, and another wave of dizziness and nausea came over him. He stopped walking for a moment, trying to catch his breath and fight it off. "Deep breaths," Clint said, "just take a few deep breaths, and you'll be fine."

"I don't understand," Cord replied. He'd been drinking pretty much off and on all day, but had been spacing the beers out enough so that he never had anything more than a mild buzz. He hadn't even smoked any pot in over four hours.

"Don't worry about it," Clint said.

The feeling passed, and they started walking again. They turned the corner at Dauphine Street, walked down another block, and turned again onto Orleans.

As they climbed the steps to the front door of a house on Orleans Street, he looked across the street while Jean-Paul unlocked the door. There was a face watching from the window of the house directly across the street. He couldn't get a good look as the face was shrouded with shadows, and as he squinted to get a better look, the face moved away from the glass. The curtains swayed back into place. Jean-Paul swung the front door open and pulled him inside.

Once they were all inside, the door shut, Jean-Paul switched on a chandelier that filled the room with golden light. It was a large square room, with candles mounted in sconces on the walls and in tall candelabras all around the room. There were a couple of antique-looking chairs and sofas spread around against the walls. There was a large worn Oriental rug on the floor. One of the other guys started walking around the room lighting the candles. Once he was finished, he kicked off his shoes and undid his pants. He stepped out of them, and Cord stared at him. He was a blond and his blue eyes seemed to glow in the candlelight. His pink cock was hard under a bush of blond pubic hair. The blond smiled at him, and then one of the other guys, who'd also undressed, knelt in front of the blond and started sucking his cock.

Someone else turned off the chandelier. Shadows danced around the room in the candlelight.

Clint started kissing the back of Cord's neck. His hands trembling a little, he reached back and grabbed hold of Clint's cock. Clint reached around and unsnapped Cord's jeans, which fell to his ankles. He fumbled for Clint's zipper, but another pair of hands moved in and undid it. He started moving his hand up and down Clint's cock as Clint tugged Cord's underwear down. He stepped out of them, and Clint moved to his side, kissing his neck. He felt another tongue probing inside his butt cheeks, licking and moving in a circle. He gasped.

It felt incredible.

Jean-Paul stepped in front of him, naked. He smiled and turned his back to Cord, bending at the waist and offering him his ass.

He glanced around. Everyone was naked, the others paired off. A big hairy man with dark hair was mounting a smaller guy, sliding his cock inside his ass.

"Fuck him," Clint whispered at his side.

Jean-Paul reached behind him and grabbed Cord's cock, pulling him forward. Cord bit his lip as Jean-Paul guided his cock inside him. "Oh, my God," Cord breathed out as Jean-Paul began to slide his ass back toward Cord, wiggling a bit. He started gasping as Jean-Paul took all of him inside, resting his ass against him. Clint began tonguing his neck, and Cord almost screamed from pleasure as the tongue exploring his ass reached his opening. Cord put his hands on Jean-Paul's waist to keep his balance, and as Jean-Paul moved forward, Cord shoved himself deep into Jean-Paul. Jean-Paul gasped.

"That's the way," Clint nuzzled one of Cord's nipples. "He likes it rough, so give it to him, man. Pound his ass."

"Yeah, fuck me," Jean-Paul breathed, "give it to me, boy."

Cord began moving from sheer instinct, and started moving his hips forward faster, all the while holding on to Jean-Paul, sometimes pulling back on him so violently that the collision made his balls ache a bit. But it felt incredible, it felt so good, he'd never known fucking someone could be such an awesome feeling, it was better than beating off by far, the feel of Jean-Paul's smooth warm skin, the moistness of his ass, and all the while the tongue in his own ass continued to lap away while Clint worked his nipples, nothing was supposed to feel like this, to feel this good, this couldn't be sin, there was no way this could be wrong, it was right, it felt oh so right, and Cord gritted his teeth as he broke into a sweat and kept moving, Jean-Paul's head twisting from side to side as he moaned, swinging his ass back into a rhythm with Cord's own thrusts, and then the tongue moved away from his own ass, and Clint wasn't there anymore, and Jean-Paul moved forward, and Cord groaned as his cock broke free.

Jean-Paul turned and smiled at him, took him by the hand, and led him to a couch. Jean-Paul lay down on his back, spread his legs, and tilted his pelvis. Cord lay down on top of him, his body shivering from the delicious feel of Jean-Paul's skin against his own, and he slid inside Jean-Paul again, and Jean-Paul grabbed Cord's head with both hands and pulled him down into a kiss, and as Cord began pounding away he felt a little bite at the base of his throat—

and his mind opened as he looked down the top of Jean-Paul's head, and he could feel a cock inside his own ass, and it was the most amazing thing, he'd never ever imagined it could feel like this, he was being fucked while he was fucking Jean-Paul and he closed his eyes, and it was as though he was some-how feeling what Jean-Paul was feeling, as they continued to pound together in a rhythm of passion and pleasure, of lust and desire, and he opened his eyes, and could see Clint watching

them while another man was on his knees in front of Clint, wor-
shipping his cock, and Clint's right eye closed in a wink, and
then Jean-Paul stopped nibbling on his neck—

Jean-Paul smiled up at him, his lips and teeth slightly reddish in color, but he had to be imagining that, it wasn't possible,
and he felt his own urgency building, he started moving faster
and deeper, he was going to come and he wanted to get there,
he wanted to know how that would feel, and Jean-Paul's eyes
closed, he was moaning, he could hear Jean-Paul's moans over
his own, and then Jean-Paul was shooting, cum started spraying out of Jean-Paul, one shot getting into Cord's mouth and he
loved the taste of it, and swallowed it, still pounding away, and
then—

He threw back his head and screamed, a low guttural howl
from the deepest part of himself, as he finally came, and his entire body convulsed and shook with each shot inside of Jean-
Paul, there was nothing like this feeling, and he kept shooting,
it was like he had loads of cum stored up inside of him waiting
just for this very moment, and he kept convulsing, his entire
body rigid, the pleasure roaring in his ears, his mind couldn't
focus on anything other than what he was experiencing, and it
was so much more than he ever thought it could be—

And then it was over, and Jean-Paul was gently pushing
him out.

Cord collapsed at the end of the sofa, trying to catch his
breath.

"Come with me," Jean-Paul whispered, and Cord allowed
him to take his hand and lead him through the house, not really
aware of anything, until he opened a door and led him into a
bedroom with the biggest bed Cord had ever seen in his life,
and then Jean-Paul was pushing him down onto the bed, and
straddling him. Jean-Paul leaned down and whispered into his
ear, "That was incredible, pretty boy."

Cord couldn't answer, so he simply nodded.

Jean-Paul put his mouth on the base of Cord's throat again, and the pleasure was so intense he couldn't help but to cry out.

and in his mind, he saw Jean-Paul leading him down a hallway, and unlocking a door. "Would you like to stay with me?" Jean-Paul whispered inside his mind, and he could think of nothing he wanted more than to stay with Jean-Paul, as long as Jean-Paul wanted, and he said yes, and then Jean-Paul stopped kissing his neck—

and Jean-Paul was pushing him down on the bed, and offering him his own throat, and Cord kissed it, and it tasted strange.

his mouth was filling with liquid, and Jean-Paul whispered, "Drink, my pretty young boy," inside his head and he swallowed, he would do whatever Jean-Paul wanted him to do, anytime, anywhere, all Jean-Paul had to do was ask and he would do whatever he wanted, and he kept swallowing and he could hear Jean-Paul's moans in his head, then Jean-Paul moved his throat away

Jean-Paul smiled down at him. "Are you tired?"

Cord nodded, feeling a yawn coming on, and covered his mouth. Jean-Paul slid off him and curled up next to him in the bed.

It felt very right.

Jean-Paul also yawned. "Go to sleep, young Cord. And don't leave here—even if you awake before I do. You mustn't leave."

Cord nodded, his eyes feeling as though they weighed a thousand pounds.

They closed, and he slept.

Chapter Two

Cord finally gave up on sleep and opened his eyes.

He winced and shut them again immediately. The sunlight coming through the open blinds pierced his eyes like needles. Involuntarily he threw his right forearm across his eyes and rolled over, hitting his left shoulder hard on the slate floor. He tried opening his eyes just a slit, and that worked a little better. The glare of the sun was still intense, but he could actually see without feeling like his head would explode.

He'd fallen asleep at Jean-Paul's, but had woken with a start with the first gray light of morning coming through the windows. He'd slipped out of the bed, his head spinning and nausea churning his stomach. Jean-Paul just moaned in his sleep and turned over, and he'd walked out of the bedroom stark naked, feeling his way down the darkened hallway. The entire house was silent, and when he reached the front room, he saw that the tapered candles were still burning. Clothes were scattered all over the floor, but he located his and got dressed—having to stop a few times to sit down because he was dizzy. *How much did I drink?* he'd wondered as he took some more deep breaths to ward off nausea. He'd never felt that crappy in the morning, even after spending the entire night doing shots. He finished dressing and slipped out the front door. The morning was cold and damp, and he'd shivered. The gray morning light hurt his eyes, but he kept them down. He'd been lucky—a United cab came cruising down Orleans Street almost immediately after he'd walked out of Jean-Paul's house. He flagged it down and climbed in, giving the address of Jared's parents.

"Fun night?" the cab driver asked as he pulled away from the curb.

"Uh huh," Cord replied. He slid down into the seat and closed his eyes.

In spite of how awful he felt, he was elated. *It was better than my wildest fantasies,* he thought as the cab headed uptown. *If only my head didn't feel like it was going to explode at any minute—and if I didn't feel like throwing up every other minute.* Several times he'd had to open the window and gulp down the fresh cold morning air to fight it, and every time he did he noticed the cab driver looking at him in the rearview mirror. As the cab spun around Lee Circle, the cab driver said, "Look, man, if you need to throw up, let me know and I'll pull over."

"I'm okay," Cord lied. "And I won't puke in the cab, I promise."

Despite the headache, despite the way the light was hurting his eyes, and the nausea that came and went, his skin somehow managed to feel tingly. A couple of times the caress of the wind coming through the window on his skin made his dick—which was also a bit sore—hard.

After paying the cab driver and walking around the main house to the back where the carriage house was located, he wondered how—or if—he would be able to ditch his fraternity brothers again and head back down to the gay area of the Quarter. He felt incredibly pleased with himself. The Holcomb house was dark and silent, and when he walked around to the carriage house in the back, he'd been about to slip his key in the lock when another wave of nausea swept over him. He'd sat down on the stoop, buried his face in his hands, and took some deep breaths. The nausea finally passed, and he unlocked the door and went inside. His three friends were all inside their sleeping bags, sound asleep. He gently shut and locked the door behind him, and he poured himself a glass of water at the sink. He gulped it down, noticing a slightly metallic taste to it, and unrolled his own sleeping bag. The heater was running, and despite the coldness of the slate floor, the warmth also felt good. As he undressed and climbed into his sleeping bag, he smiled for a bit. Gordon was snoring in his sleep—not so loud that it would disturb anyone else's sleep, and as he looked at Gordon's sleeping face—

an image of Gordon stark naked flashed through his mind. He'd seen Gordon in the shower before, and had often wondered what girls saw in him. Gordon had never exercised a day in his life, and his entire body was soft, pale, and fleshy. His man boobs needed a bra. Gordon's entire face was covered with acne and acne scars, and his personality wasn't the greatest, either. Yet somehow he always managed to coerce some girl into his bed, then bragged about his conquests all over the fraternity house. Cord thought about waking Gordon, shoving his cock in Gordon's mouth, and making Gordon suck him off—that would shut him up once and for all—

He'd looked away quickly. Where had that thought come from? Jared was sleeping with his mouth open—

but Jared was no Gordon. Jared was good looking, with deep dimples and a cleft in his chin, dark bluish-black hair, and green eyes that, he claimed, were hallmarks of his Cajun ancestry. He had olive skin that turned golden brown in the sun, and he, like Cord, had been a bit of a jock in high school, and also like Cord, still worked out with weights regularly to keep his body toned and in shape. He'd been a bit in lust with Jared when they'd first been assigned the room together at the Beta Kappa house, and Jared was definitely not shy of his body, walking around either naked or in just a pair of his tighty-whities that always showed off his hard little muscle butt. Even after Cord had confessed to him about his own attraction to other guys, Jared hadn't changed his habits. As Cord watched Jared sleep, he wondered how Jared's cock would taste in his mouth, what it would feel like to kiss Jared, to shove his tongue inside Jared's ass. Would Jared moan and like it as much as Cord did?

He looked away, feeling shame. How could he think that way about Jared after he'd been so good to him? His sore cock was hard again, and he thought about running upstairs and beating off really quick before trying to sleep, and he was about to head for the stairs when Brad made a noise in his sleep—

Brad had one of the biggest cocks he'd ever seen outside the porn movies he watched online. Like Gordon, he went through girls like Kleenex, but unlike Gordon, Brad was secure enough in himself that he didn't have to brag to everyone about his conquests. Brad was tall, was on the swim team at Ole Miss with the hard long lean muscles from years in the pool, and he was really good looking in a way that Cord only wished he could be. He could never resist looking at Brad when they were in the communal shower together—especially in the morning when Brad had his "morning wood." Brad was not self-conscious at all about the other guys seeing him with his long thick cock semihard in the shower, and when he soaped up his crotch it would get even harder and longer. Cord had fantasized about that giant cock any number of times, and he suspected that Brad wasn't averse to letting a guy suck him off—as long as he got his cock sucked, Brad wouldn't care who was doing it.

He gulped and closed his eyes. He undressed and climbed into his sleeping bag. He closed his eyes and willed himself to sleep . . . and as he drifted off he wondered what was happening to him—he'd never had such erotic daydreams about his friends before . . . in fact, he reined those in tightly and always stopped himself whenever his mind went into that direction.

This morning, he couldn't control his thoughts. He couldn't turn them off anymore.

And after a few moments, he managed to finally fall asleep.

His sleep had been troubled by erotic dreams, of cocks being sucked and asses being fucked, of men with muscles glistening with sweat dancing under the flashing lights of the dance floor. He dreamed of candlelit bodies glistening in the soft light and of his cock being inside Jean-Paul again, the way Jean-Paul had reacted to being fucked by him, the way Clint had played with his nipples and the way whoever it was had tongued his ass. He tossed and turned in his sleep, waking himself up more than once when his hard cock hit the cold, hard floor beneath the softness of the sleeping bag.

He sat up, rubbing his aching eyes. He glanced around and saw that he was alone in the carriage house. All around him lay crumpled sleeping bags, and as his eyes painfully adjusted to the brightness, he noticed junk-food wrappers, empty bags of chips, and empty beer cans scattered all around. He stood up, and his head swam for just a moment before it cleared. *I don't understand, I don't really remember drinking all that much*, he thought, trying to remember what exactly he had had to drink at Jean-Paul's house after they had left the bar and gone back there. He didn't remember drinking anything other than water, but maybe he was wrong. He'd had a couple of beers before heading down there, and there had been that huge beer he'd bought on Bourbon Street—but he could only remember the beer that Clint had bought him in Oz, and nothing beyond that. He'd had much more than that on other occasions without suffering in the morning the way he was now . . . which didn't make a hell of a lot of sense to him.

Hell, this was the worst he'd ever felt the morning after—

and that included the night he and Jared had done tequila shots till they both puked. *That* morning, he'd prayed for death.

Prayed for death.

It was Sunday.

He was supposed to be in church in Oxford.

He smiled to himself. *After last night, if I walked into a Church of Christ, the roof would probably cave in,* he thought to himself, *but if that's what hell is going to be like, I'd rather go there than to heaven. And if the preacher calls my parents— or they call the preacher to check up on me, I'll just tell them I had the flu.*

As long as they don't call while I'm at one of the parades.

The door to the carriage house opened, filling the room with bright light. He winced, turning his head away from the unbearable brightness. "Dude, you're finally awake!" Jared said. He was grinning. "You must have had a hell of a time last night."

"Morning, Jared." He didn't turn around. His mouth was dry and gummy, and he dry swallowed. He staggered to his feet and walked over to the sink, filling a glass with water.

"I'm assuming you got laid at long last?" Jared shut the door and walked over to him.

Cord swallowed a huge gulp of metallic-tasting water, and nodded his head as he set the glass back down on the counter. "Oh, yes, I did." He gave Jared a weak grin. "It was—it was incredible."

Jared clapped him on the shoulder, and Cord grinned at him. Jared was wearing an Ole Miss muscle shirt and a tight pair of jeans. For a moment—

—an image of Jared naked flashed into his mind, Jared's hand on his shoulder. "I've always wanted to know what being with another guy was like," he was saying, *his erection brushing against Cord's bare leg, "and who better to try it out with than my best friend?"*

—and it was gone, and Cord turned back to the sink. He splashed cold water on his face. *What is wrong with me this morning? Why am I so goddamned horny? I better get myself under control.*

"You need to get a move on," Jared went on. "The Okeanos parade starts at eleven—" he glanced at his watch—"and that's about twenty minutes from now. It's going to take us a while to walk down there. Brad and Gordon are making a beer run right now."

Just the mention of beer made Cord's stomach roil, and he choked down a gag. "I'm going to get in the shower."

"So, who happened?" Jared asked. "You must have been having a hell of a time. Gordon and Brad were going nuts with jealousy—they struck out with every girl they tried to hook up with—and when you disappeared, and I told them you'd texted me, I thought they were both going to explode, they were so jealous." He winked. "Of course, I didn't tell them what you were really up to."

"I don't know what time I got back."

"It was almost six in the morning, dude." Jared laughed. "You kind of woke me—"

"Sorry."

"—but I just fell back asleep—I figured you wouldn't want to talk about it right then in case Gordon or Brad woke up." He whistled. "Dude, from the look of those hickeys on your neck—let's just say they're going to want all the dirty details. You got a story ready?"

He gave Jared a weak smile. "I don't kiss and tell."

"Good luck with that one."

He didn't answer. Instead, he reached down into his duffel bag and dug out underwear, socks, a pair of jean shorts, and an Ole Miss T-shirt like Jared's. He straightened up again, his head swimming, and he swayed a little bit.

"Dude, how much did you drink last night?" Jared stared at

him. "You going to be okay? Maybe you should lay off the booze today. . . ."

"I'll be fine." He crumpled his clothes into a ball and forced a smile on his face. "I just need a shower and to eat something."

"Mom's got food set out at the house." Jared clapped him on the shoulder, and he almost lost his balance again. "I'll go make a plate for you. Pancakes are what you need—something to soak up the alcohol." The front door shut behind him.

But I didn't really drink that much, Cord thought as he started trudging up the stairs. The bedroom and bathroom were on the second floor of the carriage house, but they'd all decided to camp out and sleep on the first floor. His legs ached with every step, and his head felt like it weighed a thousand pounds on his neck. But the thought of pancakes didn't make his stomach revolt, and maybe that would help him to feel more human. He turned on the shower to hot and let it run while he brushed his teeth. He turned on the light over the sink, wincing just as little as the light hit his eyes, and looked at his neck.

Jared had been right. There were two bloodred welts at the base of his neck.

Clint, he remembered, *or Jean-Paul. Both had nibbled on my neck. Weird.*

He touched them, and the skin was extremely sensitive to the touch—sending a jolt of what felt like electricity through his body, and despite the nausea and the tiredness, his cock got hard.

He remembered entering Jean-Paul again, the feel of someone's tongue lapping at his asshole, Clint playing with his nipples and nibbling on his neck. His balls began to ache from desire, from the need to unload, despite the fact that his cock was sore, he dropped his other hand down to his cock and began to pull on it, and through the soreness it felt good, the soreness even seemed to feel good, and he took his hand away from the welts—

And was staring at himself in the mirror, his erection going soft in his hand.

Another wave of nausea hit him, and he bent over the bathroom sink. The glass of water he'd just drank spewed out of him in a stream, splattering and splashing up out of the sink. He stood there for a few moments, trying to catch his breath, willing the nausea away.

"That's strange," he thought. "Just how fucked up was I?" He spat and rinsed his mouth out. He brushed his teeth, but he could still taste that weird metallic taste in his mouth. *Maybe I should just stay here and not go to the parades,* he thought to himself, and climbed into the shower. He stood there under the hot spray, rinsing up his body (wincing a bit as he soaped his groin; his cock was very sensitive) and then letting the water rinse it all down the drain. He got out and grabbed his slightly damp towel from the night before, and began drying himself. He did feel better, but his eyes still were a little sensitive to the light. He blow-dried his hair and got dressed. When he came back downstairs, Brad and Gordon were drinking beer and there was a steaming hot plate of pancakes on the counter. He smiled at them and poured syrup on his pancakes.

"So, who was this chick?" Gordon took a swig from his beer and belched. "Where'd you find her?"

Cord put a forkful of pancake into his mouth and chewed, swallowing it down. Another wave of nausea washed over him, and he lowered his head, taking some deep breaths. When it passed, he said without turning around, "I went to the bathroom and ran into her—literally—on Bourbon Street. I think she goes to LSU. At least she was wearing an LSU sweatshirt."

"Did she have a big rack?" This from Brad. He was obsessed with big breasts. As long as the girl had big ones, he didn't care what she looked like or what the rest of her body was like. He often caught a lot of shit for fucking "fat chicks," but he just smiled lazily and replied, "But did you see her tits?"

Hating himself, Cord turned and grinned at him. He held his hands out in front of his own chest. "Nice ones."

Brad whistled. "Damn, does she have a friend for me?"

"Like any girl would set up a friend with you," Cord teased, amazed at how easily the lies were coming out of his mouth.

Brad walked over to him and whistled. "Damn, she got ahold of your neck, didn't she?" He reached out and touched the welts before Cord could pull away—

—*Brad was naked, his broad hairy chest about level with Cord's, and that huge porn-star cock was hard. "Go on and touch it," Brad whispered, "I want you to, Cord. I've always been attracted to you, you know, and no one ever needs to know. Go on, touch it, I promise I won't say anything to anyone—"*

—Cord pulled away from Brad. Brad just stood there, his eyes wide, his mouth open in shock. Their eyes met, and the *what the fuck just happened* look on Brad's face made Cord almost laugh out loud. Instead he turned back to his pancakes and put another forkful into his mouth. Brad took a few steps away from him, shook his head, and went back to where he'd set his beer down, and finished it in one gulp, opening another.

He felt it, too, Cord thought, washing the mouthful down with a swig from the huge mug of coffee Jared had also brought over for him. *It's not just me, but what the hell is going on around here? What's wrong with me? Why have I gone so crazy with this stuff? Can't I even look at one of my friends without imagining*—but Brad had felt something, too. It isn't just me. What the hell is going on?

You need to pray for guidance and the Lord's help, he heard his father's voice inside his head again, *you have sinned and you've been marked by the devil for your sin. You have to turn your back on the devil and your sin and find your way back to God, or it's going to get worse.*

He dismissed the voice and finished the pancakes. Despite the weird metallic taste—*and what's that all about?*—he felt a lot better. He finished the coffee and rinsed the mug out.

"Did she give you head?" Gordon belched again, cracking open another beer can.

"Mind-blowing," Cord replied with a smirk. *Tell them the truth, tell them you were in a gay orgy, that you fucked a guy and had your ass eaten in addition to having your cock sucked, and it was better than anything you could have ever imagined, it was better sex than any of them had ever had, would ever have in their entire lives, who cares if they turn their backs on you, they're no different than your parents, they don't know you, they don't know anything about you, they aren't really your friends.*

"Awesome!' Gordon high-fived Jared, who winked at Cord. Cord winked back and rinsed his plate off in the sink.

"Better?" Jared asked him with a big smile, opening another beer. "You look like you've got some of your color back."

"Yeah, man, thanks. " He nodded. "So, what's the plan for today?"

"Well, I thought we could head down to the Avenue with a cooler and watch Okeanos and Mid-City, then carry the stuff back here and walk up the parade route during Thoth, and then hang out on Canal to watch Bacchus tonight—and then we could head into the Quarter and party."

"Four parades today?" Brad said, not looking at Cord and still staring at his fingertips. "That's cool." He finished the beer he was holding, crumpled the can in his hand, and tossed it at the garbage can. It missed, hitting the wall and clattering on the floor. "Nice as it is, there should be lots of hot chicks out there."

"It's warm out?" Cord said, staring at Brad, who still wouldn't look at him.

"Gorgeous!" Gordon crowed. "It's sunny and in the high seventies. I might have to give the ladies a treat and take my shirt off."

"Do us a favor and leave it on," Jared shot back, and they all laughed.

"Fuck you, Jared," Gordon replied good-naturedly. "See if we can't get some trim tonight." Gordon leered at him. "You can't be the only one of us to get laid in New Orleans."

"If you boys can't get laid in New Orleans during Mardi Gras, you might as well go gay," Jared drawled, giving Cord another wink.

Gordon laughed, but Brad didn't—and he looked at Cord. Their eyes met, but Cord couldn't read the expression on Brad's face. "Well, I'm no cocksucker, so I'd better find me a chick tonight. You think you're going to see your piece from last night again?"

Cord shrugged. "I don't know. If I see her, I see her. It's not like I got her number or something."

The other three boys laughed and high-fived each other, and Cord turned away so they couldn't see his face redden. He hated it when the other guys talked liked that—it was one of the reasons, he knew, that they all kind of suspected he was gay, why some of them called him a fag behind his back. He never seemed to be interested in getting some girl drunk at a party and then taking her up to his room and fucking her—on the rare occasions when he was drunk and horny enough to allow a girl to make all the moves on him, he also didn't like to brag about it the next day in the fraternity living room as everyone nursed their hangovers and exchanged stories about the unfortunate girls they'd scored with the night before. Some even went so far as to display stained sheets or panties they'd kept as trophies.

He smiled to himself. It had been easy enough to ditch them the night before—surely he could do it two nights in a row?

Surely Jean-Paul and his friends would be out at Oz again. He smiled to himself. Much as he hated to do it, he'd have to play the game with his brothers so they wouldn't suspect anything.

"She was good but I think I can do better tonight," he said, winking at Jared and turning to give Gordon a big smile.

"Come on, guys, let's get out to the parade route—the parade's on its way already and we don't want to miss it," Jared commanded. He started dumping bags of ice into their cooler on wheels, and Gordon and Brad started loading beers into it. Cord walked over and cracked one, taking a tentative sip.

It tasted perfect. There was no metallic aftertaste, and he turned the can back up and guzzled the entire thing down, spilling some out of the side of his mouth. It ran down his neck and when a stream of cold beer touched on the hickeys, his entire body stiffened again. His cock grew hard, his nipples poking against the T-shirt.

He crumpled the can and threw it into the garbage can and let out a manly belch. "Yeah, there's chicks down there ripe for the plucking." He wiped the sides of his face, and rubbed his neck dry with his T-shirt. Again, when he touched the hickeys, an electric tingling went through his body.

He was horny. He wanted a man. And if it meant pretending to want to fuck girls for the few hours before he could reasonably ditch his fraternity brothers, well, it was a small price to pay to get his cock sucked again.

He watched as Gordon grabbed one end of the cooler and tilted it up onto the wheels and stepped out into the sunshine, pulling it along behind him. Jared followed him out the door, and Cord walked toward the door.

Brad blocked his way. "Can I talk to you for a minute?" He glanced over his shoulder at Gordon and Jared, who were laughing and talking as they walked up the driveway toward the street.

"Sure," Cord replied. "What's up?"

Brad rubbed his eyes. "Um, this is going to sound weird."

Cord raised an eyebrow and smiled. "It would be weird if you said something that didn't sound weird," he teased.

"Before—" Brad hesitated, biting his lip and glancing back at the driveway. Jared and Gordon were no longer in sight. "Before, when I touched your hickeys—" He swallowed. "Would you mind if I touched them again?"

"Yeah, that is weird," Cord replied.

"Please." Brad shifted from one foot to the another, his eyes focused on his feet.

"But why?" Cord asked. "Why would you want to do that?"

"When I touched them before, I—I kind of *saw* something."

There's something weird about my hickeys, Cord thought, remembering the erotic charge he'd felt when Jared had touched them, when the beer had spilled on them, when he himself had touched them—and when Brad had. "What did you see?"

Brad swallowed again. "I—I'd rather not say."

"Oh, for God's sake," Cord snapped. "You know how crazy you sound?" *But he isn't crazy, is he? I feel something every time someone touches them—I have erotic daydreams, my cock gets hard—and you know you saw Brad naked coming on to you when he touched them. So, let him touch you again, see what happens this time.*

"All right, but if you tell anyone, not only will I deny it, I'll kick your ass," Brad said in a quiet voice. "When I touched your hickeys..." his voice trailed off, and then he added in such a rush the words all sounded run together, "... when I touched your hickeys my dick got hard and I saw us, you and I, I mean, in bed together naked and I was ..." He stopped, his face aflame with embarrassment, misery and shame.

"You were sucking my cock," Cord said quietly.

Brad nodded his head.

"And you want to touch them again?"

"I'm not a queer!" Brad burst out. "I mean, yeah, I've messed around a couple of times with guys, you know, when I was fucked up and horny and no pussy was around, but I'm not a queer!"

"I never said you were." Cord reached for Brad's hand and raised it to his neck. "Go ahead, Brad, touch them."

Brad swallowed, and reached out his fingers—

—and there they were, in bed together in Brad's room at the Beta Kappa house. On the desk next to Brad's big bed was a mirror with lines of coke mapped out, a straw and a razor blade off to one side, and they were kissing, and underneath the covers they were stroking each other's cocks, and on the television screen across the room some saggy-breasted blond woman was riding some skinny hairy guy's cock, but they were paying no attention to what was playing on the television, they were focused too much on each other, and Cord was stroking that monster cock while their tongues explored their mouths, and then Brad rolled over on top of Cord, and Cord's arms went around Brad's back, slid down the long smooth expanse of smooth skin to the hard white little ass, and his index finger probed inside the butt cheeks and found the spot, and his finger went inside Brad, and Brad moaned and started kissing his throat as their cocks ground together, and he started moving the finger in and out of Brad's asshole, until Brad reached down and grabbed his wrist to stop him, and he smiled down at Cord and said, "no, I want your cock inside me" and he straddled Cord, and reached down and guided Cord inside him, and his eyes closed and he moaned as he slid down onto Cord's cock, and Cord closed his own eyes because it felt really good as Brad rode him, he wanted to pound himself deep inside Brad, but Brad's weight was pressing down on him and he couldn't really do anything except just lie there and let Brad ride him, and Brad was stroking himself, that huge cock just inches away from Cord's face, and he tried to bring his head forward so he could take it in his mouth, but he couldn't reach, and Brad kept riding, sliding up and down on Cord, and

Cord could feel that he was close, he was going to come really soon if Brad kept it up—

With a little cry, Cord pushed Brad's hand away.

His cock was aching inside his jeans.

Brad licked his lips. "You saw it, too, didn't you?" Brad swallowed. "What the hell, Cord? I mean—" he sighed. "I mean, I could even feel you inside of me." His eyes filled with tears. "And I liked it, man. I liked the way it felt." He placed a hand on the crotch of his jeans. "And I'm hard, man, hard as a rock."

What happened to me last night? Cord wondered. *What did Clint and Jean-Paul and their friends do to me?*

"I—I want you." Brad stepped closed to him. Cord could smell his deodorant, the cologne Brad had put on that morning. He could smell the sweat under Brad's arms.

Everything was silent, other than the soft rustling of the wind in the trees just outside the carriage house door.

"Brad—"

"What the hell are you two doing?"

It was Gordon, yelling from the driveway, and the spell was broken. Brad, a stricken look on his face, backed away from Cord. With a strangled cry, Brad bolted through the door.

Cord watched him go. *I have to go and find Jean-Paul tonight. I have to lose them again on Canal Street, and find Jean-Paul and find out what the hell they did to me, what the hell these hickeys are.*

Pray to the Lord, his father's voice echoed in his head, *make yourself right with God, you have the marks of the devil on you.*

"Shut the fuck up," he said aloud, and stepped out into the sunshine.

This time, the light didn't hurt his eyes more than a little bit.

In the distance, he could hear a marching band.

He slipped on his sunglasses and walked to the end of the driveway, where his friends were waiting for him. Once again, Brad was avoiding his eyes. Cord opened the cooler and took out a beer. He cracked it open and took a swig. Nope, it tasted just fine to him now. They started walking toward the parade route. Gordon and Jared were joking about something, but Cord didn't pay any attention—he just made sure they were in between him and Brad.

It was, in fact, a beautiful day for parades.

And as soon as we get down to Canal Street tonight, I am going to slip away from them and find Jean-Paul and his friends, find out just what exactly happened to me last night.

He remembered the last thing Jean-Paul had said to him before he fell asleep: *Don't leave here. If you wake before I do, you mustn't leave.*

At the time, he had just thought it was nice; that Jean-Paul didn't want him to go away, that he wanted to spend more time with Cord when they woke up—maybe even have sex again.

Maybe there was something more to it than that.

Maybe there was a reason he wasn't supposed to leave.

Now you're thinking crazy shit, he told himself as he finished the beer and tossed the empty into a garbage can. *You think they cast some kind of a spell on you or something? That kind of shit only happens in bad movies. There's no such thing as magic.*

But, still—Brad had seen it, felt it, too. Just from touching the hickeys or whatever the hell they were.

The marks of a vampire is what they are.

"There's no such thing as vampires," he told himself as they turned onto St. Charles Avenue and flagged a cab. He climbed into the front seat—he didn't think Brad would be comfortable sitting next to him in the back. "The parade, please," Jared said breezily as they shut the doors to the cab.

There may be no such thing as vampires, but maybe they'd drugged me—that beer at Oz had tasted funny, and I'd felt weird after I'd drunk it. But what kind of drug would allow me and Brad—no, that doesn't make any sense. No sense at all.

But there was only one way to find out for sure, and that was to find Jean-Paul and ask him.

"Beautiful day," the cab driver said to him.

"Yes, it is." Cord smiled back at him. "A great day for parades."

And finding out what the hell happened last night.

Vampires, he thought to himself again with a bit of a chuckle, accepting the beer Gordon passed to him from the back seat. *That's just crazy. There's no such thing as vampires.*

In his jeans pocket, his cell phone vibrated. He pulled it out and looked at the caller ID.

It was his father.

He put the phone back in his pocket. Plenty of time to deal with that later, he decided. All he was going to do was bitch at him for missing church, and he wasn't in the mood for dealing with that right now.

He wasn't sure he'd ever be in the mood to deal with it ever again.

He remembered the feeling of his cock deep inside Jean-Paul, and he felt his cock getting hard again.

Oh, yes, he was definitely going to look for Jean-Paul.

What had happened with Brad was weird, but it wasn't his problem.

Let Brad figure out his own sexuality.

The cab came to a stop near the corner of St. Charles and Napoleon. A float with what looked to be the Queen of Okeanos was rounding the corner.

Party time.

Chapter Three

"They aren't there," a voice said from behind him.

Cord paused with his hand in midair, resisting the urge to pound his head against the door in frustration. He'd been pounding on the door of the house on Orleans Street for at least five minutes, maybe more, but he refused to accept that Jean-Paul and his friends weren't there. They *had* to be, that was all there was to it.

He felt an overwhelming urge to start kicking at the door. *Where the hell are they?*

It had never occurred to him that he wouldn't be able to find them.

It hadn't been as easy escaping his friends as it had been the night before—it was almost as if they were determined to keep an eye on him and not let him out of their sight. Brad avoided him completely after whatever it was that happened between them in the carriage house, which was perfectly fine with Cord. *Nobody made you touch me, asshole,* he thought angrily one time when their eyes had met and Brad quickly turned away. His anger had boiled up inside him, and in his mind—

—he'd seen himself standing over Brad, fists clenched, with Brad looking up at him, blood running from his nose. Brad looked terrified, but the blood, oh the blood, how delicious it looked, and he'd felt the desire, the urge, the need rising inside him, triggered by the oh-so-delicious-looking red blood flowing from Brad's swelling nose, and he saw the blue vein in Brad's neck, pulsing with the beat of his heart, and it would be so easy to just bend down and sink his teeth into his neck, tear into the skin, and taste the warm intoxicating liquid flowing through his veins—

He'd shaken that off, shivering. *That's just crazy, what the hell is wrong with me? I'm not a vampire, I don't want to drink blood, there's no such thing as vampires, and besides I'm out in the sunlight.*

But he had to admit that the sunlight felt hateful to his skin.

He'd gotten a corn dog slathered with mustard and ketchup at one of the big trailers with the flashing yellow lights and choked it down. All around him, people were laughing and drinking and catching things, shouting at the parade riders on their floats. He felt apart from it somehow, noticing good-looking men and watching them, desiring them, wondering how their skin tasted, how it would feel to enter them and ride them, imaging their smell, the feel of their hot skin on his as he—

What is wrong with me? he wondered, time and again as they kept walking on their long voyage up St. Charles Avenue to Canal Street. He'd always noticed men before, always, but never with such desire, with such fantasies running through his mind, his cock hardening as he watched them.

The need to find Jean-Paul was overwhelming. He kept looking at his watch, as time passed by slowly as they walked, the second hand of his watch barely seeming to move around the dial as the sun slowly disappeared in the western sky and the oh-so-cool and sensual caress of the night began. Mist formed around the streetlights, and the damp felt so good against his skin.

When they reached Canal Street, they'd climbed over a barricade and ran across to the Quarter side. Jared and Brad walked off to get them all beers, and he and Gordon had managed to get a good spot alongside the barricades. Gordon kept elbowing him in the ribs and pointing out girls to him. "Check her out, I'd like to tap that," on and on until he finally stopped listening, stopped reacting and answering, and Gordon eventually shut up until Jared and Brad came back. He sipped the big cup of beer Jared handed him, but it didn't taste right, it didn't quench the overpowering thirst he was feeling. He itched to escape from them, to get away from the shouts and noise of the crowd.

Finally, as the Bacchus parade arrived, the floats with the King and Queen and maids passing, he grabbed Jared's arm and said, "I'm going to go look for a bathroom."

Jared glanced at him and smiled. "There's a bunch of port-a-potties on Chartres Street behind the Supreme Court building."

"Okay," Cord replied, returning the knowing smile.

"I'll come with you," Gordon said, tossing his own beer cup into the gutter. "I'm about to explode."

Cord almost screamed in irritation, but there was nothing to be done about it. So, the two of them had fought their way through the crowd and walked a block up Bourbon Street, turning and heading for the big building. Gordon kept trying to hit on girls as they walked, trying Cord's patience. But they turned the corner on Chartres Street, and got into separate lines, waiting their turn. And once Gordon stepped inside one and shut the door behind him, Cord slipped out of line and walked hurriedly up Chartres Street, resisting the urge to run, the need to get away as quickly as he could. He crossed in front of the cathedral and turned onto St. Ann Street, avoiding the shower of beads coming down from the partiers on the balconies. He reached the crowd at the corner by the gay bars, scanning the faces for Jean-Paul. Not seeing him, he walked into the darkness of Oz.

His phone vibrated in his pocket, but he ignored it as he walked through the crowded bar, ignoring the bikini-clad muscle studs shaking their asses up on the bar, ignoring the smiling men who wished him a happy Mardi Gras, searching faces for Jean-Paul and his friends. They weren't there, they weren't on the dance floor, so he slipped back out and crossed the street, fighting his way through the crowds in the Pub. He ignored the hands brushing against his ass.

They had to be here.

But they weren't there, either, downstairs or upstairs. He went out onto the balcony and scanned the crowds down in the street.

Almost ready to cry in frustration, he went back inside and back down to the street.

Maybe they're at the house.

He walked there, retracing his steps from the night before, climbed the steps, and started pounding on the door.

He turned and looked at the man standing at the foot of the stairs. He was of indeterminate age; his shaved head gleaming in the light. He wasn't handsome, but there was something about him, the way his greenish-brown eyes danced in the mist-shrouded light from the street lamp that Cord couldn't look away from. He was tall and thickly built, wearing a red sweater that hung from powerful shoulders and a tight pair of faded jeans. "Do you know where they are?" he asked finally. "I really need to find them." He looked into the man's eyes—

—*and an image of him naked flashed through Cord's mind. He was thickly muscled, with blue veins decorating the hard muscles like a road map, blue veins that pulsed with every heartbeat, and he felt the emptiness again, the need, the hunger, the desire. His body was smooth, the cock that stood out from the wiry dark bush of hair at his crotch thick and large, a huge head oozing a drop of clear liquid, the balls hanging heavily beneath, and he needed it, he needed to take it in his mouth and taste it, he wanted to worship it, run his tongue up and down the shaft while the man moaned and groaned from the pleasure Cord was giving him, and then the man turned and bent over, presenting his pale ass to Cord to take, to enter and pound and—*

He shook his head and cleared his mind.

"It's Sunday. They aren't anywhere you'll find them." The man laughed, a musical sound that didn't seem to go with the depth of his voice.

"I don't understand," Cord replied. His head was starting to hurt, and he felt the nausea from the empty feeling inside him growing. He sat down on the top step. "I really, really need to find them. Please."

"I don't expect you to understand, at least not yet." The man held out his right hand. "My name is Sebastian."

"Cord." He accepted the man's hand, which was strong and powerful and seemed to close over his. "Are you sure you don't know where they are?"

Sebastian gestured back across the street, to the house where Cord had noticed someone watching him the night before. "I live right over there. Would you like to come in for a drink? To get out of this wind and warm up a bit? I can tell you a few things about Jean-Paul, if you'd like. Help you to understand." He smiled, his teeth even and white.

Cord shivered. It was colder than it had been the night before, and he wasn't wearing a jacket. He wanted to—needed to—keep looking for Jean-Paul, but at the same time getting inside and out of the cold damp wind sounded very appealing. "Okay," he replied, standing up.

Sebastian smiled. "Come on, then." He turned and walked

back across the street, fitting a key into the lock on a old wooden door.

Cord followed him into a darkened house that smelled faintly of lavender and some other spice he couldn't quite place. A wide, orange candle was burning on the coffee table, set in the middle of scattered newspapers and magazines. On top of the television set, a black cat slowly licked one of its paws. The walls were bare of decoration, but there were candles everywhere. In sconces on the walls, on candlesticks and candelabras, and votives placed in small saucers on various flat surfaces around the room. They were all red or white, and were unlit.

"What would you like?" Sebastian gestured to the sofa. "Have a seat and get comfortable."

It was much warmer inside than outside, and Cord sat down on the couch. He crossed his legs and blew out a breath. *Relax, Cord,* he told himself, *you'll find them, and you'll see that all this nonsense you've been thinking all day, these weird connections you've been having with people all day, has just been your imagination, and what happened with Brad—well, there's an explanation for that, too, once I can relax and get my head on straight.* There was something comforting about this house. Maybe it was just the warm air or the scent in the air, but he did feel himself starting to relax a bit. *You've been acting crazy all day—and Gordon is probably going nuts trying to find you. How are you going to explain disappearing to them again?* He stifled a groan and buried his face in his hands. His neck was sore from the weight of the many strings of beads he'd caught at the parades, and he slipped them over his head, dropping them into a pile on the floor. "Do you have beer?" he asked, not looking up. It didn't sound good, but he was so thirsty . . .

"*Certainement.*" Sebastian walked through the huge double doors into the next room and then through a door in the distance.

Cord relaxed back into the sofa, leaning his head back and staring at the ceiling. *You're acting weird,* he told himself for what had to be the thousandth time that day, *just chill and get your head on straight.*

You need to find Jean-Paul as soon as you can, a voice whispered inside his head, *he's the only one who can answer your questions for you.*

Another wave of nausea gripped him. His head was spinning a bit, and he took deep breaths, willing it to go away.

His stomach was so empty.

Sebastian walked back into the living room carrying a glass of red wine in one hand and a bottle of beer in the other. He passed Cord the bottle of beer and sat down in a reclining chair on the other side of the room. He lifted the glass in a mock salute, said, "Cheers," and took a sip.

Cord gave him a weak smile in return and sipped the beer. The weird metallic taste in his mouth was back, and he almost gagged but managed to swallow the beer. *Maybe I'm coming down with something, that's all—some kind of flu, maybe,* he thought as he put the beer down on top of a magazine on the coffee table.

Then another thought rushed through his mind. *We didn't use condoms last night.*

His entire body went cold. *Oh my God, oh my God, what if—*

Sebastian was saying something, and Cord willed the horrible thoughts out of his mind. "I'm sorry?" he replied, "I didn't hear what you were saying."

Sebastian gave him a crooked smile. "You're quite worked up, aren't you?" He took another sip of the wine and gave him a slight nod in return. "Why are you looking for Jean-Paul? Why is it so important that you find them?

"I met him and his friends last night," Cord replied. "I had a great time hanging out with them, and was hoping to run into them again tonight. That's all."

Sebastian laughed, a warm low sound of genuine amusement. "You went back home with them last night, didn't you?"

Cord's cheeks flushed. "You already know the answer, don't you?" He waved at the window behind him. "You were watching us, weren't you?"

"Touché." Sebastian smiled back at him. "Yes, I was watching. I've been watching what goes on in that house across the street for a very long time."

"Why?"

Sebastian put the glass down. "It was your first time being with another man, wasn't it?" He raised his eyebrows.

"So what if it was?" Cord replied, reaching a trembling hand for his beer. "What business is it of yours?"

"If you're worried about not using condoms—"

How did he know that? Something's not right here. I need to get away.

Sebastian shook his head slightly. "Jean-Paul and his friends, they aren't like other men, you know. Condoms are the least of your worries as far as they are concerned."

"What do you mean?" Cord swallowed. The nausea was coming back, so he put the beer back down.

"You've felt weird all day, haven't you?" Without waiting for an answer, Sebastian went on, "You're wearing sunglasses after dark—or at least you were outside. Did the light hurt your eyes? Does food and drink taste off to you? And the sun didn't feel too good on your skin today, did it?"

Cord bit his lower lip. "How—how did you know all that?" He resisted the urge to get up and walk out the front door, to run back to Canal Street and forget anything had ever happened to him on Orleans Street.

"I'm right, aren't I?" Sebastian just smiled. "And you've

been having weird insights about your friends all day as well, am I right? Like you knew what they were thinking?"

"Well, yes." Cord felt goose bumps coming up on his arms, and a chill went through him. "It's nothing, though." He forced out a laugh. "Just a bit of a hangover, is all. And good pot. That's all it was. Really." He stood up. "I think I'd probably get back to my friends. They're probably wondering where I am."

"After all the trouble you went through to get away from them?" Sebastian raised an eyebrow and finished his wine in a gulp. "You got away from them and headed down for the gay section of the Quarter. You don't want them to know what you're doing, right? And it wasn't easy getting away from them tonight." Sebastian stood up and slipped his sweater up over his head and folded it neatly. His torso was smooth and hairless, the chest strong and muscular over a well-defined stomach. A trail of golden-brown hairs descended from his navel to the waistband of his jeans. His arms were corded with muscle, bluish thick veins landscaping his shoulders and arms.

Just the way I thought he would look.

"What's—what's happening to me?" Cord whispered, and in spite of everything, he felt his cock thickening inside his own jeans. He wanted to touch him, to feel his skin. He swallowed. "Um, wow," he finally said, cursing at himself as an idiot.

Sebastian walked around the coffee table until his face was next to Cord's. He reached up and touched the base of Cord's neck, his fingers pressing into the spot where the welts were.

Cord gasped, and the room began spinning around. His breath started panting as electric volts of pleasure shot through his body, his cock straining against his underwear and jeans. His knees felt weak, and in his mind—

He was lying on his back on an incredibly soft and comfortable bed. His legs were apart, and he looked up into Sebastian's face. The room was lit by candles, and in the soft light he doubted that anyone in the world could be as handsome as Sebastian was in that moment. He gasped a bit as he felt slight pain down in his rectum, and then Sebastian was entering him and he couldn't seem to let his breath out, the pain was too much, and then he expelled the air and his own resistance seemed to melt away in that moment. Sebastian slid deeper inside and the pain—the pain was melting away into pleasure, unmistakable, unbelievable pleasure that rode over his body like waves, and he began to tremble. Sebastian was whispering to him in his soft velvety voice, words he couldn't understand, words that made no sense to him, but seemed like French, and then he began to understand what Sebastian was saying, he was saying that he loved Cord, that he thought Cord was the most beautiful man he had ever seen, that Cord was giving him more pleasure than he ever thought possible from another man's body, and the sliding was going deeper, and deeper, and the pleasure was intense, the feeling was so amazing, so deep and intense that he thought the top of his head was going to blow off at any moment, that his heart would explode because he couldn't handle it anymore and everything was right, nothing else in the world mattered other than having Sebastian inside him—

Sebastian pulled his fingers away.

Cord gasped and sat back down on the sofa as his knees gave way completely. "What—what—what did you do to me?"

Sebastian sat down beside him on the couch and rested his hand on Cord's knee. "I did nothing other than touch your wounds."

"Wounds?" Cord wanted to pull away from him, to get up and walk out of the house, but somehow he couldn't find the energy to do so, or the desire to make his body move. "They're just hickeys."

"Poor sweet innocent boy from Mississippi." The words lightly mocked him, but the voice was kind. "You really don't know what's happening to you?"

"Nothing's happening to me," Cord insisted, but he heard a voice inside his own head mocking him, *you do know, don't you, you just don't want to face up to it.* "Just a bit of a hangover—granted, one of the worst ones I've ever had, but that's all it is. And I'll be fine in the morning."

Sebastian's left hand moved to Cord's mouth quickly, and before Cord knew what was happening Sebastian had pushed his index finger past his lips and into his mouth. Cord pulled his head back. "Hey, what's the idea?"

Sebastian shrugged. "My apologies." He held up his index finger. A drop of bright-red blood was in the pad of the finger—and getting larger. As Cord watched, it began to run down toward the palm.

And it excited—and sickened—him.

"Have your canine teeth always been sharp enough to draw blood?" Sebastian pressed a tissue to his finger, and Cord watched as the tissue turned red. He couldn't take his eyes away from it.

And he felt—he felt *hungry.*

"My—my teeth aren't sharp." It was a trick of some sort, it had to be, he didn't know what this Sebastian wanted from him or why he would play such a trick on him, but that's what it was, what it had to be. He ran his tongue over the bottoms of his upper front teeth, and sure, the canines seemed sharp to him, but no sharper than usual. *This is crazy, this guy is crazy, I just need to get out of here—*

He couldn't take his eyes away from the flowering bud of red blood in the tissue Sebastian was holding.

Sebastian just smiled at him. "You know the truth, you just don't want to face it." He shrugged. "I don't blame you. It is hard to face the truth when it flies in the face of everything you've ever believed in your life." He tossed the tissue away, and the blood welled up on his finger again. "You want this blood, don't you? You want it, but at the same time the desire for it sickens you."

"Stop," Cord whispered. "Just stop."

"Jean-Paul gave you an extraordinary gift last night." Sebastian went on as if he hadn't spoken. "A gift that many would want, would desire. He drank from your neck—and let you drink from his."

"That's not true!" He cast his mind back to the night before, the night he'd sworn he'd never forget. He remembered Jean-Paul nuzzling at his neck in the living room of the house across the street, but—he didn't remember anything like Sebastian was suggesting.

"Jean-Paul and his friends are a fraternity of vampires," Sebastian said, waving his bleeding finger over the candle in the center of the coffee table. He closed his eyes and mumbled a few words—

As Cord watched, the wound in his finger closed.

He gasped and pulled back from Sebastian.

Sebastian tossed his head back and laughed. "It's just simple magic, my friend."

"What are you?" Cord whispered, his head spinning. *None of this is real, none of this is really happening, I am going to wake up any minute and be back in the carriage house with my friends, this is all a dream I am going to wake up from, this day never happened, really, this has to be a dream, there's no such thing as magic. . . .*

"Magic is very real, Cord." Sebastian stroked the side of Cord's face. "As are vampires. Your faith—your religion— teaches that there are no such things, but witchcraft and vampires are far older than your religion. You don't really believe in your religion, anyway—it has no use for boys like you anyway. Your ministers believe boys like you are sinners, destined for hell. Which is what made you ripe for Jean-Paul—you've denied who you are for so long . . ."

"What's happening to me?" Cord cried out. His head felt

like it was splitting, he was so hungry he thought he might faint, the desire was so strong—

—and he could see the pulse pounding in the artery in Sebastian's neck.

Blood, beautiful, sweet, delicious blood was there, there for the taking, just a thin layer of skin separating him from what he needed, what he desired, what he had to have.

"You're transitioning," Sebastian replied. "Your body is changing from what it once was to what it will be. You will no longer be human, you know—you are no longer completely human right now. That's why the sun hurt your eyes, stung your skin. The transition from human to vampire is a very dangerous time, and you have to make a choice. You have to choose whether you want to be a human or if you want to complete the transition, my young friend."

"I'm dying?" *No, all of this is crazy, none of this could be true, there's no such thing as vampires, or magic.*

"You know it's true, don't you? Everything I've said is true, isn't it? You can't deny it, can you? Poor sweet little Mississippi boy. You've stumbled into something that you have to face up to—you don't have a choice." Sebastian laughed, but it was a kind sound. "And you're not dying—at least not in the sense that you mean. Vampires aren't the undead, but rather a mutation of humans. When you drank from Jean-Paul, it was like being infected with a flu. Right now, his vampire-infected blood is converting you—your blood, your cells, your organs, from what you were into what you will be."

"Can it—can it be stopped?" He heard the words coming out of his mouth, but still he resisted. It couldn't be true, vampires didn't exist, maybe Sebastian had drugged his beer, that was why it tasted funny, and all of this was just some hallucination, he was imagining it all.

"Is that what you want?" Sebastian asked. "There are many

advantages in being a vampire, you know. Vampires exist out of normal human time, you know." He caressed Cord's chin. "You're young and beautiful. A vampire stays young for hundreds of years, doesn't age the way humans do. And there's the power—you've already had a taste of it, haven't you? You experience things more deeply." Sebastian traced his index finger along Cord's inner arm and sat down beside him on the couch. "You can see into the minds of others—once you learn how to use that power. And my touch—" he slipped his hand onto Cord's knee, "just the mere touch of another can make you ravenous with sexual desire."

Sebastian's hand on his knee felt hot, as though electricity somehow flowed through his hand into Cord's leg. His cock was aching.

"I don't know what you're talking about."

"Don't you?" Sebastian moved his hand to Cord's chest, and through his sweatshirt flicked at the nipple.

Cord moaned, his eyes closing, and he sank deeper into the couch. *He was right, it felt incredible, just his touch was like fire. . . .*

"If you really want to stop the transition, there is a spell I know—but in order to make it work, we have to perform the sacred rite."

"A spell?" Cord opened his eyes. "What are you?"

Sebastian laughed. "Me? Well, I'm a witch, Cord, descended from a long line of New Orleans witches." He gestured to the window. "I've been watching Jean-Paul and his friends for years, waiting for them to try to turn another unsuspecting soul into one of them." His eyes flashed. "They did it to my younger brother, you know. They took my brother and made him one of the damned." He looked away from Cord. "We—we had to destroy him, Cord. And I swore on my brother's grave that I would never allow them to do the same thing to someone else."

He stood up and held out his hand. "So, if you truly want to be human, come with me and we will perform the sacred rite. It's the only way to save you, Cord."

Cord closed his eyes. *This is crazy, this is crazy, everything that's happened to me since I met Jean-Paul and his friends is crazy, I'm going to wake up in my bed back at the fraternity house in Oxford and this whole thing will have been some kind of nightmare, that's all it is, and I'll laugh at myself.* "Sacred rite?" he asked, "what's that?"

"We have to pray to the gods with our bodies." Sebastian ran a hand from his own throat down his torso to his crotch. "We must make love first." He smiled and undid the front of his pants, revealing a pair of red cotton underwear. "Will making love with me be such a hardship for you?" Sebastian's hand dropped to Cord's crotch. "You're already ready for me, aren't you, Cord?" His voice echoed inside Cord's head. "Even if you don't believe, you want me, don't you? So what harm will my little ritual do?"

Cord opened his eyes. What, indeed, harm would it do? None at all. And Sebastian was sexy, his body amazing, and he was right, Cord admitted to himself, he wanted him.

Cord stood up. Sebastian was slightly taller and opened his arms. Cord put his own arms around Sebastian, and their lips came together in a kiss. Sebastian's lips were warm, firm but somehow soft at the same time, and his tongue was pushing through into Cord's mouth, and he sucked on it.

Sebastian moaned, sliding his hands inside Cord's sweatshirt and coming to his nipples, pinching them.

Cord's head went back. "Oh, my God." His body and skin felt as though they were on fire, and then Sebastian was slipping his sweatshirt over his head, tossing it aside, and Sebastian lowered his mouth to Cord's right nipple, teasing it with his tongue, licking at it, flicking it, pushing it against his teeth until

Cord could barely stand it, his entire body starting to stiffen to keep from trembling uncontrollably, and he grabbed ahold of Sebastian's ass, which was hard to the touch, and squeezed it.

Sebastian smiled at him, taking him by the hand. "Come with me," he said.

Cord followed him through darkened rooms barely lit by candles, through a kitchen, and into a huge bedroom. Sebastian dropped Cord's hand, struck a match, and walked around the room lighting candles, all of them white, and turned and smiled. He kicked off his shoes, undid his pants, and slid them down, taking off his underwear at the same time, and stood there, naked in the candlelight.

His own hands shaking, Cord knelt down and untied his shoes, slipping them off. He stood back up, sliding his pants down and off his feet, and then removed his underwear.

"You are so beautiful," Sebastian breathed, taking a few steps toward him. He took Cord in his arms and they kissed again, their hard cocks brushing against each other as Sebastian's tongue entered Cord's mouth again, and the pleasure was so intense—

—and as Sebastian moved his mouth down to Cord's throat, his tongue licking the wounds at the base of his throat, Cord was vaguely aware that Sebastian was mumbling something as he licked the wounds, and the feeling grew intense, so intense that he could barely stand it, but at the same time he didn't want it to stop, no, he didn't want it to ever stop, he wanted to just stand there and let Sebastian work at his throat with his tongue forever, and he felt Sebastian's teeth nipping at his skin, and it was pleasure unmanageable, like nothing he could have ever dreamed of when he was masturbating to *Playgirl* centerfolds and wondering what another man's skin would feel like, what a cock would feel like inside him, it was beyond his wildest dreams and fantasies, and still he heard Sebastian mumbling even as he worked on Cord's throat, and then his mouth was moving down Cord's torso, his tongue playing with his navel, darting in and out as though giving him a saliva bath, and Cord moaned deep and low in his throat, his head going back, and then Sebastian's tongue was exploring his cock, and Cord was trembling, his balls clenching and aching and then—

It stopped.

Cord opened his eyes and looked down at Sebastian, who was still on his knees in front of him. "Please don't stop," Cord whispered.

Sebastian rose to his feet, placing a hand on Cord's cock and running his index finger over the wet head.

Oh, my God, that feels incredible.

"We mustn't let our desires interfere with the great rite," Sebastian whispered, leading him by the cock to the bed. He pressed his hands into Cord's chest, pushing him back down onto the red and black quilt. Cord lay back, swinging his legs up onto the bed.

Sebastian climbed onto the bed and straddled him.

"Oh great Mother of us all, hear our prayer and heed our rite, answer us with the thing that we desire of you." Sebastian closed his eyes and turned his head up to face the ceiling. He grabbed Cord's cock and positioned himself above it. "As I take this beautiful young man inside me to connect us further in your eyes, please hear us, please heed us, we do this in your name."

He slid down and Cord gasped as he entered Sebastian. He closed his eyes, and Sebastian's chanting became noise, a comforting rhythm of syllables and sounds, and as Sebastian slid down further on Cord's shaft, images starting dancing through his mind—

—he was in the showers back at Beta Kappa, late at night, watching as Brad stroked his own soapy cock as he let the hot water course over his body, and then Brad morphed into Jared, and Jared was reaching his hands out to Cord—

"Hear our prayer, O Great Mother!"

Sebastian was sliding up and down now, and Cord grabbed the quilt with both hands, it was incredible, it was better than what he'd experienced with Jean-Paul the night before—

—*and he could feel Clint's tongue inside his ass, lapping at his hole again, and it was awesome, Clint was taking little nibbles at the skin around the hole and Cord's cock ached for release, his balls aching*—

and still Sebastian kept riding him, riding and chanting in the candles. Every so often the chant was interrupted by moans of unbridled pleasure as Cord's cock reached that place so deep inside Sebastian that controlled his desires and needs and urges, and it was hot inside him, and it felt as though their souls were somehow merging, their very selves merging into one—

—*this can't be sin, I don't care what anyone says, they don't know, they couldn't know, unless they'd experienced the joy of melding with another human in this way, it wasn't a sin, this couldn't condemn me to eternal hellfire, this was the greatest feeling possible in the world*—

—and Sebastian's ass gripped Cord's cock like it would never let it go, and still he chanted on and on, saying words that now sounded like another language, and somehow, somehow Cord knew it was an ancient tongue, the ancient tongue of the witches, a tongue that was old when the pyramids were young, when Christianity was thousands of years in the future, and he felt so free—

and he was standing in the desert, with the glittering waters of the Nile beyond, and Sebastian was standing in front of him, his eyes painted the way the statues in the history books of the pharaohs were painted, with the black lines above and below the eyes coming together into a single line at the corners of the eyes, and Sebastian was turning around and offering that smooth and hard ass to him, and he plunged inside him—

—and he felt himself building, he felt the urge the need the desire welling up inside his lower bowels, and knew that he was close, oh so close, and Sebastian was gasping and moaning and convulsing and he felt the warm drops raining down on his chest and then with a cry he felt his own rising, and his balls ached and that low pain mixed with pleasure and his mouth opened and a scream of sheer pleasure erupted from deep inside him as he came, and he thrust himself up inside Sebastian even deeper and deeper and it didn't seem like he was ever going to stop—

And then it was over and he collapsed back onto the bed.

Sebastian's hand caressed his cheek. "Sleep, my beautiful young Cord, sleep."

He wanted to ask if it had worked, if he was human again, but his mind was going dark, his eyes couldn't focus and stay open, sleep was welcome, sleep was what he needed. . . .

And the last thing he heard as he drifted off into the darkness was Sebastian's pleased laugh.

Chapter Four

Cord opened his eyes slowly, not really sure where he was at first—other than that he wasn't on the slate floor of the Holcombs' carriage house.

The dream he'd been having had been intensely erotic.

It was almost, he thought as his groggy mind worked itself awake, as though finally experiencing his true sexuality had opened the floodgates of fantasy and eroticism in his mind—that actually *knowing* what it felt like to have his cock in someone's ass had intensified his fantasies.

As the dream faded, he was left with a vague memory of naked male bodies.

The glowing numbers on a clock across the room read 11:47. The room was dark other than the glowing numerals. His nose itched. He tried to move his right hand to scratch it—and found that he couldn't move his right arm, or his left.

His wrists were tied to the bedposts. "Hey!" he shouted, but there was no response to his call. The house was completely silent. He tried to move his legs—they were lashed to the posts at the foot of the bed. He turned his head from side to side, and as his eyes adjusted to the gloom—*they were doing more than adjusting, he was able to see, that couldn't be, he couldn't see in the dark, that just wasn't possible*—he realized he was still in the bedroom.

And he *could* see in the dark. Clearly, in fact. He could see his clothes had been neatly folded and placed in a chair with his shoes on top of them. He could see the patterns on the curtains on the window behind the chair. He could see the unlit candles in the sconces on the walls.

And if it was, in fact, 11:47, he'd been asleep around three hours.

Three hours.

Plenty of time, apparently, for Sebastian to tie him up before he went wherever it was that he went. How long had Sebastian been gone? How long had Cord been tied up?

And more importantly, *why* had Sebastian tied him up?

"You're an idiot," he said aloud with a groan. He tugged at the ropes holding his wrists to no avail. He wasn't actually tied very tightly—he had some movement, but tugging at them made them go taut and dig into his wrists. He let his arms go limp again and sighed. "He sure saw you coming."

Stay calm and don't panic, he told himself. *Think this through. If he tied you up, obviously he didn't want you to leave, but don't think about that. See if you can instead figure out a way to get free. And if you can see in the dark—*

But he didn't want to think about that. Human beings can't see in the dark—

But vampires can.

He dismissed that thought as soon as he had it. That was all just crazy bullshit. There was a logical explanation for the weird things he'd been experiencing all day—*sure there is,* an inner voice taunted, *you just suddenly developed the ability to read minds or see into other people's*—but he could think about all of that later. Right now, he had to focus on getting loose, on getting out of here before Sebastian came back. He shouted again, but his voice simply echoed in the silent house. No one would be able to hear him outside—there was just too much noise from Bourbon Street a few blocks away. He could, now that he thought about it, hear Bourbon Street himself. *And even if someone walking by could by some chance hear me, what are they going to do? Call the police?* The police were busy working Bourbon Street and the parade routes. How fast would they respond to a call about hearing someone calling for help inside a house? They'd probably dismiss the call as a prank.

He groaned again. *Think, Cord, you're not a fool.*

"A fool wouldn't be caught like this, either," he said out loud. He groaned again and closed his eyes. All of Sebastian's talk about vampires and magic; all of it was just a trick to get him off balance, so he could wind up tied to the bed. He remembered being groggy after the so-called "great rite"—remembered Sebastian encouraging him to go to sleep, and once he had, Sebastian had tied him up and gone somewhere.

In fact, he'd probably been drugged—the beer had tasted a little funny, he remembered. Which also meant that Jean-Paul or one of his buddies had drugged him, too, since the beer Clint had bought him last night at Oz had also tasted funny. The taste in his mouth had still been there that morning—but had gone away after he'd eaten the pancakes and drank some coffee. *Some kind of date-rape drug—that's what it all was, the funny taste, the hallucinations and so forth, all drug induced, and then Sebastian gave me another dose of whatever it was last night,* he thought grimly. Vampires and witches. If he could, he'd smack himself in the forehead. *Oh yeah, Sebastian had definitely seen me coming—hell, he may have some kind of connection to Jean-Paul and his friends, or he knew the kind of things they did to unsuspecting tourists when they took them back to their house.* But Jean-Paul and his friends hadn't tied him up, at least—he fell asleep but when he woke, he was free to go home. *And I lis-*

tened to all that idiocy about vampires and magic. "Great rite," indeed—what kind of religious rite could fucking be a part of? What religion? He laughed bitterly. "I deserve to die just for being so fucking stupid," he said out loud.

But I am NOT going to die in this fucking house.

"*Help!*" he screamed at the top of his lungs, and kept shouting until his voice went hoarse. There was no answer—and then he remembered, his heart sinking, that the bedroom was in the absolute back of the house. No one would hear him, especially with all the noise from the celebrating going on in the streets.

And even if by some miracle if someone did, what could they do? Would they even pay attention?

Probably not—it was Mardi Gras, after all, and crazy shit was going on all around the city at that very moment.

No one knows where you are. You can't move, you can't get off the bed, so how exactly are you going to get loose, anyway?

He was completely at Sebastian's mercy, for whatever it was he had planned. And whatever Sebastian's intentions were, they couldn't be good.

He's going to kill you, is what he is going to do.

He tugged at the ropes holding his ankles until his leg muscles screamed from the exertion. The ropes didn't budge, didn't move.

He tried rocking, pulling his torso up as far as the ropes would allow, then throwing himself back onto the mattress and throwing his legs up.

The bed didn't budge.

Panic rose in him, and he fought it down. Panic wouldn't help him. He pulled his head up and looked around the room.

There was a pair of scissors on the dresser only a few feet from the bed.

Biting his lip, he judged the distance from the side of the bed to the dresser. Two, maybe three feet? If he could just get the bed to move—

But how?

And even if he got the scissors somehow, how would he use them?

"Worry about that once you have the scissors," he muttered to himself.

He took a deep breath and tried to raise his torso again, throwing himself back into the mattress as soon as he had gotten as high as the ropes would let him. As soon as his back hit the mattress, he strained up again. He kept going, over and over again, breathing out as he propelled himself back into the mattress, taking a deep breath as he pulled himself up again—

—and the bed moved a bit. Maybe an inch closer to the dresser.

He stopped, panting and almost ready to cry. At this rate, he would wear himself out long before he got the bed close enough to the dresser.

And there was the matter of how to use the scissors with his hands and feet tied, anyway.

He closed his eyes and tried to catch his breath.

How long would it take before Jared and everyone got worried about him? The next morning? They wouldn't worry about him tonight—not after he'd ditched them and came home so late the night before. They'd assume he was off getting laid again. The next afternoon? The next night? The next day? And what would they be able to do during Mardi Gras? No one would even know where to start looking for him—

—and by then, he'd almost certainly be dead.

Just another dumb tourist who'd gone off by himself and wound up a corpse. He remembered the lecture Jared had given them all on Saturday night before they'd headed out for the evening:

New Orleans is a very welcoming and fun city, but at the same time, it's a dangerous city filled with some crazy people and criminals who prey on tourists. You always have to be aware of where you are, what you're doing—otherwise you are going to wind up as a victim. If you get so drunk that you aren't really capable of taking care of yourself, the best thing to do is to grab a cab and come back here. Even the French Quarter has areas that aren't safe—and don't trust strangers. Always keep your wallet in your front pants pocket whenever you're in a crowd because there are pickpockets. If we get separated by any chance, remember the address here and just get in a cab.

His parents didn't even know he was in New Orleans.

Oh, Mom and Dad, I'm so sorry. He felt tears rising in his eyes. No matter their differences, no matter how badly he wanted to get away from them and their church and live his own life, he loved them and they loved him and this was going to kill them.

Don't give up, Cord! Try it one more time! You don't know how long Sebastian is going to be gone—and if he comes home before you get the scissors, it doesn't matter. At least you didn't sit here feeling sorry for yourself and waiting for death.

He started the whole thing over again. Only this time, when he pulled himself up as far he could, he heard a slight cracking sound.

He stopped, the only noise his labored breathing. Had he imagined that? Or had he actually managed to crack the post? Tentatively, he pulled with his right arm again.

He heard another slight crack—and he was able to move the arm more.

Elated, he tugged with all the strength he could muster. There was another slight crack. He relaxed. Okay, he'd cracked the post. He wasn't strong enough to completely break it—but if he used the same method that had cracked it in the first place, only instead of rocking backward and forward, if he instead tried rocking from side to side, built up enough momentum—

He heard the front door shut in the distance.

Too late.

Whatever Sebastian had planned for him, he had to remain calm. He had to figure out a way to get free, to get out of here. If Sebastian didn't kill him right away, he could try the rocking from side to side. Anything. But the most important thing was to stay alive, not do or say anything that might trigger Sebastian into killing him sooner rather than later. If he had to beg and plead, he would do it.

Footsteps approached through the house, and each step heightened his anxiety. It was seeming to take forever for Sebastian—or whoever it was who entered the house—to get back there. *What if isn't Sebastian? Maybe I should call out for help* . . . but he decided to just wait and see who it was—if it was Sebastian, calling for help might be the very thing that would to make him angry enough to kill.

The bedroom door swung open. Sebastian stood there, holding a candelabra. He smiled. He was wearing the same clothes he'd been wearing earlier, but had a knit cap on his bald head and a black leather jacket on over the sweater. "Ah, you're awake." He set the candelabra down on a table. "How are you feeling?" He took the jacket off and dropped it over the pile of Cord's clothes.

"Why did you tie me up?" Cord tugged on the ropes again. Was that another faint crack he heard from his right side again? If so, he hoped Sebastian hadn't heard it.

Sebastian smiled at him. "I didn't want you going anywhere. I had to go out for a while—" He held up a bag. "—I went out and got a few things I needed for the spell I am going to cast." He put the bag down on the dresser next to the scissors, and started removing jars from it. "It took a little longer than I'd hoped, sorry. I'd intended to be back before you awoke." He turned and smiled at Cord. "I'm sorry if it freaked you out to wake up and be tied to the bedposts. You're perfectly safe, you know."

And what if the house had caught fire with all these candles everywhere? Cord took a deep breath and forced a smile on his own face. "Well, yeah, it was kind of freaky, frankly. I've never woken up like this before." He tugged on the ropes again. "Well, you're here now, and this is kind of uncomfortable. Can you untie me, please? Could we—" he swallowed, "—you know, like before?"

Sebastian laughed. "Oh, you liked that, did you? I'd be lying if I said I didn't. But untying you right now? I don't think that's such a good idea." Sebastian shook his head. "No, I think it's best that you stay there until I finish with you." He walked over to the side of the bed, and with his left hand began stroking Cord's inner thigh. "You really are quite beautiful, my young friend."

In spite of himself, Cord felt himself getting aroused again.

"I'm not going to kill you," Sebastian went on, his voice silky smooth, "if that's what you're afraid of."

"Then why won't you untie me?" Cord strained his arms again against the tight ropes, and definitely heard another crack. Maybe a few more tugs, and the post would break free. For a brief moment, he imagined swinging the post against the side of Sebastian's head. *Careful, careful, and be more quiet about it,* he told himself, allowing his arms to go slack again. He closed his eyes and rested his head back against the pillow.

Sebastian's fingers continued to lightly stroke his inner thigh. Cord began to shiver. It felt so good, almost unbearably so. But the restraining ropes kept him from squirming, from trying to move away from those gentle fingers, and his breath started coming in gasps.

"Relax, my pretty young boy," Sebastian smiled, and bent over. "Oh, you're quite beautiful, aren't you? You don't even know how beautiful you are."

Cord's breath left him in a gasp of pleasure as Sebastian's tongue began to flick over the skin of his inner thigh. His semi-aroused cock got fully hard, standing up and straining. One of

Sebastian's fingers began rubbing the head, gently running the ball of the finger over the slit, down around the bottom, and tears filled Cord's eyes, it felt so good, and he closed his eyes and bit his lower lip. He was completely at Sebastian's mercy. He should be afraid, not turned on, but there was something about the restraining ropes, his own sheer helplessness, his inability to do anything to stop Sebastian's teasing tongue and fingers that was—well, *exciting,* so exciting and pleasurable that he almost didn't want Sebastian to stop.

Carefully, he tugged slightly with his right arm.

"What are you doing?" Sebastian brought his head up. His eyes narrowed to slits. He looked at the post. He got up and grabbed the candelabra and examined the post. He laughed. "Ah, you do have the strength of a nascent vampire, don't you? You've cracked the post." He looked more closely. "A few more tugs and it would break. Good thing you're not at your full strength, eh? Mere ropes wouldn't have held you."

"Please let me go."

"Not yet, my beautiful young vampire." He lightly allowed his free hand to trail from Cord's neck down to his groin. "When I'm finished with you, certainly. And don't worry. I'm not going to kill you." His eyes narrowed. "You'd be of no use to me dead."

Cord swallowed. "What are you going to do? What use do you have for me?"

"It's almost time," Sebastian replied. "I am going to drink from you."

"What?" Cord shook his head. This was just getting crazier and crazier. *He does think I'm a vampire, that Jean-Paul and his friends are vampires, he is insane, I can't believe anything he tells me, he is going to drink from me and then he is going to kill me. He can't let me go in case I go to the police—*

But would the police believe his crazy story?

Sebastian turned back to him and smiled. "You are transitioning—even though you don't want to believe it, you know in your heart that it's true. You drank from one of them last night—perhaps Jean-Paul, perhaps another. I doubt it was Jean-Paul—he would have never allowed a transitioning vampire out of his sight for a moment."

Cord swallowed. He heard Jean-Paul telling him again, *whatever you do, you mustn't leave this house before I awake. Promise me you won't leave before I wake up.* But he had left the house. *No, don't listen to him, you know this is all crazy nonsense.*

"You have perhaps another twenty-four hours at best before the transition is complete and you become a vampire. Then it will be too late." Sebastian went on.

"Too late for what?" *Keep him talking, keep him talking.* "What do you mean, too late?"

"I've waited years for an opportunity such as this." He went on as though Cord hadn't spoken. "Years I've lived in this house, watching and waiting for the moment Jean-Paul or one of his little circle decided to convert another human."

"I don't understand. None of this makes any sense to me. Please, untie me and let me go. I won't tell anyone."

"How could you understand, my pretty young boy?" Sebastian laughed lightly. He was crushing something in a pestle. Tendrils of smoke began to curl out of the stone pestle as he continued to grind away. He added something else, and the smoke turned from gray to green. "Vampires and witches, my young friend, are the two most powerful creatures in the world. Our powers, of course, are different—vampires are more like what you would think of as mutant superheroes—super sight and hearing, able to move without being seen, and some of them, after centuries of feeding, can even fly. What is the movie? Ah, yes, *X-Men.* Vampires are very real, my young friend, no matter how hard your world tries to deny their existence. They—and witches—move among you every day. You may even know some already in your life; we guard our identities from humans very carefully. Despite our powers, we can be captured—and killed.

"Unlike a vampire, a witch's power is more from the mind; it has always been so. It is our mind, and the use of spells to focus that power, that gives us the ability to control the minds of the weak, to fly, to see the future and look into the past. We aren't physically a match for vampires, of course; but our minds are more than a match for theirs. But if a witch were to become a vampire . . ." his voice trailed off. He set the pestle down, opened a small vial, and poured a few drops from it into the pestle. There was a slight fizzing sound, and the smoke coming from it became thicker. He leaned forward and breathed in some of the smoke. Sebastian smiled, his eyes glittering. "To have the physical strength and powers of a vampire! Coupled with the power of the mind, a witch-vampire would become a god." He snapped his fingers. "No one, mortal or immortal, would be able to control such a creature. And that is what I desire of you. No fully developed vampire could be overpowered by a witch, but one who is transitioning?" He gestured to Cord. "As you can see, that can be done. And your blood is transitioning. If I ingest some of your blood, I, too, will begin to transition."

He's insane, Cord thought frantically. *I've got to get out of here.*

"No witch would ever train a vampire; no vampire would ever convert a witch." Sebastian sprinkled some crystals from another jar into the pestle. "But a human, transitioning, could be captured, and a witch could drink his blood, and start to transition himself." He smiled down at Cord again. He rubbed his stomach. "I have already taken your seed into my body, which has started to give me some of your nascent power." He threw his head back and laughed. "Ah, the power! It is intoxicating, more so than I could have ever believed before. And once I ingest your blood, your transitioning blood, it will be all the more intoxicating. I will become the most powerful creature in this world. No one will be able to stop me."

"Why? Why would you want to be so powerful?" *Keep him talking, he's crazy, but if he wants to drink your blood—my God, my God, this is all so crazy.*

"Have you never wanted or desired power, my beautiful one?" Sebastian asked, wonder in his voice. "To be able to do whatever you wished? With no one able to stop you from taking what you want, living the way you want?" Sebastian flicked one of Cord's nipples. "You cannot lie to me, Cord. You *felt* Jean-Paul's power last night; he gave you a small taste of it— and you came looking for him again tonight because you want it as much as I do." He leaned in close to Cord's face. "Aren't you tired of living the lie of a life that your parents have created for you? Imagine if you could be yourself, live the life you've always wanted. Believe it or not, young one, we are very alike— much more so than perhaps you'd like to believe."

"You are going to kill me, aren't you?" Cord replied, trying to ignore the truth in his words. *Freedom, to live the life I've always wanted, not the lie of a life my parents have planned out for me? What would I do for that freedom? How far would I go to have it?*

Sebastian shrugged. "That isn't my plan, but if it happens, it happens." He placed an index finger on one of Cord's nipples and pinched it, pulling it until ripples of pleasure went through his body. He felt his cock begin to harden again.

Cord shuddered unwillingly. It was insane. He was in the power of a crazy man, someone who was going to kill him, but his body couldn't help but react to his touch. He strained against the ropes again, pulling as hard with his right arm as he could. But the post didn't move more than just a little bit.

His eyes filled with tears of frustration.

Sebastian smiled at him again and bent down, flicking his tongue over Cord's nipple.

Cord moaned. His lower back arched slightly as Sebastian's tongue slithered from his nipple to his navel, darting into it and moving around. The pleasure was intense, incredible. His balls began to ache for release. *I've got to get out of here* kept running through his mind, alternating with the animalistic reaction of his body to Sebastian's touch. Sebastian took Cord's cock into his mouth, licking the tip, and Cord let out a sobbing moan from the core of his being. *It feels so good, oh my God, it feels so incredible, suck me, oh, God, suck me.*

As Sebastian's mouth began working its way up and down Cord's shaft, he could feel a finger probing at his asshole. He clenched his ass cheeks together, but the finger slithered inside him. He gasped out, and then the finger was working at his inside. A wave of pleasure rolled over him. He closed his eyes.

In the distance a bell began tolling.

And suddenly, he was aware of something *different* in his mind, edging into his consciousness over the pleasure.

He wasn't alone in his mind, there was another consciousness there.

For a brief moment he thought he must be crazy, everything that was going on was making him lose his tenuous grasp on reality, but he couldn't deny there was something there that wasn't there before the bells started tolling.

He opened his eyes. Sebastian's head gleamed in the candlelight as he worshipped the cock in his mouth. His tongue was lapping at Cord's cock, the finger moving around inside Cord—

He closed his eyes again.

In his mind he was somewhere else, in two places at the same time. His eyes were opening, and when they finished opening he was in a different place—he was not in Sebastian's house, he was not tied to the bedposts, his arms and legs were somehow free. The other mind, the other consciousness, wasn't quite awake, he could taste sleep in his mouth, he could feel the grogginess and it made him dizzy, but the eyes opened all the way. The curtains in this room were closed, there was no light, but somehow he could make out the details of everything in the room.

He was awake, a little groggy, the bells had woken him, and he felt a hunger deep inside of him, a need for *blood*.

Help me, he screamed in his mind, hoping that the other consciousness would hear, whoever it was.

And he felt the other consciousness there recoil.

What the hell?

He saw muscular legs being swung out of a bed, and a pair of jeans being pulled up those legs that were his but somehow weren't his. It didn't make any sense, he didn't know what the hell he was seeing, what he was experiencing, but there was something telling him this was his salvation, that somehow he was seeing through someone else's eyes, and—

His eyes turned to a sleeping form, naked and curled up on another bed.

Clint.

And he knew, somehow, that he was seeing through Jean-Paul's eyes.

Help me, he pleaded again in his mind. *Jean-Paul, please please help me.*

Cord?

He almost wept with relief.

Just relax, Cord, just relax and let me see through your eyes.

He opened his eyes. Sebastian slurped his way up to the tip of Cord's cock, and let it go. A string of spittle connected the tip briefly to Sebastian's lips and then spun away.

Sebastian grabbed the base of Cord's cock and squeezed. "You're very close," he breathed out, the smile never wavering.

Cord tried to slow his breathing, but it didn't work. Sebastian began sliding his hand up and down Cord's cock.

His entire body stiffened, the ropes digging into his ankles and wrists.

Sebastian lowered his mouth onto the tip of his cock as he shot his load, Sebastian drinking it down thirstily in gulps, licking the shaft of his spasming cock. His body shook and twisted, his mind completely blank, unable to focus or think about anything else but the incredible feelings of release sweeping over him, as he spurted again and again into the witch's mouth—

—and then he was finished.

His entire body went limp and fell back against the bedding.

Talk to him, Cord, keep him distracted, Jean-Paul instructed. *I am wakening the others and we will come for you. Whatever you do, do not let him drink your blood. Keep him occupied, do you understand me? It's more important than you could possibly know.*

Sebastian smiled and backed away from the bed. He picked up a dagger and dipped it into the pestle, swishing it around in the mixture inside.

He's going to kill me!

Stay calm, Cord, we will come for you. Keep him distracted! Do as I say and you will be safe! Keep him talking!

He closed his eyes and saw Jean-Paul shaking Clint and the others awake, barking out urgent commands in a language he couldn't understand, but the words inside his head made sense to him somehow—*wake up, wake up, the neophyte is in danger and we have to help him, we have to save him from a witch, a witch who wants to drink his blood and transition, they are just across the street—*

Sebastian turned and faced him, the dagger glinting in the glow of the candles. His eyes were closed, and he was chanting something Cord couldn't understand.

"No, no, no!" Cord pleaded. "Please, Sebastian. Won't you just lay here and hold me for a while first? There's no hurry, right? I'm not going anywhere."

"Ah, but my young Cord, you don't understand. I've been waiting an eternity for this moment, and I am not going to wait another moment." Sebastian walked over to the bed, and smiled down at him. The point of the dagger came down to the base of his throat, where the wounds from Jean-Paul's feeding were, and the tip of the dagger flicked one scar, then the other. The metal felt hot to his skin, and he could feel the wetness leaking down to his chest.

Sebastian lowered his face to Cord's throat and began to drink.

Cord closed his eyes, and

Jean-Paul was gone, there was no sign of him, but he could see himself on the bed, tied, could feel his own hot skin against Sebastian's skin, could taste his own blood as Sebastian lapped at his throat, could feel the changes coming over him as the transitioning vampiric blood settled into his stomach, changing the cells it came into contact with, could see through Sebastian's eyes as the darkened room somehow became lighter, somehow the dark shapes in the room began to take form in his eyes, his awareness of everything around him was heightened, and he could hear a conversation in his head—

"You want to head down and get another hand grenade?" a male voice asked.

"I think I've had enough," a woman's voice slurred back.

—and he felt a rush of triumph as Sebastian continued to suckle at his neck. It was Sebastian's triumph, all the power and glory he'd wanted all his life coming to him at long last, he was going to be a god, and he was going to make everyone pay for all of the hurts and slights, he would track down the ones who had killed his parents and make them die in excruciating agony, and he would cast spells to bring storms—because with vampiric blood he could control the winds and the rains, and he would rain destruction on all those who stand in his way, with each gulp of Cord's precious blood he could feel his power growing,

the seed he'd ingested was nothing compared to the power com-
ing from the blood, and he would make the humans worship
him, he would cloak himself in the religions that so mindlessly
followed, the empty hollow faiths that had drifted so far from
what they originally meant, what they were originally for, and
he would track down the vampires and kill them all, and then
the witches and the warlocks and the werebeasts, until all of the
creatures with powers greater than humans were dead, and
there would be no one, no one powerful or strong enough to stop
him, no one would be strong enough to stand against him, he
would be more powerful than any being this world had ever
seen or experienced before and he could remake this world in his
own image, make it a paradise, take it out of the hands of the
stupid humans who with their shortsightedness and greed and
stupidity were turning paradise into a quagmire of garbage and
trash, he would make himself lord and master of everything he
saw, of every living thing on this world, and the power would
be his . . .

Cord felt himself losing consciousness. He felt weak and
dizzy. His arms and legs felt cold, and he could hear his heartbeat in his ears, but it seemed too slow. He opened his eyes, and
could see the top of Sebastian's head as he thirstily kept drinking from the open wounds, his strength growing with each
swallow, even as Cord steadily grew weaker with each swallow.
His eyes began to unfocus and everything in the room seemed
to grow dark, what he could see so clearly just a few minutes
before was fading away into nothingness.

Please, someone, please help me, Cord thought. His feet and
legs were growing cold, his fingertips as well. *I'm dying.*

He was being drained of his blood.

Sebastian was going to drain him completely.

He closed his eyes.

Forgive me, Heavenly Father, I just wanted to have a good

time, I just wanted to have some fun, forgive me my sins and trespasses, forgive me. . . .

And then Sebastian wasn't there any longer.

He opened his eyes, but didn't have the strength to open them all the way. His head was spinning, he was light-headed, and all he could make out were shapes, but he could hear crashing and swearing and things breaking.

And then he heard Jean-Paul's voice in his ear. "Are you alive, my beautiful young Cord?"

He lolled his head to the sound of the voice and struggled to get his eyes open. "Jean-Paul." His voice sounded like a croak, sounded like it was a thousand miles away.

Jean-Paul raised his own wrist to his mouth and bit through the skin.

He thrust the bleeding wrist into Cord's mouth. "Drink from me, my beautiful boy."

"What?" Cord weakly allowed his mouth to fill with blood. He swallowed, gagging a bit at first, but as he drank, he felt the warmth coming back to his extremities. He felt rather than saw Jean-Paul cutting the ropes. His arms, numb and tingly, fell limply to the bed.

Jean-Paul removed the wrist from Cord's mouth and cut the ropes on his ankles. "Can you stand?"

Cord closed his eyes and felt strength flowing through his body. It reminded him a little bit of the absinthe he'd drank on Friday night. His entire body was coming back to life, and the darkness was fading. Jean-Paul wrapped him in a blanket, swept him up into his arms, and carried him out of the bedroom. "I told you not to leave my house, didn't I? Maybe next time you will listen to Jean-Paul?"

In the next room, Clint and the others were restraining Sebastian. "What should we do with this one?"

"My power is growing with every second!" Sebastian

screamed, spittle flying from his lips. His eyes were glowing in the dark. "I will destroy you all! You won't be able to contain me! I will be a god!" He was gasping for breath, hatred written all over his face.

Jean-Paul kissed Cord on the cheek, and said simply, "Kill him. And destroy this house once and for all."

He carried Cord out of the house.

Chapter Five

"How are you doing?" Jean-Paul asked. He gently stroked the side of Cord's face. "I'm so sorry this happened. Can you ever forgive me?"

"I've been better," Cord replied, shivering. He was still naked and wrapped in a blanket. He was sitting on a love seat in the front room of Jean-Paul's house, where he'd been put down after being carried across the street. "And what is there to forgive you for?" His teeth started chattering.

Jean-Paul walked over to the sideboard, poured some liquid into a glass, and handed it to him. "Here. Drink this—it'll help warm you up."

Cord lifted the glass and looked at it. "What is this?"

"It's just whiskey," Jean-Paul replied. "Don't you trust me?"

"I don't know what to think, to be honest with you," Cord replied, but he drank from the glass. It burned as it went down, and he gasped as the warmth in his throat began to spread through his body. "Are they really going to kill Sebastian? I—" he stopped. Yes, Sebastian had taken him prisoner, and yes, it was likely that Sebastian had intended to kill him one way or the other, but he wasn't comfortable with the entire notion of murder.

Jean-Paul gently kissed his forehead. "We don't have a choice. It's forbidden for a witch to become a vampire."

"He said he would be as powerful as a god." Cord closed his eyes and shivered again. "Vampires, witches. I don't know what to think anymore. I thought he was insane, but . . ." Everything that had happened to him in the last twenty-four hours seemed unreal—it seemed like much longer than twenty-four hours. *This time yesterday you were catching beads at the Endymion parade and wondering when you were going to be able to get away from Jared, Gordon, and Brad,* he thought, *and now . . .* He was still having trouble wrapping his mind around it all. Vampires and witches didn't really exist; they were out of fairy tales. Tied to the bedposts, he'd been able to convince himself that it was all just a warped fantasy of Sebastian's mind. But when he'd seen into Jean-Paul's mind, when they'd been able to communicate with their minds—all of that had gone out the window. It was true, it was all too true, no matter how insane it might seem.

But you believe in God, and you have your entire life. You don't question the existence of God, you never have. Your only questions about your religion have been about how the Bible is interpreted, how Jesus was all about love and peace, so why was the church named after him so steeped in intolerance and hatred? So why isn't it possible for there to be witches and vampires?

When Jean-Paul didn't answer him, he ran his own tongue over his incisors, which seemed too sharp. And there was that hunger inside him—another wave of dizziness went over him again, and he closed his eyes and asked the question he didn't know if he really wanted answered. "Sebastian said—he said that I drank your blood, that I'm transitioning, which was why he wanted to drink my blood. Am I really becoming a vampire?"

Jean-Paul looked away from him for a moment, before saying, very quietly, "Yes, Cord, you are. That's why I owe you an apology."

Cord opened his eyes, and the hunger brought another wave of nausea. "And this hunger I feel—it's for blood, isn't it?" He bit his lower lip. "I'm dying, aren't I? That's what Sebastian meant by transitioning." A tear slid out of his right eye that he quickly dashed away.

"It isn't what you think." Jean-Paul took one of Cord's hands in his. Jean-Paul's hand was warm. "You think we are the undead, that in order to become a vampire you have to die. Those are legends, mere stories, created by humans with no real understanding of the truth to try to explain what we are, how we exist, how we go on." He sighed. "You do die, in a way—you cease to be human. But you don't die in the sense that most humans die. Your soul won't be leaving your body for heaven or hell."

"Is there a heaven or hell?" Cord asked, taking another sip of the whiskey. It didn't burn as much as it had the first time, and it was helping to warm him up. "And do I need to drink blood?"

"I don't know about heaven or hell." Jean-Paul smiled slightly. "As I said, we don't experience death to go from being a human to a vampire. I don't know what happens when a vampire dies. I do know we've been around since the beginning of time—vampires, witches, werebeasts, and so forth. We are real—but we have spent thousands of years convincing humans that we aren't, so that we can live in peace amongst them. But being a vampire isn't like the legends you've heard, what most humans believe to be the truth of our existence. You have a reflection in mirrors. You won't need to sleep during the daylight hours in a coffin—sunlight will not kill you. You don't need to drink human blood, or even to kill to get what little human blood you actually do need to survive. You can exist in the sun without burning to death. You can walk into Christian churches, and a cross will not harm you." He leaned over and kissed Cord again on the cheek. "I'm very sorry, Cord. I should have never had you drink from me last night."

"Then when did the sunlight bother me so much today? Why did it hurt my eyes?"

"Because you're transitioning," Jean-Paul replied patiently. "The sunlight hurt your eyes because your eyes are more powerful now then they were when you were just human. You can see in the dark now; it's just a matter of adjusting your light perceptions to daylight, that's all. Once your transition is complete, your eyes will automatically adjust to the sun's light, the way they do now. You won't have pain from sunlight. Same with your skin. Yes, your skin is more sensitive to sunlight when you finish the transition, but all it means is you need a stronger sunscreen when you lay on the beach." He gave a half-laugh at the weak joke.

"And it's too late now?" Cord tried to wrap his mind around it again. "There's no stopping it now?"

Jean-Paul shook his head. "Once the transition starts—and it started last night, almost from the moment you ingested vampire blood—the only way for it to stop is to kill you." He got up and walked over to the front door, peering through the blinds. "Do you want to die?"

"No," Cord replied. "I don't want to die." He didn't. "But I can't go back to my life, can I?" He closed his eyes and pictured the faces of his family, his friends from school. "How could I?"

"No, you can't." Jean-Paul turned away from the door. "Your aging process has slowed down dramatically. You'll still age, of course—but one year in human terms takes a hundred years, more or less, for a vampire. You are what? Twenty-one now? It will take a thousand years for your body to age ten human years."

"How old are you?"

Jean-Paul laughed. "In human years, I am over six hundred years old. I was born in Paris during the Hundred Years' War. I became a vampire when I was twenty-five in human years. Now," he shrugged, "I'm about thirty, the way humans measure such things."

"And how old will I be when I die?"

Jean-Paul hesitated. "I've never known of a vampire to die from age."

"Ah." Cord sat up. His head swam for a moment, but he closed his eyes and took a deep breath. He opened his eyes and was fine. "I'm hungry."

"You need human blood." Jean-Paul crossed the room and sat down beside him, putting an arm around his bare shoulders. "You can't have more vampire blood. You can never drink from a vampire again." He ran a hand over Cord's hair. "You've probably had too much vampire blood. It's why the transition is making you so sick. I gave you enough blood last night to make the transition, but had I not let you drink from me to replace the blood Sebastian took from you, you would have died. There was no other choice, do you understand? There was no time to find a human . . . you were dying, and I couldn't let that happen."

"Why not?" Cord pulled away from him. "Why didn't you just let me die?"

"Is that what you wanted?"

"I don't know." Cord covered his eyes with his hands. "I don't know what I want—but this . . ." his voice trailed off. "You said I can't go back to my old life. I can never see my family or friends again. I am cut off, alone in the world now. Would I have chosen that?"

"You weren't happy," Jean-Paul whispered. "I saw that in

your mind last night. You felt trapped, you wanted to escape that life. You were living a lie, and you wanted to be able to live your life the way you wanted to live it. Now you have that chance." He put his arms around Cord and pulled him in tightly. Cord's bare skin tingled at his touch. "You can be whatever you want to be now. You can be honest. You don't have to live the life your parents had planned for you. You can love men if you want to. You can love women if you so choose. But now, the choices are yours for the making."

"But what if I want to go back to that life?" Cord shook his head. "That's a choice I can't have anymore."

"You would voluntarily choose misery?"

"I love my parents," Cord replied simply, and felt tears welling up in his eyes. "I love my friends. You're telling me that now I can never see or talk to them ever again. My parents— I'm their only child, Jean-Paul. And even though they would never accept me as I am, they do love me. I'm just going to disappear, right? Is that how this is all going to work? Cord Logan is just going to vanish off the face of the earth, and for the rest of their lives my parents will wonder if I am ever going to show up again. Every time their phone rings they'll wonder if it's me calling at last, or someone calling to tell them my body has been found. . . ."

"And what do you think they would do if they knew you loved men?" Jean-Paul gave him a crooked smile. "Do you think they'd welcome you with open arms? Do you think they would love you anyway?"

"No," he admitted. "They wouldn't." He closed his eyes, and remembered the time his mother had caught him with Ray.

Ray had been his best friend at Hubbertville High School; it was funny how he'd put this all out of his mind until just now. Ray had been taller, standing just under six three, and he had one of those bodies without the least amount of fat on it. After football practice, out of the corner of his eye he'd always watched

Ray undress and shower. His waist was narrow, his butt hard and round and small. His body was plated with lean defined muscle, and if he wasn't the best-looking guy around in the face he wasn't offensive to look at. His parents were divorced; his father remarried and was living in Birmingham while Ray and his sister Emma lived with their mother in a trailer behind Four Corners General Store, where she worked the cash register. Ray wasn't a good student, but he was a good athlete; his hope was to somehow get a scholarship for either football or basketball to a small college like Troy or South Alabama, or maybe even Alabama-Birmingham. He didn't want to end up working in the honey factory or the rubber-glove plant over in Fayette.

Ray was spending the weekend with the Logans because his mother and sister had to go up to Nashville because his aunt was in the hospital; Ray had stayed behind so he could play in the football game on Friday night. Saturday night they'd driven over to Winfield to watch a movie, and they were camping out in the basement of the Logan house. Ray had managed to sneak a bottle of cheap whiskey out of his mother's trailer; they were sitting cross-legged on the cement floor taking turns drinking the nasty rotgut straight from the bottle. Cord had never drank before; and it only took two swallows before he was light-headed and giggly. Ray had a little more experience with liquor—and after the third drink, when Cord had lost his balance and tipped over onto his back, giggling uncontrollably, Ray had grabbed his hands and tried to drag him back up into a sitting position—with the result that Cord had pulled Ray down on top of him.

Their crotches somehow wound up together, but the alcohol had loosened Cord's mind enough that he didn't care if Ray noticed the body contact had gotten him hard.

Ray was also hard, and as they lay there on the floor with Ray on top of him, Cord wondered when Ray was going to get off him.

But Ray didn't make a move, nor did he seem embarrassed.

And after a few moments that seemed like an eternity passed, Ray reached down and took hold of Cord's cock.

Cord had stiffened, alternate thoughts competing in his brain. "I should punch him or push him away" fighting against "oh, how I have always wanted this to happen."

Then Ray kissed him, his lips tasted of sour cheap whiskey.

Cord kissed him back, and they started grinding their crotches together.

Cord reached down and placed both of his hands on Ray's ass, and it was warm and hard just as he'd always imagined it would be. He slid his hands inside Ray's underwear, and Ray's butt cheeks clenched, grinding his cock into Cord's even harder.

And then their underwear was off and tossed aside, and they were naked, and Ray had his mouth on Cord's cock, and it felt even better than Cord had ever imagined it would in his wildest fantasies, as he masturbated to Playgirl centerfolds he'd shoplifted from the truck stop just outside Winfield, and even though Ray was inexperienced, Cord was, too, and he was ready to shoot a load in a just a couple of moments, and he pushed Ray's head aside as he came—and then he was returning the favor to Ray, licking and sucking his long thin cock until Ray came with a moan, and droplets of cum rained down on Cord's bare chest.

They cleaned themselves off and fell asleep in each other's arms.

But after Ray's mother had picked him up after church on Sunday, and Cord's father had driven in to Fayette to get some things from the hardware store, his mother had sat him down in the kitchen.

"Ray is no longer welcome in this house," she said, her lips compressed together into a thin line, her tone grim and threatening.

"Why?"

"I heard you two last night." She wouldn't look at him. "I

won't tolerate that in my house, Cord. You know it's an abomination in God's eyes, and I won't have it in my house. I will
pray for you, and I will pray for Ray—but he is not welcome in
this house anymore. I tried to be charitable—he can't help who
and what his mother is—but I won't have him leading you
down the road to hell. And if that's the path you want to take,
then you can just pack your clothes and get out of here as well. I
won't have it." She got up from the table and lit a cigarette,
blowing the smoke out the window over the sink. She wouldn't
look at him. "I'm not going to tell your father—but I will if I
have to. And he will kill you." And then she did turn around
and look at him. "And I'd rather you were dead than have you
lead that kind of sinful life." She flicked ash into the sink.
"Have I made myself clear?"

"Yes, ma'am." Now he'd been unable to meet her eyes, and
he slunk from the room, walking down the hall to his bedroom
and shut his door. He lay down on his bed, burying his face into
his pillow. God made me the way I am, he thought to himself,
tears falling from his eyes, using the pillow to muffle his sobs. I
wish I were dead.

"How many times have you wished that very thing?" Jean-
Paul asked. "How many times have you wished you were dead?
When you were a little boy, didn't you used to wish you'd been
born a girl so you could be with boys?"

Cord didn't answer him. It was true.

"Cord, I am offering you the life you've always wanted."
Jean-Paul went on. "You can be whoever you want to be, love
whoever you want to. You don't have to have a job—you don't
have to worry about being judged for who or what you are.
You can see the world, travel wherever you want to. You no
longer have to worry about all the mundane things that humans
have to worry about—you are free from that now."

"Free," Cord murmured.

"And your parents?" Jean-Paul's voice was bitter. "You know as well as I do that if they knew the truth about you—that you're a sinful homosexual—they'd never speak to you again. They've made that clear, haven't they? So don't waste your pity on them." Jean-Paul laughed harshly. "Their love for you, their only child, is *conditional*. They only love you if you do what they want. That's not love, Cord."

He was right, and Cord knew it. Yet it wasn't easy to imagine his parents suffering.

You have no choice, he told himself. *It's too late for that now, anyway. I can't go back to Ole Miss, I can't go home now. I have to get used to this idea that I am a vampire—something I didn't even think existed a day ago.*

The front door opened, and the other five vampires walked into the living room. Cord looked at their faces, trying to remember their names, but couldn't—other than Clint. *I have all of eternity to learn their names. I will live forever. I will only age one year for every hundred that passes. Almost a thousand years will pass before I reach thirty.*

"It's done," Clint said. "And we've set the fire."

Through the curtains, it seemed brighter out in front of the house and they could hear a siren blaring in the distance, drawing closer.

"You'll die in the fire, Cord," Jean-Paul whispered into his ear. "They will find two bodies in the house—Sebastian's and one other—and when they compare the dental records, they'll identify the other body as yours."

"But who—" Cord stopped. He didn't want to know how or why Jean-Paul would pull this off. "How is that possible?" He whispered.

Somehow, he knew it would work just the way Jean-Paul had said. Someone else would die in that fire, someone who would vanish off the face of the earth, and people will think it was Cord who died in the fire. His family and friends would wonder why he was in the house, how he had known Sebastian, but they would never get an answer. They would mourn, and they would move on with their lives. His parents might not, but his friends would—he knew that in a few years Gordon and Jared and Brad would only remember him from time to time, and the more time passed he would simply fade from their minds as they moved on with their lives. Maybe Brad would come to terms with his conflicted sexuality someday; maybe he never would and would take a wife and have kids and never explore that side of himself. Jared and Gordon would marry, have children—and all of them would die in their time.

While he lived on.

It was almost unbearably sad, and he felt his eyes welling with tears again.

"For the rest of Mardi Gras, you cannot leave this house." Jean-Paul went on. "On Ash Wednesday, we will leave New Orleans and head for Miami. I will have some papers made for you there, and you can begin your new life with us."

Cord stood up and walked naked over to the front window. Flashing red lights glowed against the curtains. He peered around the corner of one and saw the firemen drenching the houses on either side of Sebastian's with water, while still others trained their hoses on the burning house.

Clint moved up to his side and put an arm around him.

Cord rested his head on Clint's shoulder and began to cry.

"There, there," Clint patted his head. "Everything's going to be fine. You're one of us now."

A new life, a new beginning, Cord thought to himself. *Yes, everything is going to be fine.*

I'm free.

This is what my life is from now on, he thought, allowing the tears to flow. *I wanted to be free, I wanted to live my life the way I wanted to, and now I can do exactly as I please, no more worrying about hurting or disappointing my parents.*

"Are you hungry still?" Jean-Paul asked.

He wiped at his face. "Yes."

"You will learn the difference between the need to feed on blood and hunger for food," Clint said, taking his hand. "We still need to eat food." He looked up at Jean-Paul. "Shall I take him out to feed?"

"Get him some clothes," Jean-Paul instructed. "I will take him."

Clint walked out of the room, and Jean-Paul took his hand and led him back to the sofa, pulling Cord down beside him. "Are you going to be all right?"

He nodded. "I think so."

Ten minutes later they stood together on the stoop of Jean-Paul's house, watching the fireman fight the blaze across the street. A young man came walking down the sidewalk, weaving a little bit. "Hello there," Jean-Paul called out to him, with a smile on his face.

"Bad fire, huh?" the young man replied, taking a drink from his beer. He was handsome, maybe in his late twenties, and just starting to run a little to fat. He looked like he'd been an athlete in high school but hadn't kept himself up in the intervening years. He leaned against the house.

Nervously Cord went down the steps and stood in front of him. "Too much to drink?" he stammered out in a low voice.

"Maybe." The young man leaned back against the house and closed his eyes.

Cord leaned in and sank his teeth into the base of his throat, where the big blue vein pulsed.

The young man resisted at first, but then just moaned and—

—*as his blood rushed into Cord's mouth, images started flashing through his mind; images of this young man and some young woman, naked and coupling in a bed, and then this faded away and was replaced by an image of the young man, much younger than he was now, maybe thirteen or fourteen, with an-*

other young girl of about the same age, and they were in a darkened room, and he was sliding his hand inside her panties and she was whispering no, no, no, but she didn't try to stop his hand, and then with his index finger he found what he was looking for, and he pressed against her, feeling her soft small breasts against his own bare chest, and then—

Cord stepped away from him. The young man continued to moan low in his throat, and as Cord watched, the angry red wounds on his throat began to close.

In a matter of seconds, they were gone.

He looked up at Jean-Paul.

He felt warm.

He felt *powerful.*

He walked back up the steps, and they stepped inside the house.

"You have so much to learn," Jean-Paul whispered in his ear. "But I will teach you what you need to know to stay safe in this world." He put his arms around him. "Come to bed with me."

Clint and the others were smiling at them.

"Welcome, Cord," Clint said.

May God have mercy on my soul, Cord thought as he followed Jean-Paul to the bed they'd shared the night before.

But I am free. Truly free.

He felt like he could fly.

And then Jean-Paul was undressing him. He gave in to the pleasure, allowed Jean-Paul to pull him down onto the bed and kissed him back.

And when he came, he wept real tears, which Jean-Paul kissed away. "Hush, my love," Jean-Paul whispered, "don't cry. The world is yours now. Make of it what you will."

He cuddled up next to Jean-Paul's hard body. "Sebastian said that vampires can fly. Is that true?"

Jean-Paul nodded. "I will teach you, dear Cord, everything that you need to know to survive, to live your life to the fullest."

I never have to go back to Fayette County. I never have to set foot in the Church of Christ ever again. I can do whatever I want to. I can love whomever I choose. I can do anything I want.
Freedom.
Jean-Paul's skin felt so good against his own.
He closed his eyes and slept.

Land of the Midnight Sun

Chase Masters

Chapter One

As the pale wedge of morning sun advanced across Jacob Cameron's threadbare summer coverlet, an oscillating fan raked his torso with cool air, intermittently offsetting the heat of the late August morning. Ultimately, it was a losing battle, and the naked boy was sweating lightly, the moisture on his downy face glistening like the dew that bejeweled spiderwebs among the cattails along Penn's Creek.

Jacob stretched and yawned as the leading edge of sun inched its way across the broad expanse of his hairless chest. Below his waist, the thin fabric of the coverlet rose gently like a puff pastry. He turned on his side, the better to camouflage his early morning excitement should one of his four younger brothers unexpectedly enter the room. Reaching down, he grasped himself and mimicked the practiced motions he had long ago learned when milking cows—his grip firm but gentle, his movements fluid. *Grasp, squeeze, slide . . . repeat.*

The clamorous sounds of the household receded, save for the occasional squeal of his youngest brother, Ahron, at the breakfast table. The aroma of waffles and sausage—a Sunday-morning favorite—made its way up the stairs, but Jacob's mind wandered to the loamy scent of the barn, of earth and leather, of horses, and most of all the briny tang of Marcus Curvin, the hired hand, who at twenty-eight was ten years Jacob's senior and who had been, for as long as Jacob could remember, the unwitting recipient of a complex and increasingly obvious sort of hero worship.

Marcus tended to go shirtless in summer, but when he covered up out of modesty during outdoor lunches served by Jacob's mother, he wore a blue chambray work shirt with the sleeves torn off at the armholes, displaying biceps as round and hard and lethal as the cannonballs Jacob had seen stacked for display at the Gettysburg national military park. Jacob adored the damp whorls of hair that clung to the pale deltas of flesh beneath Marcus's armpits, and the dangerous, razor-wire tattoo that coiled around his biceps.

While Jacob was enthralled with Marcus's masculine attributes, he had only the faintest inkling of his own attractiveness. He thought of himself as awkward and gangly, which in fact he had been when he was eleven or twelve, but he had grown into a young man of surpassing grace and beauty. In rural Centre County, Pennsylvania, where his parents were struggling to hold on to the century-old family farm, none of that mattered—to Jacob, to his parents, or to anyone in the town of Tisana, save for the girls aged fourteen to eighteen at Penn's Valley High School, to whom Jacob was as sexy as any of the men who graced the covers of the romance novels they devoured like slices of shoofly pie à la mode. This past spring, he had been crowned prince of the junior prom and was a sure bet to be king of the senior prom next year. As such, he would be the consort of the Centre County dairy princess at the Grange Fair next August, which in Tisana, Pennsylvania, was the best a boy could hope for short of a football scholarship to Penn State.

"Jacob!" his father shouted up the narrow wooden stairs. "Where are you? Those cows aren't going to milk themselves!"

Throwing back the coverlet, the excited youth hastened the work he was doing, making sure to aim the fruits of his labors upward toward his chest and not onto the bedclothes.

Not milk themselves? he thought with a smirk. *Why not? It works for me.*

Chapter Two

As Jacob Cameron was stepping into his underwear that morning, William Wallace Reid IV was slipping out of his at Midnight Sun, the Santa Monica Boulevard flagship of his sunless-tan salon and spa chain.

"I've always thought the perfection of the spray-on tan was the best thing to happen to vampires since Anne Rice," he said to his companion as he stepped into the bronzing booth.

It was three a.m. and William had just enough time for a quick touch-up before the thirty-minute ride to his Hollywood Hills home along now-deserted Laurel Canyon Boulevard and Mulholland Drive before the first coral blush of dawn painted the mountains above the city. Never having to deal with rush-hour traffic in LA was a vampiric perquisite he cherished. On Santa Monica Boulevard, his vintage Rolls-Royce Silver Wraith gleamed curbside, its engine purring imperceptibly to maintain the deliciously cool temperature within its expertly light-proofed passenger compartment.

Forever thirty-one years old, William regretted only one thing about his immortal metamorphosis—that it had not happened two years earlier, at twenty-nine. He knew it was vain, especially considering that in "dog years," as vampires sarcastically referred to mortal lives, he was rapidly approaching 118. Why quibble over two years? But it was irksome. He was just thankful he was now near the beginning of his fifth twenty-year life cycle and could return to the youthful look of a thirty-something following his "death" at the age of fifty in a mysterious sailing accident off Catalina Island two years ago.

Having chosen to live more in the public eye than most of his vampire compatriots, William went to extraordinary lengths not only to look good but also to age appropriately during the span of each two-decade life, a limit he had imposed on himself when he realized in 1943, twenty years after his mortal death and first public reinvention of himself, that those around him were commenting with suspicion—and with increasing frequency—about his persistently youthful appearance. At that point, he recruited to the vampire brotherhood Jock Price, Hollywood's then-reigning makeup artist, first as his personal stylist and later as head of his "ageless" cosmetics line, Dermí Éternale. They also had become best friends and housemates, and it was Jock who was now in the adjacent bronzing booth.

William was proud of the discipline he had imposed on himself, ending each life cycle more or less on time, depending on personal entanglements and the complexities of his far-flung financial empire. It was difficult enough to look young as one genuinely aged, but to look authentically old while forever frozen in relative youth—that was more challenging by far. William was unwilling to make of himself another Pat Boone or Dick Clark, both of whom were so enamored of their current public personas that they had chosen to "age" well into their seventies with no apparent plans to "retire" anytime soon. Their masquerades were becoming grotesque. Come to think of it, Tab

Hunter was pushing the envelope, too. And they would all spend the first twenty years of their next "life" privately mourning their previous incarnations.

Becoming a vampire at thirty-one allowed William more flexibility in his appearance than making the transition at fifty-seven, as Jock had. But Jock was philosophical about it. Fifty-seven was not *that* bad. He was grateful to William for "sponsoring" him and thankful he had not progressed into his sixties . . . or beyond. But then, William said, Jock always had been a "goblet-half-full" kind of vampire. Jock frequently pointed out that he needed to undergo the complicated ordeal of reinventing himself much less regularly—once every thirty or forty years was sufficient, especially given his lower visibility. With minor adjustments and limited daily maintenance, he could make himself look forty-five or seventy. The fact that Jock was actually two years older than William, having been born in 1889, was the source of endless "big brother" jokes among those in the know.

"I forget," a catty vampire friend would say in jest as William approached the self-imposed end of an age cycle, "which of the two of you is older?"

As they often did on languid Saturday nights in summer, William and Jock had passed the evening among a gaggle of West Hollywood "bois" on the patio of the Abbey, commenting to one another on how remarkable it was that each new generation was both more beautiful and more vapid than the one that had preceded it, as if some perverse Darwinism was at work perfecting potential victims for them to snack upon guilt-free.

"Did you see that angel with the dragon tattoo on his deltoid?" William asked Jock over the hum of the spray that gently burnished his sinuous physique. A smile spread across William's face as he thought about the boy with long, luminous brown hair and bee-stung lips, a sexy S-curve to his spine that thrust his bony hips ever so slightly forward when he slouched insouciantly against the bar drinking exotically hued cocktails paid for by men twice and three times his age. "That dragon tail ran right down to his middle finger."

"I prefer the more discreet 'Mom' and 'Sacred Heart of Jesus' tattoos of our youth," Jock replied.

"Our *youth?* Honey, in *our* youth the tattoos read: 'Remember the *Lusitania*'!"

William had a tattoo fetish. Most vampires did, since the undead were unable to acquire tattoos themselves. To be successful, the process requires living tissue to interact with the ink injected under the skin and activate the immune system, which engulfs the pigment with phagocytes and traps it beneath the skin. A vampire who tried to get a tattoo would end up with little more than perforated skin and an ugly purple rash, but that had long been common knowledge and none but the most freshly minted or ignorant undead would attempt it. Those who did sport a tattoo already had it when they metamorphosed.

Despite some interesting menu items, not limited to the boy with the dragon tattoo, neither William nor Jock had fed that night. In reality, feeding was required considerably less frequently than suggested by the B-movies of the 1950s and '60s (many of which William's "father" and "grandfather" had produced). Like most responsible vampires, they fed fully only once or twice a year, supplemented every few weeks with nonfatal, between-meal snacks from sex partners who were devotees of blood sport or from a small group of highly paid, discreet "donors." Research at Eastern European vampire institutes had shown that was all that was necessary to survive.

In fact, William was an underwriter of the Zero Vampire Growth Association's "Curb Your Appetite" public service campaign. With the rapidly expanding vampire population, particularly here in the undead capital of the United States, traditional nightly feedings would spawn an epidemic of homicide and missing-persons investigations, resulting in a witch hunt that would certainly drive the vampire population to extinction. Perhaps their cousins in China and India could afford to indulge themselves more frequently—what loss is a rice farmer or untouchable among a population of billions?—but modern American and European vampires had for nearly a century been evolving to survive on a more restrictive diet. Limiting exposure to blood-borne diseases, including those fatal to humans though merely irksome to vampires, was an added benefit of a more conservative regimen. Spontaneous, "recreational" vampirism was exceedingly rare, at least in the circles in which William and Jock traveled.

William also did not believe in stalking prey, playing a deadly game of cat-and-mouse with his intended victim. As tasty a morsel as dragon boy might be, he would be safe from William unless their paths crossed at a scheduled feeding time. A less scrupulous vampire might have chatted up the boy, gotten his phone number, and penciled him onto his menu for his next meal. Those with even less self-control might have impulsively—and unnecessarily—taken him that night. William had seen at least one vampire of dubious character circling him, and it was entirely possible he was breathing his last at that very moment. There was simply no way of telling.

Chapter Three

In his soundproof Desert Hot Springs playroom, Mr. V reclined in his Jacuzzi after toying with two promising Abercrombie & Fitch models. The pair, a heterosexual couple, had gotten separated from their party while returning from a photo shoot in the Joshua Tree National Park and shortly after sunset had knocked on the door of V's remote desert hideaway seeking directions. Ever the gracious host, V had invited them inside, and they had partied long and hard before he had fed on them. So delicious were they, V had decided to allow them to live long enough to serve as the centerpiece of his celebrated autumnal Equinox fête and had ordered them confined in his subterranean dungeon, where they would remain while their blood replenished itself.

It had been a splendid party. For much of the evening, the comely blond female wore only a thong, the chiseled boy just his Calvins, provocative attire that intensified V's lust in a way mere nudity did not. The boy's white cotton briefs, wet from immersion in the heated pool, clung to the delicious, meaty orbs of his ass and outlined a generous pouch. V feasted his eyes on the plump cock head and the thick shaft, which he would feast on, literally, soon enough. The couple had cavorted poolside, drinking and doing line after line of cocaine. Although V was a discerning epicure, blessed with the trappings of wealth and power that attracted countless ambitious young men and women to him, rare was the occasion he ensnared two such lovelies simultaneously. That they were besotted with one another and predisposed to exhibitionism made the evening all that much more pleasurable.

The pair was almost boring in the uniformity of their perfection, inhabiting preternaturally lean, angular bodies. The boy's deep surfer tan and lustrous dark hair contrasted pleasingly with the girl's blond locks and fair complexion. V, who was sexually as well as sanguinarily omnivorous, enjoyed them both and had persuaded the exceptionally well-endowed straight boy to fuck him. While vampires are the ultimate sadists, they also are quite willing bottoms. Unable to produce the essence of the life force themselves, they seek to become its receptacle, and semen is nearly as important to the vampire lifestyle as blood.

At three a.m., the couple sought the privacy of the poolside cabana and made love like it was their last night on earth—which, while not quite the case, was closer to the truth than they might have imagined. Almost as soon as the boy had come, for the third time that night, V emerged from the shadows and sprang into action with a fervor that surprised even himself.

The models were clueless—as models so frequently are. Suddenly the mouth that an hour earlier had been lovingly sucking his cock and her breasts, rimming their delicious pink rosebuds, was sinking deep into strategic arteries. The hands that previously had caressed and worshipped them now tightened round their throats with unexpected power, choking their screams, holding them immobile as their blood drained away.

V had taken the female first, while the male was subdued by

two of the Mexican blood slaves he kept in his thrall to do the gardening, light housecleaning, and disposal of such unfortunate young beauties as these. The stunningly handsome male watched, his eyes a universe of fear, writhing against the grasp of his muscular captors while his lover struggled with V until she lost consciousness. When it came his time, his blood had tasted of both adrenaline and testosterone. V could not drink it fast enough and very nearly passed the point of no return until his protégé, Rodrigo, intervened.

"*Papi,* enough!" Rodrigo said, his hand on V's shoulder. "You want to save them for the Equinox, no?"

"I do, Rodrigo, but he is *so* delicious," V said. "I'm barely able to control myself."

Rodrigo gently tugged on V's shoulder, though not forcefully enough to appear disrespectful, which would have angered his master. V reluctantly disengaged from the boy, his canines crimson, his cock rampant.

"Take it away," he said angrily, reducing the beautiful boy to the status of an unfinished plate of food—human leftovers.

As Rodrigo carried the perfect body of the male lover to his cell, a string of bloody surfer's beads still around one wrist, he bent forward to kiss him and sensed a stirring in the boy's groin. Even as the boy hovered near death, his cock had swelled at Rodrigo's kiss. Something about this boy moved him—his beauty, his will to live, what certainly must have been a strong and faithful heart. When Rodrigo had seen the boy torn from his lover as the blood orgy began, he had turned away, unable to watch.

For a moment, he thought about finishing off the boy on the spot and telling V he had succumbed unexpectedly. It would be a far better fate than the one that now awaited him. The Equinox party was still several weeks away, and when the boy grew strong enough to regain consciousness, he would inevitably comprehend his unspeakable fate and live his last days in unrelenting terror. To make matters worse, V most likely would feed on both of the young victims at least once more.

It was extremely dangerous to cross V, fatal to overtly disobey or betray him, but if anyone could get away with it, Rodrigo could. Although he appeared to be in his mid-twenties, Rodrigo was pushing fifty in "dog years" and had been in V's employ longer than any of the other Mexicans, many of whom were family and all of whom he had personally recruited. V was one of the largest traffickers in illegals in the Southwest, a sideline that had not only enriched him immensely but also provided a reliable and largely untraceable source of kills for him and his bloodthirsty cohorts. Most of the human contraband arrived safe and sound—V was a businessman, after all—but those unlucky enough to make the transit when V needed to replenish his larder found themselves in deep trouble. Rodrigo, with his command of the Spanish language and many connections south of the border, was more than useful to V's operation—he was essential.

Nonetheless, Rodrigo knew the boy was past redemption, had been past redemption from the moment his sandaled foot had crossed V's threshold twelve hours ago. One small corner of his heart, or what was left of it, blindly hoped that V might allow him to turn the boy, to welcome him to his family eternally. He had been without a companion for several years now, since his most recent protégé had gone out into the desert to make a kill among a group of partying college students and had not returned to the dark folds of safety in time. He knew that if he asked V for such a thing—if he allowed V to even *think* he desired it—his wish would be denied. Such was V's cruelty.

The truth was, V personally enjoyed destroying beauty. He loathed the living—and especially the aesthetically privileged, denied as he was a pleasing countenance himself. It was primarily the pursuit and destruction of the beautiful and the vain that had drawn him to LA from New York in the first place. He sought them out. He stalked them. He took unnecessary risks to ensnare them. And when he feasted on them, he came as close as possible to reexperiencing human joy. After all, he had at one time been known by the name "Vicious." He was unlikely to dispense mercy—or what passed for mercy in his world. V had seen the light die in Rodrigo's eyes as he lifted the boy's nearly lifeless body and carried him to his cell, and he had been unmoved.

With all his heart, Rodrigo wished he had not known the boy's name.

Chapter Four

Before dawn on Wednesday morning, Marcus Curvin received a phone call from his mother, who had in turn been called late the night before by the Los Angeles Police Department. Marcus's younger sister, Allison, had failed to return to her West Hollywood apartment from an Abercrombie & Fitch photo shoot near Palm Springs over the weekend and had been reported missing by her roommate, Cerise.

Jacob immediately knew something was wrong when the usually punctual Marcus showed up late for work at the Cameron farm. He had spent an hour on the phone attempting to calm his panicked mother and another forty-five minutes trying to get information out of Cerise at the ungodly hour of five a.m. West Coast time. When he finally arrived at the farm, he parked his battered Ford F-150 at a haphazard angle and walked straight into the barn to find Jacob's father. He didn't respond to or even acknowledge Jacob when he called out his name and waved to him. Moments later, when Isaac Cameron and Marcus emerged from the barn, Jacob's dad wiping machinery grease from his hands with a blue bandanna, Jacob followed them into the house. Concerned by the look on Marcus's face, Mrs. Cameron banished Jacob and his brothers from the dining room, so he eavesdropped on their conversation from the hallway.

"I've got to go out there," Marcus told the Camerons as he concluded his unsettling tale over a cup of coffee, which sat untouched on the kitchen table. "I've got to bring her home."

"Of course you do, dear," Mrs. Cameron said, standing beside her husband's chair, battered coffeepot in one hand, the other resting on his shoulder. "We'll manage here without you, won't we, Isaac?"

Jacob's father nodded but scowled into the bottom of his mug, not looking at Marcus. The harvest was still more than a few weeks off, but late summer on the farm was a busy time. Things would not quiet down until well into November. He could ill afford to be without Marcus, especially now that the boys soon would be returning to school.

"I won't be able to pay you for the time you're gone," Isaac Cameron said, still avoiding eye contact with his hired hand.

"I understand that, Isaac. I've got some money set aside that will see me through."

In the hallway, Jacob flushed with anger and embarrassment. He was ashamed his father had even brought up money, when it was obvious Marcus was distraught. As he had explained the situation to the Camerons, he twisted the red calico napkin in his hands until it was knotted over on itself. Jacob wanted desperately to be able to hug Marcus, to cover his face with kisses, but all he could do was stare at the pulsing muscles in Marcus's bronzed forearms as he twisted the limp cloth in his hands.

No one in Tisana had been surprised when the principal of Penn's Valley High announced at graduation two years earlier that Allison Curvin, the school's head cheerleader, homecoming queen, and prom sweetheart, had been "discovered" on a senior class trip to New York City and signed to an exclusive modeling contract by Zyzzyva, an agency with offices in Manhattan, Los Angeles, and Paris. In elementary school plays, she had been cast as the lead in *Sleeping Beauty, Cinderella,* and *Snow White* (the production in which Jacob had stolen the show with his antics as the dwarf Sneezy). In her senior year, she starred as Dorothy in *The Wizard of Oz.* When, the day after graduation, she left Tisana to go to LA, she had been given a parade along the two-block stretch of Route 45 that served as the town's main street. As the sun set that day, turning the two-lane asphalt road into a band of gold that undulated between rows of green cornstalks, it was as if she had set off on the yellow brick road. No one had expected she would fall prey to the Wicked Witch of the West.

"When are you going to leave?" Mrs. Cameron asked.

"Tomorrow morning—early," Marcus said.

Jacob stepped into the room from his hiding place, startling his mother.

"Can I come with you?" he asked, looking imploringly at Marcus.

"Not on your life, boy," his father said, standing up abruptly. "With Marcus gone, I'll need you more than ever."

"But . . ."

"I'll have no more of this nonsense," Isaac Cameron said. "Now let's get to work."

"Don't you breathe a word of this to your brothers, Jacob Cameron," his mother scolded. "I don't want them fearful of such things, which could never happen here in Penn's Valley."

"Yes, ma'am," Jacob said as he followed his father and Marcus out the door. He would not tell his brothers about what had happened in California or how it made him feel. He vowed that he would not tell *anyone.*

Chapter Five

Like most vampires, William Reid disliked summer, with its interminably long, bright days, the nights that vanished in the blink of an eye, and the heat—the blistering, withering heat. First spawned in the dark and damp forests of Transylvania, vampires like neither light nor intense heat, though at least the latter was not lethal to them. Light, in doses not large enough to kill him, gave William migraines and generalized fatigue. He spent most of his waking hours in the cool depths of the luxurious bomb shelter constructed by his home's previous owner amid the Cold War paranoia of the 1960s and used in several James Bond films as the lair of one maniacal villain or another. Seamlessly integrated into the main house, its décor was a juxtaposition of rough, unfinished stone and gleaming expanses of polished stainless steel and brushed aluminum. It boasted an artificial waterfall and expansive koi pond, which for one of the films had been stocked with piranha, the better to dispatch the traitorous or inept minions of the resident evil genius. But even thus protected from the brilliant, brittle light of an LA summer, William chose to spend most daylight hours in his darkened bedroom, with its moss garden, artificial moonlight, and piped-in night sounds.

He realized in this respect he was the polar opposite of mortal humankind, who reveled in the long summer days, wantonly scorching their winter-white skins in a mockery of his vampiric Achilles' heel. Which is not to say that when he fed in summer, William did not enjoy the warmth of his lover's body against his own cool flesh, some muscled surfer aromatic with cocoa butter or the cheap tropical tang of Coppertone. He would not change his sheets for weeks after such a feast, allowing his heightened olfactory senses to revel in the sweet smell of surf and sweat, blood and sex, until it was no longer detectable.

It was just such a lover who now stared out at him from the front page of the *Los Angeles Times*, a gorgeous Abercrombie & Fitch model who had gone missing on his twentieth birthday along with an equally alluring female companion. William at first thought it was an advertisement, but the words beneath the photo said it was among the last shots taken of the pair, Kevin Cassidy and Allison Curvin, before they vanished somewhere between the entrance to Joshua Tree National Park and their destination, Los Angeles. Helicopters from the Marine Corps Air Ground Combat Center at Twentynine Palms were scouring the area between Yucca Valley, where they reportedly had gotten gas, and Morongo Valley, Desert Hot Springs, and Palm Springs.

"I have a bad feeling about this," William said, tapping a curved finger against the picture of the missing models, his lips pursed. "You don't simply disappear on the road to Palm Springs unless you do something stupid like drive into the desert."

"Probably felt the need to fuck," Jock said, peering over the top of the entertainment section of the *Times*.

"For five *days?*" William sneered.

"I'll agree it doesn't look good for them," Jock said half-heartedly.

"I think I've seen this boy before. I'm not sure about the girl, but I think we rep him."

"You're kidding," Jock said. "That would be bizarre."

Among William's financial holdings were a number of businesses related to the fashion and film industries. He was sheltered from their day-to-day operations by the holding companies he had established to grow and preserve his wealth during his transitions from one identity to another. In this instance, he thought of his modeling agency, Zyzzyva, which repped several Abercrombie, Hollister, and Ralph Lauren models on the West Coast. Even if the missing models were in his employ, he might not hear about it for some time as the news made its way upward through the Byzantine channels of his empire. Had the news not been so shocking—had it been merely another tragic but all-too-frequent death of some self-absorbed model by overdose—he might never have heard of it at all. He could not be expected to concern himself with such minutiae.

Sighing, William continued to read the story, mumbling barely audible fragments from time to time. *Birthday . . . red Porsche Boxster . . . rising star . . . film contract.*

"Not good. Not good at all." He picked up the cell phone that lay nearby and absentmindedly tapped it on the glass surface of the dining table as he continued to read.

Even without the potential personal connection, William had something of a sixth sense about such things, or at the very least a heightened sensitivity to them: young people coming to the city and disappearing. Sometimes their bodies would turn up in a craggy ravine in the Hollywood Hills or on a filthy embankment of the urban Los Angeles "river." Mostly girls—young girls, some not more than fifteen—obviously raped and murdered. It was more rare to hear about boys and young men disappearing. Either it happened less frequently or the editors of the newspapers and producers of television broadcasts thought it less newsworthy. There was something eternally compelling about a damsel-in-distress story, less so a wayward youth.

Powering up the phone, William scrolled through his address book and selected the home number for Xavier-Yves Zander, the head of Zyzzyva. At this hour, the office would be closed. He covered the mouthpiece of the phone as he waited for Zander to answer.

"Do we know of any ... *activity* ... in the Palm Springs area?" William asked Jock in a confidential whisper.

"I don't think so," Jock said. "At least not at *this* time of year. It's off-season."

"So then you don't think ..."

"It seems highly unlikely."

"A shame, then. What a delicacy this boy would have been."

Chapter Six

Jacob knew what he had to do. That night, while the rest of the family slept, he slipped out of the house carrying his backpack and made his way down the mile-long unpaved driveway, rolling his bicycle beside him. By the light of the late summer moon, he pedaled the length of Long Lane to Paradise Road and then into Tisana on Route 45 to Penn Street, where Marcus lived in an old Victorian house that had been turned into a duplex by two spinster sisters. He left the bicycle on the far side of the garage so Marcus would not see it in the morning and stowed away beneath the canvas tarp he knew Marcus kept in the bed of his pickup. As Jacob had suspected he would, Marcus had packed the truck before going to bed: a battered leather suitcase and a sleeping bag already lay under the tarp. Jacob unrolled the sleeping bag and stretched out on it, resting his head on the scuffed leather suitcase, and fell asleep beneath the musty canvas of the tarpaulin. He had left a note to his parents in his bike's small saddlebag explaining that he knew what he was doing was wrong, but that he felt he had to go to California with his "best friend," Marcus, who, he pointed out, had known nothing of his plans.

Jacob awoke with a start when Marcus slammed the door of the pickup and turned the ignition key. He remained motionless, afraid even to breathe as Marcus eased the truck out of the garage and headed west on Route 45. By the time the truck stopped at the red light in Old Fort, eleven miles away, he had fallen asleep again, drifting in and out of consciousness for the next four hours, only vaguely aware of the increasing heat beneath the tarp and the drone of the truck's tires on asphalt. When Marcus stopped for gas in Wheeling, West Virginia, Jacob knew he had to show himself before he suffocated or died of heat exhaustion. Startled when Jacob threw back the tarp, Marcus nearly dropped the gas pump hose with which he was filling the truck.

"Goddamn it, Jake, what the *hell* are you doing here?"

"I wanted to be with you," he said, his lower lip trembling. "I wanted to help."

"Your Pa will kill me . . . after he's done skinnin' *you* alive," Marcus said. "I trust he doesn't know you're gone?"

"I left a note."

"You left a *note?*" The gas pump clicked off with a thump. Marcus yanked out the hose and jammed it back into its slot. "Just what did this note say?"

"I told them it wasn't your fault . . . that you didn't know I was planning to come with you. I'll take the blame for this, I promise. My dad won't fire you."

"You're damn right he won't fire me. You're going home, now!"

"Please, Marcus! Don't send me back. I want to help you find Allison. And I've never been anywhere in my life. I want to see California. I want to see what's between here and California. I swear to God, I won't be any trouble. I'll do everything you tell me to do."

Marcus said nothing until the driver behind them honked his horn, wanting access to the pump.

"Get in the cab," he said. "We'll get out of this asshole's way and then call your folks."

Jacob breathed a sigh of relief as he clambered out of the pickup bed. He knew that at this hour—ten a.m.—his father would not be in the house. His mother answered the phone and nearly broke into tears when she learned it was Jacob. No one had found his note yet, and coming a day after Marcus's news about his missing sister, she had let her imagination run wild. After giving him a good tongue-lashing, she asked to speak to Marcus. She ultimately agreed to let Jacob accompany him to California rather than have him travel back to Pennsylvania by bus on his own.

"At least he'll be with someone I can trust to look out for him," she said. "Now put the boy back on the phone."

She warned her son that he would have to face the full extent of his father's wrath when he returned.

"Have fun while you're out there," she told him, "because you can pretty much kiss any semblance of a personal life good-bye when you get back, at least until you go off to college next year."

For the rest of the day, Marcus said not one word to Jacob unless it was to ask if he were hungry or needed to make a pit stop. The only sounds in the truck's cab were the rumble of the engine and the hum of the tires as they headed west on I-70 through Columbus, Indianapolis, St. Louis. Marcus was not *that* pissed off at Jacob—if pressed, he might even grudgingly admit he was glad for the company. What had bothered him most was his guilt over feelings he had for the boy that might be considered inappropriate. He knew he had enough self-control to restrain himself, but he was concerned that tongues might wag back in Tisana, at least among the very small number of people who knew him intimately—closeted men, some married, who frequently commented among themselves about young Jacob's exceptional beauty and his particularly delectable ass. Marcus did not want such talk to reach the ears of Isaac Cameron—and certainly not with *his* name attached to it.

Marcus's silence surrounded him like a force field and expanded to fill the cab of the truck, crowding Jacob to the far side against the passenger door. When he was not intently studying the map, Jacob kept his head turned to the window so steadfastly he could feel the muscles on the left side of his neck beginning to stiffen. Occasionally, the hot, humid air that shuddered through the truck's open windows carried with it the scent of Marcus's sweat—he was wearing the chambray work shirt with the sleeves hacked off—and Jacob yearned to be sitting closer to him, dreamed of innocently falling asleep on his shoulder as they drove through the orange afternoon heat.

For now, just being alone with Marcus on the way to California was enough. He could never have imagined that he would find himself in this situation. He'd had a crush on Marcus for as long as he could remember and had been masturbating to thoughts of him for years. Recently, thoughts about other boys and young men had begun to intrude on those sessions, but it was always Marcus's face he saw when he came, always Marcus's name he called out as he climaxed. He did not think much about the mechanics of lovemaking with another man— who put what where. All he knew was that he wanted to fall asleep with Marcus and wake up next to him every day for the rest of his life.

Jacob could not tell if Marcus was mad or if he simply was worried about his sister. They stopped twice for gas, and Marcus called his mother both times to see if she had heard from Allison. The answer was always the same: there was no word from her—and none from the police. By nightfall, they had covered some six hundred miles and camped on the edge of a cornfield west of St. Louis. As they cooked hot dogs on a small campfire, Marcus finally broke his silence.

"You know, this ain't goin' to be a pleasure cruise," he said, spinning his sizzling wiener over the flames. "As soon as we find Allison, we're coming home."

"I know," Jacob said. "I'm having fun just being here."

"Well it isn't *fun* for me," Marcus said.

"I'm sorry about Allison, but I'm certain she's okay," Jacob said. "You sure you don't want to spend a little time with her once we straighten things out? Not even one day?"

It did not seem insensitive to suggest that he hoped to have some fun. In fact, he thought he was doing Marcus a favor by looking on the bright side, thinking about the trip as an adventure or, at the very least, a rare vacation from the chores that awaited them upon their return.

"Maybe a day or two," Marcus said, sipping coffee from a tin cup between draws on a Marlboro. "I haven't thought that far ahead."

"I'd like to see Disneyland."

"Too expensive," Marcus said.

"I've got money," Jacob quickly countered.

"Go ahead and give your money to Mickey Mouse. I'll drop you off at the gate."

Going to Disneyland would be no fun alone. He wanted to see it with Marcus. He imagined sitting next to him in the dark as they made their way through the Haunted Mansion or Pirates of the Caribbean, gripping Marcus's thigh or grasping his knotty biceps when a ghost or buccaneer popped up out of nowhere.

"Maybe Allison would like to go," he suggested hopefully, and Marcus seemed to like that, since it implied all would be well in the end.

"Yeah," he said, "maybe."

"It'll be okay, Marcus."

"I guess so," Marcus said, but he wasn't at all certain this trip would have a happy ending. When Allison told her mother she wanted to work out of the Los Angeles office of Zyzzyva, Mrs. Curvin had worried, but Marcus had convinced her Allison was sensible—and mature enough to take care of herself. Those words came back to haunt him now, and he would never forgive himself if something had happened to her.

They slept side by side on the ground, covered by Marcus's unzipped sleeping bag. Jacob turned his face toward Marcus so he could fall asleep looking at his rugged profile glowing in the dying embers of the campfire. He hoped Marcus would not see the way the sleeping bag tented above his groin.

Later that night, Jacob awoke to find himself spooned in Marcus's embrace, pressed against Marcus's hard cock, separated by only the thinnest cotton fabric. He felt the sandpaper of Marcus's stubble against his cheek, the welcome warmth of his breath on his neck, suffused with the scent of late-night coffee and cigarettes. He wriggled an inch closer, straining to press Marcus deeper into his cleft, his own cock painfully hard. Marcus shifted and his hand drifted aimlessly down to Jacob's pouch. Minutes later, Marcus's hips began a slow, almost imperceptible undulation. Jacob shivered once, stiffened, and spent himself in four seismic shudders.

Chapter Seven

Rodrigo grew increasingly anxious in the days that followed the arrival of the Abercrombie & Fitch models. He was convinced V had acted even more impetuously than usual in choosing to feed on them and that no good could come from it. They were not like the tragic, unknown beauties V regularly savaged after picking them up, starry-eyed young men and women who had struck out for Hollywood with a few dollars in their pockets and dreams of fame and fortune in their pretty little heads, who found the City of Angels an unexpectedly harsh, unforgiving place, and V a welcome, if ultimately untrustworthy, savior. No one missed those runaways, who more than likely had left home under cover of darkness, fleeing abusive, perhaps even predatory, fathers and stepfathers who would be loath to report their missing progeny for fear of prosecution themselves.

But these kids, Kevin and Allison, already were making news. Photos from their final modeling shoot had appeared in the *LA Times* showing the pair embracing next to a Joshua tree. It pained Rodrigo to see them so carefree, to see once more Kevin's brilliant, trusting eyes staring out at the camera, unaware of the horrific fate that awaited him just hours after that photo was taken. Naked and unwashed in their cells, they were far from glamorous now. In fact, they were nearly out of their minds with fear. For the first two days, the girl could not stop crying. And even in his weakened state, the boy shouted deliriously for hours at a time.

"Let us go," the girl begged him each time he brought her food. "His parents have money. They'll pay anything you ask."

Rodrigo hardened his heart against her pleas. Under the best of circumstances, he did not have the stomach for V's sadistic games, but his attraction to this boy made it nearly unbearable to contemplate his fate. In the privacy of his own quarters, he repeatedly imagined scenarios in which he helped the lovers escape, but each one ended badly. V was powerful and cruel, and he was surrounded by minions who were both more loyal to and more fearful of him than Rodrigo. There was little he could do on his own, save making the young captives' last days as painless as possible, and so he had begun crushing increasingly large doses of Xanax into the food he served them.

To be sure, there was almost certain to be at least a perfunctory visit from the police, since V's home was one of just a few along the young couple's now well-publicized route. But there was nothing to connect them to V. The red Porsche Boxster already had been dispatched to a Los Angeles chop shop, and there was no discernable evidence of them at the house. V had spared no expense in making sure his subterranean playroom and adjoining holding cells were soundproof, perfectly camouflaged, and virtually impenetrable in the unlikely event his lair should be searched.

Although V had impulsively fed on the pair in the cabana before moving to a tiled room designed just for such things, the site was antiseptically clean now, as spotless as a surgical operating theater. If there was one advantage to being a vampire, it was a heightened sensitivity to blood—and other bodily fluids—that came in handy when swabbing up a kill. What might escape even the most practiced investigator's eye would not elude a vampire's nose. Nonetheless, Rodrigo thought it might be wise to close up the house and return to LA for a week or two. A trusted member of the mortal household staff could stay behind to feed the captives and to deflect questions from the police—that is, if he could convince V it was necessary.

"I'm not going anywhere," V said forcefully when Rodrigo suggested a strategic retreat. "I'm certainly not afraid of the bobble-headed beach bums who make up what I've seen of Palm Springs' finest. Take it from me, a bunch of failed Hollywood wannabes with a uniform fetish poses us no threat. Besides, we've got our Equinox orgy to think about and there is *much* to do in the next several weeks."

For vampires, the autumnal Equinox is a major celebration, a combination of New Year's Eve and the Fourth of July. It marks the onset of the annual descent into darkness, when the balance of day and night is tipped toward the nocturnal. And it begins the countdown to the high holy day of Halloween and the promise of the bloody orgies of Anti-Lent, the seven deadly weeks between All Soul's Day and the winter solstice, the longest—and darkest—night of the year. No self-respecting vampire ever fails to mark the observance, and vampires of ancient lineage or exceptional means do so with unrestrained spectacle. V had taken the event one step further by throwing two parties simultaneously, one for the living, one for the undead.

To the uninitiated, V's Equinox celebration was a bloodless fête, a traditional end-of-summer blowout to welcome back the Hollywood elite from their European vacations. Many of the guests unwittingly had a little added vampire protection in the form of their recent Botox injections at Swiss health spas.

If there was anything that put a vampire off his meal, it was botulin toxin, even in the trace amounts used for cosmetic procedures.

"Botox is the new garlic," V joked.

For V and a few choice friends, there would be an invitation-only "after-party," held in the privacy of his dungeon. As V's wealth and influence had grown, his Equinox celebrations had evolved from mere blood-drenched orgies of sex, drugs, and death into legendary epicurean spectacles financed through and supplied by his trade in illegal aliens. It was no wonder, then, that they often had a macabre fiesta theme. Rodrigo had been culling shipments of illegal immigrants for some time now, separating the choicest specimens from the remainder of the cargo. Several beautiful young men would be strung up in V's playroom like human piñatas, naked except for garlands of tropical flowers around their necks, wrists, and ankles, their purple cock heads dangling like exotic fruit, their femoral arteries exposed to the diamond-sharp incisors of the most elite of V's guests, who would drain them of their lifeblood over the course of the evening. Sedated, bound, gagged, and hoisted aloft by pulleys, they gradually emerged from their dreamlike states to the ministrations of eager mouths on their cocks and the insertion of sex toys into their macho virgin asses. They struggled at first, ashamed at their nakedness, but mercifully unaware of their fate until it was too late.

V gave Rodrigo specific instructions for selecting his Equinox "party favors." He wanted masculine, rough-hewn victims, at the peak of their sexual potential. He told his Mexican procurers to gather virile young men who had begun chasing tail at thirteen or fourteen. Each year at midsummer, the most handsome Lotharios in Chihuahua, Ixtapa, Oaxaca, would disappear as if struck down by a mysterious plague. In the week before the event, Rodrigo provided them with spicy food so their cum was as piquant as Mexican white sauce—redolent of red pepper, cumin, oregano. The subtlety of the flavors might be lost on mere mortals, but the sensitive palates of vampires would easily detect—and savor—them. If they could be tasted in the young men's saliva, their sweat, and their sperm, they surely would be evident when their tormentors first punctured their arteries, loosing a river of *caliente* crimson. Their spicy blood would drench the demonic revelers, whose orgiastic excesses would continue until nearly dawn.

This year, Allison and Kevin would be the centerpiece of the bloody buffet, the pièces de résistance of a sort of *tableaux morte*. Bound to St. Andrew's crosses, they would be physically and sexually abused by the increasingly rabid claque of vampires. Rodrigo had witnessed unspeakably sadistic mutilations of previous victims. For maximum effect, it was essential that those chosen for this "honor" be beauties of the highest order. Capturing a matched pair of similar caliber was rare indeed.

In light of the approaching Equinox, Rodrigo knew he could not change V's mind about Kevin and Allison. He hoped that preparations for the party would distract him and he knew that he ultimately would have to accept the fate of the doomed pair, as he had done so often in the past. Rodrigo was grateful that only a small percentage of vampires were sadists like V, who kept their terrified victims confined in stark, uncomfortable cells or caged in dog crates, sometimes feeding off them for days or weeks until they grew tired of the game.

"Fear is an acquired taste," V once told him. "It imbues the blood with a metallic tang, which is appreciated only by those of us with more refined palates."

V liked his meat lean, like himself. Before his death at the age of twenty-one, he had never had more than a twenty-eight-inch waist, and his biceps were no bigger around than his wrists. His modeling studio, Agence Sanguine, specialized in waiflike talent and recently had become extraordinarily successful with the new vogue for anorexic models. Undernourished Czech, Hungarian, and Romanian models were all the rage now, and V imported many of his finds from the traditional vampiric homelands of central Europe. A few of them had come to V's attention as potential kills, spared from execution—at least temporarily—by an unexpectedly perfect physique, a unique tattoo, a smoldering gaze that made them surprisingly photogenic. If they became superstars, or approached it, they generally were spared. If not, they eventually were rotated out of the agency—permanently—usually at the autumn Equinox event.

V already had gone over the agency's balance sheets and selected the models to be culled. Rodrigo had been ordered to issue the "invitations." The kill this year would be exceptionally large. The demand for anorexic males was on the wane, and V, ever-alert to fashion trends, had decided to harvest much of his roster and start fresh next season. The Equinox promised to be a literal bloodbath.

Chapter Eight

When Marcus and Jacob arrived in LA early on Sunday morning, they went straight to Allison's apartment in West Hollywood. It was a modest, faux-Spanish complex with a pool that looked as if it were not particularly well maintained. A couple of residents were sunbathing, but no one seemed willing to dive into the water, which had a greenish, oily sheen to it. Allison's roommate, Cerise, looked mad when she swung open the door, but relaxed when she saw Marcus, whom she remembered from a previous visit.

"Sorry, I thought you were another cop—or another fucking newspaper reporter," she said. She took a step backward and to the side, but did nothing else to invite them in.

"I can imagine," Marcus said, stepping past Cerise. Jacob followed. It took a moment for their eyes to adjust to the darkened interior. Cerise went around the room turning on lights, but did not open the Venetian blinds.

"I've been keeping the blinds drawn. We've had a couple peeping Toms in the past few days. Low-rent paparazzi."

Jacob thought Cerise probably was an attractive girl under

normal circumstances, but at the moment she looked like one of those pictures of "Stars Without Makeup!" he sometimes saw in the tabloids in the grocery checkout line—a bleary-eyed Britney or ghastly Gwyneth caught while walking their dogs or returning from the gym. Cerise caught him staring and looked questioningly at Marcus.

"He's a friend," Marcus said.

"I knew Allison at school," Jacob added.

"Oh, right."

"So the last time you saw her was a week ago Friday?" Marcus asked.

"Uh-huh. The shoot was going to last two days. Apparently, everything went fine, they checked out of the motel, and headed back to LA. They got gas in Yucca Valley—some closet-case cashier told a TV reporter he remembered Kevin because he was so hot—and then they just disappeared."

"Yucca Valley?" Marcus asked. Jacob thought it was a funny name for what probably was an ugly place. Yucky Valley.

"It's close to Joshua Tree National Park, where they were shooting."

"And this guy . . . Kevin? He's okay? Not a psycho? It couldn't be that he's like, kidnapped her or something?"

"Kevin? Oh, no. Not in a million years. They were in love."

"So we can rule him out? If something happened to Allison, it probably happened to him, too."

"Yeah," Cerise said. "Which would be a real shame."

Cerise invited them to crash at the apartment. At Marcus's insistence, Jacob took Allison's room while he slept on the couch. She gave them the address of Zyzzyva, the agency where Allison worked, and the first thing Monday, they made arrangements to meet her agent, Xavier-Yves Zander.

Jacob's only knowledge of what a modeling agency might look like came from watching a television comedy about a fictional New York fashion magazine, and the décor of Zyzzyva surpassed even his wildest expectations. The entire façade was an aquarium—so thin that Jacob wondered how the brightly colored tropical fish managed to turn around. Waterfalls lined the reception area, where a man with fishlike eyes and an almost unintelligible accent greeted them.

"We're her to see Mr. Zander," Marcus said.

"Have you an appointment?"

"I'm Allison Curvin's brother."

"I see. *Quelle dommage.*"

Minutes later, in his office, Zander had little to offer Marcus except his condolences.

"Of course, I was not on the shoot," Zander said. "You do understand that, don't you?"

"I didn't," Marcus said. "I just knew she worked for you."

"Allison had an exclusive contract with Abercrombie and Fitch. I did not see her often. The last time she was in the office was . . . I don't really know. Ennio, at the desk, could probably tell you."

Zander said he had been very fond of Allison and thought she certainly had a great future in LA. He spoke with a sense of finality that Jacob found disconcerting, as if he had already given up on her.

"And you, young man," Zander said to Jacob. "Are you also Allison's brother?"

"No, I'm just a friend."

"I see," Zander said, his palms pressed together, the tips of his fingers touching his lips. "Are you under contract?"

"Contract?" Jacob asked.

"Yes. Have you signed with anyone?"

"I'm sorry, I don't understand."

"My dear boy," Zander said, exasperated. "You're not a model?"

Marcus laughed, which seemed to annoy Zander.

"Um . . . no. I'm sorry."

"Well, I realize this is neither the time nor place for this," Zander said, "but how long will you be in LA?"

"Until we find Allison," Marcus said.

Zander reached into a drawer and withdrew two business cards, handing one to Marcus and the other to Jacob.

"If I can be of any help, just let me know," Zander said. "And you, young man, I'd like to see you in here again once this is resolved. I daresay I could sign you to a contract with Hollister today."

Jacob carefully pocketed the business card—it was the first time anyone had ever given him one.

"I can give you the name and telephone number for the photographer who worked the shoot with Allison and Kevin," Zander said. "But I'm afraid that may be a dead end. From what I've been told, everything was fine when Allison and Kevin left. And then . . ."

He shrugged and held out his hands, palms up. After a pause, he added, "Is there some way I can reach you?"

Marcus gave him the telephone number at Allison's apartment.

"Very well," said Zander. "I'll be in touch if I hear anything."

As they were leaving, the elevator stopped on the thirteenth floor and the doors opened to reveal a lobby clad in highly polished, bloodred marble, with two obsidian-black glass doors on which was etched the name Agence Sanguine. Four young men boarded together. They were tall, pale, willowy, exotic, and they moved in unison, as if they were some sort of half-human octopus. The elevator was suffused with a sweet, spicy scent, like cloves. All four spoke simultaneously, in a quick, fluid, utterly incomprehensible language. It was not French or Spanish, of that Jacob was sure, since he knew a little of both from school. Their lips were crimson, their faces elegant and elongated, with a barely perceptible hint of what looked like Persian or Asian ancestry. One had raccoon-like circles around his eyes, and Jacob wasn't sure if it was natural or some sort of makeup. Another, in a tank top, sported a dragon tattoo, with a fire-breathing head at his shoulder and a body and tail that extended all the way down his arm to his right hand. Two stood behind Jacob, one to his right, and one directly in front of him. On the eleventh floor, more people boarded and Jacob found himself pushed backward against the two boys behind him. He would swear that he felt fingers fluttering around his buttocks like a hummingbird seeking nectar.

"What a bunch of freaks," Marcus said when they had left the elevator and their fellow passengers dispersed.

"I thought they were kind of cool," Jacob said.

"Yeah, 'cool'—like they've been trapped in a meat locker for the past six months."

Chapter Nine

When William learned that the Abercrombie & Fitch models were indeed under contract to Zyzzyva, he was by turns both angry and fearful. It angered him that something that was, even in some small way, his "property," was missing, and he worried that a police investigation would raise questions about who had been responsible for their safety and security on the photo shoot. The last thing any vampire wanted was scrutiny by the police—or any regulatory agency. Layer upon layer of mortal bureaucracy separated him from Zyzzyva and the missing models, but overzealous questioning by a persistent LAPD detective ultimately could lead to his doorstep. The logistics of meeting with the police only after dark was bound to raise suspicions and was to be avoided at all costs.

He also could not shake the feeling that something was amiss—and that the vampire community might be involved. Despite a warning from Jock that he should distance himself from the situation, especially now that he had a tangible link to it, he placed calls to friends in Palm Springs to find out what they knew. No one would admit to any knowledge of the attractive couple, although a few professed interest in the pair and cursed under their breath at the missed opportunity.

"I've seen their picture in the paper," said a legendary Hollywood composer, "and they are *extraordinarily* delicious! Do you have reason to suspect it was one of us?"

"I have reason to suspect nothing of the sort," William said. "They're not even officially dead at this point. But my vampdar is pinging."

William's interest was more than personal. As chair of the western district of the American Vampire Council, it was his responsibility to make sure his vampiric brethren did not draw attention to themselves unnecessarily by flouting generally agreed-upon rules of decorum. As the vampire population had increased, particularly in Southern California, high-visibility kills had been discouraged, lest a vampire be exposed by a police investigation, or worse, the tabloids. If this were indeed a kill, it would fall into a gray area. Technically, the victims were not genuine celebrities yet, but the clamor around their disappearance made them such.

"What about that unsavory character who owns that modeling agency with the oh-so-transparent name?" William asked.

"Agence Sanguine?"

"That's the one. Put him on our suspect list. What does he call himself? Q?"

"V. For Vicious," Jock said.

"That's the one. The erstwhile talentless punk rocker. Shaved his head a few years back. Very *Nosferatu*."

"And a big drama queen—loves attention. He throws that Red Party in Palm Springs every year about this time. I think our invitations came last week."

"Maybe we should go this year to check things out," William said. "I've always tossed the invites. He's raided my talent one too many times. I've warned Zander not to have anything to do with him. I wouldn't trust him as far as I could throw his skinny little bloodless body. Wasn't there some scandal about him before he turned?"

"Claims to have woken up at the Hotel Chelsea in New York and found his girlfriend dead. V was charged with her murder and 'died' a few months later. I'm convinced it was some twisted vampiric love triangle. Apparently, he feeds constantly—and carelessly—although he's been able to escape detection by the authorities so far. Must have *some* smarts."

"Or minions," William said. "Good minions."

"True, a vampire is only as good as his minions."

Chapter Ten

V was beginning to worry about Rodrigo. He was going soft. It happened sometimes. Instead of distancing himself from his human past—his friends, his family—Rodrigo remained somewhat sentimental. Over the years, he had increasingly lost his edge, had begun to regret, even reject, the gift he had been given. If that was what was happening—and if the process continued—he would either destroy himself or force V to destroy him. Either way, it would be a tremendous loss. V had once been quite enamored of Rodrigo's beauty and had invested a great deal of time and money in him. He relied on him to run the household, to plan and "cater" events, to oversee the lucrative traffic in illegal immigrants. He would hate to lose him.

But he could tell the recent incident with the delicious young models had troubled his protégé. The decision to allow the pair to live until the Equinox had probably been a mistake. It may have planted crazy ideas in Rodrigo's head, thoughts of betrayal, rescue, escape. And now Rodrigo had actually been bold enough to confront him, to suggest it could have potentially disastrous consequences. He was right, it could. But coming to V to tell him about it bordered on insubordination.

And then there were the discrepancies in the human cargo ledgers, small and infrequent, to be sure, but troublesome nonetheless. The money was always right; Rodrigo was not a thief. But among those shipments destined for consumption, there would occasionally be an inexplicable shortfall between the cargo manifest signed in Mexico and the one certified upon arrival. Rodrigo generally explained it away as "spoilage," a death in transit, something that certainly was to be expected. V was aware of the misfortune of other immigration entrepreneurs, when entire shipments had gone bad in unrefrigerated trucks abandoned in the desert. There were no specifics attached to the records, nothing more than a head count, so V did not know to whom Rodrigo was showing mercy. It was only when a particularly tasty morsel (as noted by his Chihuahua procurement specialist) disappeared en route that V took notice and questioned Rodrigo. He had denied any wrongdoing, but V could see he was lying. He'd interrogated the road crew who helped with the transport, but none could say what had happened to the missing livestock and could not authoritatively implicate Rodrigo. In any event, it would bear watching.

Despite Rodrigo's concerns about the Abercrombie models, V was positively gleeful about the capture of two such perfect specimens. The male, in particular, was among the most compelling victims in his two decades as a vampire. Not only was he extraordinarily handsome, with a flawless, perfectly proportioned physique, he also exuded a scent that inflamed V's passion, a pheromonal amalgam of sweet milk, brine, and fresh-cut grass. Ignoring cautions from Rodrigo, V visited the boy on several occasions, drinking deeply, almost deliriously, of his vitality. He never failed to quench his sexual thirst as well. The boy grew weaker with each visit and the quantity of both his blood and semen diminished, infuriating V and causing him to take out his frustration on him with escalating brutality.

V's taste for males had come as a surprise to him. In life, he had been interested sexually only in young women, but his creator told him that "blood has no gender" and at his insistence he had begun to sample the pleasures of male flesh as well.

"Can you taste the difference a rush of testosterone makes in their blood?" his vampiric mentor had asked him twenty years earlier as together they drained a teenaged Latino hustler they had picked up in Spanish Harlem. "Isn't it delicious? For me it's the difference between a white wine and a red. The males' blood is so much richer and more full-bodied."

V's creator was a master vampire, none other than Donatien Alphonse François de Sade—the Marquis de Sade, himself the vampiric spawn of the "Blood Countess," Elizabeth Báthory, a lineage second in demonic prestige only to that of Vlad Tepes himself. Shortly after his reported "death" in France in 1814, de Sade had arrived in New York, sustained during his transatlantic voyage by an ever-dwindling retinue of household help, whose bloodless corpses were tossed overboard at regular intervals. He had been preying upon the hapless citizens of Gotham ever since and was the oldest vampire in New York and one of the richest, most powerful, and most perverse men in Manhattan.

By the end of the 1950s, de Sade had grown world-weary. As difficult as it was for him to believe, the creator of the erotic atrocities of the *120 Days of Sodom* had at last been sated. His senses had become so jaded it was increasingly difficult, despite his wealth, to orchestrate the kinds of debauched bacchanals he needed to drench himself in sex and blood with any degree of satisfaction. But the sexual revolution of the 1960s piqued his interest again and brought a flood of fresh meat to his boudoir in the form of swingers and wife-swappers, advocates of "free love" who, to his amazement and delight, somehow managed to again arouse his ancient cock.

The 1970s brought a bounty beyond his wildest expectations: newly liberated gay men he stalked in countless numbers at bars and bathhouses and along the piers beyond the West Side Highway, with convenient access to the Hudson River for disposal of his offal. To his surprise, the ease with which they capitulated to him did not diminish his appetite but increased it, especially those whose deeply masochistic impulses complemented his own twisted urges. Almost to the end, they begged for more and more and *more* pain.

The latter years of that decade delivered the ultimate gift: punk, with its devotees' sepulchral pallor, pale-skinned waifs who celebrated homeliness and cultivated disfigurement, who painted and pierced their bodies and subsisted on a diet of rotgut and cocaine, who engaged in sex that ranged from the nearly anesthetized to the intensely brutal. And it was among them he found his first true acolyte since the loss of his beloved manservant and coconspirator, Latour, a century and a half earlier. His new protégé was plain and pockmarked, with a beaky nose and perpetual sneer. His fright wig of unruly black hair lent him the appearance of a fledgling vulture. The fact that this creature had created a violent stage persona and christened himself with the name Vicious made it all seem preordained.

Once he completed the punk rocker's deadly metamorphosis, de Sade rigorously cultivated Vicious's innate sadism. How it thrilled the old reprobate through the years to know that an entire perversion had been named for him. Vicious had been a quick and eager study. He had become adept at death-by-a-thousand-cuts, one of the most sensual ways de Sade had developed to slowly savor his victims, and he shared de Sade's fascination with the slow, cruel, and relentless destruction of the beautiful.

After a decade of debauchery with de Sade, V decided, with the Marquis's blessing, to strike out on his own and establish himself among the growing vampire population in the City of Angels. The prey was as abundant there and infinitely more attractive. And with his entry into the transportation and exploitation of illegal aliens, his wealth and power expanded exponentially, all to feed his ravenous hunger for sweet, young flesh.

Chapter Eleven

William initially was skeptical when he received a phone call from Xavier-Yves Zander about two "extraordinary" visitors to the Zyzzyva offices—a "cowpoke and an angel," as he had put it. But such breathless indulgences were rare, so William had agreed to view a security tape of the pair in the reception area, which Zander wanted to courier over.

"I expect nothing less than a genuine halo and wings on your 'angel,'" William cautioned him.

"You won't be disappointed, I assure you," Zander countered. "And the cowboy is no ordinary chuck-wagon Romeo."

William was more than a little intrigued by what he saw of the "angel" on the tape. Even ill lit, in low-resolution black-and-white, the boy compelled you to look at him. William was reminded of the first time he had seen Richard Gere in a small role in *Looking for Mr. Goodbar* and Brad Pitt in his cameo appearance in *Thelma & Louise*. But this boy was young, *very* young, and unformed. Whatever potential greatness awaited him, it would have to be cultivated. The boy needed time to grow into his beauty. He was "cute" now, puppy-dog cute, but he had the potential to be truly remarkable.

But it was the boy's companion who interested him sexually. Dark, intense, either nervous or angry, he paced the reception area exuding a raw sexuality that was barely contained by his clothing: a sleeveless blue chambray work shirt that revealed sledgehammer biceps encircled by a razor wire tattoo; tight, well-worn jeans that hugged the twin globes of his ass like a second skin and lovingly limned his obviously large cock in faded denim. Beneath a weather-beaten cowboy hat, his matinee-idol face was shadowed with stubble. Decades ago, William might have cast him as the Marlboro Man or given him the lead in one of the many subtly homoerotic television westerns he produced—*Sugarfoot* or *Cheyenne* or *Bronco*. William could only imagine the shockwave that had rocked the Zyzzyva offices when the cowboy had arrived: queens shrieking as if they had seen a mouse, phone conversations abruptly terminated, coffee mugs dropped. And for those few who did not respond to his intensely masculine aura—for the chicken queens in the office, of which there were at least a few—there was always the blond sylph at the cowboy's side.

He wondered about the relationship between the two. Zander said the cowboy, Marcus Curvin, had identified himself as the brother of the missing girl, Allison. The boy, Jacob Cameron, was "just a friend" who had accompanied him. But was it possible they were lovers, that the cowboy was also a cradle-robber? He would be able to tell when he met them in person. His heightened olfactory sense would allow him to determine their relationship simply by smell. If they emanated two distinct aromas—the boy sweet as summer corn, the cowboy redolent of sweat and leather—it would mean they were not lovers. If their scents commingled into a shared perfume that was theirs alone, each indelibly marked by prolonged proximity to the other, then obviously they were lovers.

Of course, romance would be the last thing on Marcus Curvin's mind. The young farmhand was here to find his missing sister, and William was determined to assist in any way possible, not merely to ingratiate himself with this handsome man but to ensure that no illicit vampiric activity was involved, or if it was, to sanction the perpetrators.

William quickly scheduled a meeting with the pair at his home at nine p.m., the better to allow himself the liberation nightfall brought with it. He wanted to appear both welcoming and expansive, which would be difficult in his hermetically sealed subterranean living quarters. Despite the ingenuity of his home's design, the underground rooms could be a bit claustrophobic, which would serve only to make his guests ill at ease, however subtly.

By the time they arrived, the sun had sunk safely below the horizon. William greeted them at the door, wincing at the sight of the dilapidated two-tone pickup they had parked in front of the house. As they entered the foyer, William surreptitiously sniffed the air around them and determined, definitively, that they were not intimates.

His assumptions about the boy's beauty had been somewhat conservative. He was absolutely breathtaking. The attributes that made the living so appealing were, in this boy, particularly vibrant: the sparkle of his eyes, his miraculously unblemished complexion radiating vitality with each confident beat of his heart. His assessment of the cowboy's appeal was likewise validated. William had fed from a donor earlier in the day and his proximity to the cowboy now made the new volume of blood pulse through his body with increased power. He could feel his cock grow plump, and at the same time he became more aware of the sharp points of his canines. Lust and bloodlust always went hand in hand.

"I appreciate you agreeing to meet me at this hour," William said once they were inside. "But as you may be learning, the *real* business of Hollywood almost always takes place after dark. We like to call it the Land of the Midnight Sun."

"No problem," Marcus said.

"I hope you didn't have any trouble finding the house. The hills can be a perplexing maze to the uninitiated, especially at night. I recall one couple who arrived here so unnerved I had to dispense medication!"

"We made a couple of wrong turns," Marcus said. "But we're here."

Jacob had been awestruck on the ride up the canyon from Los Angeles as they wended their way along narrow, switchback roads past multimillion-dollar mansions clinging to the dusty hillsides that rose steeply on each side. When they had finally found the address they were looking for, they were at the very top of a mountain ridge. From the front, the house looked elegant and expensive—Italian cypress trees lined the curving driveway—though relatively small. Once inside, he realized it was cantilevered over the edge of the ridge on which it sat, and also included several levels that were built into the side of the mountain below the main floor.

His host was younger than Jacob had anticipated. Cerise had told them the man they were meeting was a member of one of the wealthiest and most powerful families in the entertainment industry—she was stunned that he had offered to see them personally—so Jacob had been expecting an older gentleman, at the very least, someone with a bit of gray at the temples, like his father. But at first glance, William did not appear any older than Marcus. As Jacob eyed him more closely, however, he noticed things that made him suspicious. Perhaps, through plastic surgery or an expensive beauty regimen, this guy only *looked* younger than his years. He was unusually skinny in a way that seemed somewhat unhealthy, as if he had an eating disorder or was addicted to drugs. His complexion looked a bit unnatural, too, as if he were an actor who had left the movie studio while still wearing makeup. He was not ancient, Jacob thought, but he might be as old as forty.

"I am genuinely concerned about this frightful situation, and I want to offer you whatever assistance I can," William said, once they were seated in the living room looking out over the LA skyline.

"I appreciate that," Marcus said.

At William's request, Marcus told him everything he knew about Allison's disappearance—what the police had told his mother, what he had learned from Cerise, and what little Xavier-Yves Zander had been able to offer.

"I'm not sure I can tell you anything more about Allison and Kevin's disappearance than my subordinate at Zyzzyva," William said. "As I am sure Zander told you, Allison is not exactly an employee of mine, but we do have a contractual relationship. Of course, my concern extends far beyond that. I like to think that anyone with whom I work is a member of my extended family, especially the young people, and among them, particularly the ones who come out to LA from distant parts of the country and are away from their own families."

"My mother would appreciate that," Marcus said. "Mom didn't really want Allison to come out here. But I convinced her it would be wrong to pass up an opportunity like this. If anything's happened to Allison, I'll never forgive myself."

"How are you proceeding with your investigation, if that is the right way to put it. Your . . . *search?*"

"First thing tomorrow, we're going to drive out to the area where they disappeared. Retrace their steps."

"Ah . . . isn't there already a search ongoing? Helicopters and the like?"

"Yes, but I'd like to see the area for myself," Marcus said. "I'm a hunter. I'm good at tracking. I have a vested interest in finding Allison that these other folks, as professional as they might be, don't."

"I understand. The truck you came in . . . is that what you will be driving to Palm Springs?"

"It's all I've got."

"Might I offer the use of one of my SUVs? A new Cadillac Escalade? It will be far more comfortable, and far more reliable, than your pickup, which, it would appear"—here his sniffed the air, reconfirming his earlier detection of the not unpleasant bite of Marcus's sweat—"does not even have air-conditioning."

"It doesn't, but . . ."

"Please, it's the very least I can do. I can also offer you a driver, should you want one."

"No, I can handle that myself. But, yes, it might be useful to have a better vehicle."

"What else can I do for you?"

"That will be plenty," Marcus said.

"Please believe me when I tell you I want to find Allison and Kevin as much as you do," William said. "I feel somehow responsible for them. I have resources—money, connections, influence—all of which I will put at your disposal. I'll put up a reward—say, $100,000—for information leading to their safe return, and I'll pay for newspaper advertisements and television spots. I'll divert some of my staff to help with the logistics, screen out the inevitable kooks."

"That's very generous of you," Marcus said. "I don't know how I'd ever be able to repay you."

"No need, my boy. No need at all. I want this to have a happy resolution. I'm looking forward to getting to know you—and your sister, of course—much better, in happier times."

"I guess we'd better go, then. It's getting late and we have a lot to do tomorrow."

"Where are you staying?"

Marcus described the living situation at Allison's West Hollywood apartment, with Jacob sleeping in Allison's bed and him dozing fitfully on the couch in the living room. William insisted— it required considerably more persuasion than the offer of the SUV—that Jacob and Marcus stay with him. At the very least, it would save them a ride on the dark and confusing streets at this late hour. He would provide them with toiletries. They could decide in the morning whether they wanted to stay for the duration of their trip. And they each could have their own room, with large, comfortable beds.

"That is, unless you'd like to *share* a room?" William said.

"No, two will be fine."

William smiled. Jacob looked crestfallen.

Chapter Twelve

Marcus knew William was trying to determine if he and Jacob were lovers when he offered them the choice of sleeping in one bedroom or two. Though he immediately had opted for separate rooms because he did not want to be tempted by intimate proximity to the boy, he just as quickly regretted his knee-jerk reaction. With Jacob asleep in another room, he would be vulnerable to William's advances, should he make them, which seemed likely.

Their host was gay; that much was clear almost immediately. In a city where ambitious young starlets were plentiful, especially to men with William's connections to the film industry, he was living alone in a multimillion-dollar home in the Hollywood Hills without so much as a trace of a woman in sight. All of the household help—driver, gardeners, houseboy, security detail—were attractive young men. And he had seen the way William looked at Jacob. Now he had subtly telegraphed to their host that he had no romantic interest in Jacob, when in fact precisely the opposite was true.

A couple of years ago, Marcus had become aware of a deepening friendship with Jacob, who like most boys his age had begun the process of differentiating himself from his parents. Jacob had begun to turn to Marcus for advice on things like sports and school, and Marcus sometimes brought up the subject of girls. Given Jacob's looks, it was not surprising that he was popular with the young ladies at school, and Marcus wondered if the feelings were mutual. Likewise, there was some curiosity on Jacob's part about the women he imagined, incorrectly, that Marcus must have been dating.

Marcus was gratified by Jacob's interest in his life and by what appeared to be a growing affection, brotherly or otherwise. He had acknowledged his attraction to men in his late teens and had since been with many men, especially during his four years as a marine, when he learned the real reason recruits were called "grunts." Marcus had never been physically or emotionally attracted to hairless little boys, but in the past year, Jacob had matured from the boy he once knew into a stunning young man, and Marcus found himself thinking of him in sexual, or more precisely, *romantic* terms. He did not know how long he would be able to resist his urge to make love to him, especially as it became clear that Jacob might welcome his attentions. The boy had at last celebrated his eighteenth birthday, and if something were to happen now, he could scarcely be accused of being a sexual predator, especially if Jacob initiated it. But there remained a psychological barrier. His feelings for Jacob were complicated by the fact that he had known the boy since Jacob had been twelve or thirteen. He could not look at Jacob without thinking of him as the boy he once was and not the young man he had become.

He had come close to acting on his impulses in Missouri on their way to California. The night had turned unexpectedly cool, and they had spooned for warmth beneath the sleeping bag that covered them. Both had been wearing sweatshirts and underwear but had removed their boots and jeans before slipping under the sleeping bag. Marcus's cock, constrained by the reinforced mesh pouch of his boxer briefs, was rock hard as Jacob's ass, covered only by a thin layer of white cotton, snuggled against him, seeking warmth. He wondered if Jacob had been awake as he gently pulled the boy close to him and pressed forward his hips, ever so slightly, over and over and over again, to make contact with him, aligning his cock with the crevice between the two snowy mounds of his ass. He felt the boy quiver, perhaps because he was cold, and pulled him closer. It was all he could do not to groan or bellow when his own explosive orgasm opened his floodgates, saturating the fabric of his briefs. Stricken by a sense of guilt the next morning, he could not look Jacob in the eye. He vowed he would not allow himself to lose control on the trip again, and he forced himself to keep a check on his emotions—and his lust—even at the risk of hurting Jacob's feelings by appearing distant.

Now the urgency of finding Allison had at last put his feelings for Jacob on the back burner. When Marcus and Jacob awoke in William's home the next morning, they each made their way separately to the kitchen in search of coffee and found a note from William telling them he had left for his office in downtown LA to put into motion the plans they had discussed the night before. He would not be home until sometime that evening, but his houseboy would provide them with anything they required. In addition to the keys to the Escalade and access codes to the driveway gate and house, he left them two cell phones and a printout of a map and directions to Joshua Tree National Park. He had highlighted in yellow a long stretch of Twentynine Palms Highway and circled in red the towns of Morongo Valley, Desert Hot Springs, and North Palm Springs.

The Cadillac, a luminous ivory vehicle with dark, smoke-tinted windows, was parked at a jaunty angle on the latticework brick driveway, shaded by a row of Italian cypress, looking for all the world like a magazine advertisement, save for the jarring presence of their now-abandoned pickup. Marcus unlocked the driver's door and hauled himself into the high-riding SUV almost as if he were mounting a horse. He popped the lock on Jacob's door.

"You navigate," he said, handing Jacob the directions.

As they waited for the gate to open at the bottom of the driveway, Jacob reoriented the map to face the direction in which they were headed.

"We need to take Mulholland Drive to Laurel Canyon Boulevard, then look for signs to route 134 East," he said.

"How long does it say it will take to get there?"

"A little more than two hours. Looks like most of the drive is on I-10."

"It's a good thing we have this ride," Marcus said as he adjusted the A/C. "Most likely, the pickup would have taken at least three hours, maybe more, and we would have been totally baked when we got there."

Jacob stared intently at the map, guiding Marcus turn-by-turn until they got onto I-10, when he put the map down.

"We're good for something like seventy-five miles now," he said. "I guess we can relax."

They rode in silence for a while, with Jacob checking their progress against the map with each new municipality they passed. The scenery was pretty similar: bungalows, strip malls with red tile roofs, a lot of churches, some traditional, some looking like something from another planet.

"So, do you think we'll find her?" Jacob asked. "*Today*, I mean. I know we'll find her *sometime*, but do you think it might be today?"

Marcus sighed. Jacob silently counted the number of times the tires thumped expansion joints in the roadway . . . *three, four, five.*

"It's been a week, Jacob," Marcus said. "I think it's highly unlikely we'll just drive out there today and find them alongside the road, out of gas or with a flat tire. Something is seriously wrong here."

Jacob thought he sounded angry, as if his question had been stupid or careless.

"I'm sorry, I was just . . . ."

"No . . . *I'm* sorry. I know it sounded like I was mad at you for asking. I'm not. I'm just *mad*. In general."

"Do you think . . ."

"There are some bad people out there, Jake. Some *very* bad people. And they tend to gravitate toward people like Allison. They're jealous of them or they think they're entitled to something from them, some form of attention, acknowledgment, whatever. It's completely irrational. They seem to think that because people like Allison have been given so much, they ought to share the wealth, which is to say, *themselves,* with anybody who wants a piece of them."

"Kind of like the photographers who chased Princess Diana?" Jacob had only been seven when the princess died in Paris, but he had been heartbroken.

"Kind of, but worse, Jake. Much worse. Selfish people. People with evil intentions. Kidnappers, rapists, murderers."

"You don't think . . ."

"I don't know. I'm hoping for the best and preparing for the worst. This does not look good. Two people don't just simply disappear without someone or something *intervening*. You saw what the desert was like on our way out here. No one in their right mind would drive off-road in a little sports car, especially not this time of year, in this heat, for no good reason. And if they had, I'm sorry to say they would probably have died of heatstroke and dehydration by now. That's simply a fact. But in any event, someone would have found their car, one of the search-and-rescue teams, someone in a helicopter. It's a red car, for God's sake. A bright red car."

"What do you think happened?"

"I don't know. But I can tell you this much: They were *not* abducted by aliens. And while we're on the subject, Jake, I don't think it's unreasonable to warn you about this character William."

"What? William? What about him? You don't think he had anything to do with Allison's disappearance, do you?"

"No, I don't. What I'm getting at is, well . . . I think he might *want* something from you."

"From me? What?"

"Come on, Jake. I'm sure you know there are guys who like boys like you. You're a very handsome young man."

"You mean gay guys? Yeah. So what? That doesn't make him bad."

"You're okay with that?"

"Well, not with *him*. I mean, it's okay if he's gay, but I don't like him in that way. He's kind of, I don't know, a little creepy."

"Exactly."

"I don't mean creepy-*pervy*. Yeah, he's gay, but I don't think there's anything wrong with that. I'm cool with it. I think he's really trying to be helpful to us. But he seems kind of, I don't know, *old-fashioned*, in a weird, spooky kind of way. Don't you think? The way he talks sometimes?"

"I don't know, Jake. I think it may just be that he has money. He's not like you or me. He probably went to the best schools, traveled around the world by the time he was your age. You know what Cerise said: he's Hollywood royalty. His grandfather worked with people like Judy Garland and Mickey Rooney. His father's studio did a whole bunch of television shows like *The Munsters*, *The Addams Family*, and *Bewitched*."

"How about the way he always refers to Allison and Kevin as 'young people'? He's only thirty-one himself, but he makes it sound like he's a hundred years old."

"What are you suggesting, Jake?"

"I'm not sure. I guess the fact that his father made *The Munsters* and *The Addams Family* does sort of explain things."

As they drove through the San Gorgonio Pass near Cabazon, they saw two dinosaur statues in the distance, including a gigantic tyrannosaurus rex, which seemed odd and kind of frightening to Jacob, though Marcus thought they were funny. Beyond the mountain pass, the landscape was uniformly brown and barren, the desert floor covered with scrubby vegetation extending for miles in every direction and acres of wind farms with spinning turbines. The heat shimmered off the faded surface of the roadway.

They spent the better part of the afternoon driving Twentynine Palms Highway between the intersection of I-10 and the entrance to Joshua Tree National Park, with Jacob peering through a pair of binoculars they had found in the car, his eyes peeled for a flash of red metal in the desert. On the return leg of their third round trip they stopped to question the owners of a few run-down businesses—a dusty fruit market, an isolated post office, a faded souvenir stand. They showed them pictures of Allison, but no one could remember seeing her, or a red sports car, the week before. Finally, they headed back to LA, driving into the glaring sun as it set into the Pacific, out of sight.

They made the trip again two days later and then a third and final time before Marcus was satisfied they had scoured the landscape along every inch of the drive between Joshua Tree and I-10, where Kevin and Allison should have turned right and headed back to Los Angeles but instead had simply disappeared.

Chapter Thirteen

The e-mail address William established for tips on the where-abouts of Allison and Kevin received more than a hundred messages in the first day it was operational, and the rate at which they arrived increased hourly as news of the reward spread virally across the Internet. William assigned three members of his staff to screen them in eight-hour shifts twenty-four hours a day, with instructions to pass along only the most credible leads. Many messages were accompanied by photos to validate their claims, but in each case, William's assistants quickly were able to determine the images came from one advertising campaign or another, downloaded from the Web and doctored in Photoshop to remove the product brand name or logo.

"What kind of idiot thinks he can fool us with pictures from an Abercrombie and Fitch advertising campaign?" William asked. "Do they *really* think we're going to believe Bruce Weber kidnapped them?"

"The world is full of desperate people," Marcus said. "The reward is bound to bring out the kooks and crazies, but hopefully it also will flush out someone who really does know where they are or what happened to them."

While they waited for their first real lead, they simultaneously pursued other avenues of investigation. William hired two private detectives, one mortal, one vampire, to assist them, and he arranged a meeting with Kevin Cassidy's distraught parents, who added $25,000 of their own money to the reward fund.

At the end of the first week, after more than a thousand messages had been logged in, read, and dismissed as worthless, one arrived with two large files attached, labeled simply "K.wmv" and "A.wmv." After viewing the attachments, the employee on duty forwarded them to William and simultaneously placed an urgent call to his private number. William, in turn, asked Marcus to come into his private office. He cautioned him not to say anything to Jacob regarding what he was about to see.

"These are pretty disturbing, but they look authentic," William said. "I hate to ask you to watch them, but you're the only one among us who can identify Allison with absolute certainty. I'll play the video of the boy first, so you can brace yourself for what we are dealing with."

William double-clicked on an icon and a media player appeared on his monitor. It seemed to take forever for the video clip to load and buffer, but then the small onscreen window filled with white light, flared, and faded to a uniform, pale, greenish gray. The image was black-and-white, as if it had been taken from an inexpensive video feed. There was no audio. The room was stark, cell-like, with unfinished concrete walls, a small sink, and a rudimentary toilet with no seat. The camera was focused on a simple cot, on which lay a naked male in his late teens or early twenties. His features were somewhat indistinct, but he was tall, lean, and well-built—if pale and motionless.

"This would appear to be Kevin," William said. "In a moment or two he'll move, as if he's responding to a noise or a voice. And then someone appears with a tray of food."

The boy seemed dazed and weak. In the lower right corner, the person with the tray materialized, a muscular, dark-haired male. He pulled a folding chair next to the bed and sat down, his face never visible to the camera. Propping the boy's head up with a doubled-over pillow, he spoon-fed him a thick, dark substance from a plain white bowl. When the boy would take no more nourishment, the dark-haired man set aside the tray and examined what appeared to be a bandage on the boy's leg, near his groin, removed it, applied some sort of ointment, and dressed it with fresh gauze.

William said nothing to Marcus, but the video only reinforced his gut feeling that a vampire was involved. He was distressed at the way the boy looked and acted. It had been only two weeks since he had disappeared, and his captors were obviously feeding and caring for him, but he looked deathly pale and unresponsive to his surroundings, as if he had been ill for some time. His caretaker had to coax his lips apart with the spoon. The bandage near the femoral artery also was cause for alarm. William had seen mortals in a similar state and was almost certain the boy's condition was the result of a combination of massive blood loss and the shock of surviving a near-kill by a vampire. The physical aspects of such an attack alone were life-threatening, but the emotional devastation of being alive and conscious while being nearly drained of blood were much, much worse. It resulted in a type of shock and helplessness that left such victims without the will to fight and thus vulnerable to subsequent, more than likely fatal, secondary attacks. His captor clearly had plans for him, plans that may have been even more terrifying than the ordeal he had—barely—survived so far. The thought infuriated him.

"Do you recognize him?" Marcus asked. "Can you be sure it's him?"

"I'm not *certain*," William said. "He certainly looks like someone we would represent. I'll forward this to Zander as well. But hopefully, you'll recognize Allison—if you're still willing to try, given what you've seen so far. If you can positively identify her, we can assume this is Kevin."

William closed the media player window. He paused and looked at Marcus, who nodded, before he double-clicked on the icon labeled "A.wmv." A similar scene booted up and Marcus gasped as he saw a naked young woman in an identical room, her breasts exposed, her lower torso covered with a sheet. She was sitting up on the bed, propped against the wall, apparently at least marginally stronger than the young man. William suspected she had been fed upon only once, while the boy may have been nearly drained multiple times, possibly to sap his strength and make him less of a threat or because his captor had an affinity for young male flesh. Even now, it might be too late for him.

"That's her," Marcus said, pushing himself away from the screen with one arm and turning away. "I'm sure of it. I don't need to see any more. Turn it off."

"You're absolutely certain?" William asked. "I know it's painful to watch, but we need to be sure—100 percent sure—before we pursue this. Remember, we're in Hollywood. Some USC film student could have created these videos like a homegrown *Blair Witch Project*. If this is a scam or a wild goose chase, it will divert us from the real mission of finding them."

Marcus forced himself to look at the computer display again, moving in closer and squinting at the low-resolution image. The same figure who had delivered food to the young man brought a tray in to Allison, who had the strength to swing her legs to the floor, place the tray on her lap, and feed herself. She pushed her long, disheveled blond hair back from her face with her right hand.

"That's her, all right. She was always doing that with her

hair. She liked it long. *Likes.* She *likes* it long. . . . She's alive! I can't believe it."

What had been painful had turned unexpectedly joyful. Tears rolled down Marcus's cheeks.

"Where did you get this? And what do we do next?" Marcus asked.

William quit the media player program and put the monitor into sleep mode.

"It arrived anonymously via e-mail. I doubt we'd be able to trace it, even if we tried. They're probably smarter than that. But the message contained instructions for signaling our intentions to rendezvous."

"Any demands? What do they want? How *much* do they want?"

"There *are* no demands, other than a claim on the reward, which I'll be happy to pay—if indeed they are safe. Whoever sent it claims to be a not-quite-innocent bystander who needs the money and apparently genuinely wants no harm to come to either Allison or Kevin. It's a somewhat damning admission, but that makes me think it's genuine. I don't think someone who didn't know where they were or who didn't have both the means and the intention to lead us to them would have spelled things out so candidly."

What William didn't say was that he suspected the person who had sent the message was either a terrified mortal, in which case he would most likely be powerless to thwart the vampire who was holding Kevin and Allison and deliver them safely, or a subordinate vampire bent on betraying his master and creator, which caused problems of a magnitude he could not even begin to contemplate. Trust and loyalty were highly valued precepts among the vampire brotherhood, critical to the clan's survival, and such betrayals were not taken lightly. Indeed, they often resulted in the trial and execution of the protégé while his master was censured, at most, for losing control and allowing such a thing to happen. In any other circumstances, William would find it difficult to participate in such a scenario, let alone bestow $100,000 on the accuser. But because of his personal interest in recovering Allison unharmed for Marcus's sake, he communicated his willingness to meet with the author of the e-mail at the appointed time and place: midnight, two days hence, at a small, little-used scenic overlook on Crest View Drive just below the Mulholland Tennis Club. With its panoramic view of Los Angeles in the valley below, it was public enough that passing cars could see them, but was poorly lit, affording a modicum of privacy and anonymity to everyone involved.

William knew Marcus would insist on accompanying him to the rendezvous, and he agonized over how much to tell him about his suspicions. While he could not be *absolutely* certain vampires were involved, his level of confidence was extraordinarily high. For Marcus to enter into such a situation unawares would be dangerous, perhaps even fatal. If he lost control of himself and attacked the man he blamed for his sister's disappearance, and if that man were a vampire, Marcus easily could be killed, despite William's swift and decisive intervention. Sometime in the next forty-eight hours, he would have to decide whether or not to reveal his true nature to the man that he had unexpectedly, almost unwillingly, come to love.

Chapter Fourteen

With each passing day, each hour spent in Marcus's company, William found himself drawn more passionately to the handsome, down-to-earth farmhand. Over the years, he'd had many mortal lovers and a few long-term relationships with other vampires (long-term being subjective; in vampire life spans, they were barely the blink of an eye). A few of his shorter relationships with mortals had run their course without him ever revealing his true nature, although that required a master-logistician and significant compromises when it came to avoiding daylight. He had lost count of the number of relationships that had ground to a halt when he repeatedly was forced to decline to take sunny, beach vacations. Others had ended when he had "come out of the casket" to his partners. One such lover had gone mad upon comprehending the news and had to be institutionalized. Now in his eighties, he remained heavily medicated. Another, tragically among his greatest loves, had to be destroyed to protect William's secret, an act which, in the lonely years that followed, had caused him to consider extinguishing his own life.

Perhaps it was only because his relationship with Marcus—
or his *hoped-for* relationship with him—was new, fresh, and
full of optimism that he felt it had the potential to be the deepest and most meaningful love affair of his life.

"You poor, deluded monster," Jock had said to him recently,
patting his hand as they sat in the darkness of William's private
screening room like a film production team viewing the daily
rushes but instead watching a live video feed of Marcus sunning
himself at the pool just a few yards away. "You're only tortur-
ing yourself."

William was close to tears. Reclining on a chaise longue,
Marcus glistened with tropical oils as he took a rare respite
from his search for Allison. Watching Jacob apply the lotion to
Marcus's back and legs aroused both William and Jock, for different reasons.

"Have you ever seen anyone—any *thing*—so beautiful, so
alive?" William asked.

"Truth? I have. James Dean. The young Marlon Brando.
Errol Flynn. *Sean* Flynn. Oh my God, the poor, tragic Sean
Flynn. Even more delicious than daddy."

"Stop it!"

"Rock Hudson. Cary Grant."

"I said, stop it!"

"You asked."

"It was a *rhetorical* fucking question."

"Still, my dear, this isn't doing you any good. The young
man is here for one reason only: to find his sister, and you and I
both know that's going to end badly. These things always do.
However things turn out, he will be returning to whatever
charming little burg he came from back in old Pennsyltucky
when it's all over. He's not the Hollywood type, I think you
know that. And he will probably take that charming little boy
home with him and fuck his brains out . . . 'til death do *they*
part."

"He's not interested in Jacob."

"*Yet.* . . . But Jacob is certainly interested in him, and the boy has many charms."

"I intend for Jacob to stay here."

"Oh, you *do?*"

"I intend to make him a star."

"And what do you intend to do with Marcus? Turn him from cocksucker to bloodsucker?"

"No, but I . . . I *want* him. For however long I can have him."

This intensity of yearning was relatively unknown to William, who like most of his blood brethren was by necessity quick to rouse to passion and equally quick to quench it. A soulful longing was rare among their kind. It was not that vampires did not *have* souls, but rather that as the decades passed they grew inured to the human emotions they had largely been forced to abandon on the day they had been transformed. The fact that they invariably outlived their inamoratos, saw their youthful, beautiful lovers wither and die, and in some cases even ended up destroying them, had sheathed their own ravenous hearts in granite. What remained were the most primal urges—blood, sex, sleep.

If it had been merely lust, William could have taken what he wanted from Marcus forcibly. However strong he was, the mortal would be no match for him. And despite William's outwardly pacific nature, the forceful taking of some of his earlier lovers had proven to be quite the aphrodisiac. He likewise could have used his fabled vampiric wiles to bewitch Marcus. But like Kim Novak in *Bell, Book and Candle,* which William had coproduced, he wanted his lover to come to him of his own accord, unbidden.

"I think you may just be hungry," Jock said. "What you need is a good, long, feeding. To *completion.* You're overdue. We both are. I know you're trying hard to set an example for the rest of the community, but these 'light bites' just aren't doing it for you anymore. If not for your sake, do it for Marcus and Jacob. If we don't feed soon, they might not be safe here. Seriously. You know your inner beast has a mind of its own when it is denied for too long. And that sweet boy makes my canines tingle."

William knew it was more than that, more than simple hunger. Although he had no doubt that sipping a bit of Marcus's blood, especially at the culmination of a long night of steaming sex, would be nothing short of ecstasy, he wanted so much more than that. He found himself considering, for the first time in at least a decade, the possibility of *turning* Marcus in a couple of years, if they proved compatible. But for now, for this night, anyway, the simple pleasure of an all-too-rare kill would have to suffice. It would clear his head. And it would provide him with the physical strength he needed for his encounter with the man who held the key to Allison's future.

"Perhaps you're right," he said to Jock. "Tell you what, I'll split one with you tonight. Something beefy and full-bodied. A stevedore from Long Beach. Big, butch, and greasy."

"*Now* you're talking," Jock said, rubbing his hands together theatrically. "But no sharing. I'm famished!"

Chapter Fifteen

When William returned from Long Beach at three a.m., he was surprised to discover the lights were on in Marcus's suite, and he decided it was as good a time as any to reveal his true nature. The rendezvous was scheduled for that evening, and there was little time to waste.

He was feeling strong and confident in the wake of the kill, which had gone particularly well. He and Jock had approached two longshoremen as they were leaving the docks, offered them a lavish sum for the pleasure of their company "for an hour or two," and plied them with alcohol while their chauffeur drove them to the Laguna Coast Wilderness Park, where it would be easier to dispose of their bodies. Vampires are accomplished cocksuckers who take as much pleasure in draining their victims of semen as of blood—and provide almost unspeakable ecstasy in return. They use their considerable cocksucking skills to disguise their true intentions, to distract their victims from their impending doom. Having achieved what may be the greatest climax of their lives, their victims are scarcely aware that their lifeblood is being drained from them via their femoral arteries in what seems like an endless orgasm. In fact, the feeling is as pleasurable as it is deadly. Such was the case with the two sweaty, strapping stevedores, whose last moments on earth were ecstatic, and whose lifeless, bloodless bodies were left behind in the Laguna dunes.

It had been a long night, but it had been worth it. The large volume of fresh blood cleared William's head and calmed his spirit in ways his more measured feedings did not. It was an exhilarating feeling and one it would be only too easy to indulge again. He was reminded anew why he allowed himself such extravagances only occasionally. But for tonight, he was sated. He showered and changed clothes, then appraised himself in the mirror approvingly. He could look Marcus in the eye knowing his own cheeks were flushed with life and health, but more importantly he would not be distracted by his need for blood or sex.

He arrived at Marcus's suite carrying a red leather folio, rapped lightly on his door, and barely whispered his name. It would be enough to summon him if he were awake, but not to disturb him if he had fallen asleep with the lights on—or to rouse Jacob in the suite across the hall. He heard footfalls and the door opened. William was glad he had drunk as deeply as he had, because Marcus was standing in front of him in black boxer briefs and nothing else, his dark hair tousled, his chin shadowed with stubble.

"What is it?" Marcus said, eagerly. "Do you have news?"

"No, no, nothing new. I just saw your lights on and thought I'd see how you were doing. Are you up early or late?"

"I slept for a while—three or four hours—but I can't get those images of Allison out of my head. Come in. Let me put something on."

"No need. Don't trouble yourself," William said.

The suite was in the wing that was cantilevered over the cliff and offered an unobstructed view of the city. William made his way to the conversation group near the floor-to-ceiling windows and sat down in the Barcelona chair.

"You're comfortable here?"

"Way more than comfortable. I just wish I could enjoy it."

"You're always welcome to return or to stay awhile once this affair is satisfactorily resolved, as I know it will be."

"Thanks, but I'm sure Allison will want to get home."

"Then you'll come back soon, I hope."

Marcus poured a cup of the coffee he had been brewing at the wet bar when William had interrupted him. He offered his host a cup, which he declined.

"I'm wide awake already," William said. "I am most definitely a night person."

"So what's on your mind? Given any more thought to our meeting tonight?"

"I've thought of very little else. In fact, that's what I want to talk to you about now, before Jacob wakes up. It's not the type of thing we need to trouble him with."

"I agree. The less he knows about the details the better."

William paused. He had difficulty knowing where to start. In preparation for this conversation, he had replayed similar dialogues from years past, most of which had turned out badly. But this situation was different. He was not coming out to a lover who had invested a great deal in him, so there was less at stake. He doubted Marcus would become overly emotional. What he was doing could be seen as a warning, an attempt to protect Marcus and Jacob and to assist with the safe recovery of Allison. He supposed Marcus could choose to believe him or not, but at least he would not be entering into the night's event unprepared.

"Marcus, surely you know the story of Dracula. . . ."

"The vampire? Sure, everybody knows Count Dracula. He's right up there with Frankenstein and the Wolfman."

"Ah, yes, the holy trinity of Hollywood horror movies. But unlike the far-fetched Frankenstein and Wolfman, the story of Dracula is more than mere myth, more than fairy tale. It is truth, Marcus, historical fact. Vampires *do* exist. They walk the earth to this day. Increasingly, they walk the streets of this very city."

"You're shitting me, right?"

"Unfortunately, Marcus, I am not, as you say, 'shitting you.' But colorful expression, that. The fact is, I believe there is a very real possibility that vampires are responsible for the disappearance of Allison and Kevin."

"I'm sorry, William, but as you might imagine, I'm having a hard time swallowing that."

"What if I told you that *I* was a vampire, Marcus? That I am 118 years old?"

"I'd say you don't look a day over forty."

"Touché. But I'm thirty-one, Marcus. Or I was, when I became a vampire in 1923."

As grateful as Marcus was for William's help, he had never been entirely comfortable with him. He had known from the beginning that William was gay, and his first concern had been that he was interested in Jacob, although that no longer seemed to be the case. But ever since the conversation with Jacob on the drive to Joshua Tree, Marcus had been thinking about some of the things he had said about their benefactor—his somewhat old-fashioned turns of phrase, his references to "young people" not that much younger than himself. The idea that William was a vampire would go a long way toward explaining that, but it was preposterous! More than likely, William was a nut case, plain and simple. He was the third or fourth generation of a family who had been in the film industry since the beginning. That kind of insular wealth and power was sometimes crazy-making. Maybe a doting, overprotective mother had kept him isolated in their Sunset Boulevard mansion, where he passed the time watching old horror movies in his grandfather's screening room. Maybe he was the result of Hollywood inbreeding. In all other respects, he seemed sane enough. He was obviously rich and powerful, a clearheaded and astute businessman. His home was modern and beautiful, something out of *Architectural Digest*, not a cluttered old cliché out of one of his father's Gothic horror sitcoms. What could he possibly gain by making up something like this? He wasn't going to extort money from Marcus, who had none anyway, in the false hope of rescuing Allison.

"Well, if you say it's true, William, I'll believe it. Or at the very least, I'll believe that *you* believe it."

"I see, so you're still not quite convinced, but you're willing to go along with my . . . delusion. Is that right?"

"I guess so," Marcus said. "Naturally, I have a lot of questions."

"Such as?"

"Such as are you going to kill me, now that I know?" He laughed.

"I see. . . . No, Marcus, I am not going to kill you. Both you and Jacob will always be safe with me. Of course, I do ask for your discretion about this matter, your silence outside the walls of this house."

"Of *course*. Your secret's safe with me."

"I can see that you still need convincing. I thought you might," William said, placing the folio on the coffee table between them and untying its red ribbons, revealing yellowed pages of century-old documents, crumbling letters written in a spidery hand, and sepia-toned photographs.

"I was born into a show-business family in 1891. My mother was an actress and my father a screenwriter and director in the early years of Hollywood. I wanted to be a director, but the executives at Vitagraph thought I was leading-man material. I didn't believe it myself, but I suppose they were right. I ultimately was featured in both of D. W. Griffith's signature films, *Birth of a Nation* and *Intolerance.*"

Marcus looked at him blankly. He had never heard of either film or their director.

"D. W. Griffith?" William asked, incredulously. "No? Really? Ah, how fleeting is fame. Tell me you've at least heard of my dear friend Gloria Swanson."

"Heard of her but couldn't pick her out of a lineup. I *have* heard of Joan Crawford, though."

"Ah, the lovely Lucille LeSueur," William said. "But I see the reference is lost on you."

"I got nothing," Marcus said.

"In those days we ground out movies the way McDonald's grinds out hamburgers. I was in Oregon making a picture called *The Valley of the Giants* when I was injured in a train wreck. The studio doctor gave me morphine for the pain and I got hooked. He kept me supplied so I could continue to work, and I went downhill, fast, but I continued to turn out picture after picture. I was practically on my deathbed when an old friend who in life had been a renowned Victorian actor turned me. Drained of my tainted blood, I went through a brief withdrawal but completely recovered.

"Edwin and I lived together for nearly ten years, investing in film production companies and Southern California real estate, but I grew morose about my lost family and abandoned career, and I felt constrained by his Victorian attitudes. He was a hundred and three at the time.

"We split up, amicably, in 1935," William concluded. "Edwin said it was to be expected. Apparently most vampires in time come to regret their metamorphosis and turn against their creator. He called it 'the seven-year bitch,' but we lasted for nine.

We remain friends to this day, although the poor dear has been growing increasingly aloof for the past forty years, and rarely sees anyone socially anymore."

Marcus had seen photographs of William's "grandfather" discreetly displayed in nooks and crannies around the house and realized now they were actually William himself. He stood up and went to refill his coffee cup.

"You might need something stronger," William suggested.

"Not on your life," Marcus said. "My head is already spinning."

A moment had come and gone, a moment from which there was no turning away—or back. William could see that Marcus's hands were unsteady, the surface of the coffee rippling with concentric circles.

"Relax, dear boy."

"I don't know.... What you say sounds so ... *real,* as if you believe it yourself. What you're telling me is that you are actually a vampire? A real, live, bloodsucking vampire? I guess that would explain why I've never seen you in daylight."

"Indeed it would. I am precisely what you think I am. Bram Stoker got it right, by and large. No sunlight, garlic, or stakes through the heart, please. But we are far more vulnerable than you might think, more superhuman than supernatural. We *will* die if you cut off our heads or set us alight. Who wouldn't? And the whole shape-shifting thing? Ridiculous. We cannot alter the laws of physics that govern the conservation of matter and energy. And even if I *could* turn into a bat, why would I?

"We do drink blood and eat nothing else. We can tolerate water—and alcohol, some of us more readily than others. If we are absolutely *forced* to consume food in some social situation, we invariably purge it. As we have grown in number over the years, we've learned more about who we are and what we need to survive. We must feed no less than once a fortnight, but not necessarily to completion."

"Meaning?" Marcus asked.

"Meaning we do not need to *kill* to survive. A couple of pints, at regular intervals, will suffice. But it must be fresh blood, warm, living, and it must be taken orally. No blood banks, no transfusions. Most responsible vampires maintain a cadre of donors—well-paid, I might add—who willingly provide us sustenance."

"But some vampires kill?"

"Alas, yes. For some of us, feeding satisfies more than hunger. It's a sexual experience. For one thing, as we feed, the nourishment we take in rushes to our blood-starved extremities, including our sexual organ."

"Oh my God, so you throw wood when you feed?"

"Throw wood? No. Why on earth would we do that?"

"I mean you get hard, you get an erection, a woodie!"

William laughed softly. "Ah, yes, Marcus. We get a . . . woodie. You have *such* a way with words."

"Not really. I think maybe you're just a little out of touch."

"Unfortunately, those among us with less self-control can get a bit crazed. They continue feeding until it is too late. Occasionally, accidents happen even under circumstances that were intended to be controlled. The donor often is to blame. The outflow of blood induces euphoria in the donor, who urges the vampire on. There is a parallel to the practice of partial asphyxia during sex: the lack of blood, like the lack of oxygen, makes the victim light-headed, 'high,' if you will. But sometimes, in both practices, things go terribly wrong. It is only when their hearts begin to fail that they suspect they have made a fatal miscalculation—and by then it is too late.

"But there are also vampires who kill willfully, wantonly, brazenly. They live on the edge, outside our established communities, and when they are discovered, they are sanctioned. Some of the older, more established vampires have political connections within the community and get off with what amounts to a slap on the wrist. Others, those more recently converted to our ranks who fail to grasp the rules by which we live, are exterminated. The vampire I suspect of taking Allison seems to be to very immature, 'young' in vampire years, bloodthirsty and arrogant, unable to control his impulses. I suspect he may be the relatively recent spawn of an old and powerful vampire who adheres to more traditional mores and practices and who passed on his bad habits to his protégé.

"I suspect this particular vampire delights in tormenting and destroying things of beauty. 'Things' like Allison and Kevin. And his modus operandi seems particularly cruel. This is another sign of vampiric immaturity. Either that, or his is simply a very twisted, evil, perverted demon. I believe he must be sanctioned, and I am trying to get the approval to do so before he can harm anyone else, including Allison and Kevin."

"You have to get approval? There's, like, paperwork?"

William laughed.

"No, Marcus, we are not a bureaucracy like the federal government, more like an ancient Byzantine court of intrigue. But there are still channels through which we must go, approvals we must get. This vampire must be declared a rogue and his death warrant must be signed . . . in blood, ironically."

"I see. So you're like some secret society. A college fraternity like Skull and Bones."

"That's one way to look at it, I suppose. We are not as different as you might think. Vampires are people, too. We have our own needs that are not entirely different from those of you mortals."

It was impossible for Marcus to fully comprehend the implications of William's revelations. The complexity of his confession, the level of detail, carried the weight of authority. Either he was utterly mad—and dangerously delusional—or he was what he said he was. Both options were equally disturbing. But he seemed rational and had been kind and generous to both him and Jacob. He was obviously concerned about Allison, and as a result of the $100,000 reward they had their first solid lead to her whereabouts. Even if he were crazy, he had been helpful. Marcus could not successfully move forward without him—or his money. The man they were meeting that night certainly would not believe a farmhand in a twenty-year-old pickup was capable of producing $100,000. And if what William said were true—that vampires existed and Allison was at the mercy of one—his help would be crucial.

"You've convinced me," Marcus said. "As hard as it is for me to say it, I believe you. But do me a favor: Don't say anything about this to Jake."

"Certainly not. Not only do I not think we should tell Jacob anything about this, I also believe we should send him home, immediately, to get him out of harm's way. The fact is, Marcus, we may not be successful in our attempt to rescue Allison. We may die trying—both of us. I cannot in good conscience leave him here alone, even with Jock, who, by the way, also is an immortal. If we fail, and if the vampire we are battling survives us, he will likely seek revenge. This house will be among the first places he comes to wreak havoc. And if he finds Jacob, that beautiful, *beautiful* boy, he will destroy him in the most unspeakable manner."

"I'll put him on the bus myself."

"Bus, oh my no. I've already purchased him a first-class plane ticket home. You see? I've thought this out quite thoroughly."

"Now all we have to do is convince *him*, which won't be easy."

"A certain amount of candor is called for. Not, as we both agree, complete honesty. But we need to make him understand the gravity of the situation."

It was nearly dawn, and William needed to make his way back to the safety of his private quarters. As he left Marcus's suite, he noticed that Jacob's door was ajar, and he wondered, fleetingly, if he had been eavesdropping on his revelatory conversation with Marcus. But he had no time to investigate. His feet barely touched the floor as he raced to his subterranean suite and closed the door behind him. It had been a very long night, and although the blood of the stevedore had renewed him, he lay down and willingly relinquished himself to the pull of sleep.

Chapter Sixteen

While William rested, Marcus went to the private gym and worked out, concentrating on stretching his muscles, increasing his flexibility, and assessing his readiness for combat with the undead. During his four years in the marines, he had been a member of a sniper team nicknamed "Nightmare One," and while most of his work had been done with deadly long-range rifles, he also had been trained in the hand-to-hand combat techniques of an assassin, skills that could come in handy if Allison's captors put up a fight. When Jacob made his way to the gym later that morning looking for him, Marcus spent an hour teaching him some of the basics of kickboxing.

Jacob was wearing only the flimsiest pale blue nylon running shorts, with a vent that ran all the way up to the waistband so the front and rear panels looked more like a loincloth than a pair of boxers. When Jacob raised a long, tan leg to kick, Marcus could see a flash of the pale half-moon of his ass, a delicious curve revealed—and just as quickly obscured. A glimpse of paradise. It made him wish he had suggested a wrestling tutorial instead of a kickboxing lesson.

Later, in the steam room, the gift of Jacob's body was offered to him unobstructed, save for the gauze of fog that rose between them. The sight quickened Marcus's pulse, flooded his cock with blood. Out of modesty, he kept a white towel secured around his waist. Jacob felt no such compunction. In his innocence, he laid his towel lengthwise on the tiled platform and reclined. Marcus thought his body looked like sculpture, not in cold, pale marble but in golden tones of oak, as if his torso had been lovingly turned on a lathe by a master craftsman seeking the perfect balance between grace and power. He found himself staring at the boy's provocative navel and the barest line of corn silk that drew his eyes downward to Jacob's prize. He silently hoped the boy would turn over so he could see the downy curve of his back, the rounded melons of his ass.

He remembered the first time he had been aware of a genuine physical attraction to Jacob. On a sultry summer morning last year, he had looked up from his work repairing a harness to see an unfamiliar figure silhouetted in the door of the barn—tall and slim but broad-shouldered, naked from the waist up, a pair of thread-fringed cutoffs slung low on his slender, prominent hipbones. The feeling that overtook him was unmistakable, the kind of primal attraction that took his breath away. Backlit by an aura of sunlight, the figure's face was lost in shadows, but when he entered the cool darkness of the barn, he left behind the golden halo that had surrounded him. It was Jacob.

William was right; such beauty would inflame the perverse passions of whoever had taken Allison. Jacob needed to be protected. Though it was the last thing he wanted to talk about—it would surely break the erotic spell he was under—Marcus decided it was time to have the conversation with Jake that he and William agreed needed to take place.

"Jake, remember the day we first drove to Joshua Tree and I told you there were bad men in the world who preyed on people like Allison?"

"Yes?" Jacob sat up and swung his legs around to the floor. He feared there was some terrible news about Allison, that she had been found, or rather that her *body* had been found.

"William and I think there is a person like that who had something to do with Allison's disappearance."

"So . . . you know where she is?"

"We don't *quite* know yet," Marcus said, "but we have evidence. Someone sent us videos of Allison and Kevin. They're alive but not in terribly good shape, I'm afraid to say."

"But isn't this kind of good news, actually? I mean, it's not like they got lost in the desert and died."

"It's not what I wanted to hear, but it does give me hope that I still might be able to save Allison, that it's not too late. Unfortunately, we have reason to believe they are being kept alive only so that they can be killed later."

"That's just sick, Marcus. That kind of stuff really goes on here?"

"I am afraid so," Marcus said. "Not just here, but apparently in many places, Jake."

"Have you told the police about this?"

"It's somewhat more complicated than that, Jake. But we are negotiating with the person who sent the videos. We think the information he can provide will lead us to Allison. Before we go get her, we think you need to go home—back to Pennsylvania. William has bought you a plane ticket."

"What? Go home? No! Never! Not without you."

"Jake, *please* . . ."

Jacob felt like a schoolboy who had misbehaved and was being chastised by his teacher.

"Jake, it is very important that you agree to the plans we've made to send you home. When this is all over, William says you're more than welcome to come back and stay as long as you'd like. But for your safety, Jake, for your very *life*, you *must* listen to us."

Jacob glared at Marcus. He felt utterly betrayed. For a moment, he said nothing. He was devastated.

"Why does this mean I have to leave? I came out here to help you find Allison, and I want to be here with you when you do."

Marcus could see that Jacob was hurt. It might be easier if he could tell him the whole story, as William had done for him. With his youth and naiveté, Jacob might even find it easier to believe than he had. Young people often were enthralled by vampires and werewolves. Fed by movie fantasies, they half-believed in them, the way they could imagine that there really were people like Batman, Superman, Spider-Man, comforting adolescent replacements for the lost myth of Santa Claus. That was part of the problem. Jacob might romanticize the notion of vampires and not fully understand the danger he was in. It might even increase his desire to stay, so he could have a little adventure. It would be better to couch it in harsher, less glamorous terms.

"Buddy, we are in *waaaay* over our heads here. We are talking about a guy who would kill you as soon as look at you. And who, according to William, would take great pleasure in harming you, in particular."

"Me? Why me? What have I ever done to him?"

"Because, Jake, you're a very good-looking boy and this guy apparently is a dangerous psychopath, a serial killer with a taste for handsome young men like you and beautiful young women like Allison. There's more to the story, Jake, more than you need to know. It's the kind of thing that will give you nightmares for the rest of your life."

Marcus did not get the reaction he was expecting: Jacob was beaming.

"Jake, did you hear what I said? You're in danger."

"You think I'm very good looking?"

"Jake, that's not the point."

"I think you're very good looking, too, Marcus."

"Jake, please."

Jacob got up. He stood in front of Marcus, his cock rising with each pulse of his heart. The time they had spent in California had erased the harsh borders of Jacob's farmer's tan, blurring the boundaries at neck and shoulder, hip and thigh, where clothing had obscured his flesh and left it mushroom white. Only the most slender and inconspicuous of tan lines against the loamy tones of sun-tanned skin betrayed the fact that Jacob was not quite ready to sunbathe au naturel beside William's pool.

"Tell me what you want, Marcus. Tell me what to do."

Marcus placed his hands on Jake's slim hips. The gift he had dreamed of for so long was at last within his grasp, the gauzy apparition of last summer finally realized.

"What I want?" he said, gently urging the boy forward. "What I want is for you to come closer."

Jacob welcomed Marcus's encouragement. It had taken all the courage he could muster merely to stand naked before him, to offer himself at last to the man he had for so long worshipped. He could not have done it at home, not in the barn or the hayloft. But here, in these steamy confines, his inhibitions evaporated. His legs quivering, he swooned forward like a breaker seeking shore, drawn inexorably to his lover by the tidal pull of lust and moon.

As Jacob stepped toward him, Marcus hungrily took the boy into his mouth, burying his face in his surprisingly thick, damp bush, inhaling the aroma of yeast and dough that rose from the youthful flesh. His desire to ravish the boy, to consume him, was overwhelming. For an instant he wondered if this urge was similar to what William felt when he fed, and his feelings for his host softened into understanding.

Unaccustomed to such passion, Jacob abandoned himself to the intensity of his feelings—sensual and romantic. Though he never wanted this moment to end, he did nothing to hold back the explosive force gathering in his tightening scrotum. Instead, he drove deeper into Marcus's velvety chasm until he lost control in a titanic shudder that reverberated through his entire body over and over and *over* again. Marcus, too, abandoned all pretense of restraint and allowed himself to erupt in great molten spumes. Jacob collapsed against his lover, slid down to his knees, and kissed Marcus, tasting himself on his lover's eager lips.

Marcus wanted more, knew he would *take* more, though for now this would have to suffice.

But it was not enough. It would *never* be enough. Not through all eternity.

Chapter Seventeen

William and Marcus arrived at the rendezvous point half an hour early. Although their contact had said he would arrive in a black Hummer, they watched warily as a man walking a yellow Labrador retriever approached the area and lingered suspiciously. After a few minutes, he struck up a conversation with a dark-haired, bearded man in a construction company panel truck, then made his way to the passenger door and urged the dog into the vehicle.

"Get in, Goldie," he said, before entering himself and disappearing into the night.

Their vigil continued, uninterrupted. At 11:57, a gleaming H2 pulled up and flashed its high beams twice before extinguishing all but its amber running lights. A lone figure emerged from the driver's side and approached the left rear door of the Silver Wraith. William rolled down the window. The young man was Latino, muscular, with dark wavy hair, large brown eyes, and facial hair that was somewhat more than stubble but would not qualify as an actual beard. William was certain he was the caretaker in the videos of Kevin and Allison, who had brought them food and spoon-fed the pathetically weakened boy. He was patrician in bearing, as if centuries ago a forebear was a Spaniard who took a royal Aztec bride. William thought his face looked almost Christlike, beneficent but sad, the way the Savior must have looked when he was denied by one of his disciples. He unlocked the door and allowed the young man to enter. One sniff of the air in the confined passenger compartment and William knew he was a vampire. Likewise, there was an unmistakable flicker of recognition in the young man's eyes as he sat down in the jump seat opposite William and Marcus.

"Ah, I see you . . . *understand,*" William said, glancing at Marcus and nodding imperceptibly. He assumed that the young man had sized him up equally quickly and knew what—if not whom—he was dealing with. "I am William Reid."

"Rodrigo Santos."

From long experience, William could guess the young man's history—a poor but handsome boy from the barrio, seduced to the dark side by a powerful but impulsive and ultimately fickle vampire who was fleetingly smitten with him and offered him riches and eternal life, to whom he was once a lover but now only a servant. He almost certainly lived in fear of his master and creator, whom he was about to betray.

"And this is Marcus Curvin, the brother of the missing girl. While he is not one of us, he is . . . well informed. You can be completely candid with us."

Rodrigo nodded in tacit acknowledgment.

Marcus was stunned by the young man's dark good looks and for an instant was deeply saddened to think he had become a vampire, possibly against his will, at such an early age. But he was not predisposed to sympathy for the man he previously had thought of as a monster who had participated in Allison's kidnapping. He damped down his anger, knowing it would jeopardize their transaction. He would take his revenge later, if he could.

"Your sister is safe, for the moment," Rodrigo said, without hesitation, looking directly at Marcus. "I'm sorry to have put you in this situation. It was not my decision. I was . . ."

"You were only following orders?" Marcus hissed.

William cocked his head toward Marcus ever so slightly, one eyebrow arched.

"I'm sorry," Marcus said. "Go on."

Perhaps as a way to at least partially exonerate himself, Rodrigo described how Allison and Kevin had arrived at V's house seeking directions.

"It's not as if we stalked them," he explained.

"I'm afraid that's neither particularly relevant nor useful at this point," William said, tartly. "Why not just tell us what you can do for us?"

"I can provide you with the location of your sister and the boy, Kevin," he said. "And I can get you past security and onto the property. Beyond that, I'll assist you to the extent I can."

"And in return?" William asked.

"In return I ask only for the full amount of the reward money, to start a new life, and depending on how things play out, temporary sanctuary until it is safe to establish myself in our community independently."

"Ah, sanctuary. That was not in your original request," William said. He could sense Marcus stiffen as he processed this information: the man who had abetted his sister's kidnapping was now seeking protection for himself.

"Forgive me, but I did not fully grasp the situation until I stepped into the car," Rodrigo said, tentatively. "I did not think a mortal would be willing or able to give me sanctuary. I was prepared to try and deal with that myself, but it would be easier for me this way and I'm afraid I must now require it."

"Duly noted, my friend. Consider it done. You will be safe with me," William said. "Is that not right, Marcus?"

Marcus nodded mutely, abashed that William apparently had read his vengeful thoughts.

"So?" William asked.

Rodrigo shifted uncomfortably in his seat for a moment and cleared his throat.

"They are being held by the one known as V of the clan de Sade."

"Clan de Sade?" William said. "A force to be reckoned with."

"You know him then?" Marcus asked.

"He was on my short list of suspects, but I didn't know his lineage. He's a dangerous man. When he was mortal, he was a punk rocker who went by the name 'Vicious.' His creator is the famed Marquis de Sade, whose taste for blood is legendary. I daresay his protégé will be a formidable opponent."

"He is a sick, sick man—a monster," Rodrigo said. "He needs to be eliminated."

"A sanction of that magnitude can only come from the highest authorities," William said. "And 'sick' is a matter of opinion among a community such as ours, with a centuries-old legacy of spilling innocent blood. But as long as the Marquis reigns in New York City—who is he now, ah yes, that real-estate-magnate-cum-reality-show-host—we might have a hard time justifying it."

"I might be able to provide you with enough evidence to convince anyone. I've seen some pretty grotesque things in my ten years with him. He does not simply feed . . . he torments and tortures his victims before he kills them. He terrorizes them with the foreknowledge of their fate. Their deaths are often slow and agonizing."

"And you've done nothing until now?" Marcus said, his anger rising again.

"Marcus, you have to understand the power dynamic here," William interjected. "There is a unique relationship between a master vampire and the subordinate he creates, familial in nature but power-based. Love and hate, life and death, commingled. It is impossible to accurately describe to a mortal in all its complexity. We should be grateful Rodrigo has come to us offering to help Allison and Kevin. What has happened in the past is done, finished, immutable. We need to concentrate on the here and now."

"Time is of the essence," Rodrigo said. "V plans to finish what he started at his annual Equinox party this weekend, if he can wait that long. He has no self-control. He's inordinately attracted to the young man. Well, *attracted* is not the right word. He's obsessed with making him suffer. V has fed on him several times, despite my objections, and has violated him in the most heinous and bestial ways. The boy is close to death. The video I sent you no longer accurately represents his condition."

Marcus tensed visibly, assuming the worst about Allison.

"No, no," Rodrigo said, shaking his head. "I assure you, nothing similar has yet befallen your sister. V's lust, and his loathing, are focused entirely on the boy. But we *must* act quickly."

"How do you suggest we proceed?" William asked.

Rodrigo reached into a pocket and pulled out a handful of red rubber wristbands of the type worn to support charitable or humanitarian causes, imprinted with the words EQUINOX XVIII.

"These will get you into the party," he said.

"I've received an invitation and just RSVPed," William said.

"Perhaps you have, but that must have been for the mortal events, based on your standing in the Hollywood community. I know all the vampires on the invitation list and your name is not among them. The red wristbands are full-access badges, for vampires only, and will allow you entry to the private afterparty. There will be heavy security at the entrance to the feeding area. I'll enter your names in the database as last-minute acceptances. The private party begins at midnight and the feeding begins immediately, but Allison and Kevin should be safe for a couple of hours, anyway. They are the grand finale."

"How many of us will there be?" William asked.

"Approximately sixty."

"Not very good odds," Marcus said.

"I may be able to convince one or two of the blood slaves to help us, if you can provide them with sanctuary, as well. They are cousins of mine."

"Blood slaves?" Marcus asked.

"Mortals who serve as donors to V and me, with the promise we will turn them at some point in the future."

"It's a kind of apprenticeship," William explained. "Unfortunately, many unscrupulous vampires, I presume our friend V among them, don't always follow through on their promises of immortality. When the blood slaves begin to get suspicious or impatient, they are drained, discarded, and replaced. Am I right, Rodrigo?"

"Unfortunately, yes. That is often the case."

"I'll sweeten the pot for your cousins. If they will join us, I will provide sanctuary, employment as donors for me and my business partner, Jock, and a cash bonus. I will not, however, offer them immortality."

"That will be more than adequate, I think. I'll explain that V likely would not have honored his commitments. But now, I need to be getting back before V misses me—and before the sun rises."

As a sign of good faith, William passed him an envelope containing ten thousand dollars.

"For you . . . or for your cousins, if it will help."

When Rodrigo reached out to accept it, William saw a beaded bracelet on his wrist similar to those worn by surfers. His nostrils flared. He could smell blood on it, though it was present in an infinitesimal amount. This was indeed a sentimental vampire.

As Rodrigo returned to his Hummer, the panel truck reappeared and the man and his dog got out. He walked down the hill with a swagger and a smile, waving buoyantly to the occupants of the Rolls as they passed moments later.

"An obviously satisfied customer," William said, waving back as he rolled up the tinted window.

Chapter Eighteen

Marcus had barely left the house with William when Jacob entered his suite looking for the keys to the Escalade. If they wanted him gone, he would go. But he'd do it on his own terms. He wouldn't be packed off like an unwelcome relative, and he wouldn't go back to Pennsylvania without seeing something other than the inside of William's fortress-like home or the endlessly boring highway between "Yucky Valley" and Palm Springs.

Although he initially had been reluctant to go home, Jacob ultimately agreed to do so because Marcus had seemed genuinely concerned about his safety—and because he had told him that he loved him. They had made love in the steam room until they had nearly passed out from the heat—their eyes stinging, their bodies slick with sweat, their swollen cocks slapping up against their bellies. Jacob had actually cried the first time he came inside Marcus, and he was glad the steam and sweat camouflaged his tears. Later, in Jacob's room, he entered Marcus a second and third time, and Marcus promised him he would return the favor once he thought Jacob was ready. And that is when he said the words Jacob had dreamed of hearing for years.

"I love you, baby. You're my little prince."

They had fallen asleep entwined in each other's arms, but in the middle of the night Marcus had slipped back to his own room without waking Jacob.

Now he knew why.

He was no fool. He might not know what had happened to Allison, but he was certain there was no psycho serial killer. Marcus and William had made that up to scare him off. He'd woken up that morning just before dawn to find Marcus gone. Without even bothering to cover himself, he leapt out of bed to find him. When he opened his door, he saw William scuttling down the hallway like a rat, shrinking from the first rays of sunlight as they poured through the sliding glass doors to the courtyard and pool. Marcus's door was ajar and when Jacob peeked in he could see him in his underwear. William obviously had spent the night! That's why Marcus had left Jacob alone in his bed. He knew it! He *knew* William had been hot for Marcus the first time they had met. But he never would have guessed Marcus felt the same about William.

Jacob had to prevent himself from slamming his door, alerting Marcus that he was awake and knew what was going on. He threw himself on his bed and waited for the tears to come, but he was so angry he couldn't cry. Instead he kicked and flailed, his screams muffled as he bit down on his pillow. He did not know which of them he hated more—Marcus for taking advantage of him when he obviously didn't love him, or William, the little shit who had conspired to steal Marcus away from him. Later, in the shower, as clouds of moisture enveloped him, he remembered how he and Marcus had clung to one another in the steam room, how they had shuddered together in simultaneous ecstasy, and he fell to his knees bawling like a child. He stayed that way until the water ran as cold as the ice in his veins.

He avoided them as much as possible for the remainder of the day, which was not difficult. They shut themselves away in William's private quarters, obviously making plans to get rid of him. And that evening they had announced they were going out and told him he wasn't invited. They said it was an important meeting related to Allison's disappearance, but he knew it was a date.

Jacob had no idea where he was going when he climbed into the Escalade and started down the driveway with the lights off. All he knew was that he was hurt and angry, betrayed by both Marcus and William. He thought he might make his way back to Allison's apartment and spend the night there if Cerise would let him. But first, he needed to find a place to sit quietly and collect his thoughts.

The moment the gates closed behind him, the consequences of his actions momentarily paralyzed him. Marcus would be pissed off. William might have him arrested for stealing his car. They would have the excuse they needed to justify packing him off to Pennsylvania. But he no longer cared. They would do it one way or another.

Cautiously nosing the SUV onto the street, he worried about what he would do if he had an accident. The Escalade was the biggest vehicle he had ever driven. It did not help that Mulholland Drive was twisting, narrow, and dark. Afraid of careening into the ravine that fell away on the right, he hugged the middle of the road, angering the speeding drivers who approached him from the opposite direction, blowing their horns and swerving dramatically to avoid him. He breathed a sigh of relief when he turned on to Laurel Canyon Boulevard, but by the time he reached Sunset Boulevard, he was nearly in tears. He took a deep breath and continued another two blocks to Santa Monica Boulevard, where he turned right and allowed the flow of traffic to carry him along until he saw a Starbucks ahead on the right. A cup of coffee sounded like a good idea. Easing into the right lane, he turned onto North Robertson and found a parking space a block from the coffee shop.

"Thank you, thank you, *thank* you, Jesus," he said, slumping over the steering wheel. "Not a scratch on it!"

He climbed out and sat on the curb, his heart pounding. Then, his concern for the condition of the Cadillac behind him, he suddenly leaped up, spun on one foot, and kicked it, the way Marcus had shown him how to attack an opponent in the gym.

"Fuck you," he shouted. "Fuck you both!"

He had sweat through his T-shirt, even with the A/C going full blast, so he pulled it over his head and laid it on the hood of the car, allowing the heat of the engine to dry it. He leaned back against the car, allowing the night air to dry the rivulets of sweat that coursed down his chest into his treasure trail. A couple of passersby whistled at him.

"Nice car. Does your sugar daddy know you've got it?" one of them said.

"Baby, you can drive *my* car anytime," his companion called, turning around and walking backward as he receded. He grabbed his crotch lewdly.

At first, Jacob was stung by the comments; he thought the men were making fun of him. But the sexual gesture made him realize they were flirting, in their own crude way. He got up, tucked his still-damp T-shirt into the back of his jeans, and, bare-chested, followed the pair across Santa Monica Boulevard. He forgot about getting coffee or trying to find his way to Allison's apartment.

The men turned and walked into a restaurant in what looked like a Spanish hacienda or mission. The Abbey, a sign said. Jacob walked past the gated entrance, then slowed and stopped. He turned back, ambling past slowly, staring at the people seated on the patio, most of whom looked like aspiring actors waiting to be discovered.

"Sweetie! Stop window-shopping and get your cute little ass

in here!" a red-faced man called out the third time he passed. Jacob kept walking but realized he had sprung an erection. These guys *were* flirting with him. On his next pass, he was caught up in a stream of young men who had piled out of a taxi and was pulled along with them into the courtyard.

"Mmm, look what the fags dragged in!" the tipsy man said, smacking his lips.

Jacob quickly moved away from him, farther into the interior. He hoped he could simply melt into the crowd and disappear, but no matter where he went men stared at him. Most of them were quite friendly, making way for him as he passed, smiling as if they knew him, offering to buy him a cocktail. Though he smiled back, he was too self-conscious to return their greetings or accept a drink. He didn't want to have to tell them he was underage. He might get thrown out.

He found a quiet, dimly lit corner and stood against a brick wall. Exhaling for what seemed like the first time since he had walked in, he allowed himself to focus on individual men. Each time, the men looked back almost instantly, as if they were somehow aware he had been studying them. Soon, they began coming over to talk to him, one by one, asking questions, offering drinks—he quickly had four Cokes lined up—and suggesting they go to Starbucks for coffee . . . or back to their apartments. He was overwhelmed by the attention. All he wanted to do was sort out his feelings about Marcus and William.

Nearby, he saw four young men who had set themselves apart from the crowd. When one of them turned and Jacob saw the dragon tattoo on his shoulder, he realized these were the same boys he had seen in the elevator with Marcus. Two had their shirts off and both had an identical tattoo in the small of their backs, something Jacob thought looked like the symbol for radiation or hazardous materials. When the boy with the dragon tattoo caught Jacob's eye and motioned for him to come over, he hesitated only a moment. In a group, they seemed less intimidating than the lone wolves who had been circling him all evening.

"Welcome to our nightmare," dragon boy said as he extended his hand. "My name is Zéphyr."

"What?" Jacob asked, unable to grasp the name, which sounded like *Zeh-fear.*

"Zéphyr. You Americans say it *Zefur.*"

"Ah, I see. I'm Jacob."

"We have met before, no? In the elevator . . . with the cowboy?"

"Yes . . . Marcus."

"And these pervy little boys are Narcisse, Adonis, and Cupidon—Cupid for short."

Between Zéphyr's accent and the unusual names, Jacob could make sense of only Adonis and Cupid, but the boys to whom those names were attached certainly deserved them. Adonis was well built, with tight ringlets of luminous, dark hair. A tiny diamond stud glittered in his right earlobe. Cupid had the prettiest mouth Jacob had ever seen on a boy, and blushing cheeks. All of them were pretty boys, downright girlish, with high cheekbones, full lips, and longish hair. But, Jacob thought, they could use a good meal.

"Are you brothers?"

They laughed in unison.

"No, we are *sisters,*" Cupid said.

Narcisse took a slice of lime from his drink and threw it at Cupid.

Zéphyr put his arm around Jacob's shoulder. "What brings you to this place tonight? Where is the cowboy boyfriend?"

"He's not my boyfriend," Jacob said. "And I guess he never will be, now."

"Ah, the heart is broken?"

"No," Jacob said defensively.

"I think it is," Zéphyr said. "Sit and drink with us. We are experts at unbreaking boys' hearts."

Zéphyr motioned to a waiter, splaying his hand to reveal five fingers.

"Where are you guys from?"

"Romania," Cupid said. "You know it?"

"Can't say as I do. Sounds like a made-up place."

"Is very real," Adonis said. "And good riddance!"

"How did you get here?"

"We are the fashion models," Cupid said.

"Like you," Zéphyr said.

"Oh, I'm not a model."

"You are not? Then what were you doing in our building, where *everyone* is model?"

"We were visiting someone at Zyzzyva."

"So you are *becoming* model?" Narcisse said.

"No. It's a long story."

Their drinks arrived, dark red and sweet, with a tang of orange and an alcoholic bite.

"This is good!" Jacob said. "What is it?"

"Is called *granatini*," Zéphyr said. "Vodka, Cointreau, and pomegranate."

The boys were cute and kind of funny and, as Jacob had hoped, they protected him from the more intimidating men who had been circling him. They also were sexy in a strange sort of way, with their pale skin, dangerous-looking tattoos, and exotic accents.

Jacob was unaccustomed to drinking, and the potent cocktail warmed his belly and loosened his tongue. He found himself pouring out his story to Zéphyr and Adonis while Narcisse and Cupid necked. Before he knew it, he had drained his glass and another drink magically appeared in his hand. The bright lights of the bar softened, the crowd receded, and he was aware only of the attentive faces of Zéphyr and Adonis floating inches away from his own. Zéphyr leaned in and kissed him.

"Adonis and I can make you forget about this cruel cowboy, Marcus."

"I don't think you can. And besides, I don't want to."

"Not even for one night?" Adonis asked.

"Well, if I have another one of these cocktails, I'll probably forget my own name."

"Then by all means you must have *two*," Zéphyr said. "We will tell you your name in the morning."

Jacob thought he saw the eyes of Zéphyr's dragon flash at him, its tongue flicker, but he decided it was only an illusion of the twinkling lights of the bar—or perhaps the effects of the alcohol. He did not need to guess at what drew his eyes to the coppery nipples that decorated Adonis's smooth olive chest and to the rounded swell in Zéphyr's low-slung hip-hugging jeans.

"Just one more," Jacob said. "And then I really must go."

An hour later, Jacob found himself naked on the satin sheets of Zéphyr's bed, his host on his right, Adonis on his left, both naked except for their tattoos. Their cocks were long, thin, and uncut, something Jacob had not seen frequently and which made them seem even more exotic. His own thick, cut cock slapped firmly up against his taut belly leaking precum into his treasure trail, his balls drawn up achingly tight in their sacs.

"We love Americans with cocks fat like corncob," Adonis said gleefully.

"We will milk you like cow," Zéphyr added.

Jacob laughed. "Go right ahead. I do that all the time myself."

Jacob abandoned himself to the previously unimagined pleasure of having two skilled and attentive lovers simultaneously.

Both the Romanian boys were beautiful and exotic. Jacob found himself drawn to Zéphyr's tattoo but was equally attracted to the crisply defined musculature of Adonis's physique, which somehow managed to seem both graceful and rugged. They, in turn, were fascinated by his all-American-boy looks: his blond hair, the sprinkling of freckles across the top of his shoulders, the farm boy strength in his arms and legs, his incongruously thick slab of a cock.

"Oh, my God, Jacob, you could fuck me into eternity," Zéphyr growled as Jacob entered him, while Adonis hungrily rimmed Jacob's tight rosebud.

Later, Narcisse and Cupidon joined them in a sexual free-for-all that was part tug-of-war with Jacob as the prize and part a perverted game of Twister. When they all were exhausted, Jacob asked one last favor, and the four Romanians surrounded him as he knelt and summoned one more generous round of cum with which they painted his grinning, upturned face.

The next morning, he awoke sandwiched between Adonis and Zéphyr, whose colorful dragon tattoo he kissed tenderly. But his heart sank as he realized how much more he would have loved to have been kissing Marcus's razor-wired biceps and smelling his distinctive earthy aroma instead of the exotic clove scent Zéphyr and Adonis exuded. His night with the Romanians had been exhilarating; he'd experienced pleasure he had only imagined previously. But his heart belonged to Marcus and it always would, even if Marcus did not love him back. Nonetheless, he was aroused again and willingly would have once more slipped inside Zéphyr, whose cleft now cradled his cock, if only he had a condom within reach.

Zéphyr awoke and turned to face him.

"Good morning, Mr. America," Zéphyr said. "Or maybe I should call you Superman, as hard as steel."

"Good morning," Jacob said. "I should probably go. Marcus will be worried."

"So let him worry. Absence will make his heart grow fonder."

"It's not a good time to play games. At the moment, I'm the least of his worries."

By now Adonis had awakened, too, and without a word he inched his way down to the foot of the bed, along the way kissing Jacob's shoulders, his spine, the small of his back, his fragrant cleft. Jacob drew in a sharp breath as Adonis's tongue probed his rosebud.

"Oh God, that feels so fucking awesome."

Jacob had never been fucked, even by Marcus. Both Zéphyr and Adonis had tried the night before, but he had not allowed it. Now he feared if Adonis's lips lingered there much longer, capitulation was inevitable.

"Stay. We have nowhere to go until we leave for a party at our boss's house this afternoon," Zéphyr said.

Jacob's urge to leave was tempered by the knowledge that when he arrived at William's home he would have to face the wrath of his host—and Marcus. In the light of day, what he had done the night before seemed foolish and insensitive. At the very least, he should call, but he had forgotten the cell phone with William's number programmed into it and he had not memorized it. Staying here with these sexy boys, at least for another hour or two, seemed preferable to climbing into the Escalade and making his way back up into the hills. And so he relaxed, allowing Adonis's tongue to penetrate him more deeply, as Zéphyr, too, moved down his torso and swallowed his cock.

Narcisse and Cupidon joined the trio in bed and Jacob played with them singly and together. They snorted coke off each other's firm, nearly hairless bodies—placing a line of white powder along Adonis's spine, running down to the small of his back and into the firm cleft of his ass; taking a hit from the well of Cupidon's deep, tattoo-wreathed navel. They dozed as the sun made its arc across the cerulean sky, spooned or splayed across the California king–sized bed. At five p.m., a knock on the door startled them.

"Oh my God," Zéphyr said, "the car is here!"

"The car?" Jacob asked.

"Our boss has sent a car for us. Come with us. It's the biggest, most glamorous party of the year!"

"I don't think so."

"Come on, Jacob!" Adonis said. "There will be many, many hot boys, lots of drugs and sex, and . . . celebrities!"

"Celebrities?" Jacob said. "Really?"

Zéphyr rattled off the names of the people he had met at the previous year's party. They included many names Jacob recognized—among them the wizened lead singer of a famed British Invasion rock band—and a few he did not.

"Cool! And it's okay if I come?"

"Pretty boys are always welcome at Mr. V's house," Zéphyr said. "He eats them like candy!"

Chapter Nineteen

Marcus discovered Jacob was missing when he went to wake him for breakfast. His room was empty, the bed still made. After an increasingly urgent check of the gym, pool, and kitchen, he sought out William in his darkened private quarters.

"Jake's gone. No note, no anything."

"Gone?" William said. "Any sign that something's amiss?"

"Nothing I can see. He's just not there, and his bed hasn't been slept in."

"Have you tried the cell phone I gave him?"

Marcus tossed him the phone. "It was on his nightstand."

William buzzed his head of security and learned that someone, presumably Jacob, had left in the Escalade shortly after he and Marcus had gone to meet Rodrigo. The car had not yet returned.

"Activate the GPS. Find it."

Within minutes, his security chief reported that the SUV had been located in West Hollywood, on North Robertson near Santa Monica Boulevard.

"That's close to the Abbey," William said.

"I'll kill the little fucker!"

"Calm down, Marcus. This has been a stressful time for all of us—and he's just a boy. I knew something was up last night. He was unusually antsy after you had your little chat. He doesn't want to leave. He did this to rebel. And I'm sure he's like a kid in a candy store in West Hollywood. He probably met someone and went home with them. At the very least he didn't do something stupid like drink and then try to drive home. But maybe you're just a little jealous?"

Marcus's eyes narrowed for a fraction of a second. Even after William's revelations about his relationship with the vampire who had created him and with whom he had lived for nine years, there had been little discussion of sexual orientation. The fact that he was a vampire was food enough for thought. Marcus supposed there had been a mutual presumption of homosexuality from the beginning, though he had not considered that it had extended to Jacob.

"I . . . I'm not jealous. A little protective, maybe. His mother entrusted me with his care. And this is so unlike him. He's usually such a responsible kid."

"Responsible enough to run away from home with you?"

"You've got a point there. I suppose he can be a little headstrong."

"He'll be back soon, I'm sure."

"There's no way this could be related to what went down last night? We weren't followed?"

"I seriously doubt that. Security said the Escalade left within minutes of our departure—so closely they assumed he was following us—and at that point we hadn't even met Rodrigo. Still, it's a troublesome and unnecessary distraction, and you and I have a lot to do. I'll send a couple of men to wait for him at the car and make sure he gets home safely."

Later that morning, William initiated a conference call with members of the western district of the American Vampire Council, which he chaired. He laid out what he knew about the situation with V and began to build consensus for his plans to rescue Allison and Kevin—and to accept responsibility for any collateral damage. He had provided each council member with the videos Rodrigo had sent, and there was near-unanimous agreement that the practices they exposed were dubious at best and probably flagrant violations of vampiric protocol. But without additional evidence, the council could not grant its permission to fully sanction V unless he met William's rescue attempt with lethal force. Some council members had been invited to the event and they agreed to boycott it. None, however, offered assistance of a more material sort.

"It's the best we could hope for," William explained to Marcus. "The council is a traditional group. There's not a member who hasn't been a vampire for fewer than seventy-five years, and many are far older than that. They remember the days when there *were* no rules. And I suspect one or two may have a few skeletons in their own closets, no pun intended. What we are about to do may not be without consequences, but I won't be declared 'rogue.' And at least they did not defer judgment to the national elders, who are akin to your Supreme Court—and about as conservative."

Marcus was surprised at the number of names he recognized on the list of vampires Rodrigo e-mailed them. Among them were an actor-turned-director known for his anti-Semitic views and a Hollywood icon associated with a reactionary religious cult.

"None of these is going to give us any trouble," William said. "They are all too self-absorbed. Vampires have an even more highly developed survival instinct than mortals. The moment they suspect something is amiss, they'll wish they *could* morph into bats and fly away."

"You make it sound easy."

"It won't be. I suspect V won't take kindly to having his authority challenged."

"Do you have any idea how this will play out?"

"It may come down to a face-off between him and me."

"I can't let that happen. This is my fight, not yours."

"You'll have no choice. Regardless of how strong you think you are or what training you have in the martial arts, he will be too quick and too strong for you—for any mortal. He and I are more equally matched."

William said Marcus should instead occupy himself with V's mortal protectors. He suspected they would be armed with traditional weaponry, likes guns and knives, but with so many mortals around, they likely would try to keep a low profile.

"Those in the dungeon area will be the greatest threat," he explained. "We'll need some sort of distraction to buy enough time to free Allison and Kevin. And they both are physically compromised, so we should be prepared to carry them out. Rodrigo's cousins can assist with that."

Rodrigo was more than holding up his end of the bargain. In addition to the invitation list, he had e-mailed floor plans of V's villa and videos of previous Equinox celebrations. The mortals' celebrity-studded party looked like an *Entertainment Weekly* special, but Marcus was appalled at the carnage that took place behind closed doors, under the unsuspecting noses of the Hollywood elite. Dozens of beautiful young men, and some women, were sexually assaulted and drained of their blood by a ravenous horde of vampires in a scene that made such grindhouse classics as *Saw* and *Hostel* look like *Sesame Street*. Marcus turned away, repulsed.

"I don't understand this," he said. "If it's the last thing I do on earth, I will take down that evil bastard. And this Rodrigo character . . . he's all apologetic and helpful now that you've waved a hundred grand under his nose, but where was he when this kind of shit was going down? He was probably the fucking cameraman!"

William tried to soothe him, reiterating his explanation of the situation in which Rodrigo found himself. He was concerned about Marcus's volatility and worried that, in the end, his anger might even turn him against William himself. It was the rare mortal who could understand the nuances of vampire existence and separate the good from the bad.

"Let's concentrate on logistics, a game plan," William said. "Getting in and out safely ourselves, with Allison and Kevin. We can work on justice—and retribution—another time."

By nightfall, when Marcus still had not heard from Jacob, he considered calling the Camerons to see if he had been in touch with them. But he could not think of a plausible excuse for calling that would not reveal that Jacob was not with him or explain why he was not able to talk to his parents. William had arranged for the return of the Escalade, which he wanted to drive to Desert Hot Springs because it was sturdier and more reliable than the Silver Wraith. He stationed two members of his security team at the site overnight to intercept Jacob when he returned for the car and to bring him home.

"Naturally I'm concerned about Jacob, Marcus, but we need to remain focused on the task at hand. He simply doesn't understand the gravity of the situation. If he did, I'm sure he would have called. You have nothing to worry about."

"Nothing but rescuing Allison from a crazed, bloodsucking psychopath."

"Well, yes, there is that."

Chapter Twenty

V was hungry and horny. The Equinox orgy would begin in a few hours, but his undisciplined appetites demanded satiation. Like a child who surreptitiously scoops a fingerful of icing off his birthday cake then smoothes the surface to disguise his pilferage, he wanted one more private taste of the delicious Abercrombie model before he shared him with his ravenous guests.

"Bring me the boy," he ordered Rodrigo shortly after sunset.

His protégé hesitated, then suggested an alternative. There were plenty of attractive young Mexicans awaiting slaughter, and they were designated as appetizers, not the main course. Why not sample one of them instead?

"*Now!*"

Rodrigo reluctantly obeyed. Kevin was too weak to walk, so Rodrigo carried him the short distance from his cell to the entrance to V's playroom. There, he stood Kevin on his feet, slung the boy's arm over his own shoulder, and shuffled in to the room. V circled them, imperiously inspecting the boy, his skin pallid, almost gray, his azure eyes vacant when V raised his sunken face with a single, crooked finger. Kevin's once magnificent cock was shriveled, almost vestigial. Bruises beneath his armpits, inside his thighs, at his groin, and on the soles of his feet marked the spots from which V had fed over the past three weeks. He never drank from the same spot twice, to avoid the macrophages and other "contagion" present during the wound-healing process.

As Rodrigo knew he would be, V was furious.

"How dare you bring me this . . . this *carcass*? There's not enough blood left in him to satisfy a vampire *bat!*"

It was pointless for Rodrigo to object or attempt to explain. V was so accustomed to acting without conscience or consequence that for Rodrigo to remind him of the times he had begged him not to feed on Kevin would be futile and would only fuel his master's rage. V's demonic lust for the once-stunning boy had blinded him to his progressive deterioration. It was as if he were an alcoholic, with no recollection of what he had done in the intoxicating crimson haze of blood lust. Only now, when the boy was utterly destroyed, could he see the results of his sadism.

With one blinding flash of teeth, V slashed the boy's carotid artery, vehemently spitting the blood and viscera into his victim's face. Rodrigo instinctively recoiled, but instead of a torrent from the torn blood vessel, the flow was thin and weak, almost watery. Kevin's heart could not withstand the assault. He collapsed into Rodrigo's unsteady embrace and uttered one final syllable, *"oh."*

"Get it out of my sight," V bellowed.

Rodrigo quaked as he carried the dead boy from the room. How much lighter he was now than he had been a mere three weeks ago.

"And bring me something else to feed on," V shouted. "One of those Romanian tarts should do nicely. On second thought, better make it two. They're not much more than skin and bones themselves."

Rodrigo returned Kevin's body to his cell, from which it

would be collected later. He wiped the blood from the boy's face, gently closed his eyelids over the now-lusterless blue gems, and kissed his blistered lips one final time. In repose, Kevin appeared to be almost smiling, as if he welcomed his end as a release from the horrors he had endured.

In the next cell, Allison watched silently as Rodrigo ministered to her lover's lifeless corpse. She tried to summon a scream but had only the strength to collapse onto her cot, her slender body racked by tears. After Rodrigo covered Kevin with a sheet and washed the blood from his own hands in the sink, he turned to look at the girl, her head in her hands, weeping.

"Allison," he called in a hushed voice. *"Allison!"*

She stopped crying and looked at him, curiously. It was the first time he had spoken her name, the first time *anyone* had spoken her name since she had been imprisoned.

"You *monster!*" she hissed. "If you're going to kill me, kill me *now!* I don't want to live like this! And I don't want to die like *that!*"

"You won't, Allison, trust me. I want to help you. And Marcus is on his way."

"Marcus?" she said. She was momentarily stunned at the mention of her brother's name, then began to sob uncontrollably. *"Marcus?"*

"Your brother's here, in California, and he's coming to get you. I'm helping him."

"You? But . . ."

"I didn't kill Kevin. It was V. I'm on your side, Allison, you've got to believe me. Try to stay calm. Conserve your strength. You'll need it soon enough. I'll send someone to remove Kevin's body."

"No!" she cried. "Not yet. Give me time to say good-bye."

Rodrigo slipped the surfer's bracelet from his wrist and held it out to her.

"Take this," he said. "It was his."

He left her in tears, clutching his gift to her chest.

Reluctantly, he made his way to the suite occupied by the Romanian models. They had arrived at the house only a few hours earlier and were just settling in. Having been honored guests at last year's event, they were innocently anticipating a weekend of carefree debauchery. He knew they were all doomed, but the idea of selecting two to die now was almost more than he could bear. He wondered if V forced him to make such decisions out of sheer cruelty, knowing he did not have the stomach for it. An abundance of imported livestock was penned up in their subterranean holding cells for just such purposes, while the Romanians were, after Kevin and Allison, the most compelling of the weekend's victims. As he had done for previous Equinox celebrations, he had carefully choreographed the timing of their presentation. Harvesting two of them early not only caused emotional distress but also logistical problems. One of the two surviving Romanians would have to be substituted for Kevin, leaving three second-tier slots empty in the intricate mosaic of slaughter. For aesthetic purposes, he would have to fill those places with three of the human piñatas, themselves the pick of the litter, then cull a trio of the most attractive males from the remaining herd as substitutes for *them*. Each successive decision would be painful, underscoring the unwelcome power he held over the captives' fates and making him more intimately complicit in their deaths. The words of Allison's brother rang in his ears: *"You were only following orders."*

He comforted himself with the knowledge that this would be the last time he would have to make such decisions. One way or another, this would be his final Equinox in V's thrall. At this time next year, he would either be free or dead.

Over the years, Rodrigo had made it his practice not to get attached to the beautiful, damned Agence Sanguine models, and this particular group made it easier than most. They had been recruited as a group and thus were more insular than those who had been assembled of more disparate elements. Their exoticism and obscure language also set them apart. They had been lionized by the media, which, hungry for a new trend, had singled them out for attention, turning the word "anorexic" into a backhanded compliment. As a result, they developed a sense of entitlement beyond anything he would have expected, given their origin in a remote area of a poverty-stricken former Soviet satellite. But as with most fashion phenomena, after two seasons their popularity was on the wane, which is why they were to be slaughtered. Rodrigo felt it was premature. He thought they had at least one more good season in them. And his personal favorite, Zéphyr, was poised to break out. Had his success only come a few months earlier, he might have been spared. They were all beautiful, young, and innocent. They did not deserve this fate.

How to choose? The two not selected would never know the fate of the pair who went before them—at least not until it was too late. Their absence would be explained away. *"They are attending a private party."* He knew two of them—Narcisse and Cupidon—were a couple, while Zéphyr and Adonis were merely fuck buddies. Obviously, the lovers should die together, so no suspicions would be aroused. Separate them and the remaining partner would soon ask questions. But which pair first?

Narcisse and Cupidon, he thought, and he was ashamed his decision was based not on mercy but on lust. He reasoned that in the heat of the orgy, he might still have the opportunity to take Zéphyr for himself, to enjoy that incredible face, those magnificent lips, that outrageous ass, before the boy died. It would serve another purpose, as well. V would be watching. If he shied away from feeding, it would arouse suspicion, and that was the last thing he wanted. V already was angry about Kevin's death; he might be looking to make trouble. If he did, Rodrigo might be unavailable to help Marcus and William when the time came. Taking Zéphyr would at least be a pleasure, and he would be merciful to him. He would die in the heat of passion, when his thoughts were of ecstasy and release.

At the door to the Romanians' suite, he knocked once, paused, and entered. Rodrigo was a familiar and trusted presence, and the boys looked toward him languidly, without fear. The room looked like a harem painted by Ingres or Delacroix. All four boys were naked—Narcisse intimately joined to Cupidon, Zéphyr reclining in the arms of Adonis.

"Narcisse, Cupidon, make yourselves presentable and report to V immediately," Rodrigo said. "You've been selected for a private party."

Sighing, the two doomed lovers untangled themselves and headed slowly toward the bathing area.

"Quickly, quickly! He's waiting."

As the pair opened the door to the spa area, Jacob stepped out, naked, his half-hard cock bouncing as he walked. Rodrigo's heart jumped, surprised at the presence of another person in the suite and taken aback by his extraordinary beauty. He had been besotted with Kevin in a way he had not been since he first had become immortal, but this boy—*this* boy could make him forget even Kevin's name. Where Kevin had been angular, chiseled, this boy was rounded and smooth, not in a way that suggested softness but rather incipient ripeness and vitality. Kevin's musculature had evoked armor, a body almost mechanical in its perfection. This boy's physique, while fluid and graceful, emanated the vulnerability of a not-quite-mature creature, the big-pawed cub of a sleek and powerful animal—a leopard or cheetah—still growing into his body. His skin was tawny, aglow with youth and health; his torso nearly hairless save for the golden down at his armpits and cock. And what a cock it was: large, beautifully shaped, capped by a full plum head, its thick, semitumescent shaft astride twin pink orbs. And his face. There were no words to describe the exquisiteness of his face, his eyes the color of cornflowers, his hair a thatch of gold. By comparison, the Romanian boys, whom Rodrigo found attractive in an odd, exotic way, seemed cold and alien.

Rodrigo was gripped by lust and fear in equal parts. Should V see this boy, he would immediately lay claim to him and mark him for destruction by the most heinous means. The man's heart was so black, so perverted, that beauty of such magnitude would inspire in him an unquenchable bloodlust. The boy would be tortured with infinite patience and infinite cruelty.

"Who are you?" Rodrigo asked, more sharply than he had intended.

"Jacob. Jacob Cameron."

"It's okay, Rodrigo, he's with us," Zéphyr said.

"It most certainly is not *okay,* Zéphyr. You know the rules. No one who is not specifically invited is allowed on the property at any time—and certainly not for the Red Party."

"I'm sorry," Jacob said. "I thought . . ."

"Not now!" Rodrigo barked. "I need time to think."

"What the fuck is going on, Rodrigo? Why are you making such a stink? We've brought guests before."

"Maybe, but not to the Red Party. And V already is pissed about . . . a no-show, for which he blames me. Just be quiet. Get dressed, all three of you. I think we need to get him out of your quarters. Find him someplace safe."

"Safe?" Zéphyr said. "What the . . . ?"

"Just do it! Get out of bed, put some clothes on, and let me think. All of you. *Now!*"

Rodrigo's first thought was to hasten the departure of Narcisse and Cupidon before V became impatient and sought them out. While Zéphyr, Adonis, and Jacob desultorily sorted through the clothes they had so readily divested upon arriving, Rodrigo followed Narcisse and Cupidon into the spa to urge haste. He found them completing the act he had interrupted minutes earlier.

"Rápidamente," he shouted, lapsing into his native Spanish. He clapped his hands together vigorously. For the second time that night, his heart broke, knowing what fate awaited the luscious young lovers. Returning to the bedroom, he found the trio in just their briefs, engaged in erotic horseplay.

"Quickly, quickly, be done with it."

His head was spinning. What to tell them? Where to take them? Could he save all three? Or just *el pequeño dios rubio?* The little blond god.

But as Rodrigo feared, V was too impatient to wait for Narcisse and Cupidon. Just as he was hustling the freshly showered pair out the door, V arrived, accompanied by four hulking blood slaves, his typical retinue during events such as Equinox.

"What's going on here?" V demanded. "Where's my dinner?"

He had abandoned all pretense, given that the four Romanians would be dead within hours. With a nod, he instructed two of the blood slaves to take hold of the pair of delicate boys closest to him, who until that moment had been prepared to go willingly to what they thought was a simple assignation. Manhandled, their natural response was to resist. Their captors tightened their grips on them and hustled them out of the room.

"Master, there's no need for this. I assure you, we were on our way."

"Not quickly enough!"

Rodrigo subtly tried to place himself between Jacob and V, to obscure his sightlines, but his keen-eyed master was too quick for him.

"Wait," V said, his right brow arching. "What have we here?"

"Nothing, sir. No one."

"Hardly *nothing.* Hardly no one," V said. "If he were not so fair-skinned, I'd say you were skimming the cream off my Mexican shipments. You *have* been holding out on me, haven't you, Rodrigo?"

"No sir. Nothing of the sort."

Rodrigo's mind was racing. He tried to think of a response that would save both his skin and the boy's. V seemed to be implying that he was aware of the way he had been altering the human cargo manifests to allow the youngest and most vulnerable Mexicans to escape. He already was skating on thin ice and needed to give V a plausible answer that would not further arouse his suspicions.

"He . . . he's . . . a replacement for the boy," Rodrigo said, hoping to buy enough time to think, to deflect V's fatal fascination with Jacob for a few hours, at the very least.

"The boy? Which boy?"

"The boy we . . . *lost* this evening."

"I see."

V circled Jacob, appraising him. His eyes narrowed as they traveled over the smooth, unblemished torso, coming to rest on the swollen pouch in the ridiculously mundane, ridiculously sexy white BVDs, admiring the fullness of his firm, boyish ass. He sniffed the air around Jacob, took his chin in his hand and turned his face left and right. He did everything but inspect his teeth like a horse trader. Jacob, feeling vulnerable in just his briefs, allowed it. He felt guilty for being someplace he apparently did not belong and did not want to offend this man and be hauled off like Narcisse and Cupidon.

"An excellent choice," V said. "You've outdone yourself. He's almost too *good* to waste on the rabble assembled here tonight. I could do great things with this boy."

Rodrigo insinuated himself between V and Jacob, placing his arm around the boy's shoulder. He sensed Jacob's rising anxiety and hoped his embrace would calm him. Zéphyr and Adonis looked on, perplexed.

"Please sir, it was difficult enough to find someone of this caliber for tonight's event on such short notice. We have standards to uphold. Please just let me do my job."

"I don't know. There is so *much* potential."

"Master, please . . ."

V took a step back. He was not sure whether Rodrigo's assertiveness was appropriate or bordered on insubordination. But perhaps he *was* just trying to make sure the Equinox party was a success.

"I suppose the show must go on. But deliver them all to the staging area without delay. These two," he said, nodding toward the remaining blood slaves, "will see that you do."

Chapter Twenty-one

From the street, V's villa presented an anonymous and uninviting face: a seven-foot cinderblock wall slathered roughly with unpainted stucco and topped with concertina wire and shards of broken glass. Only someone familiar with the prince-in-pauper's-camouflage of the homes of wealthy desert dwellers would suspect the unprepossessing façade hid a sybaritic oasis. Marcus realized he had driven past the isolated property previously, when he and Jacob had strayed from Twentynine Palms Highway searching for Kevin's red Porsche Boxster. Ironically he now was surrounded by expensive crimson vehicles—Ferraris, Jaguars, Lamborghinis. The ivory Escalade was like a lone white corpuscle adrift in a sea of red blood cells.

Guests parked in orderly rows in a sandy, scrub-covered lot across from the gated entrance. Jock Price, who had agreed to act as chauffeur and "getaway car driver," remained behind. After checking in at a white tent with acrylic mullioned windows, a chandelier suspended from its apex, William and Marcus walked along a red carpet toward the house, a low-slung, glass-and-stone affair with Aztec influences that might have been designed by Frank Lloyd Wright under the influence of peyote. Built in the 1930s for a Latino matinee idol who many years later was bludgeoned to death in his bedroom by hustlers, it had remained vacant for two decades before V purchased it, intrigued by the bloody history that had scared off other potential buyers. He had filled it with plundered artifacts of Aztec ritual sacrifice and placed at the front door two menacing stone jaguars, which had once decorated a temple devoted to the worship of Huitzilopochtli, the god of war and blood sacrifice.

In Hollywood's vampire circles, the Equinox event had become known as "the Red Party," and as the term passed into wider usage among mortal guests an unofficial red dress code spontaneously developed. Every year in early summer, starlets besieged Los Angeles couturiers with requests for crimson gowns. As autumn approached, Rodeo Drive jewelers stocked up on rubies, beauty salons created Lucille Ball clones in startling numbers, manicurists fretted about a run on Jungle Red nail lacquer. At the peak of the event's popularity, *Us Weekly* had run fashion coverage of "The Ladies in Red," and E! had reported live from the event's red carpet. V could not resist an occasional sly reference to his clandestine lifestyle in the mainstream party's theme or decorations. One event featured a Bloody Mary bar; this year, Speedo-clad waiters circulated among the guests bearing trays of crimson mojitos.

"Red rum?" they repeatedly asked. "Red rum? Red rum?"

Marcus felt a bit foppish in the gold brocade matador outfit William had worn in one of his early silent films. But it was the only excuse he had to carry a *capote de paseo,* a cape in which to conceal a sharpened wooden *estoquillador,* which William assured him would quite effectively slay a vampire when plunged into his heart. He felt like a gaudily upholstered, overstuffed chair, although his firm, shapely ass got more than a few appreciative stares. William was only slightly more conservatively dressed, in black toreador pants, red sash, and billowing white *blouson.* Compared to the ostentatious bling on the necks of female guests, they were practically inconspicuous.

"Are all vampires so wealthy?" Marcus asked.

"Most of these people are not vampires," William said. "Bloodsuckers, yes, but not vampires."

As he mingled with the guests, Marcus remained alert for the telltale red wristbands that identified the undead. The vampires tended to cluster together with those their own "age," and what made them stand out from the mortal guests was their often-dated styles of grooming and fashion. Those who led more reclusive lifestyles and, unlike William, did not have personal stylists to keep them up to date often seemed frozen in the era in which they had made their immortal metamorphosis. Love beads and Nehru jackets competed for supremacy with gold chains and polyester.

"This may be easier than I thought," Marcus whispered.

"Don't get overly confident," William said. "Beneath these leisure suits beat some of the blackest hearts you will ever encounter."

They spent the next two hours orienting themselves to the layout of the house, reviewing their plan of action, and reconnoitering escape routes. After talking further to Rodrigo, they had determined that security around Kevin and Allison would be impossible to breach prior to their "presentation" at the climax of the evening's festivities. But the timing ultimately worked to their advantage, even if it exposed Kevin and Allison to a somewhat greater risk of enduring at least the early stages of sexual and sanguinary assault. Having reviewed Rodrigo's videos of previous Equinox parties, Marcus and William knew V always reserved the first taste of his trophy victims' blood for himself before turning them over to his highest-ranking guests. By that time, the more recently transformed vampires, possessed of both less status and less self-control, would be sated, having fed on the piñatas and the Agence Sanguine models.

Like drunks, they may even have crawled off to a dark corner and fallen asleep. The more venerable among the guests, with greater restraint and more refined palates, would have saved themselves for a privileged taste of the finest blood of the evening. Though hungry, their heightened sense of self-preservation would make them less likely to resist or fight back when Marcus and William launched their rescue attempt.

The plan was to create a diversion at an appropriate time, preferably when V was preoccupied with his pleasures. One of the lesser vampires would have to die dramatically at Marcus's hands. When V abandoned his prey to investigate, William and Rodrigo and his cousins would free Kevin and Allison and spirit them away in the ensuing confusion. Marcus would follow. They would rendezvous at the front entrance, where Jock, having been alerted by cell phone, would be waiting, even if it meant crashing through the security checkpoint with the brushbar-equipped Escalade.

By 11:30, Marcus and William still had not laid eyes on their host, but Rodrigo approached and shepherded them into a quiet corner.

"Kevin is dead," he said. "But Allison is safe, for the moment."

"Dead? What the fuck happened?" Marcus demanded.

"V finished him off in a fit of anger," Rodrigo replied. "He might not have survived the evening, in any event. As I told you earlier, V has been feeding off him all along. I've replaced him with a young man who arrived with some models from the agency. You've got to promise to help me save him."

"That wasn't part of our deal," Marcus said.

"It's not negotiable," Rodrigo said.

"Marcus, it's okay," William interjected. "We'll rescue your sister first, then this boy—if we can. A life is a life, after all."

He turned to Rodrigo. "Allison has always been our first priority, for obvious reasons. We'll do what we can for this boy.

It's a shame about Kevin. I hope we'll have the opportunity to let his parents know."

"I came to tell you the doors to the security anteroom are about to open," Rodrigo said. "I'm going to make a sweep of the area and inform the other VIPs. Try to blend in with us. You'll be checked individually by security, but it may go more smoothly if you appear to be part of my group. Once we're inside, you'll be on your own for a while. I have final preparations to make. When I'm done, I'll join you."

Marcus and William fell in behind a group of vampires that included a famous cross-dressing comedian from the Golden Age of television, who had been "dead" for more than five years. Marcus thought he would make easy prey. After passing through security, they descended two flights of stairs and entered the play space, a large circular room dimly lit by jets of natural gas, its surfaces clad in black ceramic tile. In the center of the room, a low Aztec sacrificial altar, slightly higher than a coffee table, was flanked by two slings. Grooved channels in the floors sloped almost imperceptibly toward the exterior walls so blood would sluice toward drains that ringed the space.

The music of the outdoor party receded and was replaced by a deep, almost subsonic pulse, like a heartbeat. Marcus shivered. It reminded him of walking through the giant, beating heart at the Franklin Institute in Philadelphia, a mandatory field trip for all Pennsylvania middle schoolers. As his eyes adjusted to the darkness, he saw eight young Mexicans hanging from the ceiling, facedown, suspended by garlanded ropes tied tightly around their wrists and ankles. Their thick brown uncut cocks dangled within reach of passersby. They had been ball-gagged and drugged to offset the searing joint pain they would otherwise feel in their unnaturally contorted positions. If they struggled, as most eventually did as their sedatives wore off, they would dislocate both shoulders or tear their superior acromio-clavicular ligaments, which bore the weight of their glistening muscular bodies. The pain would be so intense death would be a blessing.

Two of the most handsome Mexicans and the two surviving Romanians, Zéphyr and Adonis, were tied to short pommel horses so their asses and mouths were available for abuse simultaneously. Their blood-filled cocks, bound with elastic bands and drawn back between their legs, were intended to be instruments of pain, not pleasure, for the hapless victims. Marcus found himself unexpectedly aroused. Under different circumstances—if all parties were willing and the outcome not fatal—he might have enjoyed himself. While he was not attracted to the ethereally beautiful Romanians, the Mexicans were stunningly handsome, their burnished physiques breathtaking.

All around them, vampires were disrobing, revealing largely gaunt and pallid bodies and incongruously buoyant cocks. A few looked reasonably fit, the beneficiaries of treatments at William's sunless tanning salons or relatively recent metamorphoses. Nearby, Marcus recognized one such novice, a bad-boy child star, now in his late twenties. He already was something of a has-been at the time of his recent "death," ostensibly the victim of a drug overdose.

"I wouldn't undress," William cautioned. "You're too healthy looking, and exposing that much skin is bound to give off a human scent, despite our attempts to camouflage it."

Marcus had soaked in an herbal brew of eucalyptus and peppermint, spiked with an infinitesimal amount of garlic, to simultaneously disguise his natural aroma and subconsciously repel those vampires who got too close.

"I wasn't planning to get naked," Marcus said. "But I could get rid of this jacket. It inhibits the range of motion I'll need when we're ready to rock and roll."

Marcus had barely shed his jacket when he heard a muffled whimper over his right shoulder. Someone had begun to play with the huge purplish cock of one of the human piñatas; another vampire stepped between his splayed legs and began to rim him. The crowd pressed inward around them.

"The party has begun," William said.

For an hour or so, sex play predominated. Little actual feeding took place, although now and again an isolated scream could be heard when an overzealous vampire bit down on his helpless sex partner. As two a.m. neared, the feeding began in earnest. When a jet of hot blood splashed onto Marcus's neck, it felt precisely like a spume of cum, which is what he assumed it to be until he realized the human piñata closest to him was under attack. The air grew foul with the fetid exhalations of the blood drinkers. Marcus felt suddenly light-headed. He forced himself to swallow the rising bilge in his gullet.

"Easy, boy," William said. "Let's get away from here."

They elbowed their way out of the tangle of bodies. Marcus steadied himself against a pillar and took several deep breaths. He saw that William's right hand was dripping with blood.

"Feeling better?"

"A bit."

"No more nausea?"

"No."

"Good, because you may not like what I have to do next, but it's necessary," William said. "Think of it as camouflage. Close your eyes."

"What?"

"Just close your eyes."

William quickly splayed his hand in front of Marcus's face and shook it, splattering him with blood. He then drew his hand across Marcus's lips and chin.

"Now at least you *look* as if you have fed."

William himself fed occasionally, for appearances' sake. He was acquainted with many of the vampires in attendance and frequently was offered access to one of the squirming victims. It would have raised suspicions if he had spurned them all. Marcus tried to remain inconspicuous. Within half an hour, most of the piñatas had ceased to struggle; several had been released from their restraints so they could be more readily assaulted. The Romanians and their two Mexican counterparts thrashed against their bonds with ever-diminishing intensity. Marcus was enraged to see Rodrigo fucking the boy with the dragon tattoo and was about to go pull him off when the gaslights dimmed. The heartlike rumble grew deeper and more intense. Four naked blood slaves rolled a stepped platform into a slot behind the altar, bearing two drapery-covered forms. A spotlight appeared, illuminating V rising between the two forms, wearing an asymmetrical harness that wrapped his right arm and left leg in coils of leather, harlequin style. He walked down the steps of the platform and stepped behind the altar, thrusting his pelvis forward and grasping his studded codpiece lewdly.

"Our host," William whispered to Marcus.

"My brethren," V began. "Tonight I have the pleasure of presenting two of the finest specimens of youth I have ever been fortunate enough to exhibit."

The crowd cheered.

"It is an excellent omen for a bountiful fall harvest."

He stepped aside, his left arm rising to draw his audience's attention to the crimson draperies. Behind him, pinpointed by spotlights, Jacob and Allison were gradually revealed, naked, each bound to a St. Andrew's Cross by leather restraints camouflaged with garlands of tropical flowers, their cries muffled with ball gags. Around the room, gasps of awe were quickly followed by a roar of approval. Even those actively feeding paused to acknowledge the bloody banquet's delicious main course. Some among them abandoned their sanguinary pursuits and drifted toward the center of the room to be closer to the new arrivals.

Jacob's eyes were wide with fear. His torso glistened with sweat, and his fat, flaccid cock flailed each time he struggled to free himself. After three weeks in captivity, Allison was more placid, exhausted, and resigned to her fate, but she was alert and her eyes darted around the room in search of her brother. Both had been quietly assured by Rodrigo they would be safe, but they were forced to submit to the superior strength of the burly blood slaves who bound them to the crosses. At worst, they had expected rape, but the carnage that now confronted them was terrifying: lifeless bodies suspended from the ceiling, blood-drenched revelers howling their approval and their unbridled lust. Jacob lost control of his bladder when he recognized Zéphyr's dragon tattoo on a fitfully struggling, bloodied body.

At the back of the room, William had to restrain Marcus once he saw Allison and Jacob. It had taken them a few moments to recognize Jacob, whose face was distorted by the ball gag. They had no idea how he had been captured. Marcus dropped to his knees, felled by a paroxysm of grief just as the crowd gave vent to its lust. Both his sister and the boy he loved were at the mercy of half a hundred vampires. William helped him to his feet.

"Get ahold of yourself, Marcus! Going to pieces isn't going to help."

He used his red sash to wipe tears from Marcus's eyes and spittle from the corners of his mouth.

"The bastard! The goddamned evil fucking bastard!"

V spun and cracked his whip twice. Jacob's body stiffened as if jolted by a massive electrical charge, and a red X appeared instantly on his torso, two crimson ribbons that began at each nipple and intersected at his navel. In the space of three heartbeats, they started to weep blood. Tears simultaneously rolled down the terrified boy's cheeks. The phalanx of vampires howled and advanced toward the captive pair, abandoning the Mexicans and Romanians. Those of lesser status, who had been relegated to the periphery, took their places and assaulted the squirming victims anew.

"I have it on good authority that the boy's ass is virgin, though barely. Had I not stepped in, he might have been plundered by one of our Romanian Romeos," V said, pointing his cat-o-nine-tails in the direction of Zéphyr, impaled on the crimson cock of a well-known professional wrestler-turned-actor. Nearby, a struggling Adonis also had been beset by the second wave of vampires.

"Alas, I cannot say as much for the girl, who was damaged goods before her arrival. But if your tastes run to the fairer sex and you do not mind sloppy seconds, she is an excellent alternative!"

With a dramatic flourish, V popped the rivets on his codpiece, revealing his rampant cock.

"As your host, it is my prerogative to take the boy's cherry before I submit him to your tender mercies and to ceremonially plunder this exquisite whore. Inhale the aromatic ambrosia of the liqueur that flows through their veins. And don't be greedy. You can all savor this fine vintage—in moderation."

Four sturdy Mexican blood slaves, two of them Rodrigo's cousins, released the restraints on Jacob's and Allison's wrists and ankles, carried them to the slings, and re-secured them. Under the guise of testing the restraints, Rodrigo instead loosened them, wrapping them in floral garlands to disguise his work. He whispered words of encouragement to Jacob and Allison.

William felt Marcus tense next to him, ready to attack. He placed his hand on Marcus's forearm. "Not yet."

"What are we waiting for?"

"It will be safer when V is distracted. I know his type. When he feeds, he's aware of nothing else. We'll strike then."

The pack sent up a bestial howl when V entered Jacob, who grimaced in pain and thrashed his head back and forth. After a dozen violent thrusts, V withdrew, turning to the mob with his bloody cock in hand, as if he were lovingly holding an Oscar statuette. Baring his fangs, he turned on Jacob and sank his teeth into his right leg, striking his femoral artery so all who followed would be bathed in his blood. Then, while the highest-ranking guest vampire prepared to assault Jacob's ass, V turned his attentions to Allison, his cock still dripping with Jacob's virgin blood. At that moment, her eyes found her brother in the darkness and locked on his gaze. With all her strength, she bit down on the ball gag, halving it. Spitting out the pieces, she screamed his name.

"Marcus! Help me! Please!"

Abandoning all semblance of a plan, Marcus tossed aside the *capote de paseo,* revealing the sharpened *estoquillador.* William reached out for him, but Marcus pushed him aside and he fell to the floor. With a bloodcurdling shriek, he powered his way through the pack of vampires and plunged forward toward the altar. Arms instinctively reached out to restrain him but, slick with blood, failed to gain a grip. The young has-been actor blocked his way, grinning fiendishly, his muscular torso gleaming with fresh blood, his cock hard. Without hesitation, Marcus plunged the *estoquillador* directly into his heart and he fell away. The bloody pack parted for him like the Red Sea.

Startled by Allison's scream, V hesitated long enough for her to work free of her compromised restraints. He bared his fangs and was about to bite through her carotid when he felt a searing pain in his side. The *estoquillador* entered between his sixth and seventh ribs but missed his heart. He turned to face Marcus's fury.

"You fucking bastard," Marcus screamed, his face contorted. "I'll kill you if it's the last thing I do."

"It may very well be," V bellowed, baring his canines and swiftly moving in for the kill. He sank his fangs into the taut, muscular cords of Marcus's neck. In such close quarters, the *estoquillador* was useless and slipped from Marcus's hand, falling to the floor and rolling out of reach. He tried to push away his attacker but was overwhelmed. Allison stood, trembling, on the platform, watching in horror as her brother struggled with the monster who already had killed her lover. A figure in a blood-stained white shirt and crimson sash appeared next to her. He wrapped her in Marcus's *capote de paseo* and guided her off-stage, glancing back fearfully to witness Marcus's life-and-death struggle with V.

The crowd froze for a moment but, inured to bloody struggles and convinced the scene was merely some histrionic flourish devised by V, they returned to their frenzied feast with even more vigor. Privilege and protocol now meant nothing, and they shoved aside the high-ranking vampire who was fucking Jacob and assaulted him themselves, cocks raging, canines flashing.

Rodrigo appeared, brandishing the *estoquillador*. He grabbed the hair of the vampire who was now fucking Jacob, yanked him off, and impaled him squarely in the heart. Shouting to his cousins to free Jacob, he kept the other attackers at bay with the bloody *estoquillador*. They shrank back. Dazed, bleeding from several wounds, Jacob collapsed into the arms of his rescuers.

V realized he had been betrayed by Rodrigo and was out-numbered, or at least at a serious disadvantage. He dropped Marcus and headed for an exit. Frenzied vampires crazed by the manly scent of his blood set upon Marcus. Like jackals attacking carrion, they shoved each other aside to get to his choicest spots, barking and snapping at one another. Unsure whether Marcus was dead or could yet be saved, Rodrigo nonetheless fell upon the attackers, wounding them, if not mortally then seriously enough to cause them to skulk away. It was the least he could do for the man he had caused such pain.

William had made his way to the door. He lifted Allison and carried her up the stairs. The fate of Jacob and Marcus remained uncertain, but at the very least he would complete the task Marcus had begun: to save his sister. The house was largely empty, the mortal guests having left hours ago. A few candles guttered in the desert air that blew in through full-length windows. Jock was waiting in the Escalade, engine running, passenger doors and hatch open. A black Hummer was bearing down on them, dispatched from the security checkpoint, its amber lights flashing, a blue beacon on its dash. William strapped a hysterical Allison into the front seat. She was crying and screaming her brother's name.

"Wait for me as long as you can," William shouted to Jock. "Tell the security guards this is a medical emergency. I'm not sure if they're in on this or are just rent-a-cops. If they attempt to remove either you or Allison from the car, drive off. I think she is in good enough condition to make it back to LA. Call Dr. Brock and have him meet you at the house."

"Where are Jacob and Marcus?" Jock asked.

"I'm going back to look for them. V got to Marcus. He's in bad shape. Jacob I'm not sure about."

William retraced his steps. A few naked or half-dressed vampires rushed past him in the opposite direction. One stumbled and sailed to the floor, arms and legs splayed. At the security anteroom, William encountered Rodrigo carrying Marcus, bloody and unconscious, and his two cousins bearing Jacob, in shock but less seriously wounded.

"The car's waiting," William said. "This way."

They left a trail of Marcus's blood on the polished terrazo floor as they made their way through the house. Rodrigo's cousins got into the third-row seat with Jacob between them. William and Rodrigo, bearing Marcus's body, climbed into the second row. The Escalade lurched forward, spraying a rooster tail of gravel high into the sky. Its rear wheels gained a purchase on the asphalt and bit into it with an acrid whiff of burning rubber.

Rodrigo cradled Marcus in his arms, attempting to stanch the flow of blood from his wounds. It appeared futile. William tore his shirt and crimson sash into strips and used them as bandages.

"It's no use," Rodrigo cried. "We're losing him."

"There's only one thing we can do to save him," William said.

"I'm not sure either of us has enough blood to turn him without killing ourselves," Rodrigo said.

"I'll start him, let him drink long enough to begin a transformation, then he can feed on you. Together, we should have enough. If not, there's always Jock, once we are away from here."

Rodrigo shifted Marcus's inert, blood-streaked body into a seated position, holding his head upright. William needed this man to survive—in one form or another. He dared dream Marcus would embrace this opportunity and that his metamorphosis would be successful. If Marcus would let him, he would love him eternally. Together, they would nurture Jacob, and William would make him a star. And together they would put an end to V.

"Marcus, can you hear me?" William whispered, his lips brushing his ear like a kiss. "You must listen and pay attention. Only you can save your life now."

Marcus's head fell forward and William feared the worst. But it snapped back and then forward again. He was nodding.

"Allison?" Marcus whispered. "Jake?"

"They're here, both of them, and they're safe. Our friend Rodrigo saved you. And I am here with you, Marcus. I will always be here with you. But now you must listen to me. You have a choice: to live or die. Do you understand?"

"Live . . . or die?"

"But you must decide now. We have very little time."

William brought his own wrist to his mouth and bit down, puncturing the ulnar artery. Blood bubbled up. It was strong and hot—vital. He brought his face close to Marcus's and kissed him on his lips, turning them crimson.

"Taste this, Marcus. Taste life. All you need to do to live is to drink this blood. My blood. Drink this blood and live forever."

William's kiss, the taste of blood, stirred Marcus enough to allow him to open his eyes. The interior of the car was cool and dark. He shivered. The hum of the desert wind in the car's slipstream, the song of its tires on the asphalt, were a lullaby. He wanted to sleep. He wanted to hold Jake, to make love to him.

Live or die, William had said. *Live or die.*

A hand on the back of his neck raised Marcus's head toward an outstretched arm, pale in the moonlight but splashed with crimson.

Live or die, live or die, live or die.

The car sped westward toward the City of Angels, fleeing the distant, newborn autumnal sun that was warming the verdant cornfields of the Cameron family farm at that very moment, inching its way across the bed that awaited Jacob's return, just as it would inexorably inch its way across the broad green continent.

"Live or die," William whispered as he pressed his wrist to Marcus's lips. "The choice is yours."

Epilogue

Jacob awoke in a room full of California sunlight, attended by the genial Dr. Charlton Brock, his bushy eyebrows knit with concern at the moans that escaped Jacob's lips when he first opened his eyes. Jacob was in "his" room, the room in which he had slept for the past three weeks—warm, secure, if a bit light-headed. A dark, cacophonous phantasmagoria of blood, pain, and fear swam like a dream behind a curtain of sedatives and antianxiety medications. Mercifully, the fearsome images shrank from the light.

"Marcus? Where's Marcus?" Jacob asked the stranger bent over him.

"Don't worry about Marcus," Dr. Brock said in his sonorous Southern baritone. "He'll be fine, my boy—just fine."

Jacob believed him because he wanted to . . . and because no one could doubt such a soothing voice.

"Can I see him?"

"A bit later," Dr. Brock said reassuringly. "You both need time to rest."

Beneath a sheet, Jacob wore only a pair of loose-fitting black silk pajama bottoms. White bandages crisscrossed his torso like a pair of Mexican *bandoleras*. He did not know why. His last reliable memories were of his arrival at the estate of Zéphyr's boss: a playful romp with his newfound friends, a shower—and then the appearance of some hulking, brutish men. He envisioned it as the opening scene from *Star Wars:* Darth Vader surrounded by his jackbooted storm troopers. After that, everything was dark and confused. A flash of light, a flash of pain. Deafening music, screams, a brief glimpse of Marcus, his face contorted with rage.

"Can't I see him now?"

"He's sleeping," Dr. Brock said. "I promise, you can see him tonight."

Charlton Brock had been ministering to the unique medical needs of William Reid for nearly fifty years. He had declined the dubious gift of immortality decades ago but recently had agreed to train a young replacement to serve William and the growing LA vampire community well into the future. He was glad this boy would not need his specialized services; his injuries were minor, and there was no sign he was in danger of "turning." The same held true for the young woman he had examined. But the heartbreakingly handsome man now "sleeping" in William's bedchamber was a different story. At dawn, with all but a tip of Marcus's right pinkie shrouded in light-proof cloth, Dr. Brock had done a "patch test," exposing the pale flesh to sunlight. It had turned red, and began to swell a minute later.

Dr. Brock knew what lay ahead for the new vampire and his family, his lover, his friends. He would be able to maintain his relationships with them for a time—a decade, maybe two—but eventually it would be too painful to watch them grow old, wither, and die. Soon enough, his persistent youthfulness would begin to raise questions, and he would have to disappear and reinvent himself. His only true friends would be other

members of the vampire community who shared his secret—
his blessing and his curse. The rest would fall away.

Initially, Marcus's own survival had been in doubt. Responding to a frantic call from Jock Price as he sped westward
across the desert floor toward LA, Dr. Brock knew enough to
summon a cadre of loyal blood donors to rendezvous with him
at William's home. When the Escalade squealed into the subterranean garage two hours later, Jock was nearly apoplectic. The
once-pristine white interior of the car was awash in blood,
William and a handsome Mexican named Rodrigo were per-
ilously close to exsanguination, and two young Mexican males
were dead in the back of the passenger compartment, having
been fed upon by Marcus while his hastily bandaged wounds
continued to hemorrhage. The boy, Jacob, and the young woman
required little more than the briefest attention of his nurse—
and heavy sedation—but Marcus was in that netherworld between death and immortality. It could have gone either way.
The third alternative, a normal life as a mortal, was never an option. Ironically, it was his love for Jacob and Allison that probably saved his "life," such as it would be. Half-conscious, in the
earliest stages of his difficult metamorphosis, his only concerns
were for his lover and his sister. That kept him if not *alive* then
in a sort of stasis long enough for the blood of William and Rodrigo to begin his transformation and for the blood of the donors
to sustain him. Additional "transfusions" would be necessary
tonight; new vampires were voracious feeders. And, ultimately,
he would have to make his first kill—sooner rather than later.

He knew it would be difficult for Marcus to resist turning
this beautiful boy into his eternal companion. Before he fell
into his own restorative sleep, William had told him the pull
likely would be strong on both sides. But the boy was too young
to make a mature, informed choice. The best thing to do—what
William had told him he *would* do, despite his desire to make
Jacob a Hollywood star—would be to send the boy back East

to his family, to reengage him with his life, with life itself, as far away as possible from the temptations that awaited him here.

As he watched Jacob drift back into a drugged sleep, Dr. Brock hoped Marcus would have the sense not to curse the boy with the "gift" of immortality. He hoped that Marcus would instead revel in the life of debauchery that characterized early vampirehood, which William could easily provide, given his wealth and status in the community. And he prayed that Marcus could forget about the young life that now lay before the venerable physician.

But could he? *Would he?*

THE DARK HEART

Sean Wolfe

This book, like all of my books, is dedicated to the true love of my life—my soulmate, Gustavo Paredes-Wolfe. As does Kayden with the true love of his life, I know that Gustavo and I have spent many lives together, and I'm a much better man because of his love. He didn't have a Dark Heart, or anything at all dark about him, and in our thirteen years together, he taught me so much about love and light.

I miss you so much, babies. I hope I can open myself up to seeing and hearing and feeling you again soon. *Te amo mucho, y te extraño muchisimo.*

Gustavo Paredes-Wolfe, 1969–2003

PART ONE
Kayden Ridvan—A.D. June 10, 2009

It was only an hour before the doors opened and people by the scores would flood into the club and fill it to standing-room-only capacity. Sangre was the hottest club in San Francisco, and there wasn't a single day of any given week that it wasn't packed beyond the posted limits, and a long line snaking a block long down the street. *Ridvan* was one of several Arabic words for "paradise," and Kayden took great pride in creating just that for his thousands of loyal fans, followers, and patrons. Though he had six excellent managers who could quite capably perform the pre-opening walk-through of the club, he insisted on doing it himself, making sure everything was exactly perfect before swinging the big, heavy wooden doors open to allow the stampede to barrel through and fill his club.

"How's it going, Stella?" he asked as he snuck up behind the bartender and wrapped his arms around her waist and kissed her on the back of the neck.

Stella was all of five feet tall, with long flowing curly blond hair, a waist tiny enough for Kayden to wrap his hands around, and huge round breasts that erupted from every tight blouse she wore and bounced around like gigantic water balloons. She was the only female bartender at Sangre, and her line was always three or four times longer than any of the others. Kayden didn't get his gay male clientele's fascination with boobs, but Stella kept the men happy and spending money, and so he certainly wasn't complaining.

"Do you have everything you need for the big rush?"

"Hi, boss," she said, and kissed him on the cheek, and then jiggled her boobs up and down playfully. "Yeah, I got all I need right here."

Kayden laughed and swatted her on the ass.

"Great party last night, by the way," Stella said.

"Thanks."

"You're just a big old teddy bear, aren't you? Where'd you get such a big heart, anyway?"

Kayden looked around nervously, and tried to keep the smile on his face as believable as possible. But the twitch just below his left eye was undeniable, and didn't escape Stella's gaze.

"Don't get all freaked out," she said with a smile, and caressed his face. "It's very endearing, and it doesn't hurt your badass reputation one bit."

Kayden laughed and relaxed. "It's just that I can't stand the thought of all of those kids being neglected and abused. It makes me sick. I have to do what I can to help."

"Well, word has it that we raised over fifty thou last night alone. That kind of help will go a long way to help the kiddos over at the Center. You should be getting close to the amount you need for the new building, right?"

"Almost," he said, and looked around nervously again. "Another fifty and we should be able to begin the construction."

"You'll have that by the end of the summer. And when do you become president of the board?"

Kayden smiled. "September 1."

"Perfect! And most of the idiots on the board probably think that's just coincidence, don't they?"

"Most of them don't know that I'll have the remaining fifty by then. But they don't care, anyway. No one else wants the position, and no one else can come close to raising that much money, and no one else has the extent of passion for the kids that I do. And they all know it. They're just glad to have someone else who is willing to do all the work and still keep their little names on the roster."

"Well, you're still a sweetheart, and I still think you've got the biggest heart of anyone I know, and I still love you."

"And I still love you, too, baby," he said as he kissed her on the lips. "But you're still not getting a raise, and you've still got to stock your own glasses," he said, and pointed to the empty glass rack behind her.

"Bitch!" Stella said with a laugh, and walked behind the bar to get her glasses set up for the busy night ahead.

Kayden walked away and continued his rounds. He made sure all of the tables had been polished and that the candles on each were brand new, but with the wicks lit. He made sure the levels were perfect on the sound system, and that the lights were set up with the right laser shows and were all oiled and set in the right positions. He double-checked all six bars to ensure they were fully stocked and had backup bottles easily accessible. He even inspected the restrooms and put them through the white-glove test.

It was 8:58 when he walked out of the women's restroom. As he walked toward the big wooden front doors to the bar, he noticed that every bartender and barback was in their place, waiting for the doors to open. The DJ was in his booth, hand on the button to start the music. The sound and light guys were sitting at the control panel, hands on the buttons and levers, and the four managers on shift that night were at their posts, hands behind their backs and smiles on their faces.

Kayden grinned as he reached for the doors at exactly 9:00, and made a mental note to give everyone on his payroll a 5 percent pay raise the next morning. They deserved it. He took a deep breath and swung the doors open.

His was a balancing act almost every night of the week. On the one hand, he loathed the desperate piranha who swarmed around him and screeched and giggled like retarded schoolgirls as they clamored to be seen, and even more, be heard with him. And it wasn't just the women who acted like that. Just as many men needed to be in his inner circle, but they expressed that need differently. They pushed their way brutally through the crowds, grunted like animals as they draped their arms around his shoulders, and looked uncomfortable as they tried hard not to look as if they were having an orgasm in his presence.

On the other hand, he needed to be present for his admirers. In addition to Sangre, he owned two of the hottest restaurants in San Francisco. His flock kept the lines almost a block long at all times and the reservations book filled for never less than six months in advance. So as much as he detested them at times, and as much as he wanted to pick them up and fling them across the room when they all pretended to be his best friend, he tolerated them because he needed them as much as they needed him.

"Kayden!"

He recognized the screech immediately, and turned to look for the nearest escape route. Of all the people he detested, Samantha Burton was at the very top of the list. She was in her mid-fifties, and weighed over 250 pounds, but she acted and dressed like she was half her age and half her weight. But she was wealthier than Jehovah and dropped a thousand dollars a night when she was at his club, and then always wrote a fat check for all of his charity fundraisers. And he could only dodge her so many times before she began to sulk.

"Sammy," he said affectionately, and opened his arms wide as he braced his feet for the impact.

She collided into him and covered his face with sloppy kisses. "Mon cher," she said and hugged him tightly. "Where have you been? If I didn't know any better, I'd begin to think that you were avoiding me?"

"You silly girl," he said with saccharine sweetness, and watched her giggle and blush. "You know better than that. You're my favorite gal."

"Oh," Samantha chuckled, and looked around her to make sure everyone in earshot had heard him. "I just adore you. I do hope you'll consider me your date tonight, and show me a good time."

"Now, you know I'd love nothing more that to do just that," Kayden said with a smile and a peck on the cheek. The first few times he'd played this particular hand, he'd feared he'd backed himself into a corner. After the third or fourth time, he realized that Samantha Burton always drank herself into a stupor when she was out, and never remembered or called him on his flirtations. "But I've got to make the rounds and play the gracious host. You know I'll find you by the end of the night, and we'll have some alone time."

"Oh!" she giggled loudly again, and clutched her neck nervously.

Kayden turned and walked away briskly, cringing as Samantha grabbed his ass and copped a feel. He wove in and out of the crowded room, hoping to get lost in the mob. But he was also on a mission, and stood on his toes to get a better glance around the room. There were eight to ten guys in the room for every woman, which was not unusual. Sangre was a gay bar, but it drew a relatively mixed crowd, and the women who did show up were always exquisite. Most of them were fag hags hanging around their gays, but many of them were rich socialites who just had to have their picture and an accompanying column written about them in the dailies. There wasn't a single night of the week that Sangre wasn't mentioned in the papers.

As much as he normally loved socializing and mingling with the guests, tonight he had a determined purpose. There were several friends and some of his favorite patrons there, but he needed to find Brenda. He looked around the crowded dance floor, waiting for the spotlights to land on the faces in the throng. When he finally spotted her, he worked his way through the mob, taking a moment to greet a few of the regulars, and finally to the middle of the floor, where she was.

"Hi, Brenda," he said warmly as he snuck up behind her.

"Oh my god," she yelled, and wrapped her arms around his neck and kissed him. "I didn't see you earlier. I was afraid you weren't here tonight."

"You know better than that," he said with a smile.

"Yeah, I suppose I do."

"Can you come back to the office with me for a moment?"

Brenda looked at the floor for a moment, and then back into Kayden's eyes. "Sure."

He took her by the hand and led her to the back of the club, into his expansive office, and closed the door behind them.

"Thank god you're here tonight," he said, and leaned her against the wall. "I really need you tonight. It's been four nights, and I'm getting a little weak." He tilted her head to the side and licked his lips.

"I'm so sorry, Kayden," she said, and pushed him gently away from her. "I can't."

"What?" he asked, and tried not to look too shocked. "Why not? You're my favorite and most reliable donor."

"I know," she said, and brushed her hand across his cheek. "And you know that is very special to me. Being a Blood Doll . . . *your* Blood Doll . . . is such an honor, and you know I really appreciate the privilege. I really do. Not to mention how much I love feeding you."

"Then what's the problem? Are you upset with me?"

"Oh, god, no!" she said and hugged him tightly. "You know I love you."

Kayden pushed her a few inches in front of him so he could look at her in the face. "Then what?"

"I'm pregnant, Kayden," she said, and smiled brightly as she jumped up and down.

"What?"

She nodded. "I'm pregnant. Almost two months."

"Oh my god," he said, and hugged her tightly. "I'm sure Reece is beside himself."

"Yeah," she said, and wiped a tear from her eye. "We're both so excited and happy. But I can't donate any more, at least not until after the baby is born. I need all my blood for Jasmyne."

Kayden smiled. "You know it's a girl?"

"No, not officially. I just feel it."

"I'm so happy for you," he said, and hugged her tightly.

"You're not mad?"

"Of course not. Don't be ridiculous. This is a very happy occasion, and I'm so excited for you. You absolutely must let me throw the baby shower right here. It'll be fabulous!"

Brenda laughed. "You don't have to do that."

"Oh, yes, I do. It's already done. Now get out there and dance your ass off. You have some celebrating to do."

"Thank you for everything, Kayden."

"Are you kidding me? Thank you. You're the best Blood Doll anyone could hope for. I don't know what I would have done without you these past few years. You know I love you, right?"

She smiled and nodded.

"You gonna be okay?"

"Of course," he said, and smacked her on the ass as he opened the door. "I'll call someone else. I'll be fine. Go have fun."

He waited until he saw her disappear into the crowd on the dance floor, and then closed the door. He felt a little dizzy, and walked over and sat at the desk. It wasn't often that he allowed himself to wait this long between feedings, and he knew he'd pushed his luck. The room was beginning to spin and he felt light-headed and a little nauseated. He clumsily fished around in his pocket for his cell phone and scrolled down his contact list.

He got Eric's voicemail, and Jason's, too. Dana's number was disconnected, again, and William's rang over twenty times without an answer or a voicemail message.

"Fuck," he yelled, and brushed his hand through his hair.

He stumbled to the door and walked carefully out into the hall leading to the main bar, holding on to the wall the entire way. A few people rushed past him into the restrooms, and didn't seem to notice who he was. As he got closer and closer to the big bar, the music and noise around him began to fade out, as if he were listening through a speakerphone, and the room slowly began to darken.

"Boss, you okay?" It was Janet, one of the barbacks. She looked frightened. "You're as white as a ghost, and your eyes are freaking me out."

"No," Kayden said, and leaned against the wall. "No, I don't feel well at all. I need to go home. Can you call me a cab, please?"

"Yeah, sure," Janet said, and rushed to his office, where she kept the door open and her eyes on him as she dialed the phone.

Kayden barely made it inside the door before he fell to the floor and vomited. When he was younger, and more rebellious and stupid, he'd gotten to this point quite a few times. But in the past 340 years, with a little wisdom and acceptance under his belt, he'd only allowed himself to go this long without feeding a handful of times. It was extremely dangerous and even more enormously irresponsible, and he hated himself for it. He'd recognized the telltell signs of depression the past few week; he'd experienced them a couple of times a decade for the past 100 or 120 years or so. But they'd been much worse in the past, and he didn't really think they were too bad this time around. He thought he'd had everything under control. But apparently he was mistaken.

He crawled over to the credenza and hoisted himself to his feet. The rustic wooden and iron cabinet was his mother's, and well over a thousand years old, but it didn't even creak or wobble as he leaned against it and used it to balance himself. It was solid when he was not, and for that Kayden was thankful.

The ornate 2' x 2' box that sat atop the credenza was just a few years younger than the buffet itself. It was made of polished mahogany inlaid with ivory and pearls and rubies that pre-dated Marco Polo by at least half a millennium, and lined with pure Persian silk. A container that old should have been quite dull and unremarkable, and especially considering Kayden never once polished it or cared for it in any way whatsoever. Instead, the box seemed to glow with a life all its own, and everyone who laid eyes on it was instantly entranced by it. Had a value actually been able to be placed on it, the wealthiest sultans in Arabia would not be able to afford it.

But Kayden Ridvan loathed it, and it made him ill to his stomach each time he had to open it. The box was like an iron shackle to him, and he resented and despised it with all of his being. The history behind it, and the unchallengeable force and hold it had over him, repulsed him, and he fought against it every day of his life. Even after almost half a century now, he struggled with it and his need and responsibility for it.

He reached for the box, and his hands trembled violently. He did not want to open it, but he knew the time was drawing near. When his fingers touched the wooden frame of the container, he felt an electric current begin at his ankles and swiftly travel up his legs, through his torso, and through his teeth and brain. He felt his cock respond and begin to harden, and his gums began to tingle.

Kayden ripped his fingers from the box and pushed himself away from the credenza. He paced around the room frantically, stumbling a couple of times, and using the walls and furniture to steady himself. It was now approaching 11 P.M., and he was aware that he only had a couple of hours before it would be too late. He knew this not because of the time he read on his watch, but because of the feeling he felt in his throat.

He lay on the couch for a few minutes, trying to calm down and get his bearings. He had begun to sweat profusely since he'd arrived home, and he felt his skin cooling with each passing hour. His eyes burned painfully, and his teeth and gums tingled and ached and itched all at the same time. His canines had retracted and throbbed with excruciating purpose and command that would not be denied for much longer.

When he couldn't take the pain and nausea anymore, Kayden rolled himself from the sofa onto the floor and crawled over to the credenza. He braced himself on the sturdy cabinet and lifted himself to his feet. His hands trembled as he opened the drawer and removed a key. Tears fell down his face freely as he reached for the box. A loud moan escaped his throat as his hands grasped the corners of the container, and his knees began to tremble as he felt the familiar tingle in his ribcage and the burning in his throat.

He fumbled with getting the keys into the lock, and it took him a couple of minutes to get it unlocked. His hands and fingers quivered as he opened the ornate box. A loud, animalistic screech erupted from his bowels and up through his throat as he looked into the box.

The blood-red Persian silk lining inside the box stood in stark contrast to the dark purple heart that lay atop it. Even though the heart appeared almost black, it was very obviously alive and healthy. It beat vibrantly with a steady, regular pulse, and the muscular walls of the chambers were lined with thick veins that seemed to breathe life into it. The thick venae cavae and pulmonary arteries flopped around the silk lining and bounced into the air with a purpose, as if they were seeking a long-lost partner with whom they needed to be complete. There was not a drop of blood anywhere, and yet the heart throbbed energetically as if it were sustaining a well-trained athlete.

Kayden let out another low growl that reverberated throughout the entire house. He wrapped his arms around his ribcage as strong bolts of electric shock ricocheted across and through every muscle in his body. He slammed the box shut, collapsed to the floor, and curled himself into a fetal position.

His eyes still burned painfully, but he felt them begin to roll back into his skull just as the phone rang. He crawled over to the coffee table and clawed at the table until the phone fell to the floor. He looked at the caller ID.

"Kyle," he said weakly into the receiver. "Help me."

Kayden was barely conscious when he sensed he was not alone. He opened one eye and watched Kyle shut the front door and run to his side.

"Kayden," Kyle said frantically. "What the fuck happened to you?"

"Feed," Kayden whispered.

He knew what he must look like to the beautiful boy looking down at him. He'd been there enough to know that his skin was beyond pale and close to translucent. His thick veins would be green and pounding across his skin, seeming to burst out of the thin epidermal layer. His lips would be blue and his eyes would be dark red, and his fangs would be almost two inches long at this point, not just wanting, but *needing*, to be sunk deep in the tissue of a warm host. It would frighten even the most ardent and courageous Blood Doll, and Kayden was thankful it was Kyle who'd returned his voicemail message. If anyone could handle him right now, it was Kyle.

"What the fuck is wrong with you, letting yourself get this way?" Kyle said as he ripped the shirt from his body.

Though tall and very lean, he had thick blue veins that stood out in contrast to his milk-white skin. The vein running across the underside of his triceps and across the side of his armpit was Kayden's favorite vein, because it was so large and carried the sweetest blood. He thrust it against Kayden's mouth.

"Drink," he said quietly as he caressed his friend's face and held it tightly against his arm and chest.

Kayden moaned deeply as he felt his fangs pierce the tender skin and heard the "pop" as they broke the skin and sank deeper inside. He sucked hungrily, and as the first few sips of blood rolled across his tongue, he felt his cock harden. He clamped his mouth around the underarm and sucked harder on it, drinking in larger and larger amounts of the sweet and metallic blood.

"That's it, baby," Kyle said. "Drink it. Take what you need."

After a couple of mouthfuls of the warm liquid, Kayden felt his energy return. The coppery liquid slid down his throat and immediately fed his muscles and bones. He wrapped his arms around Kyle and sucked harder on the thick vein.

"Ow," Kyle said as he jerked. "Careful, babe. That's starting to hurt."

Kayden growled low and deep, and sank his fangs in another quarter of an inch as he sucked even harder.

"Stop," Kyle cried out. "Kayden, stop it. That hurts. I'm getting dizzy."

Kayden pulled his fangs out slowly and screeched loudly. He jumped to his feet and grabbed Kyle by the throat with his left hand, lifting him a couple of feet off the floor. When he looked up into Kyle's eyes, he saw the undeniable terror. He knew that his eyes must be maniacal, and that the blood dripping from his lips was probably freaking Kyle out. But none of that mattered; his need for more blood clouded any other judgment.

He flung Kyle across the room and watched as he crashed against the wall and fell to the floor.

"Kayden, don't," Kyle said softly as he shook his head to clear the cobwebs and tried to get to his feet.

Kayden flew through the air and landed on top of his friend. He turned Kyle's head roughly to the side and sank his teeth deep into the soft skin right above the collarbone. He had the strength of ten men now, and reveled in the power he held over Kyle as the kid thrashed around and begged for him to stop. The neck was always off limits with Kyle; he always fed Kayden through his wrists or the armpit. Kayden's forceful taking of blood from the neck was akin to raping his friend, and it turned him on more than he'd ever imagined. His cock throbbed painfully against his leg as he sucked more and more blood into his mouth and swallowed it hungrily.

"Please, Kayden," Kyle begged, as tears rolled down his face. He fumbled for Kayden's hands and interlocked his fingers with his own. "I love you, baby. Please stop. You're going to kill me."

Suddenly the blood began to taste creamy, and Kayden knew that his friend was terrified of him. He pulled his mouth off Kyle's neck quickly and moaned loudly as he collapsed onto the floor next to his Blood Doll.

"I'm so sorry," Kayden said, and brushed a tear from his cheek. When he got no response from Kyle, he leaned on his elbow and pulled his friend's head around to look at him.

Kyle's face was extremely pale, and his eyes fluttered rapidly. His cheeks were sunken in and his mouth stretched tightly shut.

"Kyle," he screamed, and slapped his friend gently on the face. "Kyle, look at me. Open your eyes."

The Blood Doll didn't respond.

"Wake up, Kyle," Kayden screamed, and shook him.

Kyle moaned softly and opened his eyes slowly. "Kayden?"

"Oh, god," Kayden cried, pulling Kyle to his chest. He could feel his eyes cool down with every passing minute, and his fangs were already slowly sinking back into his gums. His skin felt warmer, and his muscles did not feel as if they'd been jolted with a taser.

"I'm so sorry, Kyle. I don't know what happened. Please forgive me. I would never hurt you, I swear." He kissed his friend softly on the lips. "Please forgive me."

"Are you okay?" Kyle asked as he struggled to sit up.

Kayden laughed through a cry as he wiped another tear from his face. "Yes, babe, I'm okay. I just went too long without feeding this time. But I'm okay now. Thank you for coming, and for feeding me. I'm so sorry I was rough. Are you okay?"

"I'm fine. But you scared me. I've never seen you like this."

"I haven't been like this for many, many years. Way before you were born. And I promise I won't get like this again. I'll never hurt you again."

"I know," Kyle said, and sat up and shook his head. "I suppose you're hard as a rock right now, aren't you?"

Kayden laughed, then pulled Kyle's hand down to feel his hard cock.

"Now that's what I'm talkin' about," Kyle said with a mischievous grin and took a long, deep breath. "Take me upstairs."

Kayden picked him up gently and carried him up the spiral staircase to his room.

There were a couple dozen candles spaced throughout the spacious bedroom, and it took Kayden almost five minutes to get them all lit. When the flame from the last candle joined the colorful flickering dance show on the walls, he turned and looked at Kyle, who was lying naked in the middle of the huge bed.

"My god, you're beautiful," he whispered as he discarded his own clothes while he crossed the expansive bedroom.

He crawled into the middle of the bed and looked down at Kyle. Kayden's taste in men had changed over the past few centuries. It sometimes seemed to sway and change with the wind and was definitely influenced by the styles and cultural values of the times. There was even a short period of almost sixty years where he was more attracted to women. But that had been just a phase, and he still wasn't convinced that he hadn't suffered from some nasty venereal disease as a result of tainted blood in Boston in the early nineteenth century. It was the most logical explanation for his lapse of judgment.

Regardless of what other phases or attractions he might have experienced over the years, there were two constants. He'd always been turned on by tall, thin men with big cocks, and blue eyes had always gotten his own dick hard with just a single glance.

Kayden smiled as he felt his cock harden as Kyle stretched his long legs across the bed and pulled Kayden closer to him. He stared into Kyle's light blue eyes and moaned with desire as he kissed a single tear from them. He'd seen thousands of pairs of beautiful blue eyes, and they had all gotten him hard and brought him to intense orgasms, but Kyle's were the most stunning and mesmerizing he'd ever seen. They were light blue, just a couple of shades from being gray. His eyelashes were long and thick and curled at the ends, and when he batted them playfully, Kayden's heart melted.

"Make love to me, Kayden," Kyle whispered, and pulled Kayden down to meet his lips.

Kayden leaned down and kissed Kyle on the lips. He'd kissed his friend a hundred times, and every one of them had taken his breath away. The boy was insatiable, devouring Kayden's lips with his mouth and desperately pulling him closer to his smooth, toned body. Kayden loved the determination and passion with which Kyle kissed and needed him, and never tired of pleasing him, even after countless dozens of times that they'd melded.

He sucked on Kyle's tongue for several minutes, and then reluctantly pulled his mouth from the soft lips. He looked down at his friend, and smiled as he saw the familiar flushed cheeks and ears, and watched the boy struggle to catch his breath as he squirmed beneath him.

"Oh, god, Kayden. Fuck me. Please."

Kayden licked his way down Kyle's body, savoring the salty taste of the cool sweat on his friend's soft skin. He rolled Kyle's big balls in his palm with one hand as he lifted the long, thick cock from Kyle's belly and sucked it gently into his mouth. His mouth was much stronger than that of even the strongest and most talented cocksucking mortal. Feeding off of humans and the extraordinary suction needed for the task developed freakishly strong jaw, mouth, and throat muscles, and made for what hundreds of men over the centuries had described as the most incredible blowjob they'd ever experienced. It was a lot of work on his part, because he had to rein in his desire to tighten his lips around the hot throbbing cock and swallow it deep into his throat. But he had to be careful and lightly roll his tongue around it instead. Anything more than that could easily result in the severing of the beautiful cock, and with him literally swallowing it. In these moments, it really was all about Kyle's pleasure and not his own, so he cautiously rolled his tongue up and down the length of the shaft and across the head, reminding himself that the boy was only human, and not to devour him.

Kyle grabbed the blanket on either side of him and wriggled beneath Kayden.

"Oh fuck, dude," he whimpered. "You gotta stop. I don't know how you do that, but if you don't stop, I'm gonna fuckin' blow my load right now."

Kayden sighed as he let his lips slip from the throbbing cock, which was already leaking a healthy amount of sweet precum. He loved sucking a hot cock, but wasn't able to do so very often or for very long at all. Humans couldn't take more than just a few seconds of his powerful mouth before shooting their loads into it. He was no headhunter. Those fucking vampires who fed on one another were incestuous and indulgent miscreants, and he despised them. Kindred blood didn't nourish its own, and so they indulged only for the sport of Blood Bonding and to gain and exert power and control over the weaker among them. Sex among vampires was not pleasurable or loving at all. It was intimate, in that it literally melded their soul and unified them in ways completely foreign to humans, but it was demeaning and belittling and humiliating for the weaker partner. It was a silly game, and one in which he refused to partake.

For Kayden, sex with his human partners was a way of bringing them complete euphoria and sharing a part of himself with them in a humble expression of appreciation for their loyalty and dedication to him. Unlike the vast majority of vampires, he held mankind in high esteem and enjoyed sharing life with them. Most of his sexual partners over the centuries had been willing donors . . . Blood Dolls . . . who gladly allowed vampires to feed on them, and who very often became their lovers. There had been a few times where he'd become fond of men, and women, who never knew that he was a vampire. But that was not a secret he could keep successfully for very long, so those relationships were short lived. Because of the difficulties of maintaining them, they were also few and far between.

"Please," Kyle begged, and wrapped his fist around Kayden's hard cock.

Kayden picked Kyle up with both hands and lifted him effortlessly off the bed. He flipped him around as if he were twirling a weightless baton, and laid him gently down on his stomach. He wedged his knees between Kyle's long legs and scooted them apart. The smooth, pink hole winked at him, and Kayden dove in. Again he had to be careful not to let his eager mouth perform at even half potential, but when he slipped his tongue slowly inside the twitching hole, Kyle moaned loudly and lifted his ass higher off the bed and deeper onto his mouth, and Kayden knew that this would not be a night of slow and tender lovemaking.

"Fuck me, Kayden," Kyle whimpered. "I need you inside me. Now."

Kayden made sure that he'd left plenty of saliva just inside and all around the pink, quivering hole. He spread the milk-white, smooth ass cheeks apart and pressed the head of his cock against the hole. At well over ten inches long and as thick as a soda can, Kayden had been legendary on every continent over the past four hundred years or so. Many men over the years had been completely unable to take him, and those that could had been broken in slowly and had required great patience on Kayden's part.

Kyle was neither of those types. From the moment he set eyes on Kayden's giant cock, he'd been mesmerized. He sat on the big dick slowly but steadily in one move and rested there for a full five minutes, allowing his body to become accustomed to the huge cock. Then he lifted himself up and bounced up and down on it, slowly at first, then more frantically. He'd later described that first session as an out-of-body experience, and was animalistic in his lust and in devouring Kayden's cock. Ever since, he'd been insatiable in his hunger for the huge dick, and was one of only a handful of men in almost five hundred years who could take as much as Kayden could give and who could match his stamina.

"Now, Kayden," Kyle said gruffly. "Fuck me now."

Kayden laughed and spread Kyle's ass cheeks farther apart with both hands as he placed the head of his fat cock against the twitching hole between them.

"Are you rea . . ."

He gasped to catch his breath as Kyle lifted his ass higher off the bed and impaled it onto Kayden's cock. Warm, wet heat enveloped his fat cock head and slid slowly up the entire rod, squeezing and gripping him every inch of the way. It felt as if a thousand tiny electric prods were worshipping his dick, and it stunned him. He stopped about two thirds of the way inside Kyle's tight ass and took another deep breath.

"Unh unh," Kyle moaned, and slammed his ass all the way onto the big dick. "Don't you dare fucking wimp out on me now. Fuck me, man."

Kayden pushed Kyle back onto the bed so that he was lying on his stomach and pushed his face into the pillow. He held one hand on Kyle's upper back and slowly slid his cock all the way out of the smooth ass. It was dark red with purple veins ribbing throughout it, and bounced vigorously up and down in front of him.

He leaned down and lay against Kyle's bare back, pressing his cock against the crack of his warm, smooth ass.

"You're so damned hot," he whispered into Kyle's ear as he kissed it, and then slowly slid his cock deep into his ass until his balls rested against the underside of the warm, sweaty cheeks.

"Oh my god," Kyle groaned into the pillow.

Kayden slid in and out of the tight ass slowly and deliberately, pulling all the way out so that only his head remained inside and forcing Kyle to suck him back inside with his clutching sphincter. He then slammed back into Kyle forcefully, knocking his head against the headboard and causing him to hold on to the sides of the mattress to keep from falling off. He loved the way Kyle's ass pulled and sucked on his dick and refused to let go of it as he threatened to pull out.

The kid was only twenty years old, but he had one talented ass. Kayden knew that even if he lived another four hundred years, he'd always remember Kyle fondly, and that Kyle would always be ranked among the best Blood Dolls of his life. Throughout history there'd always been plenty of humans who got off on allowing vampires to feed on them. It gave them a sense of power of the mystical creatures, and they got off on it. There was never a shortage of humans who were sexually attracted to Kindred, and who struggled with their unbridled desire for them. Finding one who was not just into the power and physical gratification of the relationship, and who truly understood and bonded with the vampire, was rare indeed.

Kyle was one of those rare finds, and truly loved the vampire race. He connected with them on a soul level; he identified with their strength and their vulnerability, their beauty and their hideousness, their passion and their indignity. Everyone loved Kyle, and he tended to be the center of attention whenever he was around a group of Kindred. There were many vampires in the city who had expressed an interest in both feeding on and fucking him in the past two years that Kayden had known him. A couple of them had even pretended to challenge him for Kyle's allegiance, but it was all smoke and screens. Though Kayden had always been relatively quiet and laid back, there was no arguing his heritage. Although a few of the less intelligently blessed vampires might entertain the thought of challenging him, none of them did so seriously.

Even if they had, Kyle had made it clear that, though he loved all vampires, his loyalty and allegiance would always lie with Kayden. He would have to be killed . . . or turned . . . to change that. And no vampire on earth was stupid enough to invite the war that would ensue with that action.

"Oh fuck," Kyle gasped as he tightened his ass around Kayden's thick cock. "You feel so amazing inside me."

"You like how I fuck you, baby?"

"Oh, god, yeah. You know I do."

Kayden slid his cock in and out of Kyle's ass faster and deeper.

"I love you, Kayden."

Kayden stopped thrusting, his cock buried deep inside Kyle's ass.

"Oh shit," Kyle said as he dropped his head to the pillow.

"Don't say that," Kayden said as he grabbed his friend by the hair and pulled his head up and turned it around so that Kyle was looking at him. He felt his face turning red and the beginnings of his jaw dislocating.

"I'm sorry, babe," Kyle said. "I didn't mean it. I know I shouldn't have. It just slipped out."

Kayden took a deep breath, and gently lowered Kyle's head back to the pillow. He knew the boy well enough to know that what he'd said was the truth, but also that it had been an accident, and that there was no malice behind the words. Kyle was the one person who'd been there for Kayden tonight when Kayden needed him the most. He deserved a break.

"It's okay," he whispered in Kyle's ear as he kissed it. "Just be more careful. Watch what you say, and even more, watch what you feel. You know that loving me isn't an option."

"I know," Kyle said. He couldn't look at Kayden. "I didn't mean it, you know that. It just slipped out in the passion of the moment."

"Good," Kayden said. He pulled his cock out of Kyle's ass and turned the boy around onto his side. He slid behind him and spooned him, sliding his cock back inside the warm hole until he was buried.

"Fuck me, babe," Kyle moaned as he slid his ass up and down the long cock. "I want you deep inside me."

Kayden felt his balls tighten and the familiar tingle begin deep in his belly and make its way through his loins and into his cock.

"Oh, god," he groaned, wrapping his arms around Kyle's torso from behind. "I'm cumming, baby."

He slid all the way inside one last time and held his cock

deep inside Kyle as he felt his load explode from the head of his cock.

"Fuuuuuuck," Kyle moaned, and squeezed his ass even more tightly around the big dick inside him. "I feel you filling me up, dude."

"Yeah?"

"Oh, yeah. It's warm and there's so fucking much of it."

Kayden's body quivered for a few seconds, and he lifted Kyle up and laid him across his chest. The boy was stretched out across Kayden's body and stroked his cock while Kayden slid his still-hard dick in and out of his ass slowly.

"Oh, fuck," Kyle whispered. "I'm cumming."

His load erupted from his cock like spewing ash from a volcano. Cum flew in every direction, and seemed to go on forever. Several shots whizzed by his own head and landed on Kayden's face and even the wall behind them. Some of it landed on the sheets and pillowcases on either side of them, but most of it covered his own face, chest, and stomach.

"Damn, man," Kayden said as he gasped to catch his breath. "Fucking amazing."

"Glad you liked it," Kyle said, and yawned. "I'm exhausted. Will you stay inside me again while I sleep, like last time?"

"Anything you want, baby," Kayden said.

He maneuvered Kyle so that he was lying on his side, facing away from him. His cock was still rock hard, and felt warm and safe and comfortable inside Kyle's still-twitching ass. He smiled as he heard the boy snoring softly just a couple of minutes later. He took a deep breath from his nose, savoring the scent of Kyle's sweat and desire, and closed his eyes.

A couple of minutes later he was asleep, and, as he always did, he dreamed of his distant grandmother.

PART TWO
Lilith—April 5, 40,212 B.C.E.

Lilith rolled off Cain's hard cock and lay beside him, drenched in sweat and struggling to catch her breath. She brushed her long brown hair aside with one hand and leaned up to kiss him on the cheek as she draped one naked leg across his crotch.

"Wow," Cain croaked out. "That was really intense."

"Yes, it was," she whispered as she bit his bottom lip. "I love feeling you so far up inside me."

"You do, huh?" he asked with a laugh, and slapped her playfully on the ass.

"Oh, yes, I do." She pulled her leg back to her own side, and wrapped her long fingers around Cain's still-hard cock. "This makes me very happy."

"You're insatiable," he laughed, rolling onto his side to kiss her on the lips. "I love that about you."

Cain rolled on top of Lilith and pinned her to the ground. He wrapped one hand around her thin neck and with the other hand slid two fingers inside her wet crevice. He laughed as she moaned lustfully and squirmed beneath him, then he spread her legs with his knees and slid effortlessly back into her with one move.

"No," Lilith whimpered and scooted out from under him. She scooted over a few inches from where he lay, defeated.

"What's wrong," he asked. His hard cock throbbed painfully against his stomach and bounced across the lightly hairy abs uncontrollably.

"Nothing's wrong," she sighed. "You know I love you, and I love your cock," she said, and leaned down to kiss it and suck on the head lightly. She smiled as he writhed beneath her and moaned loudly.

He was such an easy creature to control, and she did it effortlessly. Any man would wither beneath her strength and her charisma, and her charm was magical. Cain was especially weak, and very much took after his father. She'd been able to manipulate Adam almost as easily as she was now pulling the strings with Cain. She'd had him completely wrapped around her fingers until that cunt Eve showed up and ruined everything. Her shy, submissive demeanor confused the hell of the idiot Adam, and when placed between the two women, he didn't know if he was coming or going.

"Then I don't understand," Cain whined. He tried to crawl on top of her again. "Why can't I fuck you?"

"Because you just did, not even fifteen minutes ago," she said. "And from the feel of that load you just left inside me, I'm going to predict at least quadruplets, if not quintuplets in exactly six weeks from now. If you go in again before they are born, we could have seven or eight new babies this time."

Cain pulled his wife tighter against his hard and sweaty body. "So? I want a hundred babies with you. Hell, I want a thousand babies with you."

Lilith laughed, and swatted him on the arm. "Of course you do. You are not the one in tremendous pain, nor are you the one who bleeds gallons of her own life with each birth. All you have to do is take the babies away and wrap them in warm blankets and tell them how much you love them. You've got the easy part of the job."

Cain laughed. "I want ten thousand babies with you!" he yelled, and pushed her legs apart again.

Lilith swatted him away, and pushed her legs closed. "We have thirty children now, Cain. These new ones inside me will make thirty-four or thirty-five. And every six weeks, like clockwork, we have a few more. Be patient. We have plenty of years ahead of us, and you will father your thousand kids, I promise. But it hurts me to give birth to so many at once. Be gentle with me." She brushed his chin with her hand and kissed him. "Show me you're a better man than your father was. He was never able to be gentle with me."

Cain pulled her to him and kissed her lovingly on the lips, on the neck, and on the breasts. "I'm sorry," he whispered as he licked her navel. "I will be gentle with you, I promise."

Lilith smiled to herself as she noticed Cain taking in deep breaths and savoring her scent. His hands caressed her naked body, and it did not escape her that his cock was still throbbing and leaking life force all across her bare leg.

"Show me you're a better man than your father was."

She felt him flinch, and grinned. She knew his buttons, and could play him like a finely tuned harp. She'd successfully influenced him to kill his own twin brother in a fit of jealous rage, and then had convinced him that his own parents were lunatics who were out to destroy him. She'd never in her wildest dreams imagined that they'd banish him from Eden, but when they did, she had him wrapped even tighter around her fingers.

"Father was a fool," Cain said sadly. "I don't know how he could ever have denied you anything. You are intoxicating, and I can't get enough of you, Lilith. I could never resist you."

"Why would you want to?" she said, and kissed him passionately, drawing his tongue into her mouth and sucking on it.

"I wouldn't," Cain said as Lilith broke the kiss and stood up to get dressed. He watched her pick up the flowing robe from the stool and slip it slowly onto her soft, silky body.

"Your father was an ignorant man, lover," she said as she sat on the stool and crossed her legs. "Do not make the mistake of envying him or wanting to be anything like him."

"Never!" Cain said. He crawled over to her and kissed her ankle and up her leg.

"Adam was a weak man who could never handle a strong and powerful woman like me. He was threatened by me. We were made of the same dust, your father and I. Why he thought himself superior to me, I'll never know. Can you imagine a simple man ordering me to submit to him and to always lie beneath him as he entered me?"

Cain laughed. "No, I cannot. I much prefer it when you climb on top of me and command every inch of my body. I love your strength and your power, Lilith. I crave it as I do water."

"Well, you're a better man than your father," she said bitterly, and switched legs so that he could worship the other. "He was so weak and so threatened by me. And when Eve appeared, he was smitten immediately. The bitch was sweet and quiet and obedient; everything Adam wanted in a wife and thought he deserved. She blindsided him and swept him away. I'm sorry, I know she is your mother, but the bitch was cunning and deceitful."

"I have no loyalty to either of them," Cain said, and rubbed his hands up Lilith's thigh under the robe.

"I loved her, too, you know. At first. She was a beautiful woman, and something about her demureness was exciting for me. I asked her to run away with me. Did you know that?"

"What?" Cain laughed, and wrapped his arms around her and pulled her close to him.

"It's true. For a while the three of us tried to make it work together. But after a while I'd gotten bored with Adam, and something about her enthralled me. I wanted her to be my lover. And she was tempted, too. We dabbled a bit a couple of times, but then she became afraid."

"Are you kidding me?" Cain said. "My mother has actually been here," he said, and slipped two fingers deep inside her vagina.

Lilith moaned, and leaned back in the stool as she spread her legs. "Yes, and she liked it very much, but she became afraid and she told your father and they joined forces against me. Then they convinced The Source that I was bad and needed to be banished."

"That's how you left Eden?"

"Yes," she said, and pulled Cain's fingers from inside her, and rearranged her robe. "And then Adam cursed me and called me a snake. The ultimate evil. It wasn't until then, as I walked out of the garden, naked and shamed, that The Source branded me with these," she said, and recoiled her lips to display her fangs. Her upper canine teeth on either side of her middle teeth were about half an inch in length, and razor sharp.

"Oh, Yahweh, I love those," Cain said, and felt his cock throb painfully between his legs. He leaned up and kissed Lilith, licking her fangs as he did. "I adore your evil, lover. I adore everything about you."

Lilith pushed him to the ground and pounced on him, straddling his chest and stomach. She emitted a low growl from deep in her throat and bared her fangs at him.

"Do it, Lilith," he moaned. "Please, do it again." His thick cock bounced across his stomach, dripping cum as it throbbed up and down.

She leaned forward, kissed him on the lips, and slid her ass back until she felt Cain's hard cock pressing against her bare skin. She loved the way the heat from his cock head felt against her cool skin, and wiggled her lower body across it until it rubbed against her vagina. Then she pulled it into her and slid all the way down the shaft until it was buried deep inside her.

"Oh, Yahweh!" Cain moaned, and lay perfectly still.

Lilith rode the big cock and moaned as she moved her mouth from Cain's lips and down his chin and across the side of his neck. Her nostrils flared as she inched closer and closer to the thick jugular vein that pulsed erotically just beneath the soft skin of his neck. She could smell the blood racing through the big vein, and her heart raced with the excitement of tasting it.

"Please, Lilith, do it," Cain groaned and thrust himself deeper inside her.

Lilith placed her lips on the side of his neck, and flicked her tongue around it as she kissed it lovingly. His skin was warm and sweet and salty and sweaty and dry all at the same time. Her head spun and her eyes rolled back into her head as her tongue flicked across the throbbing vein and she felt the blood flowing through it and across her tongue. She no longer felt the big cock sliding in and out of her, because every nerve ending in her body seemed centered in her lips and tongue.

She clamped her lips on Cain's neck, creating a tight seal. Then she took a deep breath and let just the very tip of her fangs kiss the warm skin that pulsed beneath them. She moaned as sharp electric shocks tickled her teeth and swam throughout every cell in her body. When she bit down just slightly, she felt his skin stretch with the pressure for a short second. As she continued with the bite, she felt Cain's breathing quicken and noticed him thrusting harder beneath her. A second later she heard a "pop" as her fangs sank through the epidermal layer and pierced the thick vein.

A faint high-pitched squeal escaped her throat as the first wave of blood trickled past her teeth and rolled across her tongue. It was warm and coppery and buttery, and it caused chill bumps to pop across every inch of her skin. She swallowed the first couple of mouthfuls quickly, and felt her orgasm shoot through her lower body as she was filled with the other life fluid from the other end. The blood slid slowly across her tonsils and down her throat. She sank her fangs deeper into the vein, but was careful not to puncture the bottom of it, and sucked more of the warm food into her mouth. This time she rolled it around in her mouth for a moment, savoring the taste and the feel of it before swallowing.

After almost a full minute of feeding on Cain's blood, Lilith felt her lover's body go limp beneath her. She tried not to smile, because she knew some of the blood would spill down Cain's neck when her lips broke the seal, and she didn't want to waste a single drop. But she couldn't help it. She knew what was coming next, and every fiber in her body exhilarated in the prospect.

Lilith felt Cain's chest cavity fill with air as he took a giant breath. A couple of seconds later she heard the sounds of his nose breaking, and felt the muscles in his neck tighten as his jawbone elongated a couple of inches. When his clavicle snapped, she finally pulled her lips from his neck.

A loud animalistic growl erupted from Cain's throat, and Lilith giggled softly to herself. She felt her windpipe closing around her as he grabbed her by the neck with one long, scrawny arm and lifted her effortlessly into the air as he stumbled to his feet. He looked up at her with ruby-red eyes, and Lilith saw a couple of giant tears well up in his eyes and then roll down his cheeks, which were now flushed pink and pulsing beneath his skin. She blew him a kiss and winked at him, and then felt herself being flung across the mud and straw hut. She crashed against the far wall, and stumbled to her feet just in time to see Cain storm out the door into the cool dark night.

Lilith took a couple of deep breaths and brushed the dirt and straw from her sweat-soaked body. She heard the deep roar from somewhere in the distance, and a couple of seconds later, the high-pitched shriek of a woman. She recognized the voice when the woman pleaded in vain to be spared. It was the wretched Kali, the most self-righteous of the entire village, and the source of almost every rumor to come from the entire valley. Lilith tilted her head back, still savoring the buttery taste of Cain's blood in her mouth, and laughed hysterically. The loud cackle rose to a pitch that brought a howl from every dog in the village and drowned out Kali's desperate cries for help.

"We all live with our curses, wench," she spat out. "Yours is your mouth."

She walked out into the cool evening and crossed her arms across her naked breasts. A light wind blew across her, and she took a deep breath. She could smell the coppery blood from Cain's feeding in the wind, and envied him. Partaking of one's lover's blood had its own appeal and fulfilled her in one way. But there was nothing like the thrill of feeding on the forbidden and feeling the life drain from a useless body.

She walked to the tent next to her own and smiled. Her youngest eight children shared this tent, and the two youngest ones were crying. Sara and Shila were the two girls born with four boys ten weeks ago, and they were inseparable. They slept at exactly the same time, they relieved themselves at exactly the same time, and they cried at the exact same time, as they were doing now. The boys were all sleeping soundly through the tantrum; nothing could stir them when they slept. They were just like their father.

Lilith reached down, picked up the babies, and brought them to her breasts. The girls latched on to them and calmed immediately. They giggled as they fed, and their little feet and hands flitted around aimlessly as their bellies filled. Lilith looked down into their faces and smiled. All of her babies had been beautiful, and she supposed that all mothers thought their babies were the most stunning ever to be born. Of all thirty of her children, Sara and Shila had been blessed with something special. Their skin was milk-white, with rosy pink cheeks that glowed when they smiled. They had bright blue eyes and long blond eyelashes that matched the flowing blond hair that fell softly over their shoulders just days after they were born. They looked like angels, and Lilith loved them just a little more than she did the rest of her children.

From somewhere in the distance a crashing sound pierced the quiet night, and then a soft chatter began to grow closer and louder. Lilith balanced the babies in her arms, careful not to pull them away from her tits, and walked over to the front of the tent. She kicked the drape aside and looked out into the night.

An impossibly loud growl screeched across the sky, and a moment later it turned to a cry, and then a whimper. Lilith fell to her knees, dropping her babies to the hard ground as she recognized the voice behind the cry. Tears welled in her eyes as she clutched her stomach, which felt as if it had been punched with a giant axe, and vomited onto the ground.

"Lover," she cried weakly into the dark night.

She looked up and saw the orange glow in the sky in the distance. It was getting bigger and brighter by the second, and before long she heard the murmurs and shouts of angry men and women quickly approaching her.

Lilith jumped to her feet and ran to the two large tents to either side of her.

"Quickly," she shouted to Tara, the oldest of the children, who was just stirring from her sleep.

"Mother?" Tara said, sitting up and wiping the sleep from her eyes.

Lilith looked at her oldest daughter and cried. Tara was a striking young woman of twenty years. She had creamy white skin that was soft as a baby's. Her dark brown hair fell to her shoulders and always smelled like honey. Her hazel eyes were mesmerizing; they stopped men in their tracks. She was a mirror image of Lilith and was following in her mother's footsteps admirably. Already she was a master at manipulating every man in the village and had them all wrapped securely around her fingers.

"Help me with the younger ones," Lilith said sharply. "We must go, now."

There were thirty children in all, and one might have thought that they'd move slowly and awkwardly, especially after being roused from sleep. But the clan moved swiftly and gracefully. They'd been here before, and moved with a defined purpose. Lilith watched her older children, and saw in their eyes that they sensed something different and more urgent this time. They didn't speak a word or question her actions. They simply grabbed the cloth bags that had been prepacked, scooped up their youngest brothers and sisters, and slinked quietly and swiftly out of the tents and into the thick forest that abutted their homestead at the edge of the village.

The sounds from the distance were getting louder, and Lilith could now make out a few individual voices. She turned to look behind her, and saw that the bright orange light in the sky was now flickering. She could see smoke. The mob had entered the village from the other side, and was advancing toward them faster than she'd anticipated. Another ten minutes, and they would be here.

Lilith tilted her head back and cried. The loud screech rose from her throat and into the dark night, and then ricocheted from every tree in the forest. She heard the crowd grow silent for a moment and noticed the flickering light several yards away stop for a few seconds. Then a loud yell erupted from the mob, and she heard the stomping feet coming toward her.

She waved for the children in front of the line to run, and the family slithered deep into the black forest.

PART THREE
Kayden—A.D. July 9, 2009

Kayden paced around the living room, trying hard not to let the oncoming panic overtake him. Even after more than three hundred years of dealing with this, he still found himself sweating and struggling to breathe as the inevitable time approached. He hated it. A handful of times over the past three centuries, he had contemplated throwing in the towel, ending the history of his infamous family then and there, but that would have meant the ultimate betrayal of not only himself but also of his entire lineage. He couldn't bring himself to do it.

The phone had already rang over a dozen times, and he was just about to hang up and try someone else when he heard the click announcing the call was picked up.

"Hello?"

"Hi, Kyle," he said quietly into the receiver.

"Baby, how are you?"

Just the sound of Kyle's soft and tender voice brought his cock to attention. Even from across the phone line, Kayden could smell the musky scent of Kyle's skin. When he licked his own lips, he could taste the sweet flavor of Kyle's favorite gum.

"I'm good," he said.

"Are you sure, baby? You sound a little strange."

"No, I'm good. Can you come over tonight?"

"Of course," Kyle said anxiously. "I can leave now."

"No!" Kayden said quickly. "Come over at four."

"Four? But it's almost midnight now. Do I really have to wait four hours?"

"Yes," Kayden said shortly. "I'll leave the door unlocked. Just come on in. I'll be home a little before four. I'll be naked in bed when you get here, and I'll be horny as hell and wanting you badly."

"Okay," Kyle said.

Kayden heard the disappointment in his voice, and knew that he wanted to come over now. "Do not come over here before four. Do you understand me?"

"Yeah," Kyle said. "I like a little danger and excitement, but I'm not stupid, and I don't have a death wish. I know you well enough to know that you don't say something like that without a good reason."

"You're right. So I'll see you in a few hours?"

"Definitely. It's been too long. I can't wait."

Kayden hung up and tossed the phone on the couch, and then walked over to the credenza. His hands trembled as he reached for the box, and he shook them a couple of times to release the stress and calm his nerves. The dark polished wood was now several shades lighter than it normally was, and seemed almost translucent. The sparkling jewels lining the edges pulsed with life and shone with a light beneath them. They threatened to propel themselves from the box and rocket through the brick wall across the room.

He felt the bile crawl up his throat as his fingers danced half an inch from the box, which now seemed to be growing in size, closer and closer to his quivering hand. The tears were building behind his eyes, and he wished more than anything that he didn't have to open it, that he could throw it in an incinerator and walk away from it forever.

He couldn't, and he knew it. He felt this way every time he was forced to open the box and claim its inhabitant. Luckily, he only needed the heart once every five or six weeks. Between then he could sustain himself with just the donor feedings that were tender and ended in hot and passionate lovemaking once a week or so. He always tried to stretch that period for as long as he could, and he'd tempted fate with it thousands of times. He hated everything about the heart—the way it looked, the way it smelled, the way it felt, and the monster it made him become when he couldn't deny it one more evening.

Kayden reached inside the box and wrapped his hand around the heart. He dry heaved as it beat against its palm. The thick veins that wrapped around the smooth muscles pulsed against his skin; the aorta and pulmonary arteries wiggled around aimlessly for a few seconds, and then found his fingers and squeezed them with a loving familiarity. A high-pitched whimper escaped from somewhere deep in his gut as the tears fell freely down his cheeks, then was quickly replaced by a low and angry growl from the back of his throat.

He lay down on the sofa, closed his eyes, and brought his free hand to his chest. His fingers moved across the pecs and to the thin line of black hair that separated them. The nerves on every inch of his body felt as if they were being touched with a cattle prod as he followed the trail down to just below his sternum. When he felt the skin sink just slightly with his touch, he pushed down with his forefinger until the skin gave way and his finger slid effortlessly inside his chest. He pinched the skin between his forefinger and thumb, pulled the large flap of skin back, and laid it across his chest.

The cavity between his ribcage was empty. For Kayden it was nothing special. But for the very few people that he'd trusted enough to show, it had fascinated them immensely. It was dark and cavernous inside his chest, and they'd been amazed that they could actually see several of his internal organs and the way the muscles attached to the bones. Several flaps of raw pinkish gray tissue that had previously been lying dormant against the bones of the ribcage were now starting to float to life, stretching out a couple of inches from the bone and constricting with a life of their own. They swam out in front of the skeletal frame, searching for their companion.

Kayden noticed the flaps of tissue were now beating in perfect sync with the warm heart throbbing in his hand. He swallowed hard, forcing the acrid bile he felt trying to make its way up his esophagus back down. As he brought the beating heart closer to his chest, another low, agonizing growl erupted from somewhere just behind the muscle surrounding his spine and echoed around the room.

He dropped the heart into the vacant cavity and felt the muscles in his legs and arms begin to twitch uncontrollably. His breathing quickened and his eyes rolled back into his head as he felt the aorta and pulmonary arteries on the heart stretch desperately out in front of it. The pink and gray tubes of tissue from his chest bounced excitedly around his ribs for a few seconds, then latched on to the thick veins that were searching so frantically for them. When they connected, he gasped for breath, and his body became rigid as the two sets of tubal tissue melded. Blood immediately rushed through his body and filled the heart and arteries. He actually felt it pumping through his body for several seconds before he closed his eyes and went completely limp.

He stopped breathing for a little over two minutes, then took a sudden, frantic gasp of breath. His eyes flew open, and he knew without seeing them that his irises were bright red and ringed with a yellow-orange outer circle. He'd been told many times how they were simultaneously frightening and seductive while in this state. His jawbones separated and his face elongated three or four inches. He felt the skin stretching to accommodate its new dimensions. Agony overtook him, and he screamed as his nose snapped with the contorting skeleton beneath his skin.

His fangs were a couple of inches long, and as he opened his mouth to scream, they tingled throughout his gums and up behind his eyes when the cool air hit the sensitive nerves. His nostrils flared angrily as he scanned the room frantically. He was starving and needed to feed.

Kayden jumped up from the couch and floated a couple of inches off the floor over to the door. Beside it was a full-sized ornately framed mirror. He looked into it and roared in misery as he saw his reflection. There was still enough of him present to be mortified with the appearance of The Beast. In another two or three minutes, that part of him would be gone, and The Beast was all that would be present, so he savored the disgust he felt looking at himself in the big mirror.

He tilted his head back and opened his mouth to allow the loud, animalistic roar to escape his throat, and then flung the door open and flew out into the dark night.

From atop the roof of the Metropolis Hotel, Kayden could see clearly for a six-block radius. The ten-story hotel in the middle of San Francisco's seedy Tenderloin district was his favorite hunting perch. The corner of Mason and Turk Streets always promised an eclectic group of people from which to choose. It was only a couple of blocks from the prestigious San Francisco Center, and some of the wealthier patrons were naïve enough to park their expensive cars on the block. In contrast, the small taqueria across the street brought in a young punk crowd filled with drug addicts and prostitutes. Neither was ideal, really. The death of a wealthy aristocrat inevitably meant media attention, and no vampire was a fan of that. The punk kids weren't the best alternative, either. Their blood was always tainted with drugs of every imaginable variety, and he didn't particularly care for that most of the time. Sometimes he'd be in the mood to get high and would partake. Mostly he stayed away from the Goth kids. They were ignorant and their blood had a nasty and sour aftertaste.

Aside from the two polar ends of the spectrum, though, the hotel also offered a smorgasbord of young, healthy, and tasty yuppies on their way to the theater a few blocks away or one of the trendy restaurants that currently dotted Market Street. Those folk didn't bring along the swarm of unwanted media, nor the drunken blood of the streetwalkers, and he could always count on his pick of several warm-blooded main courses on any given night.

This night was no different. As he leaned against the wall and watched the busy street below, he caught the scent. Undeniably female, and somewhere between twenty-nine and thirty-two years old. After almost half a century of feeding on humans, he'd developed a keen nose for blood, and could describe his prey down to the eye and hair color simply by the smell of their blood even if they were still five or six blocks away.

When she turned the corner, he smiled. Her auburn hair and green eyes were as beautiful as he'd known they would be. She was wearing a stylish dark blue skirt and a meticulously pressed white dress blouse. Her stilettos clicked against the asphalt and suggested she was upper management at an insurance brokerage firm or possibly a newly appointed partner in a medium-sized advertising agency.

She was exactly what he craved that night, and his nostrils flared hungrily as she approached the hotel. The heart beat excitedly in his ribcage, a mixture of sharp pain and erotic caress at the same time. A part of him realized that he did not miss that feeling when the heart was not inside him, but another part reveled in the elation it brought to every cell in his body.

The woman stopped at the entrance of the small parking lot that abutted the hotel and looked around nervously. She brought a petite hand to her neck and rubbed it defensively, looking up at the roof of the hotel.

Kayden didn't bother to move back from the ledge of the roof. He could see the light from the street lamp sparkle in her emerald eyes, count every strand of her shiny hair, and see the blood pulsing through each of her veins. But it was closing on one o'clock in the morning, and was pitch black outside. He knew that although he could see very clearly, the woman ten stories below him couldn't make out anything higher than the second story of the hotel.

He watched the woman shudder and then reach for her car keys in her oversized handbag. He took a deep breath and flung himself over the edge of the roof. The night air enveloped Kayden and supported him as he soared quickly and noiselessly to the ground. When he was less than ten feet from the woman, she finally turned and looked at him with wide eyes.

Kayden slammed into the woman, wrapping his arms around her torso as he crashed into her. His teeth sank deep into her neck even as they fell to the ground, and he rolled several feet with her on the asphalt parking lot. She'd been taken completely by surprise, and hadn't even had a chance to scream or cry out for help. By the time she realized what was happening, it was too late, and she was unable to produce an audible scream.

He bit down harder on the woman's neck and sucked the warm blood into his mouth. He was so hungry that he swallowed the first several mouthfuls quickly, without tasting it. Then, as the flow started to slow down and he had to suck harder to get it, he rolled it around in his mouth for a few seconds, savoring the sweet taste before swallowing it.

When the blood slowed to a trickle out of her vein, he pulled his mouth from her neck and growled at her. He noticed that she was looking at him right in the eye. Her stare was vacant, and didn't register any emotion at all; not fear or loathing or shock or surprise. She blinked a couple of times, though, demonstrating that she was still conscious. Kayden grabbed her by the hair and roughly pushed her head to one side, exposing the other side of her neck. He bit down on it and sucked more fresh blood into his mouth, and gulped it down hungrily.

With every swallow of a mouthful of warm blood, Kayden felt the life drain from the woman. He sensed her body getting lighter and colder with every passing minute, and before long her heart lost its energy. He'd done this enough to know when the time came—that moment where her heart was beating only once every fifteen seconds. There was a window of about one minute once she reached this stage. If he wanted to turn her, this is the time he would need to stop. There was very little left of her soul, and it was that miniscule spirit that was needed to accept the immortality.

Kayden did not feel the need to turn her. He had more than enough bitchy cunts under his charge already, and didn't really have the time nor the patience to bring another one into the fold. This woman didn't bring anything unique to the table. She was pretty but not gorgeous, smart but not cunning, resourceful but not particularly creative. There was no reason to bother with her.

Her blood began to flow cooler onto his tongue, and he moaned with disappointment. It was too late to turn back now. The cool, thick fluid now had a milky taste to it and left a filmy texture on his tongue and throat. Kayden could no longer feel her heart beat, and he felt the last bit of her soul slip haphazardly from her frame as she took her final gasp of breath and then lay perfectly still and quiet.

He clamped down on her neck and gnawed at it, ripping into several shreds of skin and muscle that dangled across her throat and the side of her neck as Kayden lifted his head from it. He looked down at the woman and smiled as he saw her mangled neck. Her blank eyes rolled back into their sockets.

A loud and high-pitched screech escaped his throat, something that was half laugh and half sob. He stood up slowly, balancing himself on the sedan the woman had been trying to get into. He felt a little drunk with the excitement of the kill. Even after the thousands of feedings and kills he'd done, the thrill of it still intoxicated him.

It made him horny as hell. His cock was hard and throbbing in his pants. When he reached down to touch it, his body shuddered and his knees buckled beneath him. He needed to get home. Kyle would be there and waiting for him, and more than anything at the moment he needed to slide into his friend and fuck him until he lost consciousness.

From the front of the hotel Kayden heard several voices, and they were getting louder by the second. He squatted down so that his ass almost touched the ground, and then jumped into the air. His body flew upward and he landed on both feet on top of the roof a few seconds later. He looked down, watched the small group of people walk toward the dead woman, and held his breath. He hated it when his kill was found so quickly, and it stressed him out. When the four men turned in the opposite direction right before tripping over her body, Kayden took a deep breath and flew away into the dark morning.

Back inside his own home, a fire was crackling in the fireplace, and soft romantic music was playing through the overhead speakers. Kayden smiled and growled at the same time. Kyle was a sweet kid, but more than a little naïve. He'd never seen Kayden in The Beast state—Kayden had been careful of that. If Kyle had, he'd never be seen nor heard from again. He knew that Kayden sometimes had to actually hunt, rather than just feeding on willing donors, and that there was a secret that Kayden absolutely had to keep from him, and he'd been fine with that from the beginning. The kid had no idea what Kayden was like in this state, and the fact that he had a romantic fire going and soft music playing on the stereo attested to that.

Part of him wanted to rush up the stairs, to kick in the bedroom door, and watch Kyle's face as he saw him for the first time, to see the look of horror in his eyes and to watch his lips open wide in a terrifying scream. A lesser vampire would do just that, then rip into the kid and tear him to shreds, because The Beast held a powerful and undeniable hold on vampires while they were under its influence.

But Kayden was not a lesser. He was Kayden Ridvan, and as much as he wanted right this minute to rape and pummel the kid waiting naked for him upstairs, he wouldn't. As hard as the heart in his chest was pounding and pleading with him to tear the kid apart into unrecognizable pieces, he wouldn't. He'd satiated his thirst for a kill tonight, and would not indulge the heart another.

He walked over to the credenza and leaned against it as he took a few deep breaths. The heart was now beating harder, and Kayden could feel it gripping the other veins—its lifelines to his body—tighter and more desperately. The heart knew it was about to be separated from him and was fighting against it. Kayden doubled over in pain as the heart protested and clenched at the tissue around it for support and anchorage. It didn't like being apart from its host, and never gave up without a fight. It was fighting harder tonight than it did most nights, and the pain brought Kayden to his knees.

He'd been here before, though, and had the routine down to a science. He ripped his shirt from his torso and tossed it onto the back of the sofa. Pressing the three middle fingers on each hand against the center of his ribcage, he located the barely detectable slit in the skin and slid his fingers inside his chest. With one hand he held the skin back to keep it from preventing him further entrance into the chest cavity. With the other, he reached inside and grabbed the beating heart. He felt it pulse against his palm for a couple of beats, then his long fingers sought out the venae cavae and pulmonary arteries. They contracted against his touch, clamping down harder onto the muscles and veins in his chest that held the heart in place and provided entry into the rest of his body.

Kayden pinched the arteries and then pulled quickly, detaching it from its lifeline. Blood spurted out in all directions, and he swiftly tugged on the beating heart now, while it was weakened with the absence of its main support. He heard the familiar "plop" as the other arteries released their tissue hosts, and the heart was finally freed from his body. He removed his hand from his chest and pulled the heart out. It was dark purple and dripping with red blood, and it pulsed dramatically in his hand. It looked as if it were breathing.

Kayden brushed the excess blood from the sinewy muscle and opened the mahogany box, which was now multiple shades of red and orange, glowing eerily from seemingly every pore in the wood. He carefully set the beating heart in the center of the silk cloth and shut the lid. He stood leaning against the credenza for several minutes, taking deep breaths and trying to clear his head. His skull was retracting back to its normal size and shape, and the feel of his bones shrinking back into themselves and his fangs sliding back inside his gums and reshaping themselves into normal teeth always made him dizzy for a few minutes.

His long razor-like claws were always the last remnant of The Beast to disappear, and when they did so this time, he pushed himself away from the credenza and walked upstairs and into the shower.

* * *

"Well, aren't you a sight for sore eyes," Kyle said sleepily as he yawned and walked into the bedroom. His face instantly lit up and he licked his lips unconsciously as he saw Kayden's hard cock sticking straight up in the air.

"Come here," Kayden said, sliding his legs apart.

Kyle crawled onto the giant bed and between Kayden's legs, but when he reached for the huge cock in front of him, Kayden stopped him.

"I want to hold you first," he said as he pulled Kyle up to his chest. He cradled the boy in his arms, hugged him tightly, and kissed him tenderly on the lips.

"Are you okay?" Kyle asked, as he broke the kiss and leaned on his elbow to stare into Kayden's eyes.

"Yeah, I'm fine. Why?"

"I mean, don't get me wrong, I like it when you kiss me like that, and when you hold me. It makes me feel special. But you haven't done it all that much, at least not lately. And you've never done it right after a hunting feed. And I've never in the three years I've known you, ever, seen you pass up a blowjob. Is something wrong?"

"No," Kayden said, and turned away. He hated when he fucked up like this and gave up a part of himself he didn't want to share. It made him feel weak. "Nothing's wrong. And I am not passing up a blowjob. You're definitely gonna suck my dick. I just wanted to kiss you first and to hold you for a minute. Why does that have to mean that something is wrong?"

"It doesn't," Kyle said, and leaned down to kiss him. "You're right. But can I suck your cock now?"

Kayden laughed and pushed him gently by the back of the head down to his crotch. He moaned as he felt Kyle's tongue lick the head of his dick first, and then felt the warm, wet mouth envelop it. The kid was a fucking pro, and when he swirled his tongue around the throbbing head, Kayden could never contain himself. He held Kyle by the back of the head and thrust his big cock deep into his mouth.

Kyle knew the cock like the back of his own hand, and he also knew how Kayden liked to be sucked. He opened the back of his throat so the entire cock could slide deep inside, and then he held the big dick there while he squeezed the shaved balls with one hand. When he tightened his throat around the thick cock, and Kayden moaned as he thrust deeper inside him, Kyle felt his heart beat faster and a trail of precum drip from the tip of his cock.

"Oh, god, Kyle," Kayden moaned. "That's fucking incredible."

"Thanks," Kyle said, as he came up for air and wiped a hand across his mouth. "I'm glad you like it. But now I want your dick inside my ass."

"I think that can be arranged."

"Will you do it my favorite way?"

Kayden laughed. "I guess we can do it that way. It's been a while."

He hooked his hands behind his head, spread his legs apart, and smiled as he watched Kyle take a couple of deep breaths. A couple of seconds later the boy began to rise from the bed, and his eyes bulged. Kayden's eyes stayed focused on his friend's, and when Kyle floated several feet above him, suspended in the air like a limp ragdoll, Kayden stretched his legs farther out on the bed. His cock was rock hard and stood straight up in the air, throbbing visibly and leaking a large amount of precum that slid down the thick, veiny shaft.

"You ready?" he asked, but already knew the answer. Kyle's eyes were wide, and Kayden could see his friend struggling to get to the fat cock.

"Yes!"

Kayden kept his eyes on Kyle's but lowered them and watched the boy float lower in the air and closer to his anxious dick. Moans escaped Kyle's throat, and his breathing came out in short, staccato bursts as he was invisibly lowered. When Kayden felt the heat from Kyle's ass, he stopped lowering his eyes, and watched his friend squirm an inch above his cock.

"Oh, god," Kyle groaned. "Don't stop. Please."

"You want it?"

"Yes."

Kayden lowered his eyes again, and watched Kyle float down the last inch. He stopped when he felt the hot ass touch his dick head. A second later Kyle's hole twitched uncontrollably around the head, trying desperately to grab on to the fat head and suck it inside.

"Fuck me," Kyle gasped. "Please, Kayden. Fuck me."

Kayden smirked and allowed Kyle's body to slide down the big cock. Kyle screeched a little as the fat head popped inside, but Kayden felt the hot ass squeeze and massage his cock as it slid down it one inch at a time. When Kyle began breathing heavily and faster, as if he were practicing the Lamaze technique, Kayden forced him the last four inches all at once.

"Oh, *fuck!*" Kyle yelled.

"Take it, baby," Kayden said, and thrusting his dick in and out of the clutching ass slow and deep. He knew being fucked suspended in midair, held and manipulated like an invisible marionette, was Kyle's favorite position. But he'd forgotten how much *he* liked it as well.

"Ungh," Kyle moaned loudly, and shook his head back and forth quickly as he bit his bottom lip and breathed faster and harder.

"You ready?"

"Unh hunh."

A second later Kyle's feet and legs were pulled invisibly into the air, so that they were just inches from his face. His body now formed a "V," with his ass the narrow point at the bottom, and still impaled on Kayden's thick cock. He grabbed the back of his knees with both arms, and held his legs tight to his torso, like a diver about to enter the water.

"Fuck, your ass is tight in that position, baby."

"Hell yeah," Kyle panted heavily. "Spin me."

"Already?"

"Spin me!"

A couple of seconds later, Kyle began spinning around in circles, his ass anchored on Kayden's big dick. The first few 360-degree turns were slow and elicited deep moans of ecstasy from him. After four or five, though, he began to spin faster, and his moans turned to squeals.

Kayden slowly and carefully lifted himself up so that he was standing on the bed. With his feet firmly planted on the mattress, he watched Kyle rotate full circles around his cock. The boy's ass was hot and tight, and as it spun around his dick, he had to concentrate on not shooting his load too early. He grabbed Kyle by the waist, pulled him harder onto his cock, then spun him around even faster on it.

"Fuck me," Kyle moaned as he stroked his cock while spinning. "Please. Fuck me."

Kayden slid in and out of Kyle's ass faster and harder as the boy spun on his cock. He knew it wouldn't take him long to shoot his load this time. He'd been so wound up and charged from the kill earlier in the evening that he was surprised that he'd even made it home before popping one. Now, with Kyle spinning around and sliding up and down his throbbing cock, he couldn't hold out any longer.

"Oh, god, Kyle," he grunted as he pounded into his friend harder. He didn't notice that his friend was now spinning so fast around his dick that he couldn't speak, and was close to losing consciousness. "I'm cumming, baby."

He buried his cock deep inside Kyle's ass and held himself perfectly still even as the boy twirled around his cock at dizzying speed. He thrust his chest and head backward and clenched his fists together as he emptied his load deep into Kyle's quivering ass. Seven or eight giant spurts later, he slowly pulled his cock out of the tight ass.

Kyle stopped spinning immediately, and dropped limp to the bed.

"Kyle!"

Kayden fell to his knees and pulled Kyle into his arms. He brushed the boy's wet hair from his eyes and caressed his face.

"Kyle, wake up."

The boy stirred in his arms. "What happened?" he said groggily.

"You passed out."

"Well, *that* isn't sexy."

"Are you okay?"

"Yeah, just really tired and a little dizzy. Did you cum?"

"Umm, yeah. Like a gallon, I think."

"That's hot," Kyle said, and leaned up to kiss Kayden on the lips.

"You didn't cum, though," Kayden said, and reached down to stroke his friend's soft cock. "Want me to finish you off?"

"Nah," Kyle said. "It'd take me a while to get hard again." He cuddled up against Kayden's chest. "Will you just hold me and let me fall asleep in your arms?"

Kayden tensed up. "I don't think that's . . . I'm not sure . . ."

"Calm down. I don't need to spend the night. I know you get freaked out about that shit. Just let me sleep in your arms for a few minutes. Catch my breath a little."

"Just for a few minutes?" Kayden said cautiously as he looked at the clock. It was a little after five, and the sun would be coming up in about an hour.

"Yeah," Kyle said as he hugged Kayden tighter. "Twenty minutes. Half an hour, tops."

"Okay," Kayden said, and returned the hug. "Twenty minutes."

Kyle was snoring in less than two minutes. Kayden held him in his arms and brushed the long, wet strands of hair from his eyes as he stared into the kid's soft, sweet face.

"I can't do this anymore," he whispered softly to the quiet night. "I can't stand myself. I can't do this anymore."

PART FOUR
Lilith—April 12, 40,212 B.C.E.

Lilith paced back and forth around the large clearing just inside the mouth of the cave. It was cold and dark and damp, and she was shaking uncontrollably. All of the children were asleep much deeper in the cave, in three separate makeshift rooms. She and the four oldest children had ventured out and found enough sticks and leaves to place on top of the stone floor to create makeshift beds, and they'd been able to sleep relatively well.

Or, at least the children had been able to. Lilith herself hadn't slept a wink in the week since they'd been forced on the run. She also hadn't bathed or eaten; her ribs threatened to poke through her skin at any moment, and her hair clung to her scalp in mangled clumps. Her senses were all heightened. She jumped at every sound, even those she made herself, and her eyes constantly darted wildly around the cave and around the perimeter of the outside immediately surrounding it.

In the past couple of days she'd noticed that she'd begun to foam around the mouth. She usually caught it before any of her children noticed it, or at least she was fairly certain she had. It couldn't be a good sign, and it was getting worse. She knew what was wrong, and it frightened her more than anything she'd ever feared before—more than the wild dogs who'd chased her and her family on more than one occasion, more than the light of day that burned her skin and eyes until they bubbled, and more than the crazed mobs that had hunted her over the years and threatened to burn her alive.

Of all of her troubles, the worst—the one that would kill her very soon if she did not remedy the situation quickly—was that she hadn't fed since she was forced deep into the forest a week ago. She could go for several days without eating food, but more than just a couple of days without feeding was much more serious and could be her demise. Her last consumption of thick, sweet blood had been when she and Cain were in the throes of passion right before he went on the hunt himself that fateful night seven moons ago. Though she didn't have to feed on fresh blood every night, if she went more than two evenings without, she became sick and disoriented. There had been a handful of times when she'd gone up to four days without feeding, and during those times she became fevered and confused and crazed.

She'd never gone this long without blood. But she knew instinctively that her body was being poisoned by the lack of her life force, and that was why she was foaming at the mouth. She would not make it through another night without feeding. If she died, her children would be on their own. That was not an option—not with the crazed mob after them. She needed to feed in order to be strong and available for her children.

"Mother, are you all right?" Tara stepped from the dark of the tunnel that led to the back of the cave and walked into the larger living-area space.

Lilith jumped at the sound of Tara's voice and turned to look at her daughter. She gasped as she took in the beauty of the young woman. The moonlight splashed across Tara's milk-white skin and created a soft blue hue across it. She was supple and solid and looked more healthy than Lilith ever remembered seeing her. Her long black hair fell across her shoulders in luxurious waves and fell carefree across her round breasts. Her stomach was flat and firm and looked soft and inviting.

Lilith swallowed past a large lump in her throat and smiled at her daughter. Part of her was filled with pride at the beauty and undeniable power she'd brought into the world. Another part, closer to the surface than she'd like to admit, was jealous of the goddess standing before her and ached to kill her and remove the threat of competition.

"No, darling, I don't believe I am all right," she said slowly. She reached behind her and steadied herself on the limestone wall, and then lowered herself to the ground carefully. She felt the tiny bubbles of foam gathering on her tongue and spilling over onto her lips. "I must leave this cave."

"No, Mother, you can't!" Tara rushed to her mother's side and crouched on the ground with her, stroking her hair away from her eyes.

"Don't worry, daughter. I won't be long. But I must feed. Look at me. I'm dying."

"Don't say that!"

"If I don't feed, I will die. I have gone way too long without blood. I can't wait another hour."

"Please, no," Tara cried, and pressed her head against her mother's gaunt stomach.

"Be strong, daughter. I won't be long. I will avoid the mob and travel in the opposite direction. I believe there is a village not far from here."

"Mot—"

"While I am gone, you must watch over the children. You must protect them. They must not know that I am gone. If they wake, tell them I am sleeping and cannot be disturbed."

"They won't believe me. They'll know that I am lying."

"You must convince them, Tara. We have no choice. If I

don't feed I will die. Then you will have a much bigger lie and a much larger responsibility."

"You won't come back," Tara whispered as she wiped the tears from her eyes.

Lilith balanced herself on the wall and slowly stood.

"Nonsense," she said, steadying herself on Tara's shoulders. "I'll be back before you know it."

Mother and daughter hugged tightly, and then Lilith turned and walked out of the cave and into the open darkness.

Tara stood back a few feet from the mouth of the cave, ensconced in darkness. Tears streamed from her eyes, and her hands covered her quivering mouth. She stood there for a couple of minutes before realizing she hadn't taken a single breath since her mother left the cave. She pulled her hands from her mouth and took a couple of deep breaths as she played with the hair that cascaded down her shoulders and across her chest.

After another minute or two, she felt safe enough to turn and walk toward the hidden rooms in the back of the cave. She'd taken three steps when the shrill cry pierced the night and every cell in her body.

Tara fell to the ground as she heard and felt her mother's screams. Lilith had been very weak and not able to move very quickly at all when she'd walked out into the cool night. She couldn't have gotten very far at all, and her voice sounded as if it were possibly even still inside the cave.

She turned and looked at the entry to the cave, and was shocked to see the bright orange glow just outside. She heard the voices now. There seemed to be hundreds of them, and they were angry. Tara stood and looked toward the back of the cave, where her brothers and sisters slept soundly. She took a couple of steps into the dark of the cave, but when another shriek from her mother shattered the darkness, she turned around and ran toward the open mouth of their home.

She stopped just inside the opening of the cave, and stood with her eyes and mouth wide open.

The crowd outside wasn't as large as it sounded, but maybe half what she'd originally thought when she heard its roar. Still, the number was staggering, and the crazed looks on their faces made them all the more frightening. Their eyes were bulged wide open and Tara could see the fear and hatred in them. Spit flew from their mouths as they yelled obscenities at her mother, and several of them were clawing at themselves, ripping open wide sores in their own bodies as they cursed Lilith and flung themselves to the ground.

Tara felt a scream build deep in her gut and threaten to burst from her mouth. She fell to her knees and covered her mouth with both hands as she watched the crowd pull her mother out into the middle of the clearing in front of the cave. They all held lighted torches, and were holding them high and thrusting them toward Lilith as they screamed their curses at her.

Barely hidden inside the dark of the cave, Tara watched as her mother writhed around on the ground and screamed in agony. Lilith's body was trying desperately to morph; Tara could see her face contorting, trying to elongate and become The Beast. She heard the bones breaking in her mother's body but saw that the actual transformation was not able to happen. Lilith was clawing at her own mouth, and Tara knew that she was trying to release her fangs. She could also see that they were betraying her mother.

The crowd surged forward as one, and the roar grew even louder. They stopped and picked up handfuls of stones of all sizes and threw them at Lilith, who curled into a fetal position and tried to cover her head.

Tara knelt on the ground, crying and keeping her hands tight over her mouth. She watched as her mother was pelted with stones, and her body twitched and writhed uncontrollably as it was struck. After only a couple of minutes, a piercing scream floated up from Lilith's mouth, and then her body stopped moving altogether. Tara dropped her head to the ground. She prayed that the crowd would now just turn and leave, and that she could gather her siblings and flee the area.

The mob was enraged now, and could not be stopped. Tara watched in horror as several of the men in the crowd pounded Lilith's chest with sharp large rocks. She heard the bones crunch beneath the assault, and couldn't peel her eyes away as the men reached into Lilith's open chest and ripped her still-beating heart from it.

One of the men stood up and lifted the heart high into the air. The horde of angry men and women yelped in joy and victory as he thrust it higher in to the air. The beating heart was completely black but dripped bright red blood all around it as it was being heaved above the heads of the crowd. Another of the men dug a shallow hole into the ground, and buried about six inches of a long, sharpened stake in it. The rest of the wooden stake rose about five feet into the air. The man holding Lilith's dripping heart walked over to the stake and shoved the heart onto it so hard that the sharpened end poked all the way through the heart and poked out the other side of it.

A heavyset woman rushed toward Lilith's body and tossed a couple of handfuls of dry leaves into the gaping cavity that had once housed her heart. She touched the lit end of the torch she was carrying to the bundle of leaves, and then stood back as they erupted into flames.

Tara's eyes flew wide open and she clutched at her chest as dark black smoke began to rise from between her breasts. The pain was excruciating, and she felt her muscles and organs burning from inside her. She jumped to her feet and rushed out into the cool night, beating at her chest and screaming loudly.

The crowd gasped and surged backward, retreating several feet back into the forest as they watched Tara roll around on the ground and thrash at her chest. The smoke floating from her naked body and into the air was thick and black and smelled sour and rotten. Many of the men and women in the crowd covered their mouths, and some even vomited as they watched her flailing around and breathed in the acrid smoke.

Suddenly, Tara's chest exploded, and her heart burst into flames in front of the mob. They gasped as they watched her body grow still as the heart burned intensely. A couple of minutes later they heard several screams coming from deep inside the cave; then black and gray smoke spewed from the mouth of the cave, and the screams quieted all at once. The smell was overpowering, and some of the crowd ran back into the forest to escape its pungent odor.

Most of them stayed until Lilith's entire body had burned completely, and there was nothing left but bones and ashes. It burned more quickly than they'd thought it would take, and when it was done, the man who had ripped Lilith's heart out grabbed an arm bone and held it high above him.

"Take one of her bones and hide it somewhere in the forest as we return home," he yelled into the crowd. "If her body is scattered all over the forest, she will not be able to return."

Several of the crowd rushed forward and grabbed some of the bones, and passed them out to their fellow villagers. When there was nothing left of Lilith but her ashes, which were scattering in the wind, the mob turned and walked back into the forest, anxious to return home and to know they were safe from the monster Lilith.

Cain saw the orange glow above the trees from almost a mile away, and when the wind quieted and the various forest animals calmed for a few seconds, he could hear the rumblings from the crowd, who were at times chanting and at others roaring in anger.

He tried to fly through the thick brush, but had been weakened by the beating that same crowd had given him a week ago.

He'd been beaten unconscious, and the mob had made the mistake of thinking him dead. When a couple of them had returned to bury him a few hours later and found him gone, they rushed back to the group and announced "the demon" had resurrected and vanished. It had enraged the mob and mobilized them to hunt down his wife and children. And so he was rushing now to warn them and to assist them. He flew, slowly, for a few yards, and then fell to the ground. The attempt to fly had weakened him even further, so he decided to run instead.

He forged ahead as quickly as he could, but sometimes he felt confused and lost. He should be getting closer to the sound of their voices and to the orange light above the trees, but no matter how much ground he covered, it seemed like the crowd was always the same distance away. Sometimes it felt as if he were flying backward rather than moving forward. The ground was getting warmer, and the trees in front of him were becoming fewer and farther between. He knew he must be getting close to the place where the people congregated.

On his last attempt at flying, as he cleared the treetops, he caught a whiff of the acrid smoke. He coughed out a mouthful of bile and fell to the ground. As he got to his feet, he realized he was in the clearing he'd been searching for. There were still a few torches anchored to the ground, and from the flickering fire he saw the cave. There was still a small amount of black smoke pouring out of the mouth of the cave, and he wondered what could possibly smell so putrid.

He looked around groggily and noticed the stake with the heart impaled on it. It was still beating, though barely.

"Noooooo," he cried out.

He stood up and stumbled over to the stake on the opposite side of the clearing from the entrance to the cave. On the way, he passed the small pile of ashes that had once been Lilith's body and that had not blown away with the wind. The ashes barely registered in his brain. But the creamy white naked female body a few feet from the stake did register with him. It was battered and scratched and badly mangled, and more than half of the body was badly burned and charred. But the perfect white skin, the large round breasts and the long flowing dark hair were unmistakable.

"Oh, God no!" Cain cried, and dropped to the ground next to the body. "Lilith, please wake up."

He rolled her over onto her back and brushed her hair from her face. Her eyes were swollen and bruised, her lips cut and bleeding, and her nose was broken. He tried to brush the dirt and smoke from her face, and that's when he noticed the giant gaping hole in her chest, and the burned-out cavity that had once housed her heart.

Cain tilted his head back and growled loudly. It came out a cross between a low moan and a high-pitched screech, and it reverberated around the clearing. As he lowered his head to look at his wife again, he saw the stake with the beating heart once more. He stumbled to his feet and half ran and half fell over to the stake. Once there, he ripped the black heart from the wooden pole and rushed back over to the dead body on the ground.

"I'm so sorry," he cried. He looked at the beating heart in his hand, and tried hard to keep from vomiting as he felt it throbbing warmly against his palm and fingers. "I shouldn't have left you. I didn't need to feed that night. I could have been content with sharing your blood. I was so greedy, and now they've killed you."

Cain leaned down and kissed the cracked and bleeding mouth, and then dropped the heart inside the burned-out cavity between the ribcage. The muscle and tissue there was charred and ashy, and it smelled of burned and rotten flesh. It was still warm, and Cain couldn't bear reaching in and retrieving the slowly beating heart. It was too late, anyway, he thought to himself. She was dead already, and nothing he could do would bring her back. So he left the heart there in the empty cavity, and leaned down to hug her.

As he hugged the cool, limp body, and cried into her neck, he was oblivious to the activity happening in the cavity in her chest. The heart began to beat stronger and more rapidly in the burned-out ribcage. The charred and blackened muscle tissue popped and peeled away, and pink and gray tendons and arteries and veins snaked out between them and clutched at the heart. The pulmonary arteries, aorta, and both venae cavae stretched and flexed, as if looking for something to grab and hold on to. It took a couple of moments, but they eventually found the arteries and veins extending from the burned-out organs, and when they connected, the heart pumped up to double its size and beat slow and steady.

Cain took a deep breath and pulled himself away from her torso.

"I'm so sorry, Lilith," he said. "I shouldn't have . . ."

Her eyes flew open and she took a deep breath that seemed to get stuck halfway through her throat. Her body convulsed beneath him.

"Lil—"

Her eyes were wide and wild and flickered from side to side frantically. She opened her mouth wide, and her long, razor-sharp fangs sparkled in the moonlight. A deafening, high-pitched screech pierced the night air.

When Cain brought his hands to his ears to ward off the painful noise, Tara reached up with both hands and grabbed Cain by the hair. She pulled his head down to her and sank her fangs into his carotid artery. She bit down deep, and pierced both sides of the big vein; blood spurted in every direction. Tara gnawed at his neck, shaking her head back and forth rapidly, ripping out large chunks of skin and meat as she growled low and loud.

Cain's body flailed around on the ground as Tara scrambled to her feet. She looked down at the open space in her chest and watched the heart beating inside. She let out another shrill cry and rushed over to the stake on which her heart had previously been impaled. The dry wood snapped as she broke it in half, and then drove it through the center of Cain's heart.

"Lilith," Cain cried out just a second before a mouthful of blood erupted from his throat and lips. A second later his body began to smolder, and then went limp.

Tara looked down at Cain and suddenly recognized her father. She fell to her knees and held his head in her hands. As his skin burned into ashes right before her eyes, she leaned her head back and howled again into the night air.

Then she stood up and looked toward the faint orange light on the other side of the forest. Her eyes glowed bright red as she jumped into the air and flew toward the village she once called home.

PART FIVE
Kayden—A.D. August 2, 2009

Sometimes, on nights like this, Kayden enjoyed, and indeed needed, to get away.

It had been an exceptionally busy night at Sangre. The line that almost always stretched a full block from the front door never diminished, and his security team had had to put out several temper fires throughout the evening. Already the club was the largest in the city, taking up a full city block. Even so, there was never a night in which it couldn't benefit from twice the space. He was working on opening a second club, but opening up just any space wouldn't do; there were high expectations for any of his endeavors. And real estate was at an all-time high premium in San Francisco, so he was confined, at least temporarily, from building the club of his dreams, and certainly from one that would rival or even live up to the high standards set by Sangre.

For the time being, he worked with what he had and dealt with the constant stress of running the largest and most successful club in one of the hottest cities in the world. His walks across the Golden Gate Bridge helped him deal with the stress.

Every Sunday morning, at about three thirty, after the club closed and was cleaned and emptied, Kayden would walk leisurely across the great bridge. He had a way of going completely unnoticed when he wanted to, and so even the added security measure of a closed steel gate after dark and security cameras did not prevent him from indulging in his favorite stress-relieving activity.

He sat in his favorite place, high atop the 746-foot South Tower, and looked around him at the panoramic view of the beautiful bay area. A thick, low-lying fog cloud blanketed almost the entire area, save for a small patch of land where the bridge connected to San Francisco and the first third of the bridge, and another small area right around Treasure and Angel Islands, which intercepted the larger Bay Bridge on the other side of the Bay. He loved the cool, damp air in San Francisco and the beautiful fog that tended to blanket the area for at least the early morning hours on most days year round. It reminded him of his favorite cities in Europe—Rome and Amsterdam and Prague—in which fog was a major characteristic, and his personal favorite. He loved being blanketed by the cool, thick, cottony mist, and it made him feel at home and at peace with himself.

Kayden looked down at the empty lanes below him, and his eyes were drawn to the sidewalk on the westbound lanes, heading into Sausalito. Someone was down there, riding a bike slowly along the sidewalk. He watched as the person got off the bike and leaned it against the side of the bridge, then climbed slowly onto the rail. Kayden squinted his eyes and saw that the person was a young man.

He'd seen his share of death over the centuries, of course, and had been responsible for more of it than he cared to admit. He'd even witnessed a few suicides. It was part of being who he was, and he tried not to think about it too often. If he'd learned anything about life in the past half a century, it was that life was fleeting and that it went on, despite how badly we might want it not to. There were times where he felt absolutely no remorse or sadness at the loss of it. And with the other times where he did regret any death in which he played a part, it was never more than a couple of days and a few drinks couldn't drive to the back of his mind, if not obliterate completely.

He often envied humans their right and luxury of death. Having lived through both world wars as well as countless other acts of hate and violence, he knew how much they valued it and even worshipped it, sometimes. Though being immortal certainly had its advantages at times, it was not nearly as romantic as it probably seemed to those who wished for it. Over the centuries he'd gone through several periods in which he wished for death, and even thought about bringing it on for himself. The past several months were one of those periods. There was so much negativity everywhere he went, and life seemed like much more work than it was worth.

Something about the young man crawling over the side of the big bridge made him think that maybe it might be worth it after all. He wasn't sure what that something was—he couldn't even see the kid's face and had no idea what his story was. Watching him climb over the rail and prepare to jump brought a lump to Kayden's throat and made him feel anxious. He found himself standing at the top of the tower.

He watched the boy hold on to the rail with his hands behind him as he leaned forward and bowed his head. A lump formed in his throat, and he found himself breathing faster, and his head spinning.

"No," he whispered to himself.

The boy below lifted his head and took a deep breath, and Kayden knew he had to make his move. He dove headfirst off the South Tower and glided quickly and noiselessly down to the kid, who was now teetering on the outside edge of the railing. He landed right behind the boy, and reached out and grabbed his shirt collar just as he bent his knees to lunge forward off the bridge.

Kayden expected the boy to scream in surprise at having someone right behind him, and especially at grabbing on to him, but he didn't. He just grunted, and tried even harder and with more force to throw himself from the bridge. Kayden was much too strong, though, and with no effort whatsoever, he lifted the boy up by the collar and hauled him over the railing to safety on the exterior of the four-foot railing.

"What the hell is wrong with you?" Kayden asked sternly.

From this close he could see the kid was beautiful. Kayden guessed him to be between twenty-five and thirty. His dirty blond hair fell arbitrarily across his face, and he brushed it impatiently away. He wouldn't look at Kayden, keeping his eyes diverted to the ground instead, but the lashes were long and blond and thick, and trapped his tears. What looked like a three- or four-day stubble dotted his chin, and a tiny stud sparkled from the middle of his left nostril. His thin lips were pink and looked soft, even as they quivered from the cold and his crying.

"Are you okay?" Kayden asked more kindly.

"No," the young man whispered. He knelt on the sidewalk as he cried into his hands. "No, I'm not okay."

Kayden lifted him into his arms and carried him several blocks, to where he'd parked his car earlier. When he wrapped his arms around Kayden's neck and laid his head on his shoulders, Kayden felt his entire body tingle. He never asked Kayden's name, where he had come from, or where he was taking him. It probably didn't matter. He just hugged Kayden tightly and allowed himself to be carried away and put gently into the car, and said not a word on the short drive to Kayden's house.

"Who are you?"

The kid sat with his legs curled beneath him on the sofa next to the fireplace, wrapped in a thick blanket and sipping on hot tea. He'd been in that same position for over an hour and was now on his third cup of tea. These were his first words since being carried off of the bridge.

"My name is Kayden. What can I call you?"

"I'm Nathaniel."

"May I ask you a question, Nathaniel?"

The young man took a deep sigh and another big sip from his tea. "It's a long story," he said without waiting for the actual question.

"Well, lucky for us, I have plenty of time," Kayden said.

He'd known immediately that he'd be up way past dawn and had drawn all of the heavy curtains, and had slathered himself in his custom-made sunblock upon coming home at a little past four in the morning. He didn't anticipate venturing out into the daylight, but he'd learned very early on to be overly cautious rather than the opposite. For the past sixty years, with the creation of the special sunblock and the invention of his unique contact lenses, he'd been able to walk among the living in broad daylight. He didn't enjoy it yet, and was still always so concerned and stressed about the possible consequences that he was always on pins and needles. But there had been several times where circumstances mandated his presence during broad daylight, and he was thankful that he'd been able to buck the system.

"I don't know you, and this might not be very safe for me," Nathaniel said quietly.

"You were just on the verge of jumping off the Golden Gate Bridge," Kayden said, and massaged the back of Nathaniel's neck with his thumb and forefinger. "You're safe with me."

Nathaniel took another deep breath and set his cup on the coffee table.

"I met my boyfriend five years ago," he said slowly, and watched for Kayden's reaction. When his host smiled and scooted an inch closer, he continued. "From that very first night together, we never once spent a night apart. I loved him so much, and he was my whole world."

The verb tense did not escape Kayden, and neither did the single tear rolling down Nathaniel's cheek or his heavy breathing. He rubbed the kid's neck some more, careful not to come across as predatory or seductive. It was important that Nathaniel knew that he was safe here, and that Kayden was there for him as a friend.

"It took me three years to come out to my parents. My pop is a Pentecostal preacher, and my mom is the typical stand-behind-your-man kinda wife. She idolizes June Cleaver. So you can imagine that my little news was not met with open arms."

"I'm so sorry," Kayden said. He wanted to say that though it was undoubtedly difficult, that it probably didn't warrant jumping off the big bridge. Plenty of gay boys and girls were met with similar reactions from their families, and most of them found it within themselves to move past it. But he didn't.

"We didn't speak after that. They disowned me, but that didn't stop them from sending Christmas and birthday cards with Bible verses and pleas for me to repent and return to Jesus."

"They didn't really honor the disowning, huh?"

"No. Only the part that was convenient for them. Every time a card showed up in the mail, I knew what was going to be inside, but I couldn't not open it. I had to take a chance that they'd come to their senses and wanted me back in their lives. I was always disappointed, though."

"I can imagine that was very difficult."

"Yeah, it was. But I eventually came to terms with it. It is what it is."

Again, Kayden noted the conflicting verb tenses.

"A little over a year ago Roger was diagnosed with aggressive skin cancer. There was nothing the doctors could do about it, and he passed away six months ago."

"I'm so sorry, Nathaniel."

"He was my *world*," Nathaniel cried out. His entire body shook as he cried. "How am I supposed to go on without him? We spent every single day together, every hour. I love him so much."

Kayden leaned in and hugged him, massaging the back of his head.

"I didn't know what to do when Roger died," Nathaniel said, breaking the hug. He took another big drink of his tea. "I don't know why I did it, what I expected from them, but I called my parents to tell them that he'd passed away."

"Oh no," Kayden said, and shook his head. He'd seen and known enough people like Nathaniel's parents to know that sharing this information with them would not have a happy ending.

"They screamed at me, Kayden," Nathaniel said as he wiped the tears from his eyes. "They told me that Roger got what he deserved, and so did I."

"What?" Kayden was enraged, and wanted more than anything to make his parents pay for their spiteful words.

"Yeah, they told me that all fags caught AIDS and that we all died, and that this was God's punishment for me sinning with another man."

"AIDS? You said he had skin cancer."

"He did. But my parents wouldn't listen to me. They said it was AIDS and that I was in denial, or just flat-out lying to them. My mother was especially hurtful and screamed that I was next and that God would cause my skin to boil and then burn in hell. She called Roger an abomination and a 'General in Satan's army' and said that every fag on earth would suffer the same wrath of God's fury."

"Shit," Kayden said softly. "You know that that's not true, right?"

"I thought I did," Nathaniel said, and wiped his nose on his arm. "I was in so much pain, Kayden. I can't tell you how badly

I hurt. How could God make me suffer so much pain? The only thing I could think of was that my parents were right, and that God was punishing me."

"That is not the God I know," Kayden said slowly.

That was difficult for him to say, because he didn't really know God all that well. And the stories passed down from generation and generation in his family and ancestry suggested that this was exactly the way in which God operated. The story of Lilith's banishment from Paradise and the curse placed on her and her family was hard proof of that. But that was not what Nathaniel needed to hear.

"God does not punish us for loving another person, Nathaniel." Kayden bit his tongue, because he didn't necessarily believe this, either. His centuries of experience sometimes suggested otherwise. "That is our biggest challenge, and for some of us that challenge is more difficult than others. For those of us who love another man, we understand the hardship and we take it on headfirst."

"So, it's already so hard to find that love and commit to it. Shouldn't we be rewarded for that, rather than being punished for it?"

"I think we are."

"How do you figure?" Nathaniel said, and leaned forward, a couple of inches closer to Kayden.

"Our love is a little more intense. Do you really think that your parents love each other as strongly or as intensely as you and Roger loved one another?"

"No," Nathaniel said softly. "I think they tolerate one another because it's safe and it's somewhat comfortable."

"Well, they are the ones who are missing out," Kayden said. He wanted so badly to lean in and kiss the soft, pink lips in front of him. "They had no right to make you feel unwanted or unloved."

"That's all I ever wanted from them," Nathaniel cried as he

scooted closer and laid his head on Kayden's shoulders. "All I wanted was for them to love me and to be happy that I'd found someone to love and to love me in return."

"I know," Kayden said, and hugged him tightly.

Nathaniel looked up into Kayden's face and kissed him on the lips. "Will you love me?"

Kayden looked down at the naked young man lying in the middle of his big bed and gasped. Nathaniel was a little over six foot tall. His legs were long and lean, with enough muscle and definition to bring Kayden's cock to full attention. His chest was also lean and toned, with tiny nipples that were at constant attention. His arms were muscular and riddled with veins.

Over his lifetime, Kayden had seen and fucked and loved many beautiful men. Although Nathaniel was certainly stunning, he was not the most physically striking man who'd shared his bed, but something about him took Kayden's breath away and kept his cock hard and throbbing.

"My God, you're beautiful," Kayden said as he crawled into the bed and over to the young man.

"Thank you," Nathaniel said. He reached up, hooked his hand behind Kayden's neck, and pulled him down for a kiss.

Kayden returned the kiss, sliding his tongue slowly in and out of the warm mouth. He loved the faded taste of spiced tea, but was intoxicated with the sweet taste and smell of the man beneath him.

He broke the kiss and brushed the long, straight blond hair from Nathaniel's forehead, groaning as he felt like he was just fist-punched in the gut. He'd been looking at the young man for the past couple of hours, and he'd been impressed with his exquisiteness. Nathaniel had been elusive in looking directly at him for the entire morning, and he hadn't gotten a good look at his eyes until now.

They were big and round and more expressive than the rest

of his body combined. The lashes were long and thick and curly, and seduced Kayden immediately. One iris was bright blue, and the other was light violet, and together they were guaranteed to take anyone's breath away upon first glance.

Kayden recognized them immediately.

He'd seen them many times before. The first time was in London in 1584. The boy's name was Jasper, and he and Kayden were both nineteen years old. Jasper was the son of the wealthiest baker in London, and personal baker to Queen Elizabeth I. He was arrogant and demanding and energetic. In bed he was passionate and insistent and insatiable, and Kayden was powerless against his seduction. They were lovers for ten years, until their affair was discovered and Jasper was found bound and horribly mutilated inside his father's main oven.

In 1622 he saw the eyes again. This time the boy's name was Aineas. He was twelve years old and lived with his grandparents in Athens. Kayden recognized the eyes immediately, and the young boy developed a strong bond with him immediately. Kayden struggled valiantly with his love for the boy. He was patient, knowing that Aineas would eventually grow to an age that was appropriate for him to love physically, and he was willing to wait. He, after all, was not growing old, and the two would soon be seemingly the same age, and they could then become lovers again. The young boy drowned in a freak boating accident at the age of fifteen, however, and Kayden was left devastated and unfulfilled again.

While visiting Kenya in 1688 Kayden found his lover again. This time, he was the thirty-year-old newly appointed chief of a small tribe on the border with Tanzania. His sparkling light-colored eyes were startling against his ebony skin, and the superstitious clan deemed them a sign from the gods that he was destined to lead them to great power. Chief Chitundu and Kayden lived happily together for thirty years, until the chief was murdered in a bloody coup by his eldest son, and Kayden was exiled from the tribe.

Almost 100 agonizing years passed before Kayden found his true love again. It happened quite by accident as Kayden was walking down a dark alley in Boston in 1847, contemplating whether or not he wanted to put the heart in and feed. William was a nineteen-year-old thief who was fleeing an overweight policeman and an aggravated clothing store owner whom he had just robbed. He ran into Kayden, knocking them both to the ground, and when Kayden looked into those beautiful eyes, he cried for the first time in half a century. He was so overwhelmed with emotion that he didn't even bother to conceal his identity. He picked William up and flew off with him into the night. It was the only time in his life that Kayden had ever entertained the idea of turning his lover, so that they could be together forever. As much as William begged him to do so, though, he couldn't bring himself to do it. He loved William too much to condemn him to the eternal life he suffered through. In the end, the two lovers lived and loved together until William died of old age in 1906.

The last time Kayden met his lover was at Woodstock in 1969. Beau was twenty-four, and was immediately attracted to the suave and handsome Kayden. They got stoned together at the festival, and when it was over Beau followed Kayden to San Francisco, where the hippie movement was strong and powerful. They loved one another intensely, and to Kayden it seemed as if they'd never been apart. When he awoke one evening to find Beau dead with a needle in his arm, his life fell apart, and he felt he could not go on. That was the last time he'd entertained the idea of dying, and he went almost a month without placing the heart in his body and going on a feeding hunt. At the very last moment, just an hour before he would have died, another vampire from his clan burst through the door and shoved the black heart into his chest, condemning him to continued eternal misery.

He went on a three-month rampage that time, keeping the heart inside him the entire time, and killing more than sixty people after feeding on them. In addition to those he killed, he presented even more with an even worse fate, and turned them. He was angry, and it was his ultimate revenge on the cruel world that kept taking his lover from him. It was after Beau's death in 1975 that Kayden decided he would not live through that pain again. He vowed never to love another human being again. And he swore that if he ever were to find his lover again, that he'd either kill himself or he'd turn his lover. Either way, they'd be together forever, and he would never have to suffer the loneliness again.

And now, here he was staring into those mystical eyes once again, and Kayden felt as if he were going to vomit and pass out. He rolled off Nathaniel's body and lay next to him on the bed. He covered his eyes and took a few deep breaths.

"Are you okay?" Nathaniel asked as he rubbed Kayden's bare chest.

"Oh, god, oh, god, I can't do this," Kayden cried into his hands.

"What's wrong? Did I do something wrong?"

"No," Kayden said quietly, and wiped the tears from his eyes. "I'm just a little tired. It's been a long night."

"I'm sorry. I probably made it even longer, being such a drama queen and all."

"No, it's not your fault," Kayden said. "The truth is, I'm not really tired at all. That was just an easy cop-out. I'm a bit overwhelmed."

"Overwhelmed?" Nathaniel said, and looked down at Kayden's face. "With what?"

"With you," Kayden said, and pulled him down for a kiss.

He rolled Nathaniel onto his back and lay on top of him. He kissed him desperately on the mouth, licking his thin pink lips and sucking his warm, sweet tongue into his mouth. The taste of his tongue and the feel of his soft skin brought Kayden's cock to full attention. He kissed Nathaniel's chin and worked his way down his throat. When he reached the silky smooth and soft skin of Nathaniel's neck, he felt his gums tingle and throb.

His fangs pricked through the surface of his gums, and his body tensed up as he realized his canines were breaking through and demanding attention. He wanted so badly to sink his teeth into the pliable tissue between the boy's ears and shoulders—to suck on the thick vein until his mouth was filled with warm, coppery nectar, and to swallow the essence of his soul. They ached and itched and pulsed demandingly in his mouth. He closed his eyes and took a couple of deep breaths, concentrating on anything other than the smell and the feel and the heat of the body and boy beneath him.

"Make love to me, Kayden. Please."

"Oh, god, yes," Kayden moaned.

He lifted Nathaniel's legs into the air and pressed them to the boy's shoulders, forcing his naked ass into the air. Sliding down to get behind the upturned ass, he licked the twitching hole and up and down the smooth crack. When Nathaniel moaned loudly and puckered his hole even more, Kayden let a large glob of saliva fall from his mouth and into the puckered hole and watched it slide inside. He leaned down and licked at the hole, moaning when Nathaniel tightened his muscles, drawing his tongue deep inside.

Kayden's cock throbbed painfully and bounced up and down in front of him. He felt a large drop of precum ooze out of the tip and drip down the thick shaft. He knew he had to fuck the boy, and fuck him now. He stood up so that he towered over Nathaniel, and when he looked into that beautiful face and saw those achingly familiar eyes, his knees began to shake.

"Fuck me," Nathaniel mouthed, but didn't say out loud.

Kayden bent down a couple of inches and rubbed his cock head against the twitching hole, sliding the precum all around it. Once again the hole opened wide for him and then puckered shut, teasing him. He took a deep breath, and slowly slid just the head inside the warm, moist tunnel.

"Oh God," Nathaniel moaned, and lifted his ass deeper onto Kayden's cock. "I need you inside me so bad."

Kayden heard Jasper's voice, and Beau's and William's, too. And he heard Chitundu's thick, sexy dialect in Nathaniel's words. They were all there, individually and collectively at the same time, and Kayden bit his tongue to choke back a tear.

He bent down farther and moaned deeply as his thick cock slid an inch at a time deeper and deeper inside Nathaniel's ass. The hot muscles wrapped around his dick and squeezed it hard and lovingly and with stubborn determination. Kayden prided himself on his virility and his lovemaking abilities. He could easily outlast any of his partners, and he was guaranteed to cum at least three or four times. He was never insecure in his lovemaking.

Until now. The heat from Nathaniel's ass and the strength with which his muscles tugged on his cock, stroking him lovingly and demandingly at the same time, were more fantastic than anything he'd ever felt. They pulled him deeper inside, and got hotter and wetter as he slid further into Nathaniel.

"You are amazing," he whispered out huskily as his balls rested heavily against Nathaniel's ass.

He shook his head to clear the high-pitched ringing sound in his ears. When Nathaniel smiled, his ass tightened even more, and Kayden shuddered as he felt the hot muscles slide up and down his shaft. It felt as if they were kissing and licking and caressing him all at once. He felt his orgasm begin to churn deep inside his gut.

"Oh God," he moaned. "You're gonna have to stop that, or I'm gonna cum."

Nathaniel smiled even broader and winked at him. He slid his ass almost all the way off Kayden's big cock, until only the head rested inside him still, and then stopped. Then he took a deep breath and slid all the way back down the thick dick. When Kayden moaned even louder, Nathaniel picked up the pace and began sliding up and down the big pole slowly at first, then with more vigor. His eyes rolled back into his head and his breathing became shallower as he rode Kayden's cock. His own cock bounced around his stomach as he fucked the big cock frantically.

"I'm not kidding," Kayden groaned. He felt like a little boy whose desires for something . . . candy or a toy or a pet dog . . . anything . . . were so strong that he couldn't control himself. As hard as he was trying, he wasn't able to control the orgasm that was now on its way through his organs and on to his hard cock. He knew he was already beyond the point of no return. "I'm gonna cum, baby."

Nathaniel moaned loudly as his entire body became rigid. His ass clamped around Kayden's cock and squeezed it tightly, and a second later three shots of cum exploded from his cock and shot over his head and across his face. Another three or four landed on his chest and stomach. His entire lower body quivered violently as it refused to release its hold on Kayden's cock.

"Oh, *fuck!*" Kayden yelled.

He leaned down and kissed Nathaniel on the lips as he emptied his load deep inside the tight ass. He was completely breathless and struggled to catch a couple of deep ones as every bit of his energy left his own body and entered Nathaniel's. He knew the boy could feel his load entering his body, because with each ejaculation, Nathaniel moaned louder and squeezed his cock lovingly.

Kayden collapsed on top of Nathaniel, still struggling to catch his breath as he kissed the boy tenderly. His cock was still hard and buried deep inside Nathaniel. When he tried to pull out, Nathaniel moaned and pulled him back inside him. Kayden rolled clumsily onto his side, making sure not to pull out, and hugged his lover tightly.

"Oh, my god," Nathaniel said as he snuggled his naked back deeper against Kayden's torso, forcing the still-hard cock deeper inside him. "What the fuck just happened?"

"I think I fucked you," Kayden said, and kissed him on the ear.

"No."

"I didn't?"

"No. It was much more than just a fuck. I don't know exactly what that was, but it was much more than just a fuck."

Kayden swallowed hard, praying that his next words would come out without the frog he felt in his throat, and without the tears he tried desperately to blink away without the convenience of his hands, which were wrapped tightly around his lover.

"Yeah, I guess it was," he said slowly.

"Will you stay inside me," Nathaniel asked. "I just wanna fall asleep in your arms, with your dick buried inside me. It makes me feel safe."

"Of course I will," Kayden said. "I'll do anything you ask."

"Will you love me?" Nathaniel asked groggily. He snuggled up even closer to Kayden and in just a couple of seconds he was snoring lightly, not even waiting for the answer.

"I will love you, baby," Kayden said, and cursed the tear that he felt roll down his cheek.

PART SIX
Kayden & Nathaniel—A.D. November 4, 2009

Nathaniel couldn't contain his excitement, and he could tell he was working the last nerve of everyone else in the club. But he couldn't help himself. There were just some things that not only warranted everyone's attention, but demanded it. And goddamm it, his three-month anniversary with the most incredible man in the entire world was one of those things.

"Come on, guys," he whined as he wiped several glasses dry and hung them in the wineglass rack suspended from the bottom of the cupboard above the sink. "You guys are being party poopers."

Sandra spit out a mouthful of soda as she laughed. "Did you really just say 'party poopers'?"

"Stop it!" Nathaniel said, and despite his valiant efforts not to do so, he stomped his foot on the ground. "I'm serious about this."

"We know you are," Jeremy said as he walked past the bar and over to the DJ booth. "But a surprise party will not go over well. Kayden doesn't like surprises."

"That's only because he hasn't really had a reason for one,"

Nathaniel said. "You know how much I love him. And he loves me just as much."

"There's no denying that," Sandra said. "He's crazy about you, Nate. He worships the ground you walk on, we can all see that, but he doesn't like surprises. He especially won't be happy about a surprise party with a room full of people. Your anniversary is special for him, and you know that. But a party is not the right way to celebrate. He'll want to take you somewhere special. Hawaii or maybe Europe."

"Oh, I'd love that!"

"See. Let him show you . . ."

"And we can leave right after the surprise party."

Sandra shook her head and walked away, and Jeremy locked himself in the DJ booth. "You're fucking crazy, Nate," he announced over the loudspeaker. "You're gonna freak him out."

"Shhhhh," Nathaniel said, and threw a towel at the window. "He's going to hear you."

"He left twenty minutes ago, baby," Sandra said. "He won't be back for another couple of hours. You know that. If it were my husband meeting with another man at night for a couple of hours, I'd be worried."

"I don't care. I don't wanna jinx it. And you should be worried. Your husband would have a reason to play around elsewhere," he said as he swatted her on the ass with a damp towel. "My man has absolutely no reason to stray. I give him everything he wants, and more."

"Yeah, like herpes," Sandra said, and then turned to run away.

"You're all gonna help me plan this fucking party," he yelled out to no one in particular. "And you're gonna love it!"

There were twenty employees in the club, all preparing for the evening, and with the exception of their short exchange about the party, they almost never saw one another. The massive club had a tendency to swallow people up and hide them. Everyone knew their jobs, and they had them all down to a science. Everyone else came to the club dressed to work, but Nathaniel never did. He preferred doing all the prep work in his grungy jeans and an old t-shirt. But when it was time to open the doors for business, he insisted on wearing only his best shirts and most expensive jeans or slacks, and he always went home to change before the doors opened for business.

"I'm heading home," he yelled out. "I'll be back in about an hour."

"Be careful," Jeremy said over the sound system.

Kayden and Nathaniel lived less than half a mile from the club. Nathaniel enjoyed walking, so he almost always walked back to the house to change, at least when it wasn't raining. He hated routine and monotony, and made a point of taking a different route as often as he could. That night he hadn't eaten earlier, and so he took a longer route than usual so that he could stop and get a couple of his favorite hot dogs a few blocks from home.

At eight o'clock on a Thursday evening, he had no qualms about walking through the streets of San Francisco. He'd lived there for the past nine years, and despite its reputation for sometimes being pretty seedy, he never felt unsafe there. He didn't hesitate to turn down Tehama Street, the alley dissecting the dark area between the larger and brighter Folsom and Howard Streets. When he first turned the corner it was dark, and he slowed his stride a little until his eyes could adjust to the dimly lit alleyway.

When he first saw the large shadow several feet in front of him, he thought it was possibly a sheet hanging out in the night air, possibly having been hung out to dry earlier in the day and then forgotten. As he took another couple of steps into the alley, he realized the movement of the shadow was deliberate and animated, and very human. And then he heard the cries and the groans of unmistakable pain and fear.

"No, please," the male voice cried out as the large shadow split for a few seconds, and allowed Nathaniel to make out two distinct human shapes. "Please don't hurt me."

Nathaniel wanted to scream out, to yell and scare the much larger and obviously stronger man away. He wanted to help the smaller man, who was clearly in pain and in fear for his life. When he opened his mouth to shout out a warning, only a barely audible squeak escaped his lips. He felt his knees begin to shake uncontrollably, and he stepped backward, now wanting desperately to run away out of the alley and into the brighter streets behind him, where he could find help.

He brought his hands to his mouth, stifled the scream, and took a couple of steps backward. His ass brushed against a metal trash can and knocked it to the ground, sending a loud crashing noise into the air. Nathaniel's eyes bulged as he watched the smaller man fall to the ground as the larger figure turned to glare at him.

The first thing Nathaniel saw was the long and severely distorted face. The nose was long and flared wildly. The cheekbones stretched to several inches on either side of the face. But the most startling feature was the fangs. They were long and gleamed even in the dim light of the single bare bulb that hung above the back door of the liquor store that emptied into the alley. A dark, thick fluid that could not be mistaken for anything other than blood dripped slowly from them, and the man licked at them hungrily and desperately.

Nathaniel couldn't bear looking at the teeth any longer. He felt his throat tighten in his neck and struggled to catch his breath as he slowly looked away from the fangs and up to look into the man's eyes. They were bright red and glowed brightly and bored into him from about thirty feet away. Hate flew from them and slammed into Nathaniel with fierce hostility, and he knew that the monster would pounce upon him and rip him to shreds at any moment.

Then those eyes changed in an instant. They softened and twitched several times as they looked at him, and then a tear fell down the deformed cheeks as they undeniably recognized him. And Nathaniel recognized those eyes, too.

"Kayden," he whispered as his legs gave out on him and he slumped to the ground.

A low, guttural moan escaped the monster's throat, and he steadied himself on the brick wall behind him.

"Baby?" Nathaniel cried. He couldn't take his eyes off the beast only a few feet away from him. "Kayden, what's going . . ."

Kayden threw his head back and screamed into the night. The cry was loud and shrill and pierced the thick, dark night.

It pierced Nathaniel's soul even deeper.

Kayden kicked the dead man at his feet out of the way and watched him fly across the alley, stopping only when his limp body slammed against the brick wall several yards away. He turned and took another look at Nathaniel, then jumped into the air and flew away.

Nathaniel glanced down at the cell phone and read the display. Not that he really needed to. Since he'd seen Kayden kill the man in the alley and then fly off into the night screaming like a banshee nine days ago, it had been ringing almost non-stop. And eight out of ten times, it was Kayden's name, number, and picture that popped up on the LCD display.

He'd been tempted to pick it up a few times, even touching his finger on the connect button twice. But he couldn't bring himself to pick up the call and speak with his lover. He couldn't get the picture of Kayden's elongated face and the long, razor-sharp fangs with dripping blood out of his head. But the worst part was those bright red eyes that were filled with hate and rage and violence. They were so different than the soft and tender and beautiful eyes that looked so passionately into his own when they made love, and that cried salty tears when he laughed so hard his stomach hurt.

Nathaniel's heart hurt and he had barely been able to eat anything since the incident. A couple of people from Sangre had called the first couple of days, and then those calls abruptly stopped. He was sure Kayden had told them some half-believable story and had insisted they stop calling him. He'd not returned to their home after that night, and since he'd given up his own apartment when he moved in with Kayden, no one knew where to find him. After wandering around aimlessly for a couple of hours that night, he eventually found himself at a rundown motel, and he'd been there for the past nine days.

He hadn't left the room at all since he'd checked in. He showered every couple of days, ordered pizza and Chinese food on delivery, and spent the entire day in bed watching mindless television. Up until now, he'd been okay with that routine; in fact hadn't given much thought at all to any alternatives. But when he woke up that morning, something was fundamentally different. He woke up on his own less than an hour after sunrise, with more energy than he remembered having in a month. He showered and dressed and walked out into the cool morning light before he thought about it or could stop it.

Once outside he realized how badly he missed engaging in life. The sun felt warm on his skin, the cool air felt like fingers caressing his face and arms, and the sounds of the city around him energized him. He strolled down to the wharf for his favorite lunch at In-N-Out Burger, and bought several t-shirts and a couple pairs of jeans while he was there. After lunch he spent a couple of hours at the Ripley's Believe It Or Not! museum, and walked up and down Pier 39 several times.

Eventually, he had to head back to the motel, though. He opened the door and walked into the room, reaching for the light switch as he shut the door behind him. He'd kept the blinds and curtains drawn since he'd arrived, and with the sun setting outside, the room was very dark. The light didn't come on when he flicked the switch, and he tried it again.

"I took out the bulb," he heard from the bed across the room. "I'm a little sensitive to light right now."

"Oh, god," Nathaniel moaned, and leaned against the door. "Kayden."

"I've missed you so much, babe," Kayden said. "I was so worried about you."

"What are you doing here?"

"I came for you."

"You *came* for me? I'm not going anywhere with you, Kayden. You can't make me."

He felt his heart pinch in his chest, and his eyes began to water as he watched Kayden stand up from the bed and walk toward him. He pressed himself closer against the door and cringed as Kayden leaned in to within an inch of his face.

"Please don't hurt me," he whispered as he closed his eyes tight and began to cry.

"Hurt you?" Kayden said. "Oh, my god, babe, don't be afraid of me. Please don't be afraid of me. I would never hurt you."

"Yes, you would," Nathaniel sobbed. His knees were shaking and he felt as if he'd faint. "You'd kill me, just like you did that poor man."

"No, baby, no," Kayden said, and pulled Nathaniel to his chest and hugged him. "Never. I would never hurt you. I love you."

"Don't say that!" Nathaniel yelled. He tried to pull himself from Kayden's embrace, but couldn't. "You don't love me. You can't love me. You're not even human, are you? You can't be human. What are you?"

Kayden held Nathaniel's face in his hands and tried to kiss

him on the lips. But Nathaniel cringed and cried again and refused to open his mouth or kiss him back. Kayden picked him up, carried him to the bed, and laid him down. He crawled into bed himself and spooned his lover into his torso.

"I'll tell you everything, babe," he whispered into Nathaniel's ear, and kissed it. "But I need you to be objective about all of this, okay? I need you to keep an open mind."

"Just tell me," Nathaniel said between gritted teeth.

"I'm a vampire."

Nathaniel's body tensed from head to toe, and he took in a sharp breath, but didn't say anything.

"I'm sorry I didn't tell you sooner, babe. I was just afraid you wouldn't understand, and I didn't want to lose you."

"You can't be a vampire."

"I am."

"We've been out in daylight several times, Kayden. Everyone knows sunlight will kill a vampire."

"It takes a lot of exposure to sunlight to kill us, baby. It is harmful, and it's painful. But it doesn't kill us just to be exposed to it. When we go out in the daylight, I wear a very special sunblock, long-sleeve shirts and custom-made contact lenses. I take a lot of precautions."

"*Took*. You took a lot of precautions. We're not going out into daylight anymore. We're not doing *anything* anymore."

"Please, babe . . ."

"And stop calling me that. How did you get in here, anyway? I thought you couldn't come in anywhere you weren't specifically invited."

Nathaniel hated that he was asking these questions, because it lent validity to Kayden's story about being a vampire. He didn't want to believe it, but he did. Asking these questions made that fact loud and clear.

"You watch too much TV, babe. We don't have to be invited

anywhere. We can come and go anywhere we wish, and with the right precautions, any time we wish. Garlic doesn't kill us, and neither do crucifixes. Those are all myths."

Nathaniel took a deep breath. He was too tired to fight anymore. "I don't believe you."

"Yes, you do," Kayden said.

He hugged Nathaniel closer and kissed him tenderly on the neck. When his lover cringed and his body tightened when Kayden's lips kissed his neck, he felt electric shock waves course through his body.

"You do believe me. And I want to tell you the truth. I love you, Nathaniel. And I need you to know the truth."

"Right. Because that's important to you. The truth."

Kayden felt as if he'd been kicked in the gut, and he flinched. Nathaniel turned around and faced him. "So spill it."

Kayden took a deep breath, leaned in to kiss him on the lips, then pulled back just a couple of inches.

"You may have heard the story of Lilith, the mythical first wife of Adam? Well, it's not a myth. She was real, and she was my great grandmother twelve times distant."

He watched Nathaniel roll his eyes and move to get off the bed, but he grabbed his lover and pulled him back to the mattress.

"I know this isn't easy to hear and it's even harder to believe. But it's important and it's true, and you're going to listen to me."

"Or what? You'll kill me?"

"Please don't say that. I love you so much, Nathaniel," he said, and kissed him again. "Lilith was a little too independent and a little too wild for Adam to handle. She was created from the same material as Adam. She believed herself equal to him, so she refused to submit to him. They were constantly fighting, and it became clear that she would not bear him any children, so Eve came into the picture. She was quiet and submissive and more than willing to have Adam's children. Lilith was no longer needed, and so she was cursed and banished from Ridvan."

"Ridvan? That's your last name," Nathaniel said.

"It means 'paradise' in Arabic. Lilith was pronounced by God and by Adam to be the symbol of sin and of evil. On her way out of the garden they cursed her with fangs, hideous body transformations, and the unquenchable thirst for blood. She was the human personification of the serpent, the ultimate representation of evil. Lilith was ostracized and feared and never accepted anywhere she went. She moved from village to village, staying as long as she could before the villagers became weary of her and ran her out.

"She and Cain had thirty children, and several of them were born with the curse as well. One evening, while Cain was out feeding, the villagers ran Lilith and her children deep into the forest. They eventually killed Lilith by stoning her and cutting her heart out of her chest and impaling it on a wooden stake, and burning her body. When they did that, every single one of her children were killed. Their hearts caught fire right in their chests. When Cain returned, he found Lilith's dismembered body and her impaled heart, and he went crazy. The body of their oldest daughter, Tara, was lying next to Lilith's ashes, and Cain mistook Tara's body for that of Lilith. In the middle of the chaos and sadness and desperation, he grabbed Lilith's heart from the stake and placed it inside Tara's body, hoping it would revive Lilith's body.

"The heart was still beating, though barely, when he put it in Tara's ribcage. It immediately began beating stronger, and it melded with her body. When Tara was revived, it is said that it was Lilith's soul in Tara's body. She flew into a rage. She didn't recognize her husband and ripped into his neck very violently, eventually decapitating him. When she finally did recognize Cain and realized what she'd done, she became hysterical and wreaked vengeance on all of the villagers who'd murdered her family.

"Lilith moved from village to village in Tara's body, and eventually she married again and had one more child. His name was Evander, and he was born with no heart. Lilith's chest and ribcage never closed after her death, and her heart rested in the open cavity in the middle of her chest. One day, by accident, Lilith's heart fell from her chest and rolled across the floor. She ran over to retrieve it, then realized she could live without it being inside her. After a while, she realized that she only needed the heart inside her when she needed to hunt and feed. When she wasn't on the hunt, she didn't need the heart to live. Evander was born with the same hole in his chest, and so it was natural for Lilith to share her heart with him when he needed to feed.

"With the heart in his ribcage, Evander's face and body grew grotesque and disproportionately powerful. In a fit of rage one night, he cut Lilith's head off and stole her heart, swearing never to take it out. And he didn't for over a thousand years. He had over three hundred kids. They were all born perfectly healthy except for Leilana, his eldest. She was born without a heart and with a gaping empty hole in the middle of her ribs. When Evander was murdered, his heart was impaled on a stake in the public square for all to see. Leilana retrieved it, placed it inside her own empty ribcage, and lived to be one of the fiercest vampires in history.

"Each generation followed the same pattern. The oldest child of all of Lilith's descendents was born without a heart. When the elder vampire was killed, his or her firstborn child claimed the heart and was unequivocally recognized as the lead vampire. The heart has been carefully guarded and passed down from generation to generation. It's gotten blacker and more rotten with each passing."

"You do realize how ridiculous all of this sounds, right?"

Nathaniel asked. "You can't possibly think that I believe it for a moment."

Kayden ripped his shirt open and grabbed Nathaniel by the hand. He thrust both of their hands into his chest cavity, forcing Nathaniel to feel the empty cavity, even when he tried to pull his hand back.

"I'm not lying to you," he said softly. "I love you more than I could ever explain. And you love me, too. We've loved one another for many years and many times over the years. I can't stand to think that I could lose you again."

"What the fuck are you talking about?"

Kayden told Nathaniel about his previous incarnations, and talked in length about their love throughout the past five centuries. The lovers kissed and they cried together, but Kayden could tell that Nathaniel was still holding something back. He still flinched when Kayden touched him, and though he returned the kisses, they were reserved and lacked the passion they once held.

"I can't do this, Kayden," Nathaniel said as he pulled away and sat up on one side of the bed. "You're a vampire and you go around killing people. How can I be with you? How can I love someone who does that?"

"I know it's hard to accept. And if I could change it, I would. But I can't. I'm not that monster all the time, though, babe. I only need that heart once every three or four weeks. When I put it inside me I become a beast, that monster that you saw a few nights ago. It's horrible, I know, and it makes me sick every time I have to do it. But if I don't put that heart inside me, Nate, I will die. I have to."

"You're hideous like that."

Kayden gasped and blinked his eyes quickly to keep from crying. He couldn't stand to hear those words coming from the man he loved more than anything in the world.

"I hate it too, babe. Please believe me. But that's not who I am. I only need that a very small portion of the time. Ninety percent of the time I am the man you fell in love with. I am loving and caring and passionate, and I do a lot of good in the world around me. I can't do that, though . . . I can't be the person you fell in love with if I don't put the heart in me and if I don't honor that despicable creature that is a part of me whether I like it or not. Believe me, I don't. I hate it. I vomit every single time I take the heart out and put it back in its box and face the reality of what I've done. It literally sickens me. Many of my ancestors loved the heart and the monster that it made them become. They kept it inside them their entire lives. They were brutal murderers who thrived on being just that monster. I am not that person, babe. If I could, I would never put it inside me again, and I'd never feed on another human life again. But I can't *not* do it, Nate. I will die if I don't put that heart in me and if I don't feed every three or four weeks."

"I understand, Kayden," Nathaniel said softly.

"You do?" Kayden asked, and leaned in to kiss him again.

Nathaniel moved his hand to stop him.

"Yes, I do. I understand. But I can't accept it, babe. I can't love you knowing all of this."

"Please don't say that," Kayden said, and tried to hug him.

Nathaniel pushed him away and stood up.

"I'm sorry. I just can't. I need you to go now."

"Babe . . ."

"You need to go or you need to kill me, Kayden. Because I will not love you anymore."

Nathaniel walked into the bathroom and closed the door behind him as Kayden covered his eyes with his hands and cried into them. When he came out, Kayden was gone. He tried to walk over to the bed, but his legs gave out before he got there, and he fell to the floor. He curled into a fetal position and held his knees tight to his chest as he cried himself to sleep.

* * *

It had been three weeks since he'd had the conversation with Nathaniel and his life collapsed around him. He'd tried to call Nathaniel a few times the first three or four days after that night at the motel, but to no avail. His calls went unanswered, and Nathaniel never once called him or came to see him. Kayden had refused to eat or drink anything at all since then, and he hadn't fed on live blood for over a month now. He felt himself getting weaker and sicker by the day, and knew it wouldn't be much longer. It couldn't come soon enough.

Lilith's lineage and her legacy of death and fear had lived on long enough, and Kayden was resolved to end it. His death, and that of Lilith along with him, would not mean the end of vampires. Not by any stretch of the imagination. But it would mean an end to the insurmountable power that the Dark Heart gave to them. Without it they would fall into disarray and chaos, and with any luck at all they would self-destruct and eventually kill each other off in another century or two. It was possible another vampire could rise among the ranks and lead them into prosperity, of course. Kayden wasn't aware of anyone on the sidelines who could do that, and because he was Lilith's last living descendent, he would know of another powerful vampire who might be ready and able to step into his place.

Kayden's body began to convulse as he lay on the couch, and he fell to the floor. He began crawling slowly across the hardwood floor toward the credenza and gritted his teeth as he tried with every ounce of remaining strength in his body to stop and to move away from the glowing box on top of the wooden bureau. He was able to almost come to a stop, but not quite. His body was on a mission, and it trudged closer and closer to the box.

He looked up at a stainless-steel vase on the coffee table as he crawled past it. He looked at his reflection in the vase and drew in a dry, raspy gasp. His eyes were sunken deep into his skull, and the cheekbones below them jutted out awkwardly.

His skin was a pale green-yellow color, and spotted with a series of small purple lesions. His nose was twisted at seemingly impossible angles and his lips were cracked and caked over with dried pus.

"It's over," he whispered as he fell to the floor.

He closed his eyes and waited to die. Visions of his life passed slowly across the inside of his eyelids, and then the pictures switched to those of Bertrand and Tamara and Elijah and other members of the first vampire's lineage. Eventually they turned to visions of Lilith herself. The pictures of his relatives were bloody and violent, and they made him feel like he would vomit.

His body began to feel light and as if were floating an inch above the floor. His head buzzed and he found it hard to concentrate.

When was the last time he made love?

Did he remember to lock the club this morning?

The color blue tastes like pumpkin.

Thirty-two divided by four equals banana cream pie

Did Churchill kill the little white rabbit

Laundry thinks

Beau

From the other side of a very long tunnel Kayden heard a noise he recognized, and a moment later he felt something kick his foot. He opened his eyes slowly and blinked even slower through dry and sandy eye lids.

"Kayden?"

He groaned as he looked up at the handsome face. Tears formed slowly in his eyes, and then came in torrents down his cheeks in just a few seconds. They stung the scratched pupils as they passed over them and spilled down his face.

"Oh, my god, babe," Nathaniel screamed. "What did you do?"

"It's over," Kayden cried as he tugged on Nathaniel's shirt sleeve. "No more."

"Fuck, Kayden," Nathaniel cried. "What the hell are you doing?"

"I love you."

Nathaniel looked around to find a phone. His eyes landed on the glowing mahogany box on the credenza, and remembered Kayden's story from a few weeks ago. It was glowing and seemed to pulse lightly from inside. He started to get up and go to the credenza, but Kayden grabbed him by the arm and squeezed lightly.

"No," Kayden whispered.

"Fuck you," Nathaniel said as he stood up. "You're not going to die on me now that I finally realized I can't live without you."

He walked over to the credenza. The box was opened and the dark heart inside was lying shriveled inside it. He could tell that Kayden had contemplated putting it in and feeding, but had decided against it. It was completely black and drying out in several places. It was beating, but just barely, and it seemed to be struggling even with its limited activity. He looked over at Kayden and noticed the heart was beating in the exact rhythm as Kayden's raspy and labored breathing.

Nathaniel grabbed the heart and fought back the urge to vomit as he rushed back over to Kayden's side. He sat on his knees and ripped open his lover's shirt with one hand as he held the beating heart in his other.

Kayden groaned and shook his head back and forth; more tears fell down his face. He moved one hand over his chest and tried to cover it with his shirt again, but he didn't have the strength to do even that.

"You fucking coward," Nathaniel said between gritted teeth. "How dare you give up on me? I know I'm not the easiest person to love, but goddamm it, I'm worth it. You will not give up on me now. Not now, you bastard."

He pulled the shirt back again and set the heart on the coffee table next to him as he reached into Kayden's chest at the slit and pulled the flaps of skin to either side. The skin was dry and cold, and it made a sickening sound that reminded him of what he imagined a scalping would have sounded like. He dry heaved but was determined. When he was satisfied the flaps would stay open, he carefully took the heart in his hands and brought it slowly to Kayden's chest.

"No," Kayden groaned. "Please don't. Let me die."

"Like hell I will," Nathaniel said. "I love you, and I'm not giving up now."

"Don't," Kayden said.

Nathaniel's hands began to shake as he got closer to the open ribcage in his lover's chest. Tears pooled in his eyes and his lips quivered.

Kayden shook his head slowly from side to side, but couldn't muster the strength to speak.

"Please don't make me regret this," Nathaniel whispered as he dropped the heart into the vacant space in the middle of Kayden's chest.

Kayden had shared with him every graphic detail about how the heart melded with the rest of his body and became a part of him. He talked about how it felt when the aorta attached to the other veins in his chest and how the heart began to beat faster and stronger within a few seconds of being placed in his chest.

Nathaniel watched the heart lying in the cavity for a couple of minutes. Nothing happened with it or with the gray slices of tissue that were supposed to take on a life of their own and connect with the heart. When he looked back at Kayden's face, he saw that his eyes were closed and he was not breathing.

"No, no, no," he said as the tears spilled down his face. He reached inside Kayden's chest and began massaging the black heart. "Don't do this to me, Kayden. Goddamm it, don't you dare die on me."

After a couple of minutes he stopped massaging the heart

and collapsed on Kayden's torso. He wrapped his arms around him and cried as he hugged the cold and lifeless body.

"Why did you do this, you fucking bastard?" he cried as he brushed Kayden's ashen face. "Why did you make me love you and then go and fucking kill yourself? What am I going to do now?"

Nathaniel leaned forward and pressed his lips to Kayden's. They were cold and felt like dried leather, but he fought against the urge to pull away. He kissed Kayden softly and tenderly on the lips.

He thought he felt a twitch in Kayden's leg, and he broke the kiss to look down at his lover's body. The heart was now attached to the tendons and veins that surrounded it, and it was beating strongly. His own heart pounded painfully in his chest, and he found he was paralyzed and couldn't move his eyes away from the black heart beating so perfectly in Kayden's chest.

He heard and felt at the same time a slow, deliberate scratching of something hard and sharp against the wooden floor right next to him. When he looked down at the sound he saw a long and pointed dark brown talon scraping the floor. His head jerked up and looked at Kayden's face.

Kayden's eyes were huge and bright red with bloodshot veins. They glared at him unblinkingly. Long, razor-sharp fangs broke through Kayden's bloody gums and seemed to throb with a life of their own. His jaw was elongated and twisted in odd angles, and his nose was almost unrecognizable.

Kayden smiled at his lover and licked at his fangs hungrily.

"No, ple—"

About the Author

Sean Wolfe lives in Denver, Colorado, and wishes desperately that he were living back home in San Francisco . . . or better yet, was retired and living and looking young and pretty in Puerto Vallarta, Mexico.

Sean has had more than fifty erotica stories published in just about every gay magazine in print, and more than a dozen have been reprinted in several anthologies. This is his eighth book with Kensington Publishing.

For his day job, Sean is the Director of Volunteer Services and Training for a nonprofit agency that works with victims of child abuse, domestic violence, and homelessness. He is in high demand for speaking engagements on myriad subjects. He also facilitates more than a dozen workshops and seminars.

Though Sean does write other than erotica, and he loves to talk, and is a prolific public speaker, and is a Gemini who believes he is never wrong . . . he has been woefully unsuccessful in convincing others that he is not a sex maniac, because all of his published work suggests otherwise.

He is currently putting the finishing touches on his first nonerotic novel, and is about halfway through his second novel.